black tiger

black tiger

the black tiger series—book one

SARA BAYSINGER

STARFINDER
PRESS

Published by StarFinder Press
Martinsville, Indiana

This is a work of fiction. Characters, incidents, and dialogues are products of the author's imagination and are not to be construed as real. Any resemblance to actual events is strictly coincidental.

Cover Design by Sara Baysinger
Manuscript edited by Sarah Grimm
Typesetting and formatting done by Perry Elisabeth Design

Printed in the United States of America

For Michael.

Thank you for daring me to pursue my dreams.

There is a pleasure in the pathless woods,

There is a rapture on the lonely shore,

There is society where none intrudes,

By the deep Sea, and music in its roar:

I love not Man the less, but Nature more.

—-Lord Byron

PART I

the community garden

CHAPTER ONE

I always wondered what it would be like to be dirt. Dead and useless and ugly and walked on. Until a seed drops. Takes root. And grows into a sapling that grows into a tree that produces crates full of fruit every year. All because dirt gave it life.

Dad says I put too much thought into the little things. But I don't think so. Tomorrow is Career Day. I'll leave my home—my *family*—to take up a new life in the city. And I wonder. I wonder if my life will have meaning then. If a seed will be planted, or if I'll remain as useless as dirt. Unnoticed, unseen, disregarded, and overlooked.

I pick up my crate of freshly picked apples and walk through the orchard toward my cabin. The brisk November wind whisks across the Community Garden and blasts into my face, filling my lungs. I absorb every last detail of my surroundings and commit it to memory, a picture to cling to when I need to remember what it's like to live in the place city folk call paradise.

And no wonder.

My eyes scan the green rolling hills and blue sky. I've been told the surrounding megacity of Ky has gray skies and the only blade of grass for miles is planted in window boxes. As the only place that grows fresh food in this country, the Garden is like the heartbeat of Ky.

I live in the apple orchard, in the midst of a mile-square patch of trees that I pruned and harvested from since childhood. Lush red fruit dot branches the way stars dot the sky. Apple trees grow bountiful fruit and are associated with the principles of generosity and abundance. So, of course, the apple tree is the sign of our charitable government.

But to me, the apple tree means so much more than charity and generosity and every good thing Ky does for its citizens. I was born in this orchard. Mom's laughter still dances through the trees. Musical. Vibrant. *Alive.* Almost like she's still here. To me, the apple tree represents beauty and family and safety and home. But more than those, it represents *life*.

The field hands have already left for the day, but farther down the row, my thirteen-year-old brother, Elijah, crouches in the branches of an apple tree, playing his harmonica. The music washes over me like melted butter on a piece of fresh bread—which I've only experienced once, when the older chief, Chief Aden, came to visit and our school had a picnic in his honor. The best food I've ever tasted.

It was also the last meal I had before Mom was taken away.

Strange, how two completely opposite events could happen within hours of each other.

Elijah looks up from his harmonica, smiles at me, and

swings down from the tree with the agility of a flying squirrel. Elijah and I look entirely too similar. Well, all of us Ky folk look the same, really. Eyes too big for our faces, skin the color of hazelnuts, and hair the color of mud. And we all possess the same unhealthy thinness, thanks to the meager rations of food provided by the government.

Elijah picks up his crate of apples and jogs toward me.

I grin. "Hey, kid."

"Ember!" His voice cracks, and I smother a snort.

Poor Elijah, stuck in that awkward place between boyhood and teenhood, where his voice hasn't quite figured itself out yet.

"How many crates did you fill today?" he asks.

"I lost count after lunch. Thirty, maybe." I adjust my basket on my hip, then select a ripe red apple and sink my teeth into it. Sweet juice explodes in my mouth. After a long day of harvesting, the forbidden fruit—I mean, *literally* forbidden—tastes like pure goodness. I swallow and look at Elijah. "How many did you fill, little squirrel?"

"Ew." He scrunches up his nose. "Don't call me that."

"Why not?"

"Just… just don't."

I laugh and resist the urge to ruffle his hair, just to keep him in his little-brother place.

"So?" I ask through my mouthful of heavenly bliss. "How many?"

"Forty-eight. So… way more than you."

"It's not a race, you know." I roll my eyes.

"I know." He looks away, but not before I see the mischievous grin creeping on his lips. "But still. I beat you."

I shove him.

"Hey!" He laughs and regains his balance. Then his smile slowly fades, and he looks at the ground, his features more serious than I've seen in a long, long time. "You're leaving tomorrow."

My own humor dissipates like an early morning mist.

"Maybe they'll let you choose your career," he says. "And you can choose to stay here."

"When have they ever let anyone choose?"

"What if you could, though?"

"I can't."

"But, like, use your imagination." He looks at me, his dark hair falling into his eyes. "You're not careered yet, so I know you still have one. If you had the choice, what would your career be, and why?"

"What is this, some sort of interrogation?"

"Sure. So?"

He's not going to let this go, is he? "Okay. Okay." I let the question simmer as we continue walking. What would I be and why? I look ahead at the apple trees surrounding us. Farther down the rows, our cabin nestles between two hills, smoke curling out of the chimney, making it look like some painting hanging in the courthouse.

A painting.

I love to paint. If being an artist were a career, I could sketch and paint all day for a living.

But I can't tell Elijah that. I have to be a bit more practical for my little brother, set the good example of a responsible worker instead of a dreamer. Because dreams have no place in this world.

"I'll be happy with whatever career they give me, I guess." The lie comes easily, and a piece of my hope deflates, because reality. Reality is a jackal. Reality strangles the fuchsia out of hope and leaves it black and blue and bruised in the dirt. Reality, I think, will be the death of us all.

"Good answer," Elijah says, mimicking the Patrician accent. "You get a Coin of Good Service for good citizen conduct."

"Just trying to be optimistic."

"Optimism is a good trait, Ember. But if you always choose to see the glass as half full, you'll never have the incentive to change anything."

I grit my teeth. "Wise words from a thirteen-year-old. Is that something Dad said?"

He shrugs. Elijah, ever the philosopher, wanting to take credit for every intelligent bit of advice he has to offer. Well, good for him for not wanting to conform to the brainless way of thinking that the majority of Ky adopts.

"What about you?" I ask before taking another bite of my apple. "What career would you choose?" I look at him and grin. "And *why?*"

"Oh, easy. I'd be a politician."

All humor saps from the marrow of my bones, and I almost choke on that last bite. "Elijah." His name comes out in a strangled laugh-cough. "I thought I told you to stop talking about being a politician."

His jaw tightens and he shoves his hands into his pockets.

"They don't even offer that job to the Proletariat," I press.

"But, if I get good grades, they might offer it to me."

Mmm no they won't, is what I probably shouldn't say to my naive little brother.

"I mean," he says. "It doesn't hurt to hope for it, does

15

it?"

Well, yeah, it kind of does. It hurts to want something so badly, to think, dream, dwell on it so much that your soul threatens to leave your body for it. But your soul can't grasp this unreachable dream because it's trapped in this body, and so a little piece of you is sliced off every time you allow one moment of daydreaming.

Elijah, I should say, *you could never be a politician unless you were born into a Patrician family.* I should—but I don't say. Because even though it's not the law, it's just the way things happen around here. Patricians get the elite education that politicians require. And we Proletariats are far from having royal—I mean, *Patrician*— blood.

"Come on," I say instead. "It's getting late, and Dad probably needs help bagging the apples."

I walk faster, leaving him behind and fighting my growing irritation. Because I honestly don't really want to talk about dreams or careers or politicians or tomorrow. I'd be perfectly happy if this day, this moment right here, lasted forever. Because surrounding me are rows and rows of apple trees stretching over hills for a mile, and above, the sky is a canvas holding the merging colors of burnt orange, searing flames, strawberry red, and lavender wine. Right now I'm loving the way the grass brushes up against my knees, and I'm soaking in the evening serenade orchestrated by over-excited crickets. Every bit of this moment could go on and on and I really wouldn't mind.

But the city buildings of Ky rise on the horizon; uneven blocks of concrete, reminding me that my life is not my own and tomorrow. Tomorrow I'll join them. I'll leave the sanctuary of the Garden and join these cold, stone buildings and become a workaholic robot.

And maybe. Maybe a piece of me is terrified, because I've never been to the metropolis. Farthest I've ever traveled is the farmers' square in the heart of the Community Garden, one mile north of here—just a few small buildings where we store food, pick up our rations, and hang out at our own tavern.

But the city is a strange mystery of skyscrapers and factories and enclosed streets and recycled air and people people people *everywhere* and it's suddenly getting too hard to breathe just thinking about it.

The crunch of a rumbling vehicle sounds down the road when I arrive at the mailbox. I step back, coughing on the dust the jeep stirs as it drives toward the square. The delegate from Frankfort is most likely riding in that vehicle. He or she will assign me and everyone else who turned sixteen this year our careers first thing in the morning.

I just wish I were a little bit more excited about it.

When I open the lid to our mailbox, there's a letter inside. I unseal the wax and unfold the crisp brown paper, though I already know what the white ink says:

Your rations are available for pick up in the town square.

The door to the cabin creaks when I open it, and I have to shove it closed with force so it latches. Dad is in the kitchen bagging the apples we picked this morning. He stamps each bag with a label. I notice his mustache twitch like it always does when he talks to himself. He's tying a string around one of the filled bags but his fingers are struggling with the tie.

His wiry fingers.

His fingers that are stiff from the arthritis eating at his bones and his knotted knuckles. He's skin and bones from eating too little, and sometimes I wonder how he'll possibly survive against the cold and the wind and the rain and the snow that's sure to come because all that cold, damp weather seems to make his arthritis worse.

They used to have medicine for arthritis, or at least something to take the pain away, but it disappeared with all the other medicines when the White Plague struck. It takes a lot of time and brain power to recreate something like medicine, and we don't have the resources. We've taken thirty steps back into the past. We're rebuilding, trying to figure out this life thing again, clamoring back to where we were before the White Plague, and we're failing miserably.

And people like Dad are the ones paying for it.

"I can pick up our rations tonight." I drop the letter in front of him, then help him finish tying the string.

"Hm. They're finally in," he mutters. "A week late, but at least they're in."

"A week late is better than two weeks."

"Optimistic, as always," Dad says. "But too much optimism will kill your incentive to change anything."

I snort back a laugh and shoot Elijah a look. "Sounds like something Elijah would say."

Elijah pretends not to notice as he finishes tying off one of the last bags, but I can just barely make out a twitch of his lips.

"Well," Dad says with a sigh. "If they delivered our food on time, we wouldn't be forced to *steal* the apples we pick." His shoulders shake with what I think is a chuckle, but I'm not sure because the sound is a little off, a little choked, a little...pitiful. "I don't know what we're going to do in the winter when there are no more apples to keep Elijah and me fed," Dad says.

18

Elijah and me. Because I won't be here come winter. The veins around my heart tighten. What will happen to Dad and Elijah when I'm gone? We're already living on bare minimum when our rations actually *do* come in. Oatmeal for breakfast, a chunk of dried meat and cheese for lunch, and a small boxed meal for dinner—the kind where you *just add hot water.* So when our rations are late, when *Dad's* and *Elijah's* rations are late, where will they get their food? Come December, there won't be any more apples to keep their bellies full.

But, I shouldn't worry.

Because, I mean, I don't think anyone's actually *starved* to death in Ky. *They* make sure we don't. They feed us just enough to keep us from dying off. To keep us working like bees. Somehow, when someone gets close to starvation, the government steps in and fixes it.

That's what the chief does. Takes care of us like a father to his children. Chief Titus Whitcomb and his host of politicians keep the chaos under control, the rations and clothing and shelter equally distributed among us so no one is overcompensated and no one is homeless. We're all equal, all bees working for one big hive—a picture, a dream to bring this government back where it used to be. Parity is always preserved in this government and times are much easier now than they used to be.

At least, that's what the government wants us to believe.

But Dad has other theories. Dad thinks Chief Whitcomb and his swarm of politicians are just milking the system. That they're taking our resources—the apples we harvest and bag and send off—and not giving us the payment we deserve. That these rations they provide are maybe one-tenth of what they actually have stored up, and maybe they're stuffing it away for themselves, for the Patricians, for the people who are born and raised in the golden city known as Frankfort.

Dad has done the math in his head and seems to have figured out how many people are living in Ky and how much food they're all providing and how much food is actually coming back to us.

But me? I try not to question the system. Because that's what we're taught in school. Don't ask questions and you'll be okay. Don't stand out and you won't get in trouble. Blend in. Cooperate. The chief is great, the system is fixed, and don't challenge it unless you want to die at the claws of a black tiger.

And that. THAT is why I shove down my grief, swallow my anger, and force myself to look at Career Day tomorrow as a brand new opportunity full of wonderful possibilities.

CHAPTER TWO

After a dinner of baked apples and sliced apples and juiced apples and apple-everything, I take our family I.D. card and head toward the square to pick up our rations. Up ahead, our neighbor Leaf walks toward the square.

"Leaf," I call over the wind.

He turns and grins at me. "Hey, girl."

"Wait up." I race to catch up.

Leaf is exactly how one would picture a boy named leaf to appear: A paper-thin boy, flapping in the wind with wiry arms and bird legs, and he's really not any taller than me. His ivory wool shirt is too baggy, and his brown cotton pants are rolled up at the ankles, making him look even more dwarfish than he already is.

Just as I'm about to catch up, he turns around and starts jogging. "I'll race ya."

"What?" I pant. "I just caught up!"

But he's already jogging ahead of me, so I break into a

sprint, renewed adrenaline coursing through my veins, and it's not long before I'm passing him.

Running. It's my escape. My heart rate slowly picks up with each step, detoxing the anxiety of tomorrow from my bloodstream. Inhale. Exhale. Replenish bad air for good.

Everything's going to be okay.

But while I run, thoughts of tomorrow weave through my mind the way the wind weaves through my hair. And the fear makes the veins tighten around my heart and I run more quickly, breathe harder, make my blood pump through my veins faster until a calming presence demolishes all my fears. And I know everything's going to be okay.

Because sometimes. Sometimes I think there's something bigger out there. Something—or some*one* so elusive yet so incredibly present, knowing my deepest thoughts and wildest motives and most terrifying fears and unreachable hopes. I think this, because I *feel* this overwhelming presence. In the rarest moments, in the quiet, when I'm alone there's a pull. A whisper of the unknown begging to be known. And I want so badly to reach out and grasp it—but I don't. I can't. Because calling out to nothing is certifiably insane, and I'm not crazy.

So I pull back. I blink away this feeling and push away the presence while clinging to the hope that it will return.

And maybe…maybe someday I will reach out to this incredible being. I will hold onto this overwhelming power.

And I won't let go.

When I reach the town square I slow to a jog, then hunch over and plant my hands on my knees, drag air into my starving lungs. Leaf trots up behind me, his own breathing as heavy as mine.

I straighten and grin at him. "Beat ya."

"Holy Crawford," he says between breaths. "Everything's a competition with you, ain't it?"

"Hey, it was your idea to race."

"You weren't s'posed to win, though."

"I always win."

He laughs and tugs my ponytail. "Don't get too cocky now, Ember-girl."

"Oh come on, Leaf. Let me bask in the glory just a bit longer. Being the fastest girl in the Garden is really the only achievement I have to my name."

He chuckles and locks his hands behind his head, dragging in another breath. "You in a hurry to go home tonight?" His brown hair is too shaggy, whipping in the wind that sweeps in from the east.

"So I can sit in bed and sulk about tomorrow? Yeah, no thanks. Why?"

"We should hang out at The Tap or something."

"What, you don't think you'll ever get a free drink again when we're gone?" I offer a wicked grin.

"Not me. I'm not nearly as persuasive as you. Just one look at you and Judd fills whatever order you command." He snorts and shakes his head. "And so does practically everyone else."

"Hanging at The Tap actually sounds divine." Anything sounds better than returning home only to lie in bed wide awake, dreading tomorrow. Honestly, just thinking about Career Day makes me want to puke.

"So," Leaf says as we walk toward the courthouse. "You ready to be drafted into the Line of Defenders?"

"Um, no? Why do you say that?"

"Because that's what happens. Every year. Almost

everyone's given a career as a Defender. Last year it was over half the group. Remember?"

I did notice that last year. "Why would Ky need more Defenders of the Peace? They already have more than they need patrolling every corner. There's no war going on—"

"At least not that we're aware of." He glances at me and arches a thick brow. "But the government doesn't really tell us much, now do they?"

No. They don't. The only news we receive is posted on the town square board every week, and it's usually about the upcoming weather so we farmers can prepare. Occasionally it lists the names of notorious criminals scheduled for executions, rebels who verbalize their opinions a bit too loudly, or thieves who succumb to stealing food just before they starve to death. Those of us living in the Community Garden actually have it kind of easy because when our rations run out, we can always slip a bit of food from our own harvest inconspicuously. City folk don't have that luxury.

"So," I say. "You've completely resigned yourself to the Line of Defenders?"

"I don't know." Leaf drags his hand down the length of his face. "But I'm screwed if I do." He looks at me and smirks. "I mean, I'm not gonna let them make me fight for a cause I know nothin' about. There's no way."

"You won't really have a choice, though."

He shrugs. "I'll resist them."

"Whoa. That's, um, ballsy." I let out a choked laugh, but he's not smiling. He keeps his gaze straight ahead, and if I didn't know him any better, I would think he was dead serious. Because Leaf is in no condition to resist Defenders. But I know Leaf and I understand his wry humor. "They won't pick you," I say, trying to ease the tension.

"Um. Why not?"

"Because, look at you." I look him up and down and lift a mocking brow. "You'd be, like, an apple tree standing among a bunch of great Oaks."

His mouth drops open, then he clamps it shut and crosses his skinny little arms over his skinny little chest. "Wow, Ember. What a way to make me feel like a wimp."

I cringe. "You're not a wimp. I mean. I'm just trying to make you feel better."

"And a good job you're doing."

Better to just stop talking.

We have to wait in line to receive our rations. Each of our families gets a large crate that's supposed to—but doesn't—last us through the month. We gather our rations, then we head over to The Tap.

The Tap is really the only place where we can spend our meager Coins of Good Service. It's funny how food is so scarce in the country, but alcohol flows as freely as rain from the sky. As long as you have the Coins of Good Service to purchase them, you can get as many drinks as you want. I guess it's the government's way of patting us on the back and apologizing for our pathetic existence.

Smoky air hits me as we step inside. The light is dim, and someone plays a loud upbeat melody on the piano. This bar isn't nearly as nice as The Roaring Lion, the new tavern on the north side of the square. The Roaring Lion has a smooth silver floor and colorful lights hanging from the ceiling and a purifier to clear the smoke out instantly. Instead of an old, out-of-tune piano, music streams in from the city.

But The Tap matches the farmers' spirits more. I like the old smoky smell, even though I don't smoke. The piano has been here all my life, and the out-of-tune music has grown on me. The red tile floor is chipped, and some of the lights flicker, but this place is home.

"Well, well. If it ain't some of the finest young folks running this part of the Garden," a toothless old man says, tipping his straw hat.

"Hi John," I say. He raises cows to provide milk and meat for the city. Sometimes he's kind enough to slip us some milk in return for some fresh apples. This is just another reason I love The Tap: I know everyone here.

Well, *almost* everyone.

My eyes are drawn to a taller boy sitting on a stool by the bar. His short hair is the color of gold, and his skin has the undertone of butter. He must not live here, because I would immediately recognize features like those. For a moment I wonder if he's the delegate, but his clothes are rugged and worn, nothing like the neat black slacks and vests delegates and politicians wear.

I follow Leaf through the crowd toward the bar. We set our boxes on the floor and sit two benches down from the stranger.

Judd's unruly beard parts to reveal a yellow-toothed smile when he sees us.

"Can we have one Viper's Tongue?" I ask, remembering Leaf's favorite drink. "And plain old water for me."

"Sure thing."

I grin. For reasons I still don't understand—I think because Mom passed away and Judd was fond of her—Judd always gives me exactly what I want, no Coins of Good Service necessary. It's why Leaf always insists on accompanying me here: free drinks.

Judd looks at Leaf as he begins to fill the order. "You

celebrating 'fore the big day tomorrow?"

"Celebrating?" Leaf's lips twist into a disgusted smirk. "What's there to celebrate, exactly?"

Judd shrugs. "Well, don't drink too much. Don't want your head pounding the moment you're called to your career. Want to leave a good impression, y'know?"

"Don't worry about us, Judd," Leaf says. "I think we're ready for whatever tomorrow smacks us with. But let's not ruin the fun." He looks at me, lifts his drink, and grins. "Tonight, we drink."

I try to smile back, but my face is broken, the muscles in my lips refusing to be drawn up in a smile when my soul feels completely shattered. The upbeat music fades into the back of my mind at the brutal reminder that I might never see Leaf or the Community Garden or—even worse—my family again.

Leaf drinks, then strikes up a conversation with Judd about how shoddy our luck will be if we're all drafted into the Line of Defenders, to which Judd responds that if more Defenders are what the chief wants, then there must be good reason for having them.

And I have to set my glass down, swallow the tears burning the back of my throat, and stare at the stained bar. Because I really don't want to be a Defender. And Leaf really *really* doesn't want to be a Defender. But neither of us have an option to which career we get. It's the way the world works—our punishment for overpopulation.

The White Plague struck. It wiped out every last heartbeat on this continent, and every survivor found their way here—which used to be a slice of what was known as Kentucky. Our tiny country is surrounded by rivers on every side. No one wants to venture across the rivers or even to the edge of the city, which is nothing but a ghost town. No one wants to see what's left of our ruins. No one wants to risk getting what lingers of the plague when they're safe here.

And as a reward for our cowardice, we have to obey the laws of the government. We have to accept our careers with gratitude. It's not what I want, but it's the way it has to be to keep the balance of the government.

Someone clears his throat beside me, snapping me back to the present. The blond boy who sat two benches down has moved beside me, a bottle in hand, and the bluest eyes I've ever seen focused right on me.

CHAPTER THREE

I say the bluest eyes I've ever seen, but they're the *only* blue eyes I've ever seen. Like two buckets filled to the brim with water. Dad told me there used to be people with blue eyes and blond hair and skin white as milk, but they're creeping to extinction. I thought they were already gone. I mean, when they piled all the un-plagued into this tiny little country, our ancestors interbred, their genes merging until everyone came out olive-skinned with dark brown hair and brown eyes.

But this guy clearly came out of another gene pool.

He clears his throat. "Did you... um... pay for that?" He looks at my glass of water.

Fresh water is a commodity around here, and, no, I didn't pay for it. And this stranger didn't miss a thing. Oh, rot. This is usually a safe place. Judd never charges us. But this guy is foreign. With one word, he could have the Defenders on me in an instant. My heart trips over itself, and

I quickly try to come up with an excuse or some flirty pick-up line or *something* to get me out of this mess, but his eyes light with a hint of humor, and he laughs.

"Don't worry." He grins, revealing the straightest, whitest teeth I've ever seen. "I'm not going to smoke you out."

I let out a breath I didn't realize I was holding, and my heart sort of remembers how to beat. "Holy Crawford," I breathe. "You—you really scared me."

I could go to prison for stealing if the Defenders knew I didn't pay for this. And people who go to prison NEVER get out. Ky does not tolerate disobedience to the law, no matter how big or small the crime. It's how they keep complete control.

The boy takes a drink from his bottle, then holds out his hand. "I'm Forest."

I take his long fingers briefly in mine. "Ember." It's safer to remain on a first name basis.

"Ember. You from here?"

"Yes. My dad owns—*oversees*—the apple orchard. But you're obviously not from here."

His eyebrows are two slices of gold arching up. "How can you tell?"

"I've never seen anyone with hair that light... or eyes that blue... or..." Stop. I'm rambling. He is really good looking, with a well-defined chin and sculpted lips. I mean, he looks like a picture I want to paint.

Am staring. Look away.

He laughs softly and takes another swig from his bottle. "I'm from the city."

I figured as much. Besides his foreign looks, his accent is different. More clipped than the farmers' around here. Of course he's from the city.

"What brings you to the Garden?" I ask.

He sets his bottle down. "I'm, uh, landscaping."

I could have guessed he was a builder. His arms are strong and beautifully built, attesting his hard work. "Where are you landscaping?"

"On the north side of the Community Garden. Miles away by the strawberry fields."

"Ah. But the strawberry fields are way up north. Why are you *here*? Isn't The Roaring Lion closer to where you work?"

"Yes, but, you know..." He glances at the ceiling. "Cameras. I would rather not be watched when I'm off the clock, you know?"

"Oh." Of course. The Roaring Lion, with all its new technology, would have cameras hooked in every corner of the ceiling. "It won't be long before they put cameras in here, too."

"Yeah... might be a good thing though, yes?" he says.

"Why?" Why would cameras ever be a good thing?

"They keep the violence under control."

"Well, this place doesn't get very violent."

"I can see that." He leans in closer. "But if there are any criminals about, the government would need to know. How else would they find them unless there are cameras everywhere?"

I can't tell if he's kidding or serious. I'm so used to being around people I know and who know me and who I can trust completely, that I'm stumbling for words around Forest because he's a stranger. How am I supposed to act around a stranger? Can I trust him? Can I tell him everything I'm thinking and trust him to keep a secret? Or do I shut down?

"Most criminals aren't really criminals," I say, testing the grounds.

"No? What are they, then?" His eyes are inquiring, but not accusing.

"Just... people with opinions. People who want to speak their mind instead of bend beneath the will of the government."

He jerks his head back, as though this is the first he's heard such a rebellious statement. Should've kept my mouth shut. But the spark leaves his eyes, and he gives a casual shrug before taking another drink from his bottle.

"So you're one of those people who thinks the government's out to get us." He chuckles and shakes his head like I'm some stupid child.

My walls of defense come up. "No."

"No?" He looks at me, his beautiful blue eyes narrowed.

I sigh. Time to cover up my tracks before Mr. Loyalist here calls the Defenders on me.

"I-I've just heard other people talk about the conspiracies." Mainly my dad, but Forest doesn't need to know that.

"Conspiracies?" he asks. "What sort of... conspiracies?"

"You know." I shrug and stare at the rough wood of the table. "The usual."

"The usual?"

"Mm-hm."

"And what, exactly, is the... usual?"

I chew the tip of my tongue and peek at him. His questions seem more like inquiries than accusations. He's smiling and possibly a bit tipsy from whatever he's drinking, so maybe he won't even remember this conversation tomorrow.

Leaning forward, I rest my elbow on the bar and prop my chin on my fist. "Tell me, Forest the Builder, what would happen if you objected to the career given you?"

He offers a no-nonsense sort of smile. "I wouldn't do that. I appreciate that the government gives us jobs and food and shelter."

Eye-roll. Such a brown-nosing answer that pretty much everyone gives out of sheer fear.

"But, like, what would happen if you had refused your career?" I suddenly realize I sound entirely too much like Elijah.

"If I refused my career?"

"Mm-hm."

He sets his jaw. "I'd get arrested."

"Exactly." I straighten, slap the table with my hand, resting my case. "We have to do the work Ky gives us, or we die. Not only that, but we're paid with meager rations of food that, as of the past year, have been *late*. Though they sugar-coat our status as *Proletariats,* those of us with brains know we're all slaves working away for Chief Whitcomb—"

"Careful." Forest cuts me off with a dangerously quiet voice. All humor is gone from his eyes, and I clamp my overly loud mouth shut. Maybe I shouldn't be speaking so freely to Mr. Builder.

"Sorry," I say. "My da—some *people* believe Whitcomb and his politicians have us all squashed under their thumbs."

"Sounds like you believe that, too."

I pick at a deep gash in the wooden bar. "I honestly don't know what I believe."

"No? Allow me to enlighten you. We're not slaves. *No one* is a slave here. The Chief has created a... utopia of sorts for us. There are no homeless people. Criminals are being taken care of. Everyone is treated equally."

"Everyone except the politicians, that is."

His mouth opens slightly, then he closes it. "The politicians are the ones working the hardest to keep the government functioning. They deserve a little more than we *Proletariats* do for their hard work."

I snort. Usually people I have this conversation with are a bit more passive. I mean, sure, at first glance they talk about how great the government is, but dig a little deeper and they're more agreeable than argumentative. I tell them how messed up our government is, and they nod and say, "Okay, yes, yes." But Forest here is about as clueless as a stump and as stubborn as a boulder. Brainless. He's one of the brainless who just does whatever is asked of them. Well. I should probably fix that.

"What about the *criminals*?" I lean forward. Might as well plunge right in to prove my point. "If you have any measure of conscience, you can't agree with the executions. Why can't criminals just spend some time in prison and go to a trial where they receive justice? Why does the smallest little act of rebellion have to end in a dramatic death sentence?"

"Because no one would be afraid of stealing or standing up against the government if they only had to endure a few months in prison for it. Everyone knows the law. If they didn't want to get an execution, they shouldn't commit crimes in the first place."

"What's wrong with standing up for what you believe in?"

"Um…" He chokes out a laugh and returns his gaze to his drink, both hands wrapped around the bottle, his knuckles white. He's tense, maybe even angry. He has to be a Loyalist.

Oh, rot. I should have kept my shoddy mouth shut.

"I'm sorry." I should probably cover up my tracks now before he turns me in. "You're right, of course, Forest. The politicians do a good job running our government. We're lucky to live in such a prosperous society." I wince at my own sarcasm. Prosperous. That's the joke of the century. Only politicians live in prosperity, and according to Forest, they *deserve* it for all the *hard work* on their part.

Forest straightens, studies me through narrowed slits, crosses his arms, then says. "You don't have to lie to me, Miss Ember."

Miss Ember? That's a first anyone's ever called me *miss*. I kind of like it.

"I'm not going to turn you in," Forest continues. "I just—" He swallows, a look of confusion flitting through his cobalt eyes. "I've *never* heard anyone speak so forcefully against our government. I mean, I knew there were people out there who had problems with it." He shrugs, laughs a little. "But I guess since I live in the city where we're constantly monitored, no one risks talking like that."

And he seems so incredibly honest right now with no sign of resentment that I can't help but ask, "So, do you agree?"

"I don't necessarily disagree. I just need some time to think about what you said."

"Oh." How has he not taken time to process this information before? But the majority of Ky is like that. People brainlessly working for this higher power—Titus Whitcomb and his snotty politicians—without giving second thought to how they're all treated like common slaves. It's pathetic, really. Kind of embarrassing. And I'm glad Dad

35

raised me to think for myself and not conform to following society.

I pass my empty glass to Judd, who is still talking to Leaf about who-knows-what.

"I guess," Forest says. "I can see why you chose this tavern instead of the one on the north end of town." He smiles a little. "You would have been arrested within the first five minutes of our argument if they'd have caught you on camera."

Some of the tension leaves my body. Maybe he really won't turn me in.

"You've got to watch what you say, though, Ember." His smile fades and he leans toward me, so close that I catch the heady whiff of cinnamon coming off his body. "You talk so casually about the government," he whispers. "But if they hear your treason, they *will* kill you."

His gaze is so intense, blue sapphire eyes burning into mine, and I have to look away before he sees into my very soul and knows *everything* I'm thinking, including how wonderfully attractive he is and how I have to remind my heart to beat because one look from him just. Makes. Everything. Stop.

I try to breathe again. "I guess I feel so far removed from the government. All the politicians are in the city, and the city is miles away. The Tap always feels so safe—"

"This place may *seem* safe." His gaze flickers past me. "But people might be watching."

All the tension creeps back into my shoulders, and I follow his gaze. To the corner. A man sits alone at a table. He holds a paper in front of him, as though reading it, but his eyes scan the bar. He wears farmers clothes, but they're crisp and clean, not like the worn, threadbare clothes the rest of us wear. We still have three months before new uniforms arrive. On one finger, he wears a giant gold ring. *No one* in the Community Garden can afford a piece of jewelry like that. His eyes find mine and I quickly turn around. My heart is pounding so hard, I wonder if he can hear it clear across the room.

"A spy." I look at Forest. "How did you know?" All this time he acted like this place was safe.

Forest offers a sad smile. "Spies are everywhere to keep crime under control. I would think you of all people would know that, based on your..." He flips his hand in the air. "Conspiracies."

I don't know how I missed it. Of course the government wouldn't tell us they had a spy in a building. If they did, everyone would behave. And they want to weed out those of us who aren't brainless loyalists. Those like me, Leaf, and Dad. Goosebumps flesh out across my skin. How long has this place been watched? Will the Defenders come after me now? Can that man hear me from across the room? I glance at Judd. Does *he* know this place is being watched? Surely not, or he wouldn't be passing out free drinks.

Forest clears his throat and takes on a less rigid position. "So, which career do you hope to receive tomorrow?"

"Farming." The word tumbles out of my lips before I can stop it, but by the look in Forest's eyes, I wish I hadn't said it. "B-but I'll be happy with whatever career is given to me. Of-of course."

A small smile touches his lips. "If you move to the city, you'll have a lot of changes to get used to, Miss Ember."

There it is again. *Miss* Ember. Who even talks like that?

The door to the bar bursts open, and the piano music

stops. Shivers weave up my spine one vertebrae at a time, and I slowly turn around. Ten Defenders stride into the bar, their guns in hand as if ready to fire. My breath freezes in my lungs because I just said a whole bunch of things I shouldn't have verbalized, and there's a spy in this bar right now, and I'm going to be arrested. I'm going to be killed for my free thoughts. I'm going to—

"We're looking for Jonah Walker."

My lungs remember how to breathe. Jonah Walker. They're looking for some guy named Walker. I could almost laugh out loud from relief, but instead, I'm completely confused because I've *never* heard of Jonah Walker, and I know *everyone* in the Community Garden.

I look at Forest. Is he hiding his identity? He looks suspicious with his shoulders hunched, his hand up by his face, as though hiding from the approaching Defender. But when the Defender passes us, showing us the picture on his tablet, I realize Forest looks nothing like this Jonah Walker. Walker has wild green eyes, slick black hair, and a peppery beard. A deep scar runs from his left temple to his chin. Apart from his green eyes, he looks like the majority of the citizens of Ky.

After the Defender passes us, I look at Forest. "Do you know him? Walker, I mean?"

Forest frowns and gives a brief shake of his head, but something in him has changed. His jaw is set, his blue eyes frosting over like ice as they scan the room.

"But you've heard of him, haven't you?" I press.

His eyes find mine. "You haven't?"

"Um. No?" Should I have?

"He's a notorious criminal."

"What's his crime?"

Forest studies me for a long moment, as though considering his answer. Then he shrugs and says, "It doesn't matter. Doesn't look like he's here."

"I wonder why they thought he was."

"Spies. He was probably here a moment ago and then snuck out. No one even noticed, it's so crowded in here."

He's right. If there are any criminals about, The Tap would be the best place to go to blend in, even with Mr. Creepy Spy hunched over in the corner, who is now gone, his paper left discarded on the table like it didn't cost him a few precious Coins of Good Service. But…how does Forest know who this Walker guy is? There must be a lot going on in the metropolis that we country folk don't know about. It's harder for word to spread when us country folk are so thinned out. Our only news comes from the Defenders, who share only what they're instructed to share by Chief Whitcomb.

"You have beautiful eyes, you know that?"

I look up. Forest is leaning toward me, all the commotion clearly forgotten as he studies me like I'm some sort of new specimen.

"What?" I ask.

"Your eyes," he says. "They look like they're always smiling."

I blink. Twice. No boy has ever given me a compliment like that. It's far too forward a thing for shy country boys to say. And I should probably put my guard up, because Dad always says that forward city boys are not to be trusted. Nonetheless, heat invades my face, and I look away, hating myself for smiling just a little bit at the compliment.

"Thanks," I mumble.

Leaf clears his throat too loudly beside me. "Ember, it's late. We should get home. Big day tomorrow."

I quickly nod. After the scare of the Defenders storming the tavern, and now this strange confusing buzz I get just by one look from Forest, I want desperately to get out of here.

"It was good meeting you, Miss Ember." Forest stretches out his hand.

I take it, a shudder racing up my spine by the warmth of his long fingers, and for an instant, I'm lost in the ocean of his blue eyes. He smiles, his gaze searching mine as though he's trying to tell me something.

"Forget," he says slowly. "*Everything* we talked about here."

Of course. Of course I'll forget it. What he said was vital information, and I'll never rat him out for sharing it with me. Releasing Forest's hand, I follow Leaf out of the tavern and wonder if I'll ever see Forest again. But there's no way. Unless I'm given the career of a farmer, which isn't likely, I'll be headed to the city tomorrow.

Or worse, the Line of Defenders.

CHAPTER FOUR

A chilly wind sweeps in from the east as we step outside. The sky has darkened to black velvet and no stars shine. Fitting. Stars are made of fire that burns and burns and burns, transmitting endless amounts of energy amidst the infinite void of black. Stars are a sign of hope. And right now, I feel no hope. Only an aching longing for things to be different. Better. Improved and corrected. So, the fact that no stars shine tonight echoes the feeling in my soul.

"Who was that you were talkin' to?" Leaf asks when we're halfway home, far away from any listening ears or cameras.

"His name is Forest. He works in landscaping." I lower my voice. "I guess spies go to The Tap to keep an eye on things. There was one sitting in the corner tonight."

"Really?" He snorts out a laugh. A pathetic thing. "I'm not surprised. I wonder if they'll send me to the stadium for un-careered drinking. Welcome to Ky, the place where one innocent drink can get you executed."

I smile and kick a pebble into the ditch. "You had way more than one *innocent* drink, my friend."

"They don't know that. For all this spy knows, I could've been drinking water."

"Yeah, water dolled up by Judd's magic syrup." I roll my eyes and look ahead at the dark abyss in front of us. The Garden electricity has already been turned off for the night, but I can just barely make out the gravel road. Way out, the tall buildings glitter like stars offering false hope. The city never sleeps, so they say. People work all day and all night there. And that's why it makes perfect sense that the criminal the Defenders were looking for is on the loose here in the Garden. You can't find anything in this pitch black of night here.

"Hey, do you know who that Jonah Walker guy is?" I ask.

Leaf clears his throat. "No idea. But the Defenders were pretty determined to get him." He shoves his hands into his pockets.

"He's a notorious criminal. It's kind of creepy that a criminal is on the loose out here." I walk a little closer to Leaf and spare a glance at the dark fields surrounding the road.

"How do you know he's a criminal?"

"Forest told me."

"This Forest guy seems to know a lot." He offers a forced laugh. "You sure he wasn't one of the said spies in the bar?"

"Um, no. He was way too honest to be a spy. He's from the city, though, and I guess this sort of information is more accessible to him."

"I guess."

Another freezing wind whips at my shirt, announcing the too soon arrival of winter. Seasons used to be a little less cruel, a little more friendly as they merged together like a symphony, but that all ended around the same time the White Plague struck. Now winter is a brutal thing. Without much warning, icy winds sweep in at the speed of a train and wipe away the green and warmth and food and all us gardeners hibernate for a while. We hide in our living rooms, huddled together by our fireplaces while snow wages war outside our windows. And it's snow snow snow and storms and flurries and winter vortexes all through December and January and then spring.

Spring arrives with a rising sun melting away the snow and nightmares. Spring is the kiss from the universe, the proof from heaven that, if there is a God, he maybe remembers us and might still care a little.

We part ways when we pass Leaf's fields, and I make the rest of the trek alone. Running. Just in case this Jonah Walker is lurking around. When I step onto our porch, Dad opens the door before I have a chance to twist the knob.

"Where have you been?" he asks. Has he been crying? No. Not Dad. "I was worried sick about you." He wraps his arms around me and crushes me to his chest.

"Why?" I ask, pulling away. "Did you hear about the criminal too?"

Dad frowns. "Criminal?"

"Yeah. Like a *notorious* one." I use the big word Forest used. "He's loose in the Garden."

Dad stares at me a moment longer than necessary. "I was worried because my only daughter is leaving tomorrow. I might never see you again, and instead of coming home, you…you—what? What were you doing?"

My throat constricts. "I—I went to The Tap. With Leaf."

Dad sighs. Nods. Pulls me into another embrace.

Guilt is a vicious thing. It shatters dignity. You look in the mirror and see all the wrong things you did and you're left wondering why you were even born if it means hurting people all the time. I shouldn't have gone to The Tap. Not on my last night here. I should've stayed home, spent what precious little time I have left with my family. Instead I just thought of myself and what I wanted in that very moment.

"Come inside." Dad takes the box of rations from me and carries them into the kitchen.

Elijah's sitting in the living room playing his harmonica. I sit cross-legged beside the fireplace and stretch my freezing hands above the dying flames. Dad returns a moment later with a bowl of soup he made from a powder from our rations. Just add hot water, and you've got a full meal of vegetables and meat ready in exactly sixty seconds.

"So what's this about a notorious criminal?" Dad asks.

"Some guy named Walker is on the loose."

Dad stops chewing his food and looks up. "Walker?"

"You've heard of him?" Am I the only one who *hasn't* heard of him?

Dad nods and looks into his bowl. "I've heard of him."

I take a bite of my soup. "Also," I say between chews, "they have spies at The Tap."

"Shoulda seen that coming."

Of course. We all should have.

"God knows there's no escaping the giant eye examining our every move," I say.

"If there is a God, he left us to rot centuries ago." Dad

scrapes the bottom of his bowl with a wooden spoon. "He probably meant for the White Plague to wipe our species out entirely, but here we are, little cockroaches who survived the big blow out, scraping on meager rations of food and wondering what the shoddy inferno we're still doing here."

My lips twist into a cheeky smile. "Way to be optimistic, Dad." I look down at my broth and pick at the orange carrot bits in the brown gravy. But I can't stop the curiosity from picking at my brain. Is there a God? And if there is, does he enjoy watching us with cool indifference? I mean, he sure helped the Patricians get to where they are, but the rest of us? We're the dirt the Patricians build their empire upon.

These are questions that always plague me, questions that I can't bring up in front of anyone, because, well, I'd be sent to Frankfort Prison if I do. All religions were banned long ago, the churches burned to the ground. To speak of God is treason, and nowadays, ridiculous. Religions are ancient myths, something our fool ancestors believed in.

And yet...I feel the strange pull again. Like something or *someone* is calling out to me, nudging me, begging me to seek it out. And I wonder—I wonder if it's just my brittle emotions because of my current predicament, if it's my desire for something bigger, or if there really *is* something bigger out there, watching, waiting to make a move that'll wipe out our current system and completely transform the entire future of Ky for the better. It's really the only way anything could drastically change a system as established as this one.

Elijah begins to play an old song on his harmonica. Fitting. This is what we do every weekend, just before our one day off. We sit around the fire. Elijah plays his harmonica, Dad sings, and I paint—if I happen to have the

45

resources. It's a night of warmth and family, so it makes perfect sense that this is how we would spend our last night together.

"Elijah," Dad says when Elijah finishes his tune. "Why don't you play the song your mother always sang?"

I look sharply at Dad. Elijah doesn't remember Mom singing this song, of course. He was too young. But Dad often sang it to us, and every time would remind us that it was Mom's song, not his.

Elijah begins to play, and my heart stirs with an unquenchable longing. Even in her death, Mom pulls us together, somehow. The haunting melody strikes a chord inside me, making my soul ache and my spirit yearn for what could never be. Dad's deep troubadour voice fills the room as he sings the lyrics.

Follow me, little one, to land of ashes
Where death has its hold so it seems
Where rivers flow free and the water washes
Back the control of the supremes

I shudder. Because I've never given much thought about the words, which are too complex for a simple lullaby. So what does it all really mean?

Tunnels run deep by the northern line
When you follow the emerald eyes
Hidden beneath a blanket of vines
Is a place where our only hope lies

Shrugging off my apprehension, I stare at the embers, the glowing sparks for which I was named. Mom always said

Ember was a strong name. I remember the night before she was taken away, when Dad was trying to convince her to hide in the fields from the Defenders. I was only eight, but the events are fresh in my mind, as though they'd happened yesterday. It was the same day the older chief, Chief Aden, came to visit the Garden. We had a picnic at school in his honor. Mom seemed distracted all day, like there was something on her mind and she wasn't really listening to me much all afternoon.

Then evening came, and we sat right by this fireplace. The flames were out, but cinders still burned, red and hot. Mom looked at me, *really* looked at me, and she said in a gentle voice, "Ember. I gave you that name for a reason."

I pulled my knees to my chest and stared at her, uncertain.

"When the fire goes out, supposedly dead," Mom said, "the embers remain, tiny specks of charred wood and ash that have the capacity to start a fire large enough to burn down an entire city." She offered a strained smile, and there were shadows under her eyes from lack of sleep. "That's you, Ember. Everything seems calm. The fire has blown over, the White Plague wiped away, and our government established. And then there's you. Ember. The hidden flake of ash, still burning, glowing, igniting into a tiny flame that will someday blow over the entire nation of Ky."

That's what she said before she hid in the fields.

That's what she said before she was taken away.

And I still don't know what she meant. I don't know why those were the last words she chose to say to me, and why, if she knew she was about to be arrested, she didn't hold me and Elijah in her arms and whisper how much she loved us instead of going on and on about my name.

Because Ember is a pathetic name. Embers are the last thing a fire sees before it dies.

It's late when I go to my room. Rain begins pounding on the roof in a steady rhythm. I crawl into bed and stare blankly at the ceiling. What will tomorrow bring? All day I've tried to keep myself together. I've tried to adopt the mindset the government wants me to have: I am lucky to have a career. I am lucky to live in this government where food is given freely…as long as we do our part of the work to keep Ky functioning. I've tried so hard to be strong around Elijah and Dad, around Leaf and Judd…and even Forest.

But now I'm alone. In the dark. And the walls of the dam I built are chipping and cracking and the water is pushing pushing pushing until the levy crumbles completely and a tear slips. And slides down the bridge of my nose. And I'm breaking, fracturing into eleven million pieces. A sob escapes me, and I turn onto my stomach, pull my thin blanket up over my head, and curl into a ball that's strong enough to keep the whole world out.

I don't want to face the great unknown tomorrow. I don't want to go to the city where I have to monitor every single thing I say. I don't want to be a robot.

Outside rain patters against the windowpane and thunder rolls overhead.

Storms. Nature's beautiful disasters. Rain. Lightning. Thunder. One giant orchestra in the sky. A symphony of merging clouds and electric energy and anger and fury and raging winds. It's water evaporated and condensed into hard ice that's returned to its previous state that floods the earth. It's chemistry. It's music. It's power. And it's frightening and fascinating all at once.

My spirit is a raging storm. I am thunder. I am lightning. And I'm terrified that if one thing slips tomorrow, if one little thing goes wrong...

I'll snap.

CHAPTER FIVE

Mornings are strange creatures. The sun creeping along the horizon, spying on every living being, sticking its nose where it doesn't belong. It always rises too soon. It's the bearer of bad news, the grim reaper, and today—today it's taking me away from the Community Garden.

And I immediately feel tired all over. But I force myself out of bed and pull on my brown cotton pants and cream shirt, then set to packing my satchel for the big day. I don't have much, just an extra pair of clothes and an old paddle doll Mom made me when I was little. And paintings.

Lots of paintings.

I pause by my dresser and look over my paintings one last time. We're not allowed to have paper or paint or pictures. These items are too luxurious for menial farmers like us. The only way I ever painted was when Defender Shepherd covered his monthly shift in the Community Garden. The Defenders are on constant rotation as to keep them from getting too close to the citizens. Shepherd's shift before the Community Garden took place in Frankfort.

When I was young, around six, I saw him sitting by the road sketching. I didn't know any better than to approach a Defender. Or I didn't care. I saw him and Mom talk often enough, I guess I figured he was safe. I remember marveling at his picture of the orchard, so detailed and perfect. I wanted to have the ability to take a picture and capture it on paper like he did. I remember leaning over his shoulder as he drew––he was much more lenient than most Defenders today. I asked him if I could try. He laughed and taught me some basic rules of sketching. I asked him if he could bring more paper, so the next time he came, he did.

Since then, he'd gather discarded pieces of paper, pencils, paints, brushes, rare canvases, and any other art supplies carelessly thrown away by Patricians, and he'd give them to me with my word that I'd keep them hidden. I haven't seen Defender Shepherd in years. I wonder what happened to him. If he got in trouble for bringing paper and paint to the Community Garden.

I run my fingers over the rough surfaces of the brightly colored canvases. These are the pictures I've painted since I was a child.

Just another thing I'll have to leave behind.

Dad is cooking oatmeal when I step into the kitchen. My mouth waters. It's been a good two weeks since I've eaten a real breakfast. No more apples for me, please. I'll take the bland oatmeal. At least it has some consistency.

"You ready for today?" he asks while stirring the oatmeal. His voice is weak, and I know he's trying to be strong.

"I guess," I say.

He finally looks up at me, and the devastated look in his eyes rips every vein in my heart out.

"You don't have to do this, you know," he says.

Oh, no. Not this again. I carefully sit down in a kitchen chair, lean back and pick at the splintered wood of the table.

"Um. Yes I do," I say.

"You could run away."

"Where the shoddy blazes would I run?" I release a half-hearted laugh. "The city surrounds us. There's nowhere to hide."

"Hide in the fields."

"Like Mom did? See what good that ever did her." I regret the words as soon as they fall out of my mouth.

Dad looks down at the pot of oatmeal and stirs again, his lips pressed together in a thin line and his face reddening.

Why do I always say the wrong thing? I never think before I speak. The words in my brain slip from my lips like bullets and I'm left in my own cloud of regret, watching the smoke clear, seeing the aftermath unfold before me, the damage done by words that forgot to pass through a filter.

But sometimes, Dad needs to hear the hard truth. Because Dad's not afraid to risk the authorities. "Life before slavery," he always says. But if he hadn't talked Mom into hiding in the fields when the Defenders came to question her, she might still be here.

Dad takes a seat at the table and passes me a bowl of oatmeal.

"If I hide, the Defenders will find me," I say more gently now. "And then they'll kill me, just like they killed Mom."

Dad scowls. "Somebody's got to do something."

Who? I want to ask. Who will do something? Who will

stop the madness of a controlling leader, careless Defenders, and mindless workers who are more than happy to do whatever the government tells them, even if it means starving to death?

No one. That's who. Because anyone who has the guts to speak up magically disappears off the face of the earth. Which is exactly what happened to Mom. And far be it from me to inspire Dad to do something incredibly stupid all because of me getting a shoddy career.

"I'll be okay, Dad," I say. "Maybe they'll give me a good career."

"It's not your job that bothers me. It's the fact that I'll never see you again." In the brief instant his eyes meet mine, I realize that he's holding back tears. Apart from last night, I haven't seen Dad cry since Mom was arrested. He's the rock of the family. Strong. Valiant. Brave.

My heart gives a violent twist, and I blink back my own tears because nothing strikes emotion more than seeing a strong person cry. I press my lips tightly together before they betray my own grief. I already decided to be strong today. No crying allowed. It will only make things harder for Dad. So I swallow the burning in my throat and force a shaky smile. I make myself think of the boy I met last night—Forest—and the thrill he made me feel just by the look in his eyes and the touch of his long fingers. And my smile feels a little more genuine.

"I'm actually excited about getting a new career," I lie. "And we don't know that I'll never see you again. They allow annual family visits." I shrug. "I'll see you then."

Dad lets out a humorless laugh. "They allow the visits, but they don't provide rides. It'll take you a full day just to walk here from the edge of the city. And if you're drafted to the Line of Defenders—"

"I won't be drafted." Holy Crawford, why does *everyone* think I'm going to be drafted?

Elijah walks into the kitchen a moment later, his dark hair flattened on one side. He looks at me, then runs up and throws his arms around my neck.

"Hey," I say. "Easy, kid."

"I don't want you to leave."

Now I can't hold back my grief. It slides up my spine, wraps around my lungs, and a sob escapes me as I crush him to my chest. The rest of the morning is spent in tense silence. We don't want to talk about Career Day, but there's nothing else to talk about. At noon, we walk toward the farmers' square.

Today is one of those days in the middle of autumn when the weather can't decide what on earth to do with itself. The sun is hot, but the wind is cold. The grass is green, but the leaves have turned.

Summer is ending, winter beginning.

I can't help but compare this day with my life. Because my past is warm and green. But my future looks dark and cold with wiry branches and promised winter storms.

Leaf and his parents join us on the road. We attempt small talk, but it's useless. Leaf's mom tries to lighten the mood with sentences that begin with, "Hey, remember that time when…" and Leaf and I both tense up and exchange annoyed glances because we know "that time" will never happen again. So what's the point of revisiting old memories? At best, they only create a yearning deep inside us to be children again. Children without worries of adulthood and careers and the fact that one-wrong-spoken-word can get you killed.

The square is buzzing with Defenders when we arrive. They always send more Defenders out on Career Day, because there is always that one person who is shoddy enough to deny their career and make a scene. Definitely more red uniforms out today.

The black military jeep that arrived in town yesterday is parked by the courthouse. Standing beside it are two people wearing black fedoras, long black slacks, and vests over crisp white shirts. My heart begins to pound. Only one type of people wear clothes that nice.

Politicians.

I stop walking and stare in shock.

"What are *they* doing in the Garden?" Leaf asks beside me. "They never come out here."

He's right. Usually they just send a delegate—a politician in training.

Surrounding them are at least ten Defenders. The first politician to enter the jeep is the biggest person I've ever seen, proof that to the Patricians, food is easily accessible. Right behind him, an older man with graying hair slips in. The Defender is about to close the door behind them, when someone shouts from across the street.

"Hold up!"

I look across the square to another politician jogging toward the jeep. And my heart stops. With blond hair that practically glows in the sunlight, I would recognize him anywhere, even without the builder clothes.

Forest.

CHAPTER SIX

Forest the Builder…is a politician?

Unbelievable. He lied to me. There I was, talking my heart out about how corrupt the government is, and he's *running* it. The sting of betrayal heats up my face, but the one burning question is, *why* didn't Forest hand me over to the Defenders?

"Hey," Leaf whispers beside me. "Isn't that the guy from—"

"Yes." I sniff back my sudden rage.

Forest says something to a tall woman with wavy black hair. She wears a black pencil skirt and a gray vest. Another politician, obviously. And a pretty one at that. She steps closer to him and gives him a peck on the cheek, then walks toward the school, two Defenders at her heels. My fingernails bite into my palms. Forest eases into the jeep, and the vehicle takes off down the road, leaving me seething in the dust.

"I guess that verifies what we already knew," Leaf says

with a laugh as he watches them leave. "Trust no one."

I offer a slow nod and follow him toward the square. Forest is a politician. No wonder he seemed angry at my conspiracies. No wonder he knew about the spies. *Forget everything I told you here*, he'd said. What he told me about the spy was confidential, but why would he share that kind of information with me?

When we file into the gymnasium, thoughts of Forest disappear, replaced with a new anxiety. The stink of sweat and heat hits me when I walk in, and the buzzing of talking people fills the air. I hug Dad and Elijah one more time, then watch them climb the stairs to the bleachers where they will observe us getting our careers. I'll be able to say goodbye to them one more time before loading on the bus that will take me to the city, assuming that's where I'll fulfill my career.

"Good luck, Ember."

I whirl around to find Ilene Jackson step through the door behind me.

"I hope they give you a career you want." She smiles, the wrinkles around her eyes forming crow's feet. Her husband, Charlie, steps in behind her, a pillar of support.

I feel my muscles relax as I lean in to hug them. The Jacksons live down the road from me where they work the vineyard. They're like the grandparents I never had. And now new tears are stinging my eyes, so I remind myself not to cry, and I pull away from them. Offering an awkward wave, I quickly turn around before a tear slips.

I join the others my age at the front of the gym. There are only fifteen of us; the Community Garden doesn't exactly have the largest population. Nothing compared to the hundreds of thousands of people inhabiting the rest of the megacity of Ky. I sit in a chair beside Leaf and stare ahead, struggling to keep my emotions at bay. Grief, anxiety, anger, they're all there, threatening to register on my face and fracture my emotionless façade.

I keep my eyes fixed on the microphone on the stage, push all thoughts out of my head, and decide that I'll at least try to *act* appreciative when given my career.

The crowd quiets down when the tall, skinny woman with wavy, black hair steps onto the stage. She must be a politician in training, since she's assigning us our careers. She kissed Forest on the cheek. Forest is a politician. Why do I even care? I'm *not* going to think about that lying son of a jackal right now.

Her black heels click across the stage as she nears the microphone. Flipping on the switch, she offers a cold, no-nonsense smile and lifts a white envelope in the air.

"My name is Olivia Doss." Her accent is neat and clipped, like Forest's. Why couldn't I figure out Forest was a Patrician by his shoddy accent alone?

Stop. Must focus.

"I will be assigning you your careers," Olivia continues. "Here I have fifteen cards, each one containing a career that will be assigned to each person in the front row." She lowers her hand. "When I call your name, please come forward to accept your career."

I wrap my ice-cold hands around the chair arms. Here it comes, the piece of paper that will determine my fate. I watch her pinky slit the envelope open. She reaches in and randomly pulls out a blue, plastic card.

"Nathan Van," she says. She lifts her gaze to us in the front row, her eyes catching Nathan, who stands and slowly walks up the stairs of the stage.

"Nathan Van, you have been chosen for a career in the Line of Defenders."

He takes the I.D. Card, and with a faint nod mumbles, "Thank you for your generosity."

"Adriana Smith." A girl whose father works in the bean fields walks up to accept her card. "Adriana Smith, you have been chosen a career in the Line of Defenders."

Another Defender career. As far as I know, the entire outside world has been consumed by the White Plague. We Ky citizens are the only remaining survivors. Who on this forsaken planet are we fighting? Ourselves? I don't want to be drafted to the military. I don't. But my chances of getting any other career are slim as name after name is called onto the stage, each person being assigned to the Line of Defenders.

"Leaf Benedict," Olivia Doss calls out.

Leaf mutters a curse under his breath. "Wish me luck," he whispers beside me. He walks up to the stage, his shoulders rigid, his steps stiff, as though he already knows what his fate is going to be.

"Leaf Benedict, you have been chosen a career in the Line of Defenders."

The words are like a punch to my stomach. Leaf takes the card, and then, almost sarcastically, says, "Thank you for your generosity." But he doesn't look thankful with his nose pinched, his gaze dark. He returns to his seat beside me, and I'm almost afraid to look at him.

"Leaf," I whisper. "I-I'm sorry."

He stares at the concrete ground, his Career Card in his fist and his jaw clenching and unclenching, and I realize, I've never seen him look so angry. Leaf is carefree and smiling, but right now he's scowling.

"Don't be," he finally says before looking at me. "You're going to be drafted, too."

The certainty in his voice knocks the breath out of my lungs. But, of course he's right. He's right. I am going to be a Defender of the Peace. I'm going to have to learn to conceal my emotions and arrest people for stealing, arrest starving people for trying to feed their families. That's going to be me. I'm going to be a monster.

I imagine firing guns and mushroom clouds. Pictures I've seen in our history books. And then I imagine the calm life I'd grown up with, surrounded by apple trees, with the sun on my face and a warm fire waiting for me at the end of the day. But now, I'm going to have to completely lose my humanity or be killed for refusing to be a Defender—

"Ember Carter."

I jump when my name is called, and my heart drops into my stomach. I feel myself rise from my seat, though I don't remember making the decision to do so. But my stubborn feet carry me up to the stage, one step in front of the other, matching the rhythm of my chaotic heartbeat, until I'm standing in front of Olivia Doss.

"Ember Carter," Olivia Doss says.

Inhale. Exhale. Replenish bad air for good. Everything's going to be okay.

"You have been assigned the career of a—" she stops mid-sentence, blinks several times, furrows her brows and looks at me. "A... *Farmer.*"

CHAPTER SEVEN

I blink. "What?"

Olivia Doss pinches her lips together, waiting for me to take my card. I accept it, my hands trembling. I'm supposed to return to my seat. But I can't exactly move. I read my I.D. just to make sure I didn't hear wrong. Beside my name is the label: FARMER. How? They never give farming careers to girls, and why did I get this career when everyone else was assigned to the Line of Defenders?

I don't understand.

Doss clears her throat, bringing my head up. She lifts a brow. Oh. Right. Time to return to my seat.

"Th-thank you for your g-generosity," I whisper, and stumble down the stairs to my seat.

As Doss begins a short speech about how our labor doesn't go unnoticed, and how we are all part of a community bringing this country to a better place, I try to comprehend what, exactly, just happened. Because nothing is going to change for me. I'll go to the governor of the Community Garden and he'll assign me as a field hand somewhere and my training will begin. But I'll still live here in the Garden, close enough to visit my family often. My muscles relax and I look at my card once more, just to be sure. FARMER. I'm a farmer. I'm going to be a farmer. I can't wipe the smile off my face.

"Good going, Ember," Leaf whispers beside me. "Fate must really love you."

I look sharply at him, the guilt suddenly eating me from the inside out. Here I am, busy basking in the glory of my own career, I forgot that he got the career he wanted least.

"I'm so sorry, Leaf," I whisper.

"Don't be." His eyes are still dark with a certain passion I've never seen before. "Listen, you've been a great friend, and you'll be a swell farmer." He grins a grin that's so out of place for this very moment. "Keep our parents in line, will ya?"

"Of-of course."

He takes my hand in his sweaty, trembling ones and locks his gaze with mine. The deranged look in his eyes scares me.

"No matter what happens," he says. "I want you to stay strong."

"Um. Okay?" Why is he telling me this? Why can't he wait until we say our goodbyes at the end of the ceremony?

"And always remember this, Ember." He reaches into his pocket, pulls out a small piece of paper and hands it to me. There's a picture of an apple in flames drawn on it.

"What is this?"

"It's the sign of the Resurgence. Remember that Jonah Walker guy?"

The picture of the green-eyed man flashes through my mind. "The criminal?"

Leaf presses the small paper into my palm and forces my fingers to curl around it. "If you ever need anything, find Jonah Walker and show him this. He'll help you." He smiles, but it's not the boyish smile I'm used to. It's more of a sad, I'm-sorry-for-what's-about-to-happen smile.

Then he stands.

And walks toward the stage.

"Leaf," I whisper. We're not supposed to walk to the stage when the politicians give their speeches. We're not supposed to leave our seats until we're dismissed. I squeeze the paper in my hands, the shock of what Leaf is doing hitting me like a blow in the stomach.

If they draft me in the military to fight for a cause I know nothing about, he'd said, *I'm resisting them.*

Oh.

Oh, rot.

Leaf is going on a suicide mission.

Everything seems to slow down in an instant. And I'm watching him walk toward the stage, and then I'm looking at Olivia Doss who has stopped talking mid-sentence and is staring at Leaf, and then I'm scanning the room at the Defenders who are already taking aim, and suddenly I'm shouting out his name but he doesn't turn around. He doesn't even seem to hear me as he takes the steps two at a time, and bolts toward the microphone. He shoves Olivia Doss aside and begins talking. It takes a moment for my shock to subside enough for me to understand what he's saying, and it's not good.

"Spies," he says, "are watching our every move at the

bars and in the fields. Our food rations," he says, "have been late for the past six months, but if we miss one day of work, we'll be arrested. Your children's bellies," he says, "are swollen with malnutrition. And what is our beloved Chief doing about that? What kind of utopian government are we living in, people?" He speaks fast and loud and clear with the authority of a leader.

Defenders jog toward the stage and my blood runs cold.

"We Proletariats live in poverty while the Patricians live in luxury. We slave away while they do *nothing*. And when we take a tiny portion of the food *we* grew in order to hold us over until our rations come in, we are sentenced to an execution." He slams one fist into the palm of his other hand. "We have to take a stand, people! We have to rise up! There are more of us than there are of them! Let's fight!"

The Defender closest to me cocks his gun and takes aim at Leaf, and I realize I'm the only person with the brains to stop him. Because everyone else is going to just stand there and watch and do nothing. So I shove the paper in my pocket and race toward the Defender.

"Stop!" I scream.

The Defender sees me and swerves his gun to me, but he's too slow. I leap on his back and wrap my arm around his neck and a loud bang fills the air and my ears are suddenly ringing and my head is pounding, and I think I must have been shot, but I'm not entirely sure because there's no pain except my ears and the pounding pounding pounding in my head. And we're tumbling to the ground. The force of the fall makes my eyes open just in time to see his gun skid across the floor as he tries to pry my arms from around his neck.

Defenders pour in from all directions. They grab me and yank me off the Defender's shoulders. My arms are pulled behind my back. Something cold and hard wraps around my left wrist. I still don't feel the pain of the bullet, though, and when I look up, I see why. Another Defender lies on the ground, not twenty feet away, blood oozing from his chest. When I jumped on the Defender's back, I must have knocked his aim off so that he shot the other Defender.

Oh, rot.

I'm going to die for this.

The Defenders drag me toward the door. I glance at the stage, hoping to catch a glimpse of Leaf. But he lies limp.

So limp. I think...I think he might be dead.

"Leaf—" My voice chokes off and I suddenly can't breathe.

Defenders crowd around him with their guns aimed, as if he would come back to life. As if, even if he did come back to life, his lanky form could overpower even one of them.

"Leaf!" I try to twist my arms from the Defenders' grasp, but they tighten their grip and jerk me around.

I catch a glimpse of Dad in the bleachers. He's shouting something as he tries to fight the crowd to get to me, but more Defenders block him on the stairs. By the way his mouth moves, I know he is calling out my name, but I can't hear him. I can't hear him above the chaotic noise of shouting people. I can't hear him above the ringing in my ears. I can't hear him above the rhythmic sound of my pounding heart.

I try to pull free again. I twist and turn and jerk my arms and kick my legs. I feel like a wild animal, working with all my strength to get out of the iron grips holding my arms, when a hand grips my chin and forces my head up. Olivia Doss glares at me with doe-brown eyes that defy the hawklike claws of her fingernails digging into my cheeks.

"Enough," she orders. "Stand. Down."

What do I look like, a Defender? Does she think I'll obey her command like a dog, the way the Defenders obey the politicians?

I spit in her face.

Her eyes widen and she slaps me. "Enough!"

The sting of her hand on my cheek throws me over the edge, and I rip my arm from the Defender, curl my fingers, and crack my fist into her perfectly delicate jawbone.

She lifts her hand to her face and stares at me, wide-eyed. I'm about to shout out a bunch of curses on the Defenders, on Olivia, on everyone, when a shock bolts up my left arm and electricity vibrates through my body. The edge of my vision goes dark. I hear Olivia talking, but her voice is a distant echo, drowning in the haze that consumes my mind.

Then everything goes black.

CHAPTER EIGHT

I jolt awake. I'm sitting in the backseat of a military jeep. I've never been inside a vehicle. It's nothing like riding a horse. The movement is too smooth and the scenery passes by so fast until I have the sudden urge to puke.

Or maybe it's the fact that Leaf is dead that sickens me.

The thought rocks me until I'm sure I'm going to hurl. I cover my mouth and hunch over until the nausea passes. Someone is squeezing my brain, and when I look out my window the Community Garden passes by in a blur, and it only makes me more nauseous, so I look out the front window.

The city buildings draw closer than I've ever seen them. They're taller up close. A little more foreboding. A little less intriguing. Judging by the sunset on my left, we are heading north. I traveled north of square once when I was Elijah's age. Leaf and I were exploring after school one day and ventured as far as the pumpkin patch, less than halfway to the city. There wasn't much to see. The north end of the Community Garden isn't nearly as exotic as the south end, where all the trees grow. Leaf and I never bothered going back.

Leaf.

Leaf is dead.

Every thought in my head collapses at the one reality. And I'm breaking, fracturing, falling apart all over again. I want to scream. I want to weep. I want to rewind and redo the entire scene. I want to tell Leaf not to fight this time.

Instead, I swallow my grief, think of something else so I don't completely lose my sanity. We arrive at the Garden border. Giant black gates creek open. The jeep passes through them, and we're immediately swallowed up by the buildings. No fields here. Only narrow roads filled with too many people and vehicles, surrounded by the towering structures that block the sun. Weeds pop up in the cracked pavement, but otherwise there is no greenery. Only brick and concrete and people.

So many people.

In the Community Garden, everyone wears similar clothes—farmers uniforms, which are provided by the government. The people here all wear different clothes, marking their careers. The uniforms are plain. Gray, navy blue, mustard yellow. The only people wearing red are the Defenders of the Peace, and there are at least two on every corner.

The jeep steers through the city roads. Left. Right. Right. Left. The city is a giant maze. I couldn't find my way back to the Community Garden if I tried. I wipe my palms on my pants, then squeeze my hands into fists and remind myself to inhale. Exhale. Replenish bad air for good. Everything's going to be okay.

Maybe.

"Where are you taking me?" I ask the Defender in the front seat.

"Shelby Prison."

Prison? Of course. This is exactly how I wanted to spend my first day as a careered citizen. In prison.

We finally arrive at a one-story concrete building. The jeep pulls over and the Defender leads me through the doors. Behind the desk sits an older man with a graying beard and the red uniform of the Defenders. Except he has multiple pins lining his uniform.

"Crime?" the Defender at the desk says without looking up.

"Murder," my captor says.

"M-murder?" I say with a shocked laugh, but the Defender squeezes my arm, and the excruciating pain is enough to make me stifle my laugh.

The older man writes something on a slip of paper and hands it to the Defender. "Lock her up."

And without a word, the Defender leads me down a long hallway and through a door to the prison stalls, which are packed full.

"H-how long will I be in here?" I'm almost too afraid to ask.

"Not long." The Defender leads me into a cell at the end of the hall. "You'll be taken to trial tomorrow."

"So, I'll actually get a trial? Like, to defend myself?"

He gives a grave nod, then sends me into my cell. A trial. Perfect. I guess the system isn't as messed up as I thought. I'll be able to defend my case in front of the judges and prove myself innocent, and by this time tomorrow, I'll be home again, taking up my career as a farmer. Assuming everything works out okay.

When he leaves, the room goes dark, save for a dim light glaring from the ceiling where a camera hangs. The majority of the cells are full. A man in the cell across from mine sweeps his gaze across my body, then gives out a low whistle. And the look in his eyes is enough to make my skin crawl. I wrap my arms tighter around my torso, both to fight off the unnerving chill and to block off his open stare.

"What did they put you in here for?" he asks. "Prostitu—"

"Mind your own shoddy business," I snap.

His mouth clamps shut and he looks at the floor. But catcalls sound from the other cells, and no matter how much I tell them to shut up, my anger only seems to entertain them. So I curl into a ball. I face the wall and ignore the hoots and leers of these incarcerated men. The excitement eventually dies down until all I hear is the breathing of the other prisoners and the steady beat of my own heart.

I take a moment to go over the past events in my head. I try to figure out what exactly went wrong. Because it all happened so fast. And Leaf is dead.

Leaf is dead.

That thought pinches my cerebral cortex like cold steel fingers, halts all my memories, and forces this one piece of information down my throat, and I can't breathe can't breathe can't breathe—until I do. And I hunch over and cover my mouth, the shock hitting me all over again with a force stronger than a gale.

But, no. Leaf can't be dead. He—he just *can't*. I mean, we were together this morning. We were laughing. We were rolling our eyes at his mom's reminiscing. I squeeze my eyes closed, seeing Leaf as he was just before he died. Angry, passionate, and a little sad. And then I remember the last conversation I had with him.

Ember, he whispers beside me.

Yes?

You've been a great friend…

So have you.

No matter what happens, I want you to stay strong…

I will.

And always remember this…

I open my eyes. Always remember what? The slip of paper. I reach into my pocket and feel the smooth, stiff paper brushing against my fingertips. What did he say about it?

It's the sign of the Resurgence. Jonah Walker….

Jonah Walker. The green-eyed criminal. He's the leader of the Resurgence. No wonder Forest didn't want to tell me who Walker was. And no wonder Walker's so notorious.

He's leading an uprising against the chief.

Not that any of this matters now. I pull the paper out, stare at the picture of an apple in flames. So much treason in one scratched drawing. The apple represents the government, that's obvious enough. And it's burning. It's burning in flames. I scrunch the paper into a tiny ball and flick it into the corner of the cell. There's no way this Walker can help me now. I'm on my own. I'll tell the judges the truth in the morning, and if God is real—and if he's in my favor—I'll be home with Dad by this time tomorrow.

God.

Only a fool would trust their life to a god, Dad would tell me. Why do I ever even acknowledge that God might maybe be real? Is it because of this strange pull I feel every so often when I'm alone? When I allow the most bizarre thoughts to occupy my mind? Is it because of this sense that there's another presence here in this room, and not just that of the other prisoners? Is it because of the feeling that there's something there that knows me fully—knows my grief, my fear, my darkest thoughts and my wildest hopes—and still wants me to call out?

I don't know. I might be going crazy. It's been a weird day full of all my worst fears, and I think I need to rest my brain so I'll have the ability to defend myself tomorrow. So I close my eyes again. And count the apple trees in our orchard until sleep offers me sanctuary.

Too soon, though, the lights switch on, pulling me out of a fitful sleep. I shield my eyes against the blinding light. When my pupils adjust, I squint down the hall. A Defender is making his way down the cells, unlocking them while other Defenders place wristbands around the prisoners' wrists. I bolt to my feet and grip the bars. It must be morning.

My trial is this morning.

CHAPTER NINE

I begin making up a defense in my head when I notice a boy who can't be any older than me standing in the center of the room. He wears gray slacks and the vest of a Patrician. A newsboy cap sits snuggly on his head. Shaggy auburn hair falls into his eyes. His nose is slightly crooked, as though it'd been broken once, but the rest of his face is perfectly angular with high cheek bones and a sharp chin. He crosses his arms with an air of confidence while he watches the Defenders work. He seems too young to be supervising.

"Today's your lucky day, boys." His sharp gray eyes catch mine, and he offers a mocking bow. "And girls. Judges like to start the trials early so they don't miss their mid-morning coffee." His lips twist up in a bitter smile. "So let's make this quick. Chop, chop." He spins on his heel and leads the way out of prison.

A freezing wind greets me when I step outside. If the sun was shining today, the tall buildings would block it out. I look up through the narrow slit of the skyscrapers. The sky is gray with churning clouds. Dad and Elijah would be trying to get the rest of the apples picked before a winter storm rolls in.

Newsboy Cap snaps his fingers. I look at him and he stares back, his gray eyes like cold steel, hard and unfeeling. He arches a brow and jerks his chin toward the blue bus.

"C'mon, criminal." His voice is light, almost musical. "Don't want to keep your judge waiting."

Swallowing hard, I step onto the bus and sink into a cold metal seat beside an older man with long greasy hair. The stink of sweat and gasoline leaks off his body. Newsboy Cap sits in front of me. The prison bus starts with a jolt and bumps down the road and the stench of exhaust fills the air. And I don't look back, because I can't afford to look back, because looking back will only make it more painful. So I look forward, and I can't help but wonder where, exactly, we're going.

"'Scuse me." I tap Newsboy Cap on the shoulder.

He turns fully to face me, his eyes sharp and piercing. "No talking allowed." His breath smells like peppermint.

"I just want to know where we're going."

He blinks two quick blinks, and a hint of amusement weaves in and out of his eyes. "Frankfort," he says simply. "Now, no talking, please." And he turns back around, lays his head back on the metal frame of the seat, and pulls his cap up over his eyes. Does he know how lucky he is? That he gets to relax because he's not on his way to a trial that will determine whether he lives or dies?

I look out my window. And think of Frankfort. Our capital.

They say it's clean and well-organized, with silvery-blue

high rises stretching clear to the sky and huge mansions where the Patricians live. The kids receive the best education and everybody's happy. There's even a library full of books from the Old Country, leftover scraps from before the White Plague brought the world to its ruins. I can't deny that I've always been a little curious about Frankfort. I kind of always wanted to see it, but not this way. Not as a prisoner.

We drive for almost an hour through the maze of old brick buildings. A slow drizzle begins, the water weaving veins down the windowpane.

Rain. So much blasted *rain*.

I don't realize I said that out loud until Newsboy Cap turns around to face me again.

"Excuse me?" he says.

"Um. Rain," I say, sinking lower into my seat and pointing out the window. "It's—it's raining."

He closes his eyes for the briefest moment, then blinks them open and stares at me again. "I thought I told you to be quiet."

I nod and sink a little lower and look out the blur of the rain-streaked window. Rain seems to be everywhere as of the past few days, clouding my mood, putting a damper on life. Rain isn't so bad in springtime, when it's giving life to the dirt and plants and food and people. But in the winter it just makes the cold more bitter.

Eventually, the bus takes a turn onto the highway that arches over the city, then picks up speed. This road is nothing like the gravel road in the Community Garden, or the cracked pavement in the city streets. It's completely smooth, like glass. As we rise above the metropolis, I can see the crumbling city of Ky at a glance. I knew Ky was big, but not *this* big. The buildings stretch as far as the horizon. A dusty haze rises from the streets. Way out in the distance is the only patch of green this country owns. The Community Garden. Home.

The Community Garden is nestled in the heart of Shelby County, one of the six remaining counties of Ky. It's located in the center of Ky and is the only place where food is grown for all the people, so the Community Garden is literally the heartbeat of Ky. The food is harvested and sent off to the rest of the country, to the factories where it's altered and turned into wafers and boxed meals and gross blandness, stretched too thin to enjoy so it can feed the thousands of citizens of Ky. These citizens take our freshly harvested food and offer clothes and supplies in return.

The systematic machinery of a perfect government.

A yellow glowing light appears ahead. I straighten in my seat. We pass a sign that says "Franklin County," and through the front window, a strange tangerine glow hovers over the capitol, like a dome of some sort. Within the dome are tall, silver skyscrapers. These aren't like the dull, uneven shadows I've grown up looking at from the Community Garden. These buildings are immaculate, all pointing toward the sky like silver arrows.

We drive through a dusty ring encircling the outer rim of the dome.

"The outer ring," the greasy man beside me says, his tired eyes scanning the distance. He winces. "And the Rebels Circle."

I glance back out the window. Sure enough. I can barely see the iron circles from this road, but stakes, about thirty feet tall, rise in the distance with giant rings at the top. Through the hazy rain, I can just barely see the bodies swaying in the hearts of the circles by the breeze.

Shuddering, I look away. The Rebels Circle is the sort of death reserved for those who conspire against the government. Criminals get a quick execution. Rebels are burned. They're tied upside down in a circular ring, hanging by their feet with a cord. I guess they place the Rebels Circle around the perimeter of Frankfort to remind the rebels what could happen to them if they had an uprising against Chief Titus Whitcomb.

The bus crosses the ring, then stops at the edge of the dome where the driver speaks to a Defender. When we pull in through the gates of Frankfort, I don't feel like I have enough time to take it all in.

Every building is made of glass, not crumbling brick like the rest of Ky. Flowers the color of ripe plums grow in the median of the streets. Trees shoot straight into the air, their only branches long green fronds that leaf out at the top, shading the street from the sun.

When did the sun start shining?

I have never seen so many Patricians in one place in my life. It's too crowded here. Too loud. Too busy. Unlike the plain uniforms and heavy coats everyone was wearing minutes ago in the rest of Ky, the men here wear long-sleeved shirts beneath their gray vests, and women wear bright togas––fuchsia, turquoise, burgundy, lime. Their arms are bare, like they're not cold at all, and gold and silver bracelets grace their wrists.

Up ahead is a round glass building, taking up its own block. This must be the capitol courthouse. The driver takes a right turn on the road that wraps around the courthouse. When he parks on the curb, we're ordered off the bus. The

Defenders unload first, then wait to take custody of their assigned prisoners. One prisoner to each Defender because we're apparently as bad as the White Plague.

I'm last to step off the bus. I wrap my hands around my arms, bracing myself for the freezing winter chill, but no cold air greets me. I look up. The sun is still shining, the air warm, like spring. Sure, the seasons change quickly, but not within hours. A front must have hit, which means tornadoes. I hope Dad and Elijah stay safe.

"If you're planning on bolting, you can forget it."

I turn to face Newsboy Cap, the only person left to take me.

"Your electroband," he says in that musical voice, tilting his chin slightly. "Will shock you if you step more than ten feet from me. Now come on. I don't want to hear another lecture about being late."

He jerks his head for me to follow, and my heart sinks a little, but I do. Because, what's my other option? Get shocked by the electroband? Yeah, no thanks. So I stumble behind him and inhale the faint scent of peppermint that lingers in his wake. He stands a full head taller than me and walks with fast, purposeful steps, and I try to keep up, try to keep that ten-foot gap closed between us so I don't get shocked, and I can't help but feel like a dog on a leash.

When we arrive at the double glass doors, Newsboy Cap mumbles something to one of the Defenders while flashing his I.D., then he turns and looks at me. Lifting an auburn brow, he gestures inside and offers a clearly forced grin. "Ladies, first."

Such a gentleman. I look at the doorway, the threshold to the place that will determine my fate, but suddenly my feet are frozen in the concrete, and I can't get myself to step through those doors.

"Come on, *criminal*." He rolls his eyes in obvious irritation. "We're already running behind schedule because of your obsession with the sky."

I gasp. So insensitive. Doesn't he understand what this means to me? That this is a trial that determines my *life*? That, once I go inside, I might not come back out? That the glance I spared the sky earlier might have been my last? But to have any chances at survival, I have to do whatever this arrogant son of a jackal says, no matter how old he is or how mocking he is or how annoyingly condescending he is.

So I inhale. I exhale. I replenish bad air for good.

And I step across the threshold.

CHAPTER TEN

The door slams behind me, making me jump. Light filters through the glass walls, reflecting off the beige tile floor of a hallway. The first thing I notice is a balcony across the hall that overlooks a vat of sand. An arena. The balcony wraps around the perimeter of the arena, about thirty feet from the ground. The roof is open to the blue sky, the warmth of the sun pouring onto the sand.

I'm led down the hall, passing giant oil paintings of people who I imagine must be important. At the end of the hall is a portrait that stretches clear to the high arched ceiling.

"Is that—is that the chief?" I ask Newsboy.

"Mm-hm."

"He's really young." I mean, he couldn't be too much older than me. Maybe just a couple years. He stands tall, wearing a black vest over an immaculate white button-up shirt. Black bowtie, black slacks, black hair. He's onyx on ivory with green, green eyes. His face is completely void of any emotion, and one elbow rests casually on a gold-fringed shelf. The other hand holds a gun. The portrait is, in every sense of the word, intimidating. And I think that's exactly the chief's intent.

We turn down another hall. I wipe my clammy palms on my pants as we walk closer to the courtroom. It's suddenly too hard to breathe, and I can't quite focus. I try to clear my mind. I try to rehearse what to say to the judges, but my brain is a whirlwind of thoughts scattered in a funnel cloud, and I can't seem to grasp them, to put them in the right order that'll make a valid defense for the judges. Then a Defender opens the door, and all I can think is I'm not ready to face a trial.

He leads me and the other criminals in single file through the entrance. Bright lights greet me when I step through the entry. The sound of shuffling steps echoes down the tile floors, matching the rhythm of my heartbeat. I've seen the small courtroom in Farmers Square where the citizens settle their disputes. That room was small, with dim light slanting through the cracked windows. It smelled of mildew. This is nothing like that courtroom.

This room has a dome ceiling that stretches a good two stories high. It's circular with balconies wrapping around the perimeter and climbing halfway to the ceiling. In the center of the room, on the marble floor, are ten round podiums. I'm taken to a podium just wide enough for me and Newsboy to step on. A railing rises around both of us, locking us in, and the podium slowly begins to lift off the ground. The unexpected movement makes me stumble back against Newsboy. I quickly regain my footing, glancing at him just long enough to catch a glimpse of his arrogant smirk and a dimple forming in his left cheek.

How stupid I must appear to him. Though he stands a full head taller than me with his arms locked behind his back, his smile makes him look less Patrician and a little more human. But his humor infuriates me. I'm preparing to face the judge who will determine whether I live or die, and he's *laughing* at me.

I grip the railing to stop the trembling in my hands and turn back toward the balconies lining the wall. The podium stops rising when we reach a balcony holding three judges. At least with three judges, my chances of having a just trial look better.

"Ember Carter," the first judge begins reading. "Stands on trial for killing a Defender."

I bite back my reply. Chew my lip until I taste blood. Try to properly wait until he's finished reading to state my defense. And he reads. On and on and on, listing all the facts. The time of day, place, how it all happened, more details than I can remember. Because all I remember is Leaf shouting out treason on a shoddy microphone.

Defenders aiming guns at Leaf.

Leaf laying limp on the stage.

Dead.

"Verdict?" The judge's voice snaps me back to the present.

The other judges both mumble, "Guilty of murder."

"She is to be executed," the reader says with a flip of his hand, then his face breaks into a wide yawn. The podium begins to lower.

"Wait," I say. "I-I didn't get a chance to defend myself."

Newsboy snorts behind me.

"I'm not guilty," I shout.

But the judges are already turning away. The head judge shoves the paper back into a folder and laughs at something one of the others says.

My heart begins pounding until I almost feel dizzy. I grit my teeth, search my brain for the right words, the polite words, the mature words that will garner some respect but all that comes out is, "I didn't kill the shoddy Defender! I was just t-trying to save Leaf."

The older judge stops. He slowly turns around, watches me as my podium lowers the floor. He's going to hear me out. He's going to actually listen to me and maybe offer forgiveness. But then he shakes his head, turns away, and exits the balcony as my podium arrives at the floor, stopping with a click.

And I'm numb. Every last drop of hope sapped from the marrow of my bones because my life is going to end in an execution.

"Nice try," Newsboy mutters as he escorts me out of the room. "But they never hear a criminal out. Ever."

"Of course not." And why did I think they would? The politicians and Patricians and judges and chief never have been for the people of Ky, because if they were, they would try to fix the starvation issue. They would try to improve our living conditions. They would do something that would make our lives a little more livable and little less miserable. So why, why on this forsaken earth would they bother listening to the plea of a commoner? A Proletariat? *Me?*

Tears sting my eyes and my hands curl into fists when I hear footsteps behind us.

"Hang on, Rain."

Newsboy—who's apparently called Rain—grabs my arm to stop me and turns around. The older judge walks toward

86

us, his hands locked behind his back and his black robe hanging neatly down his shoulders. Maybe he wants to hear my case after all. My blood is melted butter and a smile fights its way to my lips. I open my mouth to speak, but Newsboy/Rain squeezes my arm, stopping the words from leaving my mouth.

"She murdered a Defender," the judge says, looking at Rain. "To save her friend. Leaf. The rebel. Yes?"

"No," I say. "I didn't—I didn't *murder*—"

Rain clamps his slender hand over my mouth, but keeps his eyes on the judge and offers a grave nod. "Mm-hm."

I jerk my face from his hand, relieved when he releases me.

The judge stares at me with birdlike eyes, disapproval shifting in and out of his gaze. His lips pinch into a beaklike expression. Then he looks at Rain again. "Take her to Perseus. We have plenty of criminals to feed the black tigers, and Perseus may want her to die on the Rebels Circle, instead." He looks at me again, his upper lip curled in disgust. "Anyone who *associates* with rebels should have the most inconvenient death."

Inconvenient. As if death has ever been a convenience. As if anyone ever thought, hm, I think I'll just, I don't know, *die* to today. I think I'll just take my life and see what's on the other side for giggles.

No. Death is the most terrifying concept next to loneliness. I don't care how brave and courageous you are, or how unafraid you are of spiders or heights or enclosed spaces, death is the biggest mystery of all and therefore the most terrible fear.

And I—I am terribly afraid.

87

CHAPTER ELEVEN

Rain releases me and begins walking down the hall, his hands shoved into his pockets, and I trot to catch up, careful to stay within the ten-foot, no-shock radius of him.

"I don't think I deserve a death on the Rebels Circle." I look at him, hoping to maybe find some compassion there. "I mean, I didn't really do anything deliberately against the government."

"Of course." Rain looks at me with limestone eyes—gray and hard and cold. "You're completely innocent. It was an accident. You did absolutely *nothing* wrong."

I almost feel hopeful, like he believes me and might just vouch for me, but then that mocking grin appears, and my hope deflates.

"It's not that bad," Rain says as we turn down another hall.

"Getting *burned to death*?"

He shrugs. "You'll most likely pass out by all the smoke

before you feel any pain."

"Wow." I force a laugh that sounds more like a choked, strangled cough. "That's so incredibly reassuring, *Rain*. Thank you so much for your words of comfort before I *die*."

His lips quirk up into a smile, revealing that dimple—the only thing that makes him look attractive. "Any time, Miss Carter."

I cringe at the way he calls me *Miss* Carter, because that's what Forest called me.

Forest, the lying politician.

Rain gestures a Defender over. "Captain Mcallister."

A Defender walks over, chin erect, arms by his side. He is tall and well-built with dark skin, and wears the same red jacket and black slacks of the Defender uniform. He looks surprisingly young. Too young to be wearing so many gold pins.

"Sir," he says.

"Take her to Perseus," Rain says, taking a thin band off his wrist and handing it to Mcallister. I assume it's connected to my shock band. "See if he wants to sentence her to the Rebels Circle."

Mcallister looks at me now, and apart from Shepherd, he's the only Defender that's actually really looked at me. I think I might see a hint of emotion flicker in and out of his eyes, but it's hard to tell because then he looks back at Rain, once again stoic, and says, "Is she the only one?"

"The only rebel, yes. The other criminals are headed straight to the black tigers."

A shudder rushes down my spine and Rain grins at me.

"Consider yourself lucky," he says, his voice almost exuberant. "You get to live a few days longer than the *regular* criminals." And with that mocking smirk, he shoves his hands into his pockets and leaves me with Mcallister.

"Who is that?" I ask, watching Rain as he walks away.

"He's one of the highest politician's sons." Mcallister leads me down the hall, then up a circular marble stairway. "He has a lot of authority, though he hasn't chosen a career yet. Too busy getting drunk and having his fun with the girls."

Mcallister's tone drips with disapproval. A Captain answering to someone who doesn't even have a career yet, just because he is the son of some Big Name, has to be degrading.

But something else Mcallister says grabs my attention. "He gets to *choose* his career?"

"Yes. Patricians have the option to choose."

"Well that's not…really fair."

"Life rarely is."

His blunt honesty surprises me. He's nothing like any Defender I've ever spoken to, apart from Shepherd. He talks to me like a person instead of a robot. We arrive at the third floor and Mcallister leads me down the hall, showing his I.D. to the Defenders guarding a door.

"Captain James Mcallister here to see you, sir," the first Defender says into his white wristband. He presses the earpiece deeper into his ear, then looks at Mcallister and gives a nod. "You may enter."

The doors open, and I automatically scan the room. The office is easily two or three times the size of my house. A window runs the length of the opposite wall peering out to the beautiful glass skyscrapers of Frankfort. Two politicians stand behind a black desk, both looking out the window and talking.

"Congressman Perseus," Mcallister says as we approach. "We request a moment of your time."

The man on the left turns around. He is tall and thin, with coarse white hair and skin that almost looks pink. Brass buttons make their way from his left hip to his right shoulder and his white hair is slicked back.

He thrusts his arms behind his back and nods at the Defender before sparing a glance at me. "What seems to be the issue, Mcallister?"

"A rebel, sir," Mcallister says. "Rain told me to ask you where to put her. Thought she should face her execution on the Rebels Circle."

The person standing next to Perseus turns now. Our eyes meet. And my lungs collapse. Because piercing blue eyes pierce through my defenses. And there's only one person I've ever met with hair like gold and eyes like sapphires and he's standing *here* and he's looking right at me.

And I think—I think I might pass out.

CHAPTER TWELVE

I blink, try to clear my focus. But there's no denying it. The boy standing next to Perseus is Forest.

Forest the Builder.

No. Forest the *Politician*.

He sure has a knack for being around every time my life takes a turn for the worst. Was our conversation at The Tap only two nights ago? He'd seemed so down to earth, so *normal.* I would have never guessed him to be a stuck-up politician. But maybe... maybe my knowing him will work to my benefit. A small flame of hope grows in my chest, because maybe he's different from the others. Maybe he's *better.*

Maybe he'll help me.

But where I expect to see a hint of recognition, I only see disappointment. And then he looks away. He masks any confusion he may feel with a stoic expression, and I *know* he doesn't want to be associated with me at all. Why would he? I'm a shoddy rebel.

I scrunch up my nose to fight back the unexpected tears. I guess he isn't different.

"What's her crime?" Congressman Perseus's voice brings my attention back around to him, back to my current problem, back to the inconvenient dilemma of which death suits me best.

"Murdered a Defender," Mcallister says.

This news earns me an appraising look from Forest.

Perseus, however, doesn't offer so much as a glance as he picks up his mug and takes a sip. "Anyone who has the nerve to murder a Defender deserves to die on the Rebels Circle."

"B-but I didn't kill him." All eyes are on me. Knowing I tread on dangerous ground, I bow my head as a sign of respect and ignore the pounding of my heart. "A Defender was about to shoot my friend. I tried to stop him, and he accidentally shot the other Defender. But he was the one with the gun; he's the one who shot the Defender. Not me."

Perseus frowns. "Why, exactly, was this Defender about to shoot your friend?"

I open my mouth to answer, but out of the corner of my eye, I see Forest give a brief shake of his head. I look at him. His eyes hint a warning, so I stop myself. I clamp my mouth shut. I decide to maybe trust this untrustworthy politician one more time.

"Mcallister?" Perseus says when I don't respond.

"Her friend was speaking out against the government," Mcallister answers.

And now I know why Forest didn't want me to speak. Leaf was a rebel. It's because I mentioned Leaf in my defense against the judges that I got transferred from a regular criminal's death to a death on the Rebels Circle.

"Ah." Congressman Perseus strokes his full, white beard. "And do you agree with your friend?" he asks me. "Are you a part of the revolutionaries who want to bring this peaceful government down?"

I stare at the floor. "I-I believe your people have done many good things for us." I peek at Forest. He offers a brief nod of approval. Why won't he just turn me in? He knows my honest opinion. If he was any other politician or Defender of the Peace, he wouldn't hesitate to have me sent to the Rebels Circle. He would've smoked me out the night we met.

But he didn't.

And that's what makes all these thoughts in my head get tangled up into a perfect mess that I can't quite comprehend.

Congressman Perseus takes another sip from his mug. "But you attempted to save a rebel, and that's enough reason to be suspected of working with them." He looks at Mcallister. "Have her executed on the Rebels Circle."

With a faint nod from Perseus, and absolutely no interference from Forest on my behalf, my fate is sealed. Mcallister bows and begins walking out of the office. I risk another glance at Forest, but his eyes are lowered, focused on something on the desk as he fiddles with a pen. He's avoiding my gaze.

Again, why should I be surprised?

I whirl around and stumble behind Mcallister. I force all thoughts of Forest out of my mind and think instead of what exactly might be waiting for me after I die. Because death is a cruel mystery. No one can escape it, and everyone's terrified of it. It's fear, it's dread, it's despair, and to some, it's hope. And I'm not really sure which emotion I should cling to because all I'm imagining right now is my corpse, dead and cold and pale, being thrown into an empty grave and buried beneath the dirt.

And my soul... where will it go? What's on the other side? Darkness, hunger, and cold loneliness? Hope and light and warmth and a perfect paradise of endless feasting and smiling eyes? I don't know. But I'm going to find out soon—this week, according to Rain—and that fact alone makes my stomach churn, makes my lungs tight, makes everything inside me twist.

Stop. Focus. Inhale. Exhale. Replenish bad air for good. Everything's going to be okay.

I'm not dead yet.

We pass a dozen more offices, much like the one we were in. How many people will be executed today? This week? Acts of heroism never did anyone any good in this country. That's why they advise us to stay under the radar. To remain passive, docile, and plain.

Maybe that's my problem. I'm not passive. I'm not docile. And I don't think I want to be plain anymore.

We pass a window, looking out to the sand pit below, then arrive at a metal door. Mcallister whips out his I.D. and mumbles something. The Defender opens the door to a set of stairs. Stepping aside, Mcallister gestures me to go down.

"After you," he says. I expect to see a mocking grin like the one that was on Rain's face when he allowed me to step into the courthouse first. Instead, I think I catch a glimpse of sorrow. Maybe a little regret. And guilt? But he straightens and looks away, his throat convulsing in a swallow. I still can't believe how young he looks. Like, seriously not a whole lot older than me.

Letting out a breath, I step through the doorway onto

the concrete step. The acrid stench of decay and raw sewage fills my nostrils, and I have to cover my mouth to keep from puking.

This place smells like the crotch-rot of hell.

Flickering lights line the ceiling. We arrive at the base of the stairs, and Mcallister steps in front of me. To my right, cells run the length of the wall, and inside the cells are prisoners. Beady eyes squint up at me, and I realize that these people aren't used to the "bright" lights along the walls that Mcallister switched on. They seem to have the life sucked out of them. What were their crimes? Whispering just a little too loudly about the government's injustice? Refusing a career? Accidentally killing a Defender?

As we travel deeper into the tunnels, the air becomes cold and damp. Already my skin misses the warmth of the sun, my eyes beg for daylight, and my lungs crave fresh air. We pass the last cell and turn down another tunnel. And another. Even if I turned around now, I don't think I could find my way back to the gate. This place is a maze. Tunnels branch off the hall we walk down, disappearing into darkness.

Something loud and terrifying, like a roar, reverberates through the hallways, making the ground shake. And then screaming. Someone is screaming. My body convulses in chills.

I stumble closer to Mcallister. "What, um, what was that?"

"Black tiger," Mcallister says. "If you ever try to run away, you can bet you'll make a fine meal for one of those beasts."

I've never seen a black tiger, but judging by the roar, I don't think I ever *want* to see one. Another roar makes the hairs on my neck stand on end. Mcallister opens a metal door and leads me in to a circular room. Everything is concrete—the floors, the walls, the ceiling. Fluorescent lights, half of which are working, just barely illuminate the room. More cells wrap around the perimeter of the room, just long and wide enough for a tall person to lie down in.

The walls of the cells are like glass so everyone can see each other. Each stall has a blue number glowing at the top, one through twenty, and they are all filled up from one through twelve. They burn rebels monthly. Do they really catch that many rebels a month? This month is almost over, and these aren't even counting the criminals who *aren't* rebels. But Ky is so big, and this is how the government keeps control. One wrong word, one sign of resistance, and you're brought to this hellhole.

Rough-looking prisoners fill these cells. Another Defender walks up to a metal panel in the center of the room, punches in a code, and gestures me to walk into a stall with the blue number thirteen at the top. I step into the cell. The Defender clicks a button on the panel, and I hear the electric shield come on with a buzz. Then he flips a switch so all the lights, except a blue one above the control panel, go off. And both Defenders walk out, closing the metal door behind them.

So long, Mcallister. And good riddance. All Defenders, no matter how young or seemingly humane, put me on edge.

I reach out to touch the shield that separates me from stall number fourteen, just to test the strength of the shock. An electric current zaps through me, numbing my bones, and I'm thrown to the floor. The other prisoners chuckle. I can hear them as though there were no barriers. These electric shields may keep me from going anywhere, but they don't block sound or sight. Unfortunately. I guess we don't get the luxury of a few hours of privacy before our deaths. Biting back my annoyance, I study the other prisoners for the first time.

The man in the stall to my right has pale skin and tattoos mapped across his arms. His sandy hair is cropped short, his jaw broad and clean-shaven. He must not have been here long. I don't imagine they give criminals the luxury of shaving. Muscles I didn't even know existed ripple beneath his shirt when he makes the slightest movement. Honestly, if I had met him on the street, I would probably run the opposite direction, because he could obviously crush me with one blow.

He looks at me and I quickly look away, scoot farther to the other side of my cell, just in case his strength could resist even the shock of the electric shield. There's an older man in cell four with an earring in his left ear. A girl two cells from mine catches my gaze. She has brown skin and muscles bulging out of her calves and arms. She reminds me of a lioness.

She stares at me openly, then offers a big grin, revealing big white teeth. And a smile like that is so out of place in a dungeon like this, that I have to look away, I have to fight the warmth her smile brings and remind myself that I'm dying this week.

Because optimism, according to Dad and Elijah, isn't the best trait.

So I scoot against the wall, stretch each leg out in front of me. These people…they're rebels. How many of them work for Walker? How many have never heard of Walker and still stood up for what they believed in on their own? And how many rebelled by accident, like me?

It doesn't matter. You could let one wrong word slip at the exact wrong moment, or you could be conspiring to kill the chief with your bare hands, it doesn't make a shoddy difference, because it all ends with the same death—burning on the Rebels Circle.

The room is eerily quiet. And good thing. Because I need some silence to think. Or not to think. Or just to, I don't know, let my brain shut down for a minute. And, honestly? Maybe it would be better if this day, this entire week leading up to my death, would just shut up. Just end already. Because the anticipation of facing death seems worse than death itself. But hours and hours and hours creep by like sludge, like mud oozing between my fingers, and this is only day one, and how many days, exactly, are left before I die? How many more mud-sludging hours do I have to sit here and think about my impending death?

Stop. Stop thinking about death. Because spending my last moments thinking about death is ineffective and depressing.

So I close my eyes. I think of home. Of picking apples with the summer sun warming my skin, and of racing through the corn fields with Elijah. And memories upon memories stake camp in my mind, and as an escape from this place, I grasp one and follow it.

I'm sitting on the roof of our cabin watching the sunset, Elijah by my side. Crickets make their music, and the smell of humidity and grass and fresh dirt after a rain hangs in the air. Purple and orange hues explode across the sky, and I wish I could capture the sunset and put it on paper. But even if I had the luxury of good paint and a nice, clean canvas, nothing I paint would compare to the real thing.

"What do you think the rest of Ky is like?" Elijah asks.

I look down at him. His usually smiling face is serious. His amber eyes nearly glow in the sunlight and his hair tousled by the wind.

"I don't know," I say. "Overcrowded and gloomy, probably."

"Defender Shepherd says the buildings block out the sun most of the day and the only way to see the sunset is to climb the highest buildings."

"It's a good thing we live in the Garden then, huh?"

"When I become a politician," he says, squinting his eyes against the sunlight. "I'm going to design a building in each county where people can go specifically to watch the sunrise and sunset."

I smile. "Sounds like you want to be an architect, not a politician."

"Architects can't decide what to build or where to build it, Ember. They just design it. They brainlessly follow the rules and instructions that Congress makes." He looks back toward the sunset. "I'd make sure everyone got their food rations on time." He smiles a little. "And new shoes to wear every year. Nice clothes…. We'd all celebrate Christmas like they do in Frankfort."

I snort. I can't help it. "Now you really are dreaming. You don't even know how they celebrate Christmas."

"Defender Shepherd told me they have parties and string pretty lights throughout the city."

Lights throughout the city. Two hours after sunset is all the electricity we receive here in the Garden. Why would they waste it on decorative lights? Frankfort is full of strange customs I'll never understand. I stare at the sunset beyond the buildings of the city and wonder what it would be like to fly away from this place to pure freedom.

A repetitive clicking brings me back to the prison cell. Through the dim blue light, I can just barely see the older man in the cell across from mine staring at the wall, tapping his ring against the floor. I wish he would stop. I wish he would consider the rest of us who have to endure that quiet, yet incredibly annoying sound. Because for a moment, I was free again. I was in the apple orchard again. For a moment, I was able to forget where I am and what happened today and what my future holds.

Now I have to wait wait wait for hours while I chew a hole through my cuticles and wonder what I could've done better, what I should've done better, why Leaf didn't consider how his death would affect me, and why the shoddy inferno I'm still alive.

Time is such a strange and imperceptible thing. Seconds bleeding into minutes bleeding into hours until so much of it has crept by and you're left wondering when you lost count. Every second is the same. Every second is created equal. But time...time slows down and speeds up without giving a second thought to seconds. Time slips through our fingers like minnows. Time creeps through the cracks like sap through bark. Time can seem like a heavenly blessing or an infinite march to our death.

Time controls us.

And I don't know how much time has gone by since I was locked in this cell. A day, maybe. Possibly two. Or perhaps only a few hours stretched too long. But my shoulders sag in relief when the metal door finally opens and a Defender steps through.

He lets down all the shields and the other prisoners begin leaving their cells. The lioness-girl bolts out and pushes past everyone else like she knows exactly what's going on. Are we headed to our executions? Why is she so eager to face death? But being locked up so long has made my muscles crave exercise, and I pick up my pace and follow Lioness down the hallway. She's a fast runner and it's hard to keep up. But it feels so good to run.

We reach an intersection of paths, but two of the halls are blocked off by Defenders, so I follow Lioness down the only open hallway. The other prisoners' footsteps echo behind me, and I pick up my pace as to avoid getting trampled on. We take another turn, and another, until we finally reach a hall with bright light streaming from the end.

I follow Lioness up the flight of stairs and am met with blinding sunlight. The light spills over my arms and my face. It seeps into my skin and ignites my bones until I'm quite certain I'm on fire. Closing my eyes, I take a deep breath of fresh air and let it out.

When I open my eyes again, I realize I am standing in the arena, the sand pit, the vat surrounded by thirty-foot walls. The air is warm, like spring, which is strange since it's nearing the end of November. The sun casts enough shadow to make me think it is either late morning or early afternoon. Defenders stand along the walls, watching with guns ready to shoot.

Across the arena, more doors open. More prisoners pile out, squinting against the blinding sunlight.

"Better soak up the sun," Lioness says as she saunters past me. "We've got less than a week before Death Day, and there's no guarantee we'll have another chance to get outdoors."

I stare at her as she jogs around the arena. *Thanks for reminding me that I'm going to die.* Because for the briefest moment I forgot. For a moment I was lost in the heat of summer and the sun and everything beautiful.

But now I remember. I'm going to die.

And the sun doesn't seem so bright. Everything turns a little grayer. And suddenly it's getting too hard to breathe and the world is spinning and the injustice of the system makes me angry, and the anger courses through my veins, and I'm suddenly running. I'm racing along the stone wall of the arena. And I'm focusing only on my next step, my next breath, my next heartbeat. I focus on the air rushing into my face and the sand beneath my feet. I race until the muscles in my legs burn and my lungs gasp for air, but I don't slow down. I keep running. Inhaling and exhaling and replenishing bad air for good. I keep telling myself that everything's going to be okay.

I find myself full circle back at the front gate, slow to a trot, then stop and hunch over, dragging fresh air into my starving lungs. My body hurts, but it feels good to be free. Once I catch my breath, I straighten. I don't know how much more time we have, but the thought of being locked in that cell for another night keeps me moving, so this time I choose a slower pace than a full sprint around the arena.

Inhale. Exhale. Replenish bad air for good.

Everything's going to be okay.

The main gate opens. A group of ten people steps in, guarded by Defenders. Patricians, by the pressed slacks and fancy vests they wear. I immediately recognize Perseus, the guy who assigned me to the Rebels Circle, and I slow to a stop. Why is *he* here? Why are any of them here?

Someone shouts to my left. A brawny man, the one who was clicking his ring against the concrete floor, races toward the Patricians and collides into the one closest to him and pummels him to the ground. He lifts his fist to punch him, but the Defenders are on him in an instant, pulling his arms behind his back. They don't shoot him. Instead, one of them whistles a tune, another smaller gate flies open.

And a black tiger leaps out.

CHAPTER THIRTEEN

My heart takes a violent twist, but I don't run—can't run—can't even take my eyes off the first black tiger I've ever seen. It's much bigger than I imagined, its giant head as high as my shoulders. Just one pounce, and I would lie flat beneath his weight. But it's the strangest and most fascinating beast I have ever laid eyes on.

It's the purest black, glossed with midnight hues. Like raven feathers intertwined with those of a crow. It's black ink on charcoal, obsidian on onyx, ebony cloth variegated with shades of richest velvet. It's black on black on black on black, and I can *just* make out the stripes shimmering in the sunlight like shadows in the dark.

It's beautiful. It's exquisite. It's completely and utterly terrifying.

And it's looking right at me.

But there's another whistle, and somehow, the black tiger knows exactly what to do. It crouches toward the prisoner. The prisoner that the Defenders now release. And the prisoner stumbles in the other direction, but this only seems to fuel the tiger's courage. It pounces after the prisoner, then leaps into the air, claws outstretched, and pummels the prisoner to the ground. Grabbing its victim's head with its mouth, it twists violently, and I quickly look away, but not before I hear a *snap*.

Death.

Death looks like *this*. A mangled body. Limp arms and legs. A spirit *gone*. And my hands get clammy and sweat beads on my forehead and I'm barely breathing and my heart is beating too fast. The tiger drags the criminal's limp body back into the cell. I cover my mouth, fighting down the sickening bile threatening to rise up.

And I turn around.

And run.

I bolt into the shadows of the wall where I'll remain unnoticed by these Patricians who don't seem to care that a man died right in front of them. I run, and I wish that I could disappear. Because right now, in the very moment, everything is completely hopeless. Despair is too real. I wish the planet would open up and swallow me whole so I don't have to feel this way I don't want to feel this way everything about this moment is wrong.

Someone steps in front of me, and I dart right, but too late. My shoulder collides into the intruder, and I stumble to the ground. I jerk into a sitting position and glare at my interloper.

Shaggy auburn hair. Mocking gray eyes. Chiseled features, high cheekbones, and a newsboy cap.

"Rain," I breathe.

His brows shoot up. "Twenty-four hours in the prison

pit, and you still remember me. I'm flattered." He grins and steps closer, offering me his hand.

I stand without help. "Your features are distinct." I dust off my pants. "How could anyone forget eyes so cold or a smirk as arrogant as yours?"

"Ah." He crosses his arms, taking on a casual, mocking pose. "I didn't really take you for a Bitter Betty."

"My name's not *Betty*," I snap. "And you didn't exactly help me out in front of the judges, so, yes, I'm bitter."

"Well, of course I didn't help." He leans in and whispers, "See, I don't usually help murderers."

"Interesting."

"What's interesting?"

I look at him full on and cross my arms, mimicking his casual pose. "You don't help so-called murderers, and yet, here you are, sentencing people to their deaths. Just like a murderer."

His smile flattens. "*I* didn't sentence you to death."

"No. I suppose not. You're just a messenger boy."

His auburn brows shoot up. "You have a lot of bite for a Proletariat. You do realize I'm Patrician, yes?"

"Oh my word. It's so ridiculously obvious." I un-cross my arms, plant my hands on my hips, and give him a once-over. "Shiny black shoes? Straight slacks? Button up shirt? I heard you were too callow to choose a career, yet you wear a gray vest like a shoddy politician."

He chokes out a laugh, then quickly smothers his mouth with his fist and looks away. He looks back at me. His gray eyes are shining with brilliant humor, and he removes his hand from his mouth. "I met you only yesterday, and you already know more about me than half the Patricians."

"You can thank Captain Mcallister for that," I say, not caring if I get the shoddy Defender in trouble.

He snorts. "Oh, Mcallister. He's gonna pay for talking about me like that."

I wonder what he means by that, but then decide that I don't really care.

"It's pathetic, really," I say. "To find someone who has the option to *choose* his career, and he can't even get himself to make a decision."

"Word gets around, doesn't it?" His smile vanishes. "I may not have chosen a career yet, but at least I didn't throw my life away for the sake of some *pathetic* rebel."

My veins ignite, and my anger is a train heading straight for my skull. My fist clenches, and I lunge toward him, but he grabs my wrist and twists it painfully.

"Stand down, Carter," he commands.

But my anger is blinding and my other fist cracks in collision with his jawbone.

He releases my wrist, covers his jaw, and groans. "*Son of a jackal!*"

"Enough!" A Defender grabs my arm in a painful grip. Then there's a whistle.

The small door opens again.

And a black tiger leaps out.

CHAPTER FOURTEEN

I'm dead, I'm going to die, the black tiger is sauntering toward me and it's going to *kill* me—

"Whoa, whoa, whoa." Rain steps between me and the black tiger, holding out his hand toward the tiger. "Stop."

Someone must have a remote that connects to the collar around the black tiger's throat, shocking it just like my electroband shocks me, because the black tiger halts in his steps.

"Send him back," Rain says. And Defenders immediately begin prodding the tiger back toward the door with sticks.

Rain turns to look at me. His eyes are sharp, filled with obvious surprise and maybe a little bit of anger. "Are you out of your shoddy *mind?* Do you want to die *today?* Right now? This very moment?"

I swallow my heart back into my chest. Rain nods at the Defender. "Take her back to her cell." He looks back at me. "It'll be much more entertaining to watch you die on the

Rebels Circle than by the claws of a black tiger."

The Defender grabs my arm and leads me toward the entrance to the arena. I don't know what to think. That tiger could have snapped my neck like it did to the other criminal, who attacked a Patrician. But Rain stopped him. And I'm not sure if I'm supposed to be grateful or resentful.

I glance back at Rain and try to figure him out. No mocking smile graces his features now. Instead he stares after me, his hand nursing his jaw. I turn around and feel a small smile tug my lips. I can't help it. It feels kinda good putting these snotty Patricians in their places.

The roars. They're echoing through the corridors of the prison again. Deep. Guttural. Blood-chilling. And I'm half afraid the black tigers will break down the door and devour us all. Then I hear another scream, the sound of utter fear, but it's silenced in less than a minute.

And so is the roar.

And then it's silence silence silence and the violent pounding of my heart until I feel that strange pull again. That desire of something unknown begging to be known. What is it? *Who* is it? And why didn't it rescue that poor victim just now?

"Thirteen."

I look up. The big, brawny man in the cell beside mine is looking at me. "Why'd they put you in here?" His voice is deep and quiet, like gravel. "I mean, what'd you do that earned you a spot on the Rebels Circle?"

"I—I'm accused of killing a Defender."

"You?" He snorts. "How the shoddy tarnation did a little thing like you manage that?"

My mouth drops open and I bite back a crude reply.

"I mean," he continues. "The Defenders are as big as me, and they carry guns. I'm just trying to figure out what sort of magic you cast to pull off such a crime."

"I didn't do it." I squeeze the words through gritted teeth.

"Ah, yes. We're all innocents here, aren't we?" His eyes crinkle with a friendly smile. "My name's Judah, by the way. I would shake your hand, but I don't really want to get shocked, know what I mean?"

Small talk? I gauge his expression, try to read why he's suddenly interested in talking. I mean, we've been stuck in these cells for, well, I'm not sure how long, and he's not offered so much as a scowl in my direction. But, hey, what harm could come of small talk? At least it will get me through the next few days.

"I'm Ember."

"You ready to die, Ember?"

I immediately regret talking to him. "What kind of question is that?"

"One you should probably be considering."

I look away, stare at the blue-tinted floor, at the long shadow cast by the panel in the center of the room. "I guess so," I finally say.

He laughs. "No, I don't think you are."

I look sharply at him.

"Some people in here have given up," he says. "Just a few days trapped in these cells and they're already dead inside. But not you. You've got bite. I saw you running around the pit like a soldier training for battle. And I saw you punch that Patrician." He carefully studies the stalls around us, then scans the ceiling, then he looks at me and leans in closer. "You see, Ember, I think we can work together."

"Toward what, exactly?"

He lowers his voice another notch. "I-I think we can get out of this place."

This snaps me to attention and I sit up a little straighter. "How?"

"You know that door in the arena that the Patricians come through to watch us?"

I nod.

"That door slides shut as soon as the last Patrician walks through, but it's our only escape out of here. Between you and me, we can manage to escape."

I straighten. "What would I have to do?"

"When they spit us out in the pit again, you stand as close to that door as the Defenders will allow. As soon as that door opens, you bolt in."

"And get shot? No thanks."

"So you really are ready to die then?"

"No. That's why I *won't* do it. Because I'm *not* ready to die."

He stares at me, shrugs, leans back against the wall, and stares ahead. "There goes my ticket out of here, then."

The hopelessness in his voice makes me feel guilty. "Why don't *you* do it?"

"Because you're faster than me and half my size. You'll slip into that hall before the Defenders even get a chance to know what's happening. Your small build makes you more sly than a mouse. And you're fast."

"Fast?" I can't believe my ears. "How's being fast going

to help me, Judah? You saw that tiger today. He was faster than anything I've ever seen." I blow out a breath and lean my head back. "They'll sic that black tiger right on me, just like they almost did today."

"No, listen—" Someone groans, and Judah clamps his mouth shut. We both glance across the room just to see one of the prisoners flop over. Judah's gaze locks with mine, but his voice has lowered. "The next time they let us out, you go into that hall. You press that button, and—"

"How do you know there's a button?"

"I just…I know this place."

"How?"

"None of your business. Now, when you press that green button," he says. "The doors will stay open for one minute longer. Ash and I—"

"Wait. Who's Ash?"

He groans. "So many questions."

"Well, I'm not going to blindly follow your plan until all my questions are answered. Now who's Ash?"

He nods at the cell beside his at Lioness. She's staring at us, her dark eyes calculating.

He looks at me again. "Ash is strong and swift. Between her and me, we can fight our way through the Patricians to get to the door while you keep pressing that button to keep the doors open. We might even be able to get a gun from one of the Defenders. Then, we'll lead you through the hall to freedom."

Freedom. Like, not death. This all sounds too good to be true.

"I think the three of us would make a good team, Ember," he says. "I really do."

I stare at him, and question whether or not I can trust him. And then I decide that it doesn't matter, because if I don't work with him I'm going to die anyway, so why not give him a chance? I mean, it's win-win, really. I'll either die quickly by the black tiger, or I'll escape.

"All right," I whisper. And it all suddenly sounds divine—this little plan he has.

"I knew I could count on you."

"I haven't pulled through yet."

"But you will." He leans his head back against the wall. "This time tomorrow, you'll be out of this pit."

And I suddenly have the urge to know more about my cellmate. About this man who looks like he could kill me with one glance and is now offering me an opportunity to escape.

"When did you come here?" I ask.

"Few days before you."

"Did you kill a Defender, too?"

"Mm. No. Worse."

"A *politician*?"

"Nope." He grins. "Worse."

What could possibly be worse than killing a politician? He crosses his arms behind his head and closes his eyes. "Better get some rest, Thirteen," he says, calling me by my cell number. "We've got some serious work to do tomorrow."

CHAPTER FIFTEEN

Another dream. Actually, a memory. This one's of me and Leaf when we were younger. We're racing through the apple orchard, the branches arching over the lane, shadowing us from the hot summer sun. We're kids again, too young to worry about Career Day, too free to be constrained by the worries of this world. City life is too far away for us to care about, and executions are just nightmares talked about in textbooks.

And we race through the orchard, the music of grasshoppers and cicadas merging all around us in an exotic melody. The wind tugs at my hair. I reach the end of the lane before Leaf, as usual, but he pummels me to the ground when he catches up. And we're laughing and entirely out of breath.

"Gotta get home," Leaf says when the sun begins to set. He stands and dusts off his pants.

"Why so soon?" I ask, standing.

"We've got guests."

"Guests?" Such a foreign concept. No one gets guests in the Community Garden.

Leaf looks at me warily. "I'm not really s'posed to talk about it." He grabs his worn wool cap and walks toward his house. I hurry to catch up.

"Who's visiting?"

"I told you, I can't talk about it." Leaf's voice is hard and rough. "I shouldn't have told you anything in the first place."

This is where my memory turns into a dream. In the memory, I left and hurried back home. But in my dream, I follow Leaf. He doesn't know I'm following. He enters his cabin and slams the door behind him, but I slink around the side of his house and peek into the window where warm, yellow light pours out.

Leaf's dad—short and wiry like Leaf—is leaning back in his chair at the table, his hat off and his hair matted from working in the fields. Leaf's mom hurries around the kitchen fixing dinner. A normal enough evening in the Garden, much like what our house used to look like before Mom was taken away.

But the unusual thing is, another man sits across from Leaf's dad. He has a thick, dark beard, wild green eyes, and a scar running from his left temple to his chin. I gasp. It's the renowned criminal, the leader of the rebel group.

Jonah Walker.

The sound of metal on metal jolts me from my strange dream and my eyelids fly open. The doors to the prison slide open and the lights switch on. I squint against the brightness and try to see what's going on. A Defender stands at the control panel. A humming sound reverberates from my cell, then he looks at me.

"Your shield's down, Carter," he says. "Follow me."

I blink, trying to figure out if this is another dream. Or nightmare. He lifts a brow, and I decide, dream or not, I might as well go along with whatever is happening.

"Where are we going?" My heartbeat thrums against my eardrums as I follow him.

"Congressman Turner requested a visit with you."

Congressman Turner? Who the shoddy blazes is that? Someone with the power to decide my fate, no doubt. Maybe he decided that I'm not worthy of the Rebels Circle, so he's going to feed me to the tigers instead. The guard leads me through the maze of halls, then up the stairs, out of the dungeon.

A flicker of hope fights its way back into my heart as we exit the dungeon completely. Air. Fresh air. The evening sun slants through the tinted glass wall. And it's bright and blinding but beautiful. I follow the Defender down the marble hallway, into a room with a wooden floor. It's warm in here, compared to the dungeons, and smells like cinnamon. A fireplace with two pillars harbors the far wall, a painting of an apple tree above it. Fitting. Two leather couches face each other by the fire, and a small black table takes up the space between them. There are no windows, save for a sliver running along the top of the wall.

"Ember."

I whirl around.

Forest.

Forest is here. Wearing the straight black slacks and vest of a politician, and he's staring at me with those eyes the color of the evening sky. I swallow hard.

"You have ten minutes, Congressman Turner." The

Defender leaves the room, closing the door behind him and leaving me and Forest, I mean, *Congressman Turner*, alone.

Forest takes off his fedora, places it on the back of the chair, and walks toward me, looking at me like I'm some culpable child. I don't know why. He's the one who completely ignored me when my death sentence was announced. He's the one who lied about being a builder.

My anger fuels courage. "You *summoned* me, Congressman *Turner?*"

He winces and a deep sadness replaces the accusation in his eyes. "I have a few questions." He gestures for me to sit on one of the leather couches. I refuse. He sighs and sits in one of the seats, then waits. I roll my eyes and sink into the most comfortable couch I've ever sat on.

Leaning forward, he clasps his hands between his knees and looks at me with those dazzling cobalt eyes. And his expression is so open, so honest, everything about him draws me in and makes me want to tell him every emotion I'm experiencing, but he speaks first.

"I'm here," he says. "To ask why you killed a Defender when your future was set up for you. I made sure you would have a career as a farmer. Why did you throw that away?"

"Wait," I say. "*You* helped me get that career?" Now all the pieces fall into place—the reason why I was the only person *not* to get drafted into the Line of Defenders. The reason I got the exact career I wanted.

"Yes." A short laugh escapes him. "Not that it matters. You just sealed your fate by committing one of the worst crimes."

One of the worst.

"I didn't kill the Defender," I say. "I was trying to save my friend—"

"Who was a rebel." He narrows his eyes. "Just like you."

Oh. Oh no.

"Did—did you turn me in?" I ask.

"No." His eyes widen and he leans back. "I haven't ever turned anyone in. I would like you to know I'm not like that."

"No? Well what are you like, Forest? Because the guy I met at The Tap was a little more laid back than I would expect a politician to be. The guy I met at The Tap was...*nice*."

"Wait." His golden brows furrow. "You remember our conversation at the tavern?"

"Um, yes? Do I look senile to you? I'm not *that* forgetful. And you know what? You were a completely different person at The Tap. But now? You're a *politician*. Your people oppress my people."

He regards me for a moment, jaw clenching visibly in the dim light, then says, "First of all, there is no *your* people and *my* people. We're all one community, one tribe, one *people*."

"One people," I mumble. Then laugh. I can't help it. Forest is hysterically clueless. "You pretended not to even know me in that office today. You could have saved me, spoken up for me, had the judges hear my case. Instead, you—" My voice cuts off and I snap my mouth shut. The grief and rage I've been smothering down refuses to be contained any longer, and it grows and grows and grows until I think I'm going to turn into an unstoppable waterfall. Right in front of Forest the Politician.

I bite my lip, trying to hide my feelings behind the dam I've built. I stare at the fire that is burning, raging, waging war against itself, and I think, fire is such a strange source of nature. All you have to do is touch it for it to burn. No force necessary. It's not like a needle poking into your skin. It's not like a hammer smashing your finger. You just have to *touch* it. And that simple touch sets off all the alarms in your brain, warning you that something dangerous is on your skin, and you better act now or you'll regret it. The pain is mind-blindingly awful.

Kind of like the pain I feel around Forest. Because he's seems soft and kind and honest, and almost harmless, but one touch, one wrong word, and he has the power to have me killed. Here. Right now.

My pride tells me to get up and walk out of this room. But I don't really want to return to the stinky, cold cell. I like this fireplace. I like this couch. I like the warm air that carries the heady scent of cinnamon. I wouldn't mind lying right here on this couch and taking a little nap before my execution.

"I couldn't save you," Forest says in a low voice, drawing me back to reality. And he's looking at me, really looking at me, an emotion akin to compassion flitting through his cerulean eyes. "From what I understand, you killed a Defender. That's murder, Ember, a crime from which I cannot save you."

"Didn't you hear me earlier? I didn't kill him. I tried to stop another Defender from killing Leaf, his gun slipped, and—" Why do I even bother defending myself? No matter how many times I've told the story, no one believes me. Nobody cares. "Never mind." I stand and stride toward the door, my pride overriding my brief sense of freedom.

"Ember, wait. Stop right there."

A command. From a politician. My upbringing tells me to listen, to stop and obey his orders because he's a part of the group running this country. But I don't stop. I don't want to listen to what he has to say or try to explain myself to him.

Because attempting to explain myself to a politician is about as good as talking philosophy to an apple. Patricians don't speak to Proletariats. They don't listen. They don't care. *But why would he be here if he didn't want to hear me out?*

I stop. Look back at Forest. "Why are you here?"

He rubs the back of his neck and steps toward me. "I thought I saw something different in you."

"Different from what, exactly?"

"From every other farmer. From every other person in the Proletariat."

"I'm sure if you dressed up like a…a *commoner* more often, you wouldn't be so surprised to find people different than what you *expect*."

"I suppose you're right." He lets out a heavy sigh and runs his fingers through his golden hair. With his shirt slightly unbuttoned, and his sleeves rolled up, revealing strong forearms, I almost forget he's a politician. Because he's so young, and he's so rugged, and there's something casual and incredibly attractive about him that I never expected to see in a politician. He catches me studying him, but it seems he's too deep in thought to notice my appraisal. He lowers his arm.

"There's something about you, Ember…." His voice trails off, and he looks away, presses his lips together, like he's not sure if he wants to finish the sentence. Then he gives a brief shake of his head, looks me in the eye and says, "Go back and sit on the couch."

Humiliation. I'm painted in it. Here I am, noting how attractive he is, and he sees me as nothing more than a little girl. A commoner. A *slave*. And he's not even trying to hide it.

I pick my dignity off the floor, dust it off, and say, "No."

"Yes."

"Why?"

"Just *do* it," he says. "Do I need a reason?"

"Who do you think you are? Bossing me around? I already have a death sentence set in stone and don't have to do anything you tell me."

"Remarkable."

I stare at him in shock. "What?"

"The way you don't immediately obey me."

Seriously? His arrogance leaves me speechless, because when we first met in the tavern, he didn't seem the least bit arrogant. But now he's possibly worse than I imagined any Patrician to be.

"Just because I'm from the Proletariat," I say quietly, struggling to control my temper. "Doesn't mean I have to do whatever you tell me. I do have a mind of my own, you know."

His smile fades and he searches my eyes with acute discernment. "That you do, Miss Carter."

"I'm not some brainless slave."

"No. You're not. You're a very clever girl. I suppose I thought you were smarter than to attack a Defender."

A shocked laugh escapes me. "And I thought you had more dignity than to stand by and watch innocent victims get killed."

His gaze darkens. "Don't try to blame me. You put yourself in this mess, Carter. Now it's up to you to get out of it. I can try to help you, but I doubt I'll be able to do anything."

"Aren't you a politician? Don't you have the power to change the executions?"

"I wish I did, but I don't. I'm not in charge of the

executions, like Perseus. I'm not Chief Whitcomb. I'm a simple congressman."

I smother a laugh. There's nothing simple about being a congressman.

"Even if you didn't kill the Defender," he says, more gently now, "by your actions of merely attacking one, you are guilty of death."

"I'm *sorry*! I'm sorry I attacked your precious Defender!"

"Are you?"

I look at him, about to shout *yes*...but I'm not. Leaf was being aimed at. I had to save him. Not that my actions did any good.

"Listen." Forest's eyes soften. "I know you didn't mean for the Defender to die. I understand the deep loyalties of friendship that go above the law." He steps closer, tips my chin up, and the gestures is so intimate, it leaves me breathless. And his eyes are searching mine, as though seeking a solution. He presses his beautifully sculpted lips together, and for the briefest, strangest moment, I wonder what it would be like to feel those lips on mine. I quickly dismiss the thought.

Because I have to focus.

"I apologize if I made you feel... small in any way." His cinnamon breath invades the air between us. "You have courage, Miss Carter, and I admire that. I admire your loyalty and your passion." He drops his hand, steps toward the table, grabs his fedora and puts it on. "We've a few days before your execution takes place," he says with a sigh. "I'll see what I can do to get you out of here."

And then he's out the door, leaving me with that one simple promise that offers a handful of hope.

BLACK TIGER

CHAPTER SIXTEEN

After everyone else has fallen asleep in the prison, Judah whispers my name. "What happened?" he asks. "Where did they take you? Were you tortured?"

"Um...no." I was far from tortured. "Forest wanted to speak with me."

"Forest? Who on this forsaken earth is Forest?"

"He's a... a politician."

"I've heard of a few politicians. What's his full name?"

"Forest Turner."

He almost chokes. "*Turner?* You just spoke to Congressman *Turner?*"

I'm not really sure why he's so surprised. "You've heard of him?"

"Of course I've heard of him. Everyone knows Congressman Turner. He's in the chief's inner circle." He laughs in disbelief and drags his hands down the length of his face. "And he just wanted to *talk?*"

"Um. Yes?"

"About what, exactly?"

I explain how Forest showed up at the tavern the night before Career Day. How he told me about the spies and tried to get me the farming career.

"I don't really know why he met with me tonight, though." I frown.

"So he could drag information out of you, no doubt."

"No. I think...I think he just wanted to help."

"Help?" He snorts. "So, then, why are you still here if he's so eager to *help* you?"

"Well, I mean, he couldn't get me out."

"Is that right?"

"Yeah. I mean, he doesn't have that kind of authority."

He snorts out a laugh and shakes his head. "Didn't you hear me say he's in Chief Titus's *inner* circle? Don't you think he could have just mentioned your name to Titus and gotten you out?"

"Well, no," I say. "I mean, this country is run by rules, right? Chief Whitcomb can't just decide to override the rules because of favoritism."

He stares at me, bemused. "You're sharp, Ember. You think outside the brainless way of thinking that the majority of Ky is run on. But you're still pretty naïve. This country is run by our *chief,* and he can and *does* change the rules as he sees fit. This Congressman Turner...he just has to say one word and you're safe. But he hasn't helped you out yet, then there's no reason to hope that he will."

His words leave me speechless. They steal every last grain of hope from my bloodstream and leave me an empty shell on the floor.

"I can't believe you think he's actually trying to help

you."

I don't like how Judah makes me feel like a gullible child. I don't like how he calls me naïve and looks at me with that pity in his eyes. I don't like it one bit. So my walls of defense come up. And I lift my chin a little.

"Well," I say. "He didn't smoke me out in the tavern when he had the perfect opportunity to. He actually went out of his way to change my career from being in the Line of Defenders to being a farmer, which is exactly what I wanted. So, yeah. Call me naïve or whatever. But I do actually kind of trust him."

The amusement flickers out of his eyes, and now he just looks a little sad. "Right. Okay. Just don't get too attached. I've known a few politicians in my life, and they're none too friendly."

"What do you mean?"

Two blinks. "It was a politician," he says, "who turned me and my crew of Resurgencies in."

Whoa. What? "So, wait." I try to gather my scattered thoughts. "You're a part of the Resurgence? I mean, you work for Jonah Walker?"

He nods slowly.

Holy Crawford. I knew there might be some Resurgencies in here, but I wasn't entirely sure. I mean, I've never even heard of the rebels until Leaf told me. But now I'm actually talking to a *member* of the *Resurgence*. The thought is absolutely thrilling.

"So, a politician turned you in?"

"Yes," Judah says. "We had two politicians show up in the Resurgence just a couple months ago, begging to become a part of us. The first one was caught communicating with

Defenders on his phoneband. We disposed of him quickly. The second is the guy who turned me in just last week. He was supposed to be a part of our team, he was the one who would get us through the security into the chief's offices. But he smoked us out, and it's because of him that I'm in here.

"This Turner guy may seem awfully friendly," Judah says. "But he's out to get you. He probably knows your friend was helping Walker, and he wants to use you to get to your friend's father or something. Or maybe he really thinks you're lying, that you know something about the Resurgence, and he's hoping to get it out of you. But let me tell you something, Ember, and let me be perfectly clear: Congressman Turner doesn't want to help anyone but himself. If he knows he can use you to rid the people who are a threat against *his* people, then he will. And the way he'll get to you is by pretending to be your friend."

Forest's words echo in my head. *There is no my people and your people. We're all one nation, one tribe. One people.*

"I've never met a politician I've liked," Judah says. "Never. Not once. And I've met quite a few of them. They're liars down to the bone. *All of them.*"

Now I'm confused. Like, mind-bogglingly confused. Because Forest seemed so real. And I don't really understand how a man who seemed so trustworthy, so down to earth, so completely honest, could possibly be like the politicians Judah's describing. How Forest with his sincere blue eyes and casual demeanor and non-threatening manner could be *bad*.

But maybe that's his plan. To appear innocent and honest. To gain my trust so he could help his people in the long run. It worked. I'd opened up to him that night at The Tap in a way no one ever should open up to strangers. I'd said some things against the government that could've gotten

130

me killed on the spot.

I'd *trusted* him.

"My best friend wanted to be a part of the Resurgence," I say. "His father housed Jonah Walker on the last night I was there."

Judah nods. "Walker was with us the night the Defenders raided our building. We were on our way to Frankfort. When that traitor turned us in, we were scattered throughout the city. But Walker was one of 'em who got away. He must have been on the run since, hiding in the Garden with your friend."

"The Community Garden is the best place to hide in Ky." I think of not only our apple orchard, but the cornfields in the summer and the pine forests in the winter and how the lights go out two hours after sunset, and how the entire landscape is cloaked in darkness all night.

"Try second best," Judah says.

I look sharply at him.

"I mean," he says. "It's no Louisville."

A sharp intake of breath. Louisville, the ashen city. The *forbidden* city. The ghost town of ghost towns whose ashes have been taken over by vines—according to rumors.

"Is that—is that where your group is hiding?" I ask.

His gaze shifts to the ceiling. "I can't tell you too much, Ember. Cameras and microphones might be wired all over this place. But I can tell you this, and I tell you with the full knowledge that Titus might hear this message himself, we are hiding until our numbers are large enough to match the Defenders'. And the next time we attempt an assassination on Titus, we will succeed."

The air is stolen from my lungs. Treason. Judah could be

killed for what he just said. But, oh, wait, we're already headed to our executions. Still, even I don't have the balls to make such a bold proclamation.

"D-do you think it would do any good?" I squeak, almost afraid that the Defenders will march in here at any moment and kill us both on the spot. "I mean, if Titus falls, another snotty politician will just take his place, yes?"

"Not if there's another member of the Whitcomb bloodline."

This takes me off guard. "Um. Isn't Titus an only child? His dad is dead. His mom—I don't really know what happened to his mom. But she's gone. So, I mean, he doesn't have any children, does he?" Or maybe he does.

"No," Judah says. "But he has a sister."

"Oh. Weird. I don't really remember ever learning about his sis—"

"That's because Titus's mom took her when she ran off."

"Oh." So much information left out of our education. I guess they don't consider this important for us gardeners to learn, though. "So...Titus's mom just...ran off?"

"Yes. This is common knowledge," Judah says with a flip of his hand. "Now, everyone knows Titus's mom was caught and executed, but no one's found her other child yet."

"She's not with the Resurgence?"

"Nope." He stares at me, his brown eyes filled with some sort of passion. "But when we find Titus's sister," he says. "And if she supports our cause, well, then, we'll have ourselves a new leader. And *she* will have the power to control the rise or fall of Ky. The power to give us freedom, make us stronger, and make Ky better than it's ever been."

CHAPTER SEVENTEEN

Fear. It's making me sick to my stomach. Thoughts of my impending death fill every corner of my brain, and I'm scared. Heart-poundingly terrified. And my breaths become short and quick, like I just can't inhale enough oxygen, and I press my back against the wall and squeeze my eyes shut and try to focus focus focus until I feel it.

The pull. The whisper. The presence calming my nerves and taming my thoughts. The voice begging me to call out to something, *someone* that I can't fully grasp and will never understand. I look around the dim room to see if anyone else feels it, but they're all asleep, or staring blankly ahead, lost in their own thoughts. I look at Judah, but he's out cold, the soft sound of his heavy breathing confirming he's asleep.

But the atmosphere is pulsing with energy. And it's calling out to me.

"Please," I whisper to the air.

The air.

It's just air.

But it's fully charged, alive, filled with some sort of power, a being that's so incredibly moving it brings me to my knees on the rough, concrete ground. And I hunch forward, dig my fingers into my hair, and again I say, *"PLEASE."*

And it's all I can say, but somehow I feel like I'm fully understood.

We're released outside early the next morning, and I immediately notice Patricians standing on the balconies that surround the arena. Why do they come here to spectate criminals? What can be so entertaining as to watch us stretch our legs? I don't want their critical eyes on me, so I sprint along the wall of the arena toward the door that the Patricians will soon exit.

Breathe. Plan. Judah said there was a green button on the inside of the hallway that will keep the door open as long as I keep pushing it. All I have to do is slip through the crowd of Patricians, press that button, and he and Ash will magically fight their way in, and we'll magically escape. I don't know how it's all going to work. But I also don't want to die, so it's worth a shot.

When I run past the gates, some of the spectating Patricians send catcalls down and shout obscenities at me. I bite my tongue to keep from saying anything that'll make me dinner for the tigers, and continue my trek around the arena a few more times as to look less suspicious. If I wait by the door, they'll know something's up. So I run. I breathe. I exchange bad air for good and tell myself everything's going to be okay. And I wait.

After another lap, I hunch over by the door, plant my palms on my knees and suck in sharp breaths. Straightening, I look toward the Patricians in the balcony again. When are they going to get the balls to come down *here*? Are they even going to come out? Did they happen to hear us on the microphones and cameras that Judah's convinced are wired in the prison walls? If so, of course they're not going to be stupid enough to open those doors.

I grit my teeth, fight back the despair that inches into my very being, and glare at the Patricians who stare down at us.

Is Forest among them? He said he'd try to find a way for me to get out of here, but maybe he forgot. Maybe it just, I don't know, slipped his mind. Maybe Judah was right about everything, and Forest was just trying to dig for answers, bribe me by offering freedom. And maybe, after that conversation, he decided I was useless.

Either way, I'm screwed. I almost look away from the Patricians when I spot Rain, his newsboy cap sitting crookedly over his auburn hair.

Rain. A vile creature if I ever did see one. He has one arm wrapped around the skinny waist of a Patrician girl, and holds a flask in his other hand. Another girl with perfect black curls stands on his other side, clinging to his arm. He gestures toward one of the criminals while saying something in Black Curls's ear. She giggles, then bites her lip enticingly and says something that brings Rain's hallmark smirk to his face.

That smirk. I wish I could smack it off his Patrician face. As though hearing my thoughts, he looks in my direction and his eyes lock with mine. And his smile vanishes. His features

135

become stony. Cold. Almost...*dangerous*. I want to look away, but I don't want to seem weak, so I stare him down until he looks away. One word to the girls, and he turns away from the balcony and stalks off.

If he hates me so much, why didn't he let the black tiger kill me yesterday? Is watching me suffer by the Rebels Circle really a better form of revenge? For the first time, I actually look forward to returning to my cell. I'm tired of being watched, scrutinized, judged. And it's obvious they're not opening the doors. Because they probably heard our entire plan. So I pick up my pace, and I sprint around the arena. One more lap and then it'll be time to go back inside the cell.

But just as I'm finishing my lap, the doors open. Patricians begin filing out. My heart takes an overexcited leap. It's time. I glance at Judah and he dips his chin in a nod. I pick up my pace and sprint straight toward the door. I slip through the cracks of the Patricians, and I can feel their eyes on me. I can feel the Defenders taking aim, but I keep my eye on the prize—the door, the goal, the opening that screams freedom—when someone grabs both my arms and whirls me around.

CHAPTER EIGHTEEN

"Hey, easy there, tiger."

NO!

I try to pull free, but the hands grip me too tightly, and when I look back at the door, it slams shut on my dreams and hopes and the only chance of life that I possibly had.

And life. Life suddenly seems like something I've taken for granted every single day until the one day it's slipping through my fingers. Despair is suddenly fully understood. I take a step back. Stare at the doors through the blur of angry tears.

"You all right there?"

I turn to look at my intruder, the jackal who stopped me from attaining that unattainable goal. And my heart sinks into my gut. Because mocking gray eyes are staring right at me.

"Rain." His name is spoken through clenched teeth like a curse. "Rain. You—you—"

"I what?" he asks in a very quiet, but still musical voice.

"I *rescued* you from a suicide mission?"

"You—son of a *jackal!*" I rip my arms from his firm grip, surprised that he releases me so easily. "I was—I almost—"

"Killed yourself?"

I look at him. "No! The opposite. I almost *escaped.*"

"You think you could have escaped? Right in front of everyone here?" He looks around us, and I realize for the first time all the Patricians and Defenders are staring at me.

"Show's over, folks," he says, and they go about their business.

"I had a plan," I mumble. I swipe a tear from the corner of my eye before Rain sees it.

"A plan that would have ended in immediate death." He pulls a flask out of his back pocket.

"I'm going to die anyway."

"Yes. Well, aren't we all? Peter Pan doesn't exactly welcome anyone to Neverland who's older than twelve, so we adults have to suck it up, plaster a smile on our faces, and pretend like the grave doesn't completely terrify us."

I'm so confused, and I almost ask who Peter Pan is and where Neverland is, but then decide I don't really care.

Rain unscrews the lid and takes a deep drink, and I catch a glimpse of his jaw, lightly bruised from where I punched him.

A sense of gratification fills me. "How's your jaw?"

He lowers the flask, nearly choking on that last drink, and glares at me. "It still hurts."

"Oh?" I shake my hand and flex my fist. "So does my fist."

"You think it's funny?"

"I don't think I punched you hard enough."

"No?"

"No. You can still talk."

His eyes become slits of steel, his jaw tensing. "You have absolutely no shame, do you?" He slips his flask back into his pocket and crosses his arms over his chest. "No matter. You'll die soon enough. Tomorrow, in fact." His upper lip curves in a line of pure arrogance. "Bus is scheduled to take you and your happy crew of rebels out to the Rebels Circle at nine."

I have the sudden urge to puke.

"Aw, not so happy now, are we?" He puckers his lower lip in false sympathy. "Here." He pulls his flask back out, leans in until I feel his warm breath on my cheek, and whispers, "Looks like you could use a drink."

I jerk back and look at the flask. "I don't think prisoners are allowed to drink."

"Seriously? You're worried about rules *now*?" His smile broadens. "I think it's a bit late for that. Besides, who *cares*? You're going to die tomorrow. Just drink. It'll make you feel so much better. I *swear.*"

I would think he was trying to poison me, if I didn't see him take a swig from it seconds ago. And I'm thirsty. So incredibly thirsty because they've hardly given us any water. After all those laps, I do kind of want something to drink, no matter what it is. So I accept the flask and take a deep gulp. The bitter liquid strikes sparks in the back of my throat, and fire flows down my esophagus into my stomach, and I hunch over, coughing and choking while I shove the flask back into his hands.

"What's wrong? Never had whiskey?" His grin is broad now, and a laugh escapes him. And I'm humiliated and angry and completely defeated. I call him a foul word and shove past him, but he grabs my wrist. "Wait, wait. I'm sorry."

I twist from his grasp. "Let me go!"

"Ember, I just—I have something of yours."

This stops me. I turn to face him. He reaches into his pocket and pulls out a small slip of paper, holds it between his index and middle finger.

I snatch the paper from his fingers and unfold it to find a picture of a burning apple. The slip Leaf gave me. My heart stops beating, then beats two beats too fast. I squeeze the paper tight in my fist, look around to make sure no one notices, then glare at Rain.

"Where," I seethe. "Did you find this?"

"In your cell at Shelby Prison."

"You've had it all this time?"

He grins. "It's my job to keep an eye out for Resurgencies like you."

"I'm *not* a part of the Resurgence," I whisper.

"No?" He tilts his head. "Just tell me one thing, then." And he leans in closer so I can smell the sour alcohol on his breath. "What, exactly, do you know of the Resurgence?"

"N-nothing." The bigger questions is, what does *he* know of it?

"Then why the shoddy inferno did you have this paper?" he asks like it's the dumbest thing in the world for me to carry around such a treasonous sign.

"Leaf gave it to me before he died," I say. "Said it could help me." I look away, blinking back the unexpected tears that seem to want to flood the earth every time I think of Leaf. "I don't know how it could help me, though. It's just a piece of trash." I look at Rain. "Trust me, I don't have anything to do with the Resurgence. And, honestly? I don't really *want* anything to do with them."

Rain's brows flicker. "And why not? You think you're better than them? That you're somehow above them?"

His sudden defense of the Resurgence takes me off guard. "No—no, I don't think I'm b-better."

"Then what's your beef against them, huh?"

I stare at him, speechless, while he waits for an answer. "I think—I think my mom was taken away because of them."

He lifts his brows in surprise. "Your mom was taken away because of the Resurgence?"

"I don't...I don't really know."

"Is she still alive?"

I shrug. "Dad thinks she was executed on the Rebels Circle. But we Proletariats have no way of knowing for sure how or when the so-called criminals die. I mean, her execution was never posted in the town square, so..." I sigh. "All I know is Mom was taken away and never returned to the Community Garden."

"Huh." Rain crosses his arms and skates his thumb along his lower lip. "You're from the Community Garden, yes? How old are you?"

What is this, some sort of small talk? From a Patrician?

"Why the sudden interest?" I ask, suddenly annoyed at the personal level this conversation has taken. "Do all Patricians enjoy antagonizing criminals just before they die?"

I shove past him, but he grabs my arm and spins me around. "Just tell me your age, Ember Carter."

I jerk my arm from his grip, then glance around. Defenders are watching. Better not cause a scene or they'll sic the black tiger on me.

"Sixteen." I practically spit the word out.

"What was her name?"

141

"Who's name?"

"Your *mother's*."

Why does he care? And why should I stand here and take this antagonizing from him? And then I think, these are my last hours to spend, not his. And I don't want to spend them talking about how Mom died. My death is set in stone, and I have no obligation to answer his questions.

"Aren't you a Patrician?" I snap. "Don't you have access to the execution records? Why don't you go look it up yourself if you're so interested?"

He lifts his hands in mock defense. "Okay, okay. Just trying to make small talk. No need to get all defensive. Holy Crawford. Just one more thing." He reaches over and slips the Resurgence paper from my fingers. "I'll be keeping this." He grins. "Good luck, little orchardist." He takes another drink from his flask, then bows mockingly. "I look forward to watching you die very, very soon."

He whirls around and heads back toward the gate. He wouldn't let me walk away, but he's allowed to just *leave*? What an arrogant jackal.

"Wait," I say.

He pauses, turns to look at me. I stride up and grab the flask from his hands, tilt my head back and drink deeply. The whiskey BURNS as it pours into my stomach like hot lava and my body wants to convulse, regurgitate the liquor out of my system, but pride is a strong little thing, and I brace myself until I drain every last drop from the flask. Then I shove it back into Rain's hands.

"Thanks," I say with a cough-wheeze. "I needed that more than you think."

He stares at me, opens his mouth like he's going to say something, then closes it.

My eyes watering, I spin on my heel and continue my jog around the arena, trying hard not to think about the burning liquid sloshing around in my stomach, threatening to resurface and turn me into a volcano.

CHAPTER NINETEEN

The whiskey worked. After we were called back into the dungeon, I felt...*great*. Fantastic. Even though it's the night before my execution.

But then I start thinking about Leaf. Innocent, harmless Leaf. Dead because for once—for once in his shoddy life—he actually decided to stand up for himself. He was bullied all throughout elementary school and did nothing about it, but come Career Day, he suddenly has a backbone. And look where it got him.

I don't think Leaf's mom intended for him to get bullied in elementary. I think if she knew he was going to have the paper-thin profile of a leaf, she wouldn't have named him that. But she did. And he did. And kids made fun of him at school. They told him not to let the wind blow him away. They said things that made the frail, small boy look even more frail and small. And I always felt terribly bad for him. I always wondered why he wouldn't just tell them to shod off, and then I thought, maybe he was as shy as me. Maybe, like me, he was too afraid to speak out for himself.

It was in the fifth grade that I finally got the balls to stand up for him. The bullies were picking on him, sizing him up. Leaf was standing against the wall, small and frail, yet impossibly brave. Chin held high, eyes defiant while the wind ruffled his dark hair. I didn't understand why we couldn't all just get along. And just before the bully punched him, I darted between his fist and Leaf's eye and I shouted, "Stop!"

And he did. I was so surprised that I kept going. "All of you need to stop bullying Leaf. In fact," I said, "stop bullying each other. Let's just get along!"

And we did. School was much easier for me after that. Teachers called me the peacemaker. If there was an argument, I would settle it. I don't know why the other kids listened to me. I guess because my mom died just a couple years before and they felt sorry for me.

Leaf stuck by my side like a lost puppy after that. And because the kids at school liked me so much, they did pretty much whatever I asked. Even the teachers, sometimes, would let me slide by the rules. I can't lie, I've had a pretty easy childhood. I've always gotten along with everyone, and never experienced tension with anybody.

Until now.

Because for some reason, Patricians are difficult to get along with. They're not easy going. There's nothing simple about them. They're complicated and difficult. Everything is about drama and tension and heated dialogue and one-upping.

And I hate it. I hate that I can't just settle things with a few words like I could in the Community Garden. I hate how Rain instigates me, and I can't simply tell him to shod off.

Once the alcohol finally wears off, I can't help but curse the day I was born. My body wretches and I puke on the stone floor. Some of the others groan in disgust. I wipe the acidic saliva off my mouth, then crawl to the wall, like some pathetic dying rat. My head is pounding. My stomach feels like it's literally twisting itself inside-out. And the fear of death tomorrow isn't helping any. Because in less than twenty-four hours, I'm going to be burned to death on the Rebels Circle. I'm going be fried alive. And there's absolutely nothing I can do about it.

I swallow the sour bile down my throat, close my eyes, and lean my head back. What I'd give for a glass of water right now.

"You finally sober?"

"Getting there." I crack an eyelid open and look at Judah. "My head hurts."

"Who the shoddy blazes gave you a drink, anyway?"

I sigh. "Rain."

"Rain?"

"The arrogant Patrician walking around the arena like a peacock. Capital *C* on the cock."

"You spoke to *Rain*?"

"Yes." I frown. "Do you know him?"

"No—no." He says the words almost too quickly. "Of course not. I just know he's a politician's son, is all."

I didn't know he was the son of a politician. Makes sense, though.

"I bet that was some expensive stuff you drank, then." He chuckles. "What, with the politicians making profit somewhere in the millions."

I shoot upright, and immediately regret doing so when

the stabbing pain shoots into my head. I groan. "They get *paid?*" Holy Crawford. Money is used only for luxury items like alcohol and extra blankets anything else that isn't absolutely necessary. And the only way anyone makes money is by the Coins of Good Service, which they only get when they do some extravagant form of good service. Or if they turn in a criminal, they could get a good ten Coins. But I don't get it. "Why do politicians get paid? They're just doing their work, like the rest of the country is doing theirs."

Judah snorts. "Don't you know? They believe that since they're running the country, they're somehow better than us. That every hour they put in is some form of community service. They live in mansions, own fancy vehicles, eat fresh food for every meal *all day long.*"

"You're kidding." I vaguely remember Forest saying something about how they get paid for keeping the country in line. But eating food all day long? Come on. Our country has been running low on food for decades. "Are you...are you sure? About the food?"

Judah nods. Leans his head back. "Patricians, like that boy who gave you whiskey, live like kings, Ember. And they have unlimited access to food."

That would mean Dad was right.

"But, how? Where does it come from?"

He shrugs. "Your little Garden, maybe. Possible survivors from the outside world, perhaps. Who knows? The point is, they get it, and they keep it in Frankfort."

Survivors?

"I don't understand." I stare at the concrete ground, tinted blue from the dim light above the panel, and I think about the food, the little food we receive and how it's always late and how I somehow thought maybe everyone was suffering, everyone was hungry. I thought that maybe I was sort of spoiled for living in the Garden and having a little extra food when our rations ran out. I felt guilty for it. But the Patricians, according to Judah, don't have that problem. Neither the hunger problem, nor the guilty problem.

A Defender walks into the room. "Come with me." He lets down my shield, leads me out of the dungeon, through the halls, and into the comfortable room where Forest is waiting. And despite Judah's warning, I feel a great measure of relief. I guess Forest didn't forget about me, after all. But now I'm a bit more guarded. Because Judah says Forest is just milking me for information. Judah says the Patricians and politicians don't care about us Proletariats. And right now, Judah's my closest friend.

I'm sitting on the leather couch across from Forest. He's leaning forward, elbows on knees, chin in hands, two fingers pressed together on his pursed lips. And two cobalt eyes looking at me.

"You look—terrible," he finally says.

I stare at him. Forest is usually pretty polite, and that was possibly the rudest thing anyone's said to me all day.

"What happened to you?"

"Rain," I find myself saying. "Rain happened to me. He gave me whiskey."

"Rain?" His brows flicker. "Gave you…whiskey?"

"Mm-hm."

He releases a small laugh. "Jackal."

I briefly wonder how he knows Rain, but then realize the Patrician community is quite small, really. Kind of like our Community Garden. Everyone seems to know everyone.

"If I look *terrible*," I say. "It's due to the fact that I'm dying tomorrow. And that, as of the past few days, that fact is all I've been able to think about, being locked up in a tiny cell with nothing to distract me."

"Look," he says. "I'm trying to get you out." A deep sadness fills his eyes that I don't quite understand. I mean, I barely know him. And he looks devastated that I'm going to die tomorrow. "What you should know is that I spoke to Titus."

"You did?" I sit up straighter, a sudden thrill coursing through me.

Forest nods. "He came to see you for himself today, to see if you were maybe worth saving."

"Wait. So, Titus was in the arena? *Today?*"

He nods.

Wow. The chief was in the arena. To watch *me*. I guess I didn't notice with all the Patricians looking the same with all their fancy clothes. The only Patrician I noticed in the arena was Rain. And that's only because he grabbed me. He stopped me from running away. But Titus was there. I suddenly feel self-conscious, wondering if I made a good impression. I mean, if I'd known the chief was there to decide the fate of my life, I might have been on my best behavior.

"So?" I ask, trying to fight down my growing hope. "What...what did he think?"

Forest's forehead pinches and he narrows his eyes. "Miss Carter, have you been plotting an escape? With rebels?"

Oh, shoddy rot. The wind is knocked out of me by the blow of utter disappointment, because Judah told me. He told me there were cameras and mics wired all throughout the prison, and we still planned our escape. But, of course. Of course everyone heard us plotting and that's why it didn't work out. That's why Rain grabbed me by the arms and stopped me and stalled me just long enough until the shoddy door slammed in my face.

"Ember?" Forest's voice is a husky whisper now.

"Yes." I nod once and look at him. "Yes. Judah and I—we—we wanted to get out of here."

Forest straightens. He leans back. He drags both hands through his golden hair and releases an exasperated sigh. "*Why?*" His voice is full of so much emotion that *I* almost feel sorry for *him*. "I told you—" His voice cuts off and his lips disappear completely as he presses them together. He takes a deep breath and says more calmly this time, "I told you I would help you, but by conspiring with rebels, you just proved yourself guilty."

"Just by *talking* to them?"

"Yes. Merely by associating with them. By planning with them. By agreeing to work with them to go against the system."

"To escape to *freedom!*" I bolt to my feet and begin pacing, suddenly angry. Angry at Forest. Angry at myself. "No offense, Forest, but when it comes down to life or death, I'm not going to just go with the law. I'll do everything in my power to choose life."

"And by doing so you just dug your own grave."

I stare at him, any words I might have said too shocked to exit my mouth.

He utters a curse. "I'm sorry. I shouldn't have said that." He stands, and to my astonishment, draws me into his arms. "Please, don't listen to what I just said."

I forgot how incredibly therapeutic a simple hug could be. And I melt. I melt in his arms and all my resolve dissipates. I wrap my arms around his waist, realizing for the first time just how lean and firm his body is. He cradles my head against his chest, and a tear slips. And slides down the bridge of my nose.

Forget what Judah said. I believe Forest really wants to help me. Because he hasn't asked me any questions about the Resurgence or my family or Leaf's family and he's holding me like it's the only thing he wants to do right now.

"I'm sorry," I say. "I—I didn't know—I didn't think—" I swallow. "So many days went by, I thought you'd forgotten about me."

"Ember." He pulls away just enough to search my eyes. "How in the world could I ever forget about you? You're fire and sparks and unforgettable. And I'm not giving up. I'm meeting with Titus first thing in the morning. I'll get you out of here. You have nothing to worry about. Nothing to fear. You're going to be *just fine*."

"Why do you want so badly to help me?"

He cups my face, looks at me with so much certainty I want to believe every word he says.

"Because," he says. "I know the system is broken, and I want to fix it. And after our conversation at The Tap, after seeing your passion, your strong belief in a better way, I've been wanting to recruit you to work with me. I want your help to change the government."

"You want my…help?"

What would Judah have to say to this? To a politician wanting change? To Forest touching me like this? He would say it's all a lie. I take a step back and Forest drops his hand.

"Get me out of here," I say, breathless because his touch does strange things to me. "And I'll think about helping you."

I'm led back to the prison pit and I step into my cell. The electric shield goes up, and I'm once again left wondering if Forest will actually go through with his promise, or if he even *can* go through with it. I sink down against the wall, lean my head back on the rough concrete.

"What kind of information did he try to drag out of you this time?" Judah asks.

I turn my head to look at him. "He said I shouldn't have tried to plot an escape. He said Titus was there to watch me, to decide if I was worth saving, and that, basically, our attempt to escape only confirmed my guiltiness."

And Judah bursts out laughing. He laughs and laughs and laughs and says, "I seriously hope you're smart enough to see right through this Turner guy."

"He—he didn't try to drag anything from me, Judah," I say. "I mean, he just said he was going to try again. To get me out of here. He was going to talk to Titus in the morning. He didn't ask me any questions about the Resurgence or Leaf or anything like that." I don't bother telling Judah that Forest wants me to work with him to better the government. I can't handle any more of his mockery right now.

"But he got mad at you for trying to escape?" Judah asks. "For trying to save your own life?"

"Because I undid what he was trying to do."

He snorts. Shakes his head. Leans his head back and says, "You know what? Keep thinking that. Keep imagining this handsome Congressman as some hero who really cares deeply about you. Maybe it'll be your last sweet thought before you burn to death."

I stare at him, shocked that he could be so—so *mean*. Then I look at the ceiling. And I wonder if Judah's right or if Forest is right and who's on my side and who's against me and why it even matters, since I'm going to die soon. I guess

I'll find out tomorrow, when my death is carried out. If I'm rescued, I'll know Forest really does care for me. If I'm not rescued, I'll be too dead to care whose side he's on.

A roar echoes through the tunnels and goosebumps flesh out across my skin. Then screaming. Screaming that makes my arm hairs stand on end. Then the scream is silenced.

"Judah?" I ask, looking at him.

"Hm?" He doesn't open his eyes but leans his head back against the wall.

"Why do the tigers roar like that? Like they're suddenly angry? And—and where's that screaming coming from?"

He cracks an eyelid open and looks at me. "The tigers are feeding."

"On... *what?*"

He opens both eyes now. "On the other criminals."

My heart stops. "What?"

"The tigers have to eat. Haven't you wondered what happens to the other criminals? The ones who aren't rebels like us, but who still go against the law by stealing a bit of food? The black tigers are trained to scout out criminals and hunt down rebels. And what better way to train them than to use an underground maze and criminals for them to hunt? Besides, the tigers have to eat somehow." He closes his eyes, leans his head back again. "Might as well kill two birds with one stone."

Now I know I'm going to puke. The devastation makes my stomach turn and writhe and my body is suddenly trembling, my hands are clammy, and I curl up by the wall, try not to think about tomorrow or the screams echoing through the prison.

Minutes tick by. They keep growing in number like

swarming bees. One. Then two. Then thirty, then four hundred, and I lose count until it seems like an eternity has passed.

But then something happens, and it happens so fast it takes me a moment to process it because I'm half asleep.

Sirens. Sirens are blaring all around us, piercing my eardrums and shattering my thoughts into five-million pieces. I cover my ears and look at Judah, as if to find answers there, but he looks as clueless as me. Water sprinkles from the ceiling into our cells, the cold water soaking into my hair and clothes.

"Fire," Judah says. "Those are fire alarms."

CHAPTER TWENTY

And my lungs collapse. Because we're underground. There's only one way out of here. The electric shields have us confined. How hard it would be just to leap through them? How bad will they electrocute me? I reach toward them to test the barrier when Judah shouts, "No!"

I freeze and look at him.

"Electricity and water," he says, wide-eyed. "Not a good mix."

Of course.

"Good thing we're surrounded by steel and concrete," I say. "A fire can't get through those."

"No, but smoke can seep through the cracks of the doorway."

I chew my lips. "This is a big dungeon. The fire could be on the other side of the prison for all we know." I shrug. "They'll get the fire out before it reaches us."

"Why does it matter?" Judah wipes water from his face

and sits back down, resigned, his wet hair sticking to his forehead. "We're going to die, anyway."

The wailing sirens make it hard to think, and I keep looking at the door, looking for any sign of smoke of the fire. And I realize that I'm not really ready to die yet, and maybe I would like just one more day, please. One more day to think through all my memories and my mistakes, and one more day to wait for Forest to get me out of here.

And then the door bursts open.

Through the haze of spraying water, I can see a figure dressed in a black cloak bolt to the panel. Has to be a Defender, by the way the person knows exactly the code to punch in. Two more seconds and the barriers lift.

The figure seems to look right at me, but I can't see the face clearly in the dim light and spraying water. "Follow me," a male voice shouts. "Quick!"

My heart leaps with a surge of hope, and I stand up and bolt out of my cell. He grabs my arm, then practically drags me out of the room. Why choose to grab me and not someone else? Maybe because I'm small and might lag behind. And then I wonder why the Defenders are so concerned about rescuing us if we're going to die anyway, but maybe it's to avoid cleaning all the dead bodies that would be leftover. *My* dead body. Judah's dead body.

The Defender's fingers bite into my arm. "Hurry," he shouts, obviously annoyed. I reach back and grab Judah's hand, careful not to lose him in the darkness of the halls. The Defender leads us through the maze of halls until we arrive at a small door that says "Emergency Exit" in big bold letters, and it spits us out on the street.

It's night, but the light of the street lamps floods the road. Defenders and pedestrians are crowded on the sidewalk. Alarms blare in the distance, then red flashing lights on a truck appear down the street.

"Come on!" The Defender releases me, then gestures for me to follow. Wait, what? If he's a Defender, then wouldn't he just hold us captive here until the fire goes out?

"Come *on*, Ember." Judah takes my shoulders and gently guides me behind our rescuer. "This is an escape. We're *escaping.*"

Oh. *Oh.* This guy came here to help us escape. Has he been sent by Forest? Of course. Of course he has. Forest promised to help me. This is him helping me. I pick up my pace and follow our rescuer and Judah around the corner. I look behind to make sure no guards are following, and see Ash and a few other prisoners behind me. They escaped too. Good. We sprint down the street, darting left, right, left, right, trying to lose anyone who might be tracking us. It's hard to keep up; our hero is a fast runner, but when I look back, only Ash and another runaway have been able to stay on our heels.

The sound of my own breathing fills the air around me, and I match my steps to the rhythm. Inhale. Exhale. Replenish bad air for good.

Everything *might* actually be okay.

But then another sound fills the air. A louder one than the fire alarm or fire truck. A blaring siren that could be heard for miles around. It stops blaring just long enough for an automated voice to say, *"Prisoners are on the run. Citizens are encouraged to go indoors. Prisoners are on the run. Citizens are encouraged to go indoors."* Then the siren blares again and it's loud and deafening and makes my heart want to pound out of my chest.

I don't know how much longer I can keep up my pace, but the promise of life versus death keeps my feet moving. Because if I don't keep moving, I'm going to die. If I don't keep running, I'll be captured. Rain's mocking gray eyes flash through my mind, and I remember what he said: *You're going to die tomorrow.* A wave of renewed adrenaline pulses through my veins. I've never wanted to prove anyone wrong more than I do at this very moment.

Suddenly, our leader trips and stumbles onto the concrete, rolling several times. He holds his knee to his chest and groans. In the brief instant, I catch a glimpse of his lower waist where his shirt has been shoved up. I notice a tattoo, a black symbol resembling the letter *t*. I kneel beside him, but he shoves me away, careful to keep his face turned.

"Go! Get out of here! Keep heading north."

I don't even know where north is. I feel Judah's hand clamp down on my shoulder. "Come on, Ember."

"B-but we'll get caught! We don't know where we're going."

"I do." Judah offers a reassuring squeeze. "Follow me."

I glance at our leader. Our hero. Our savior. I don't want to leave him. He's the reason we escaped. And if he's caught—

"Get outta here! I'll be *fine*."

I nod and quickly stand, then follow Judah down the street. The sirens of police cars wail down the street, coming closer and closer.

"To the shadows!" Judah shouts.

I bolt behind him to the sidewalk, glancing back to find the other two still following. And behind them, something else. Something big and fast. Something that blends in to the dark cloak of night. I squint to get a better look, but a loud roar makes my brain shudder. Chills flesh out across my skin, and I nearly stumble into the wall, because I suddenly can't take my eyes off the black tiger sauntering straight toward us. It leaps into the air and pummels the runaway closest to him to the ground, then begins tearing into the flesh.

And I. Can't. Move.

"Run!" Judah says.

Right. Run. I whirl around and my feet begin slamming into the pavement. I try to catch up with Judah. Forget my exhaustion. Forget the pain in my lungs or the stabbing in my side or the way my legs feel like jelly. Forget everything but the will to survive.

We take another turn when I hear a scream. Ash. Oh, Ash. *Don't look back, don't look back, just keep moving forward.*

We bolt around another corner. When I finally dare to look back, we have no more followers. Well, except two black tigers that are racing faster than lightning. A loud roar sounds in front of us, and I slam into Judah's brick back.

"Why are you stop—"

"We're surrounded," he says.

And I stop. I look past him at the tiger blocking our path. One tiger in front of us, two tigers behind, and tall buildings on either side.

We're trapped.

The tigers slow to a stop, shoulders hunched, teeth bared, eyes glittering in the moonlight like glowing bullets. And then another roar, and the tiger in front leaps into the air—it leaps into the air and he lands right on Judah—and Judah falls to the ground—and the tiger is on top of him. The tiger is on top of him. Pinning him to the ground. And Judah tries to shove the tiger off, but it's heavy and big and strong and it sinks its teeth into Judah's shoulder, and there's blood blood blood oozing out of his skin.

And horror seizes me by the throat, rips across my lungs, and clamors out of my mouth. "STOP!"

The tiger lifts its head, looks right at me with golden eyes, and growls, revealing long fangs stained with Judah's blood. And I can't think can't think can't think—all I can think about is Judah needing help, and I stumble to his side. I don't know what, exactly, I plan on doing when I reach Judah—when I reach the black tiger on top of him—but I don't have time to plan as I race toward the massive black beast and scream, "GET OFF OF HIM!"

To my utter astonishment, the black tiger backs down. He lays his ears flat back, but he backs down, shoulders hunched, eyes glaring. And it's Leaf and the bully all over again. It's me rushing between the instigator and the victim. And it's the instigator *listening* to me. But someone must be controlling the black tiger. Someone must have a remote that shocks the black tiger from a distance, and they must be making it back down, because they want us to die on the Rebels Circle, not by the black tigers.

I kneel beside Judah. By the light of the street lamp, I can see his left arm hanging limply by his side, twisted at an unnatural angle. Blood soaks through his shirt at his abdomen. Deep gashes bleed right at his throat. In one leap, the black tiger has practically mauled him.

And then I look at his shoulder, his chest now soaked in blood. The place where the tiger bit him. I rip his shirt a little wider and gasp because the bite marks sank through skin and muscle and—*oh*. Oh no. It's like the black tiger knew exactly where Judah's heart was. Like it was trained to rip someone's heart out with its fangs. Because the teeth marks are deep

162

deep deep into Judah's chest, right above his heart.

Sirens wail down the street. Then red and white flashing lights. A bright spotlight zeros in on me and Judah, but no one exits the vehicle. No one rushes into the street to arrest us or shoot us or, heaven forbid, *help* us, and then I see why. Because the tigers are still here. They're surrounding us, pacing in a slow, agonizing circle. The Defenders aren't leaving their vehicles, because maybe they actually do want the tigers to kill us off.

So this is it. This is how we're going to die. By the teeth of black tigers. Just like all the other criminals. My stomach twists and turns. I wait in sickening anticipation for the tigers to attack us, but they just keep walking around us, like vultures prowling around a dying carcass.

"Keep...talking to them," Judah says in a choked voice.

I look down at him. "What?"

"Talk to...the shoddy...tigers." His voice chokes off in a strangled cough. "Tell them...to leave."

Is he delirious? Officially lost his mind? Lost too much blood already?

"*Do...it.*"

I stare at the black tigers. "Go! Get out of here!"

And they do. They back down. They turn around. They leap down the street toward the Defender vehicle. And I'm not sure exactly what just happened, but when I return my attention to Judah, I notice the gashes on his throat pumping out blood. He coughs again, and this time there's blood in his cough. The shock of so much blood dazes me, it makes me dizzy and sick and terrified, and I cover his chest wound with my hand, wishing I could somehow stop all the blasted bleeding.

"Ember," Judah says through gritted teeth. "You didn't tell me y-you were...p-p—" He swallows hard, his Adam's apple bobbing, then coughs again.

"Don't talk," I say. "You're making it worse."

He covers my hands with his, but shakes his head, pins me with those eyes full of anguish and pain. "You've got that...shoddy...Patrician's blood." He spits the word out, his eyes fluttering, his chest heaving.

I don't know what angers me more, the fact that he's dying or the fact that, with his last breaths, he's accusing me of being a Patrician. What did I ever do to make him call me that?

"Stay with me, Judah." I look at the red and white lights, now blurred from my tears. "Help," I shout, my voice breaking. "Someone *help* him!"

But when I look down at Judah, it's too late. His eyes are open, unfocused. He's not—he's not wheezing anymore. I feel for a pulse, then jerk back. There *is* no pulse. Judah's not a quitter. He can't—he can't just die. He *can't*.

"Judah!" I scream. I grip his shoulder and shake him, try to shake his spirit back into his body. "*JUDAH!*"

He stares blankly at the sky like he's looking at the stars, like he's looking at the moon to save him, like he's sort of hoping he can find help from the universe. But the universe is silent. The universe looks at our tiny pathetic planet in pity, tells us there are bigger things than our puny little lives to worry about, and because of that, Judah's dead. He's dead. He's gone.

I cover my mouth. It's Leaf's death all over again and why why why do all the people I love have to die?

My hope deflates. All adrenaline seeps from the marrow of my bones. I just want to disappear. I want all these

164

problems to disappear for just a minute. I just need a short break from reality because this…this is too much.

The prison siren stops.

The vehicle sirens stop.

The Defenders leap out of their vehicle, and I brace myself for bullets. I grit my teeth against the blinding pain that's about to consume me. Hands grip my shoulders and force me to my feet. No gunshots ring out. No bullets pierce my skin. Instead, an electroband is snapped around my wrist, and I'm shoved into the jeep, the door slamming in my face.

I look out the window and watch as Judah's body is dragged away into another vehicle. All I can do is stare blankly at the events unfolding before me. Because I'm helpless and useless and weak and soon. Soon I'll join Judah and Leaf in the afterlife, and we can laugh with the universe, and we can talk about our deaths like our lives were minuscule little things that really never had a place in the universe to begin with.

The jeep pulls forward, and I stare numbly out the front window. Why won't they just end my life quickly? Oh, yeah. Because they like to make rebels suffer.

The jeep rolls up to the glass prison. No fire trucks now. No sirens. It's almost like there was no fire. Captain Mcallister appears and leads me back into the prison, and I get the dreaded sense of déjà vu and despair, and I gasp in my last few breaths of fresh air before I'm locked in the stagnant pit again.

Instead of leading me to the dungeon doors—the dreaded stairway—he takes me down another hall to the right and leads me into the same room where I met with Forest. The room with wooden floors and nice leather couches and a warm fire place. But there's no fire now.

"Mcallister..." I turn to face him, my body still trembling with the shock and grief and fear. "What's going on?"

"You made quite the impression tonight," he says, walking back toward the door. In the briefest instant his black eyes meet mine, I *think* I catch a glimpse of pity. "You'll wait here until they decide what to do with you."

Until they decide? Didn't they already decide?

"What—what are they going to do with Judah?"

But Mcallister is already striding out the door, closing it firmly behind him.

I blink. And the picture of Judah's fractured body, mangled and torn by the black tigers, flashes through my mind. And this grief and regret and fear of tomorrow is painful, so incredibly painful, I can't get rid of it, and I just want to reach inside my chest and rip my heart out so I don't have to feel anything.

I sink into the couch, bury my head in my hands, and try not to go completely insane.

PART II

the golden city

CHAPTER TWENTY-ONE

I shouldn't be alive.

But I am.

I've been locked in this room all day. Pacing. Staring at my fingers, still caked with Judah's blood. And wondering what sort of painful death they have stored up for me. I mean, if rebels get burned to death, how do rebels who rebel in prison get killed? Double rebellion has to have its consequences.

A little while ago, a maid came in and started a fire. I can only guess that means someone important is coming. I sit on the floor by the fireplace and pull my knees to my chin. I stare at the dying embers and allow Mom's words to come back to me: *The embers still remain, tiny specks of dead wood and cinders that have the capacity to start a fire large enough to burn down an entire city.*

The embers still remain...

The embers still remain...

The embers still remain…

The sound of the door clicking brings my head up. Forest Turner steps in. My shoulders relax, then tense again. What's he doing here?

He takes off his fedora and places it on the back of the chair, then strides toward me, pulls me to my feet, and crushes me to his chest.

"I'm so glad you're okay," he says in a husky voice.

I melt against him. I bury my face in his chest. And I weep. I don't know how long he holds me, combs his fingers through my hair, whispers words of comfort into my ear. When I'm spent from crying, I pull away, take the handkerchief Forest offers, and wipe the shame off my face.

"Thank you," I say. "For s-saving me."

His brows furrow. "Saving you?"

"Yes." I release a shuddering breath.

"What are you talking about?"

"That guy you sent in. To let us out. I thought he was a Defender, but he led us down the street, away from the prison. He was helping us escape. You did send him, right?"

Confusion weaves in and out of his eyes. "No, Ember. I didn't send anyone. I was going to meet with Titus. I was going to get you out of here legally. Not by going against the law. Not by letting a bunch of criminals out in the process." He presses his lips together in thought. "Tell me. What did this person look like?"

He didn't send my rescuer? Now I'm really confused.

"Ember?"

"I couldn't see his face. He was cloaked and kept his face hidden from me." Now I understand why.

"Did he say anything? His name, perhaps? Or, or if he was working for the Resurgence?"

170

I wonder why he so desperately needs to know who my rescuer is. So he can thank him? Or so he can hunt him down for going against the law?

"I don't know, Forest," I snap. "I didn't really have time to interview him while I was running for my life." I suddenly feel tired. Irritable. Annoyed that Judah died and I almost died and all Forest wants to know is who rescued me.

"I'm sorry." He blinks several times. "I'm so sorry." And he pulls me into another therapeutic hug.

We stand there for a few minutes. Because my brain is numb and Forest seems to understand my need for silence.

When an inappropriate amount of time goes by, I release him. "So, why are you here?"

He stares at me a moment. Swallows. Opens his mouth and closes it, like he's not sure how to phrase whatever he wants to say. "I wanted to know why you didn't tell me your secret."

"What secret?"

"That you're a Patrician."

"Are you kidding?"

"Do I look like I'm kidding?"

"You know who I am. Where I grew up." I release a shallow laugh. "You know I'm a farmer's daughter without a coin to my name."

"Oh, Ember." Forest offers a sad but gentle smile, his eyes beckoning me to open up to him about something I don't even understand. "You don't have to pretend anymore. The whole world saw it broadcasted on the main station. _Live._ Your secret is out. And I wanted to be the first to talk to you about it."

"What _secret?_" The words are squeezed through gritted

teeth, because right now I really just want Forest to spill whatever is on his mind and quit acting like I know exactly what he's talking about.

His smile fades. "Do you really not know? Is it possible that you don't even know?" His golden brows arch. "Or are you still trying to hide it? You can trust me, you know."

"The only thing I know," I say, "is there was a fire in the dungeon. Someone came to our rescue. And now here I am, still stuck inside this shoddy prison."

"That's only because they don't know what to do with you yet."

I study at him. Try to figure him out. Try to figure out whose side Congressman Forest Turner is on. But he just stares back, an open book of vulnerability and amazement and excitement and maybe even a little bit of regret and sadness all in his blue eyes. And I don't understand. So I look down at my hands, the only two familiar things in this uncertain place. But they're covered in blood. Judah's blood. And now I really do feel sick.

"How about set me free?" I look back at him. "I think I've endured enough punishment for my actions."

"You'll get another trial."

"Will they listen this time?"

"Yes. Yes, of course they will. I'll make sure of it. And, if they decide you're innocent, they'll want to test you before releasing you."

"Test me...for...what, exactly?"

He narrows his eyes, like he's trying to figure me out as much as I'm trying to figure him out. "Ember." He says my name slowly, carefully. "You're a Patrician. You communicated with the black tigers. Don't you understand? Only Patricians can do that."

Has everyone lost their shoddy minds in Frankfort?

"Don't you remember what happened last night?" he asks.

I look away. Yes. I remember. I remember Judah lying in the street. I remember the life gone out of his eyes. I remember blood oozing from his wounds, spilling onto the concrete like crimson tears.

Forest steps closer, tips my chin up. "You told the tigers to leave, and they did. They were in hunting mode, too, and are usually a bit harder to control when they're on the hunt. They still *listened*. Don't you understand? You have more power than the average Patrician."

"*Power?*" I jerk my chin from his fingers, hating that his mere touch makes it impossible to think clearly. And I try to understand what the shoddy inferno he's talking about. But I understand very little here in Frankfort. One thing does grab my attention, though: the possibility of freedom. "So-so they're going to give me a *fair* trial this time?"

"You'll be cleaned up." He spares a glance at my blood-coated hands, winces, then looks back at me. "The trial is this afternoon; the test will take place tomorrow. You'll definitely pass." He reaches out and brushes a strand of hair behind my ear. "Then you'll be one of us."

One of us. One of who? The politicians? The Patricians? A free person? Or will I return to the Community Garden? I let out a breath of resignation and sink back into my chair. I'm so confused and too tired and grief-stricken and just plain numb to care.

"I'm sorry for what you've been through, Ember." Forest takes the chair across from mine and studies me for a moment, then leans forward and clasps my blood-coated hands in his clean ones. "I know this is hard for you. I can set up a counseling session, something to help you forget the pain of what you went through in prison, if you want."

Forget the pain? Like three days in a tiny cell could be wiped away. Like watching my friend die by the claws of a tiger could just be forgotten.

Forest's wristband blinks. He looks at it, then releases a heavy sigh. "I have to go. I have a meeting in ten minutes." He stands and stares down at me. "A Defender will arrive to take you to your trial. I'll try to get out of my meeting early so I can be there. Then, if you pass your test tomorrow, they'll accommodate you with an elaborate hotel room in the heart of Frankfort."

"And if I fail?"

He laughs. "I don't think you'll fail. I know you're Patrician by the mere fact that you remember our conversation in the tavern." He bows formally, then places his fedora on his head. "Until next time, Miss Carter." He walks out of the room, leaving me with more questions than answers. Free? One of *them*? Tested?

Communicate with tigers?

Everything Forest told me whirls around in my brain like a puzzle that doesn't fit together. What's the test? Do I want to pass? Or do I want to stay under the radar, as I was taught, and appear as a commoner? And how can I plan on passing or failing, if I don't even know what to expect from the test?

I sink back into my chair and wrap my hands around my arms, fighting off the chill that hasn't gone away since Leaf's death.

CHAPTER TWENTY-TWO

This trial goes much better than my first. Forest meets me there, and I'm infinitely grateful for his calming presence. He takes his place beside me on the podium. The judges actually listen to my defense, and there's even a lawyer to speak for me. Just like how the first trial *should* have gone.

I'm proven innocent—my actions declared a mistake born out of hysteria and shock. Then I'm sent to a temporary bedroom until my test.

I step into the shower where I wash off the filth of the past week. Hot water pounds onto the back of my neck and slides down my spine. I've never had a hot shower before. Just cold baths. This water pours from the faucet onto my tense muscles, and I melt.

I should be excited that I'm innocent. I *am* excited. But now there's a new problem. Like me being Patrician and having to take this...test. What's the big shoddy deal, anyway? I always thought Patrician meant rich or part of an elite family. I'm neither of those, yet Forest acts like being Patrician is something people don't choose. Like it's something that's in their blood.

I don't sleep too well all night. The next morning, Mcallister enters and leads me out of the room for my test. I'm wearing fresh clothes. Elaborate clothes. A dress, to be exact. I've never worn a dress. This one is comfortable and stretchy and fits to my form like a second skin. It's midnight blue and probably the most expensive thing I've ever worn in my entire life.

Mcallister takes me outside to the street, and I breathe in the fresh air. I love the outdoors, the smell of the wind. But it's warm out here. Where's the snow? Where's the cruel chill of winter? The trees of the median…their leaves are still green. Has time flown by while I was underground?

"Mcallister," I say as he opens the door to the jeep for me. "What month is it?"

"December." He closes the door behind me and takes the passenger seat. The driver veers the vehicle down a crowded street away from the stadium.

"Are we getting a warm front?"

"No."

"Does it ever get cold in Frankfort?"

"Not with the cupola."

"The what?"

"The dome covering Frankfort. Haven't you heard of it?"

I shake my head, but I do remember seeing the gold transparent dome covering the city.

"The cupola controls the weather," Mcallister explains. "It never gets hot or cold here, but stays seventy-two degrees, rain or shine."

176

Huh? "How?"

"That's like asking how a jeep runs. The answer requires a full course on the subject, and I'm afraid I don't have the time to enlighten you."

I lean back and stare at the scenery passing by, the beautiful glass buildings shimmering in the sunlight like gold. No wonder they call Frankfort the golden city.

"I guess you didn't get punished too badly," I say.

"Excuse me?" Mcallister looks at my reflection in the rearview mirror.

"Rain said you were going to pay for talking about him, for telling me about how he can't get himself to choose a career."

I can just barely make out a hint of a smile on Mcallister's face. "Did he now?" He doesn't seem the least bit bothered. Which means Rain must not have as much power as he thinks.

When we arrive at the capitol compound, I stare in amazement at my surroundings. The median is brimming with red and gold flowers. Long-trunked trees, the kind that leaf out at the top, line the side of the road in perfect organization. A wide, perfectly kept-up sidewalk runs parallel to the tree line. On the other side of the sidewalk is a sea of green, green grass, mowed to perfection. Excellent landscape for gardening. In fact, they could grow a good amount of food on that piece of land. Enough to feed a couple hundred people for the summer. Or even fence it in and keep a couple cows on it. So why are they just using it for grass?

The vehicle pulls around a rotunda and parks on the curb, and I can't take my eyes off the capitol building. Because it's big and frightening and possibly the most beautiful building I've ever laid eyes on. Whitewashed stone walls—not glass like the majority of the buildings in Frankfort—give it an antique look. Dome roof, pillars lining the front, and so many stairs leading up to the arched doorway.

Mcallister opens my door. "This is where you'll take your test."

"Wait," I say. He pauses and looks back at me. "The test...do I want to pass it or fail it?"

He offers a smile that almost looks sad. "That's entirely up to you."

He leads me up the many stairs. We arrive at a red-brick patio, and I glance to my left. Across the green lawn, hidden behind another row of long-stemmed trees, is another stone building.

"That's the Chief's mansion," Mcallister says, taking note of my gaping. I don't know why he bothers telling me this. I kind of wish I didn't know, because the Chief's mansion is the size of a hotel, and it's kind of disgusting that one man lives in all that when my family of four was crammed in a three-room cabin.

I follow Mcallister inside. We walk through a shield, right past two Defenders, and up another flight of stairs. I'm once again standing in awe of my surroundings. Everything is made of white marble: The walls, the floor, the ceiling. In the center of the chamber we step into is a bronze statue with the name "Chief Quentin Whitcomb" engraved at the base. I can see clear up to the dome roof, a good eight stories high. Marble stairways branch off to my left and my right, and elaborate balconies overlook the foyer. I can see clearly from one side of the building to the other, everything is so open.

We cross the chamber, down one hallway, and then

Mcallister opens a large, old wooden door and gestures for me to go in.

Taking a deep breath, I step into the room. It's dark, the only light beaming in from a sliver of a window along the ceiling. Small blue lights blink in all four corners of the room. Cameras. The door slams shut behind me, making me jump, and I wonder how long I'm supposed to wait in this gray, eerie room.

"Ember Carter." An agonizingly familiar voice cuts into my thoughts. Exuberantly musical. My shoulders tense, and I slowly turn around to face Rain.

"So nice to see you again." He steps into the light. His auburn hair falls into his gray eyes, and he carries a tablet in hand. He looks every inch the Patrician, from the crooked newsboy cap on his head to his crisp vest and pressed slacks and leather shoes. His lips curve in a line of pure arrogance. "I see you've proven me wrong." His voice drips with sarcasm. "You *are* innocent. You *do* have some bite. Oh, and you can communicate with black tigers, too. How utterly fascinating."

I bow at the waist as is customary in the presence of the Patricians, though I don't hold any respect for Rain. But I have a test to pass. I offer a small smile, even though I'm screaming inside. I want this test to be finished, I want to pass—I think—and I'll do whatever I must in order to make that happen. Even if it means sucking up to this son of a jackal.

"You look absolutely dashing in that dress." Rain sweeps his gaze over the length of me, and I feel my face blush to my roots. Rain jerks his chin to a metal chair at the far side of the room. "Have a seat, Carter, and we'll get started."

I cross the room, my footsteps echoing off the floor, and sit in the chair, grimacing at the cold metal pressing against my bare legs and arms. Why is Rain, of all people, my tester? Is this some sort of trick? Some form of sick torture in itself? I would honestly prefer *anyone* to Rain. Give me cruel Defender. Give me Mcallister. I'll even take Chief Whitcomb over Rain.

"First, I have a few questions about your past," Rain says. "Then I'll need to take your blood."

"Do you begin all conversations with background questions and phlebotomy?"

Rain narrows his eyes, then types something on his tablet. The fact that he's already typing something when I haven't even answered his question makes my heart sink. I squeeze the armrests with my hands. My pulse throbs in my fingertips.

"Who are you parents?" Rain asks, not looking up.

"You couldn't find that information in the public record?"

His glances at me, his jaw clenching and unclenching. "Are you going to be this difficult through the entire test?"

"Maybe." I know I promised myself to suck up to Rain, but my patience is already wearing thin. Rain seems to have this effect on me. There's something about him that brings the worst out of me, turning me into some insolent child. I hate it. "Tell me why I have to take this test."

"Just answer the shoddy question, Carter, or I'll tell them you failed and have you sent back to the Rebels Circle."

So I *do* have to pass.

"You have that kind of power?"

His lips quirk up in a cold smile. "I have every bit of power necessary to determine your fate."

His words send a shudder up my spine and I believe him. I believe him completely. And the fact that my life is in the hands of this—this *weasel*, makes me sick to my stomach.

"My parents are Tracy and Andrew Carter," I say obediently.

"And their careers?" Rain asks, typing on his tablet.

"My dad manages the apple orchard. My mother is—was—a seamstress."

He nods, but doesn't look up. "Brothers or sisters?"

"Elijah. My brother."

"Children?"

A shocked laugh escapes me. "Seriously? I'm a little young to have children."

He looks at me and smiles a little. "Of course. So is that a no?"

"Correct," I say, mimicking his Patrician accent. "That is a no."

He smirks and shakes his head as he types something on his tablet. "Mother's maiden name?"

Maiden name? "I have no idea." That sort of information isn't important in the Garden. She was taken away before I ever got a chance to ask her. And Dad never seemed interested in talking about her past.

"So...just Tracy. Hm. Ooookay."

"Is this the test?" I ask. "You asking me a bunch of pointless questions?"

"No. This is a questionnaire. We haven't even gotten to the test yet."

Splendid. "Can I go home after the test, though? I mean, am I really free?"

"Depends."

I blow out a frustrated breath. "Depends on *what?*"

"Your results."

My results. My test results. Which I apparently have to pass.

"How do I pass?"

His lips twitch into a smile. "Wouldn't you like to know? But I'm afraid I can't dispense that information, Miss Carter. I can assure you, however, that you *want* to pass this test." He pins me with those gray eyes. "Your life depends on it."

No pressure.

Without looking at me, he asks me a few more general questions about my home, my age, where I was born. All easy answers. I'm sixteen. Born on the kitchen floor of our cabin with the neighbor's help—according to Mom. All the hospitals were too far, and that's why my birth was never documented in the city. But why does Rain need to know all this?

"I'm going to take your blood now." He presses a button on his white phoneband. "Come on in, Nando."

The door opens, and an older balding man wearing a white lab coat enters with a black kit. He kneels by my chair and pulls out a syringe. My mouth goes dry. I've never gotten a shot before, and the thought of the large needle piercing my skin makes me squirm. He expertly wraps a tourniquet around my upper arm then grips my forearm and inserts the needle at the inside of my elbow. I wince at the prick and almost look away, but not before I see blood filling the canister.

It reminds me of Judah. The blood in his cough. On his neck. His shoulder. Soaking through his shirt. Black creeps around the edge of my vision, and a faint ringing sounds in my ears, and I close my eyes, think of something else something else anything else when Rain says, "All finished. You can open your eyes now."

Nando places the cylinder full of my blood into a bag, takes off the tourniquet, and walks out of the room.

"Now we can officially begin the test." Rain steps in front of me. "Look at me, Ember." His voice is lucid and full of authority.

I do as I'm told, and look into his cold, steel eyes. Holding my gaze, he pulls out a pocket knife and switches it open. "Take this knife."

A knife. Heart pounding, I accept the blade. The small handle is cold in my hands, but my palms are sweaty and trembling, and the knife slips from my fingers and clangs across the tile floor.

Rain's lips disappear entirely in obvious irritation. He bends down, picks up the knife, and presses it into my palm. "Try not to be clumsy."

I begin to withdraw my hand from his, but his grip tightens, and he looks into my eyes and says, "Now. Slit your wrist."

"What?" I jerk away from his grasp. "That will kill me." I may have grown up in an orchard, but I'm still smart enough to know a major artery lets out at my wrist.

"Doesn't matter." Rain shrugs. "Do what I say." He wraps his long fingers around my chin, kneels in front of me so we're eye-level, and he's so close, so incredibly close that I can smell the peppermint on his breath. And he whispers, "Slit. Your. Wrist."

Then he steps back. And waits.

I'm barely breathing. With trembling hands I place the edge of the knife on my wrist, away from the artery, and lay on pressure until a spot of red blood appears. The sting isn't as bad as the shot. I've had worse scrapes. Removing the knife, I hand it back to him and force a shaky smile.

He smirks. "Not deep enough, Carter." Reaching out, he taps a long finger directly over my artery. "I want you to cut deep. I want you to cut into the *vein*."

"No way."

His eyes harden. "Do you want to pass this test, or fail?"

"I don't want to make myself bleed out."

"Cut the vein, Carter!"

"No!" I stand up and throw the knife across the room. It clangs on the floor, skipping across the tiles until it hits the wall.

Rain straightens, stares at me for a moment, then jots a note down on his tablet. "Fine. We'll just have to move on to step two of the test."

I'm surprised he's not sending me directly back to prison for my disobedience.

"How many steps are there?" I ask.

"Two."

"Did I pass the first step?"

"Do you *think* you passed?"

His question implies that I didn't. My heart sinks a little, but I don't have much time to ponder what I could have done better before Rain lifts his hand in the air and snaps his fingers. A door across the room flies open. Blinding light pours in from the outside world, then the door slams shut. It takes a moment for my eyes to readjust to the dim room, but when they do, all my thoughts trip over each other.

Because prowling around the edge of the room, crouching in the shadows, is a black tiger.

And it's staring right at me.

CHAPTER TWENTY-THREE

Memories from last night pound into my mind. Unwelcome. Unexpected. Black tigers surrounding us, their loud roars echoing through the street and make my bones tremble. And I think of Judah lying on the ground while the tiger sinks its teeth into his shoulder and now that same horrifying, terrifying, awful beast paces in front of me. Golden eyes lock with mine.

And. I. Can't. Breathe.

"Remember him?" Rain asks. I tear my gaze from the tiger and look at Rain.

"Is...is this the test?" I squeak.

He nods slowly, then walks to the center of the room, looks at the tiger, and says, "Kill the girl."

And all hope vanishes out of existence because the black tiger crouches down.

Then saunters toward me.

I whirl around, stumble in the opposite direction, race to

the door I came in, my body practically slamming into the steel as I frantically search for the handle. But it's locked.

Of course it's locked.

Behind me, I hear the paws advancing toward me, drawing nearer and nearer and nearer and then a roar—a roar so loud it's deafening and blood chilling and—

You can communicate with black tigers.

The idea is ludicrous but my only hope. Turning fully around, I glare at the beady eyes of the black tiger and shout, "STOP!"

The tiger halts to a stop just a few feet away from me. His ears lay flat back and his golden eyes watch me warily.

"Now—now, go away," I tell the tiger, struggling to keep my voice level. The tiger turns and walks toward the center of the room.

Unbelievable.

I look at Rain. He's grinning. Grinning! He was about to watch me get devoured by the tiger, and he's *grinning*. He covers his smile with two fingers and looks back at his tablet, then types something.

"Very good, Carter," he says through his smile. "For a second there, I was afraid you were actually going to die."

As if he wasn't rooting for my death.

He places the tablet snugly in a pocket on the inside of his jacket and whistles a strange tune. The black tiger walks calmly to Rain's side like some sort of kitten. Rain scratches the animal behind the ears. Then to my astonishment, he kneels down in front of it, and says something too quiet for me to hear. For a brief second, I'm terrified he might be telling the tiger to kill me and not back down. Instead, the tiger trots to the door. The door opens, and two Defenders with spears guide the beast out of the room.

I'm relieved when the door closes behind it.

Letting out a breath, I look at Rain. Swallow the saliva that's somehow gathered in my mouth, then say, "What the shoddy inferno was *that*?"

"The Black Tiger Test."

"The Black Tiger—" My voice chokes off in a strangled laugh of ridicule, but there's absolutely nothing funny about it. "So—so did I pass?"

"With flying colors." He grins. "I'll send your results to the Assembly of Politicians. They'll look over your records and all that boring stuff to figure out how you're Patrician, but yes. You passed."

Relief. It's a strange thing that makes my bones melt and my muscles relax, and now my brain doesn't have to be quite as sharp and I can actually take a breath. "So…so I'm free? I mean, I can go home now?"

Rain looks at me with an expression akin to pity. Pity? From Rain? They must have taken more blood from me than I thought.

"You won't be able to go home yet, I'm afraid." He looks away and bites his bottom lip. This is so unlike the arrogant Rain I've come to know. And I'm not exactly sure how to respond, but I don't have to before he says, "They'll want to test you."

My body goes hot, then cold. "I was *just* tested."

He looks at me, his eyes once again steel and cold. "You were tested to confirm you are Patrician, which you are. Now they'll want to know *how* you're Patrician. Apparently someone went behind the back of the government without them knowing, which is how you came about."

"What are you talking about?"

He rolls his eyes and drags his hand across the back of his neck. "Either someone slipped you an antitoxin, or someone in your family is actually a Patrician. Now the blood test will confirm whether you're fully Patrician, half, or one quarter. So you can save any lies you have to tell."

He's peppering me with way too much information, and too many thoughts filter through my mind so I grasp the one that raises the most questions. "Antitoxin?"

"Against the White Plague. You know, the thing that wiped the outside world to extinction?" He gestures with his hand impatiently.

"Y-you have an antitoxin against it?"

He blinks several times. "Well, yes. Of course."

"But, how? When—"

"There's a lot of history here. I'm afraid I don't have permission to share it with you."

His eyes swivel to the ceiling. I look up. At the flashing blue lights. In every corner of the blasted room.

Right. Cameras.

"But when I get the okay to do so," he says. "I'll tell you everything." He grins.

The door opens and Mcallister walks in flanked by two more Defenders. I look between him and Rain for any signs of bitterness between the two, but he just nods at Rain in greeting and Rain offers nothing more than a mirthless smile before returning his attention to his tablet. Then Mcallister leads me outside to sunny Frankfort.

I'm so sick of Defenders escorting me everywhere. But even more sick of this uncertainty. I want to go home to familiar territory. I want to be surrounded by apple trees, not Defenders. I want to talk to Dad and Elijah, not Rain and Mcallister. But apparently going home is out of the question until they figure out the big mystery about how I'm a Patrician. I honestly don't know why it matters. Couldn't they accept that I'm somehow Patrician and forget about it? I mean, seriously, who *cares*?

Mcallister gestures for me to enter the jeep.

"Where are we going now?" I ask.

"They're placing you in Frankfort Hotel until they figure things out."

Wow. From Frankfort Prison to Frankfort Hotel in twenty-four hours.

"In the meantime," Mcallister says. "Chief Whitcomb is hosting a party to celebrate the holidays, and he's invited *you* to attend."

"Holidays?"

He looks back at me. "This is the first week of December. We've begun the month of Christmas. You are very lucky to have been invited to his royal occasions."

The hotel we pull up to is probably a hundred stories high. The glass shines like gold in the sunlight. We enter wide doors and walk across a white marble floor.

"I can take her from here, men," Mcallister says to the other Defenders. "Wait for me in the lobby."

They both nod and march off while Mcallister leads me to the elevator. He presses a pearl button and the doors slide open. After the doors shut, I look through the glass wall at the street below as it grows smaller and smaller. When we arrive at the top floor, the door dings open, and Mcallister leads me down the hall to my room.

"This is where you'll be staying until Congress decides what to do with you."

Congress. My being a Patrician actually garners attention

from Congress. But starving people in the Community Garden don't deserve a second thought, apparently.

I step into the hotel room and stop short. This place is fit for a Patrician. A plush white carpet covers the floor. A black piano graces the wall, surrounded by black leather couches. A kitchen harbors the other side of the apartment, and a large window stretches across the opposite wall, peering out to the golden city. Plants line the base of the window, and black drapes frame the edges. Another doorway branches off the living room, probably leading to the bedroom.

My eyes automatically dart to the ceiling, looking for cameras. Sure enough, one small round globe above the kitchen, another above the living room.

Mcallister walks up to the window, his arms locked behind his back. "Your test results came out positive. You're a Patrician."

"It's a mistake. My dad manages the apple orchard. My mother was a seamstress." This is common knowledge by now, surely. "I wasn't born into an elite family. I'm a common Proletariat." I shrug. "They'll see the truth when they study my blood, I'm sure."

Mcallister shakes his head. "One of your parents lied to you."

I stare at him. "My parents wouldn't lie." I step beside Mcallister and look way down at the streets below. The wide gap from my windowsill to the street is dizzying. "Why does it matter whether or not I'm Patrician, anyway?"

He turns to face me, his dark eyes glittering in the dim light. I used to be afraid of him, this tall, built man/boy who took me deep into the dungeon. But somehow, over the course of a few days, he's grown on me. He's not as cruel as the other Defenders. Maybe because he's still significantly young and hasn't been hardened liked the seasoned Defenders. And unlike the Defenders who don't give me the time of day, Mcallister answers my questions, looks me in the eye, more like a human than a robot. He's kind of grown on me.

"The Patricians have a power over us," he whispers. "But they can't control you, and that's why they think you're Patrician." He turns from the window. He looks so stiff, his back straight, his chin high. "I should go." He eyes swivel to the cameras and he turns to leave.

"Wait," I say. He pauses, then turns to face me. "You're not—you're not as mean as the other Defenders. I mean, you actually have a grain of humanity. Why are you being so nice to me?"

A strange emotion flickers in and out of his eyes, as though holding onto some secret too valuable to share, then he smiles politely. "I'm just a Defender. I do whatever I'm told." And he walks out of the room, shutting the door firmly behind him.

CHAPTER TWENTY-FOUR

I can't sleep all night. Everything that happened the past few days—the escape, my test, questions about how I'm Patrician—keeps me fully awake. So I rise and walk to the window. By the bright lights of the city, it doesn't seem like midnight. Skyscrapers rise hundreds of stories into the air, their windows illuminated from within, making them shine like glowing pillars.

Bright yellow lights speck the buildings. Green and red lanterns line the sidewalks below. Mcallister said it's December. A holiday lingers in the air, one that only Patricians celebrate. And with that holiday comes the decor of tiny lights, spruce trees, and the heady smell of cinnamon.

A smell that now reminds me of Forest.

On the street below, musicians play lovely acoustic instruments and women wearing togas stand by and watch. Across the street is a park illuminated by lanterns and marked with lamp-lit trails. Foreign trees rise from the ground, their trunks long and bare, and fronds billow out from their tops. The deep green grass is neatly mowed in elaborate designs like artwork, and benches line the walkway. Everything is too green for winter. But if what Mcallister said was true, it never snows here, or even gets cold. The weather is controlled.

After digging around the kitchen and stuffing myself with food I've only heard about, I go back to my room, collapse on the most comfortable bed I've ever lain in, and pull the covers up to my chin. After over a week in the stagnant cell, this mattress feels divine. I close my eyes, exhausted, depleted, and mentally and physically spent.

Thoughts weave in and out of my mind and back again. And I try to decide which one to grasp onto, but sleep takes over and my thoughts dissolve into nothingness.

Mornings are beautiful creatures. The sun blooms on the horizon, searing off every last nightmare and flooding the planet with light. It welcomes the earth with a warm embrace, kisses it with sun rays, lifts our hearts and makes us look up into the sky where hope lies.

I might be going home today.

I'm not sure, but if they get the results they're looking for, they might just let me go.

My stomach growls, despite the buffet I had for myself last night, and I walk into the kitchen and open the refrigerator. The shelves are packed with more food than my entire family receives in their monthly rations. They have real eggs, not the powdered dust we get. The bacon looks like it'd been freshly sliced, not heavily salted and dried. I pull everything out, when a gentle knock sounds at the door.

"Come in," I say.

An older, plump woman steps in. She wears thick-rimmed glasses, and her black hair is pulled back into a tight bun, marked with graying streaks. "Oy. You're already awake." Her voice is bright and heavily accented, every word like a note in a song. "I was going to make breakfast for you." She welcomes herself inside, dragging a giant suitcase with her, and shuts the door firmly behind. "My name is LeighAnn. I'll be your maid during your time in Frankfort."

"M-maid?"

She frowns. "Yes. You are Miss Ember Carter, no? I'm assigned to serve you."

"Oh." I don't need a maid, or a server, but I guess she was assigned this career just like I was assigned one of a farmer. "Good to meet you."

Her frown turns into a brilliant smile. "I've a few outfits for your wardrobe in this suitcase."

"Outfits?" I look down at the dress I wore yesterday, that I slept in, that I planned to wear today, because it's so comfortable. I'm really not used to having multiple outfits.

"For the dinners and parties. The feast of St. Nick is tomorrow night. You should look your best for the chief."

I cringe. "Feast of St. Nick?"

"Yes, yes."

"Thanks, but I'm not planning on staying for any...feasts."

"Ah, but you were invited! No one refuses an invitation from Chief Whitcomb."

I briefly wonder why the chief even cares whether or not I'm there, but LeighAnn belligerently rolls the suitcase into the bedroom before I get a chance to ask. I follow, listening to her list off words too foreign for me to understand. "Emerald taffeta, black pumps, silver laden hoops..." She begins unpacking the suitcase, hanging up the most elaborate gowns and togas I've ever seen, and all I can think is, *why*? Why am I suddenly being showered with gifts? Are all Patricians treated like royalty? Why *me*?

The phone rings.

"I'll get that," LeighAnn says in her sing-song voice. Before I can object, she hurries out of the room.

I run my hand over the crimson gown on top of the pile. The fabric feels rough beneath my fingertips but shimmers like the scales of a fish. It's so beautiful, so... *rich*. Fit for one of the queens I've seen pictured in our old history books.

LeighAnn returns with an earpiece. "For you." She hands me the earpiece and a phoneband.

Who could be calling me? I put the earpiece in place and leave the room. I've never spoken into a phoneband before, and I'm not sure exactly what to say. "Um. Who's...this?"

"Hello." Forest's warm voice speaks from the earpiece, and my entire being melts. "This is Forest Turner. Is this Miss Carter?"

"Forest." Finally. Something familiar. "It's so good to hear from you."

"Are you doing okay? Are they treating you well at the hotel?"

"Yes."

A pause.

"Good. That's great to hear. I was calling because I would like to extend a welcoming dinner in your honor. Nothing big. Not like the Feast of St. Nick tomorrow night. Would you like to come to dinner at my house tonight? It'll

196

just be you, me, and my family. Something informal to help your adjustment to Frankfort."

"Um." What sort of invitation is this? I'm a prisoner receiving his pity one moment, and now he wants me as an honored guest? I swallow hard. "Sure. But I don't know how to get to your…um…house."

"Not a problem." I can hear the smile in his voice. "I'll send a car to pick you up at five-thirty. Will that work for you?"

"Of course." Not like I have anything else to do.

"Brilliant. I look forward to seeing you, Miss Carter."

I click the button on my phoneband and take the earpiece out. I have no idea how people manage to wear these things in their ears all day. Setting it on the coffee table, I sink down on the couch. Why does Forest want me over for dinner? I should be flattered.

But Judah warned me never to trust a politician. I try to see Forest the Politician through Judah's lens, because what if Judah's right? What if Forest suddenly decided that I might somehow have valuable information he wants because of my association with Leaf and his association with Jonah Walker? What if he's trying to weasel his way into my life to gain my trust?

Because it's a little bit weird that he invited me over for dinner. In the Garden, people didn't just invite guests over for meals. Ever. Food is too valuable to serve just anybody. But Judah said food isn't scarce here, so maybe Forest really is just trying to be nice.

When I tell LeighAnn about my dinner plans, she's ecstatic. "Very good! The Turners are great people. We'll make you look so beautiful, Congressman Turner won't be able to take his eyes off of you."

Five-thirty is still a long way off. It's only nine a.m., and I have nothing to do. I'm not used to sitting idle. There was always too much work to do on the orchard growing up, and it's a habit for me to stay busy. I follow LeighAnn into the kitchen, and she begins pulling food out of the fridge.

"How can I help?" I ask.

"Go relax," LeighAnn says. "And I will make you the best breakfast you've ever tasted."

I don't tell her I already had breakfast.

"Or perhaps a stroll in the park will be good for you, after being locked up for so long, hm?" she says.

"I don't think I'm allowed to leave the room. I'm still under guard."

"Ah yes." She closes the refrigerator. "Well, then. What do you love to do? What's your favorite hobby?"

Hobby? We Proletariats don't really have hobbies. But then I think of Defender Shepherd and the art supplies he would bring and the elation I experienced by getting lost in creating art. Do I dare say it aloud? "Um. I like to paint and sketch."

"Ah. Perfect. A Patrician and an artist."

I don't bother telling her my art sucks.

"Since you're a Patrician now," LeighAnn says, "everything is at your disposal. I will call room service. You can give them a list of everything you want." She looks at me and winks. "It will be here within the hour."

Everything I want? LeighAnn hands me a piece of paper and a pencil. What could it hurt? I might as well soak up these last few hours of luxury before returning to the Garden. I might as well claim my so-called Patrician blood before they realize I'm not really Patrician. So I begin listing off paper, drawing pencils, oils, paint brushes, and canvases. All the things Defender Shepherd used to bring me. When I finish, LeighAnn looks at the list.

"Hmm." She taps her pressed lips with her index finger, then holds her hand out to me. "Pencil, please." I hand it over, and she begins adding more things to the list, then hands it back to me with a big smile. "Might as well take everything you can get, yes?"

I look over the list and read the extra things she added. Things called colored pencils and water colors and acrylics and three different kinds of papers and sponges and brushes and things called glass window paint sets and crayons and coloring books.

"Look good?" LeighAnn asks.

I nod.

"Very good." She calls room service, and they bring all the art supplies within the hour.

Because of my love for books, I automatically pick up the coloring book first and flip through all the pre-drawn pictures. They're deeply detailed and intricate and I wish I could draw something like this.

LeighAnn hands me the crayons. "Why not add some color to that picture, hm?"

I feel like a kid who's been given her very first birthday present, and I don't even care. I accept the crayons, select a cobalt blue, the color of Forest's eyes, and begin filling in the shapes. Coloring is a different form of art entirely. It's almost therapeutic. I mean, the basic picture is finished, I don't have to worry about creating anything, although I like creating. I just let my brain rest and focus on the simplicity of colors. It feels good to not think about anything else right now.

When four-thirty rolls around, LeighAnn interrupts me from my art-trance. I'd just learned how to use the watercolors to paint a small, palm-sized octagonal stained glass window.

"Time to get ready for dinner." She disappears into my room.

I rise from the desk and follow her. She selects a lovely white and red toga with white sandals, and without my consent, she begins undressing me, all the while talking excitedly about the mystery of my Patrician blood.

"Everyone saw it," she says as she puts the finishing touches on my hair. "They had the cameras on you during the escape. A little slice of excitement in this city that's always hungry for drama. Everyone saw you communicate with those black tigers, just like a regular Patrician."

"So, wait, can *you* communicate with black tigers?"

She looks at me in surprise and pushes her glasses up the bridge of her nose. "I'm not Patrician. So, no. I don't have that kind of power."

"But, you act like it's common knowledge that Patricians can control the tigers. I've never heard of such a thing."

"It's not public knowledge." She finishes fixing my hair. "I only know because I've lived in Frankfort all my life. But to have Patrician blood. That's a gift."

"Why does it matter? Who cares that I have Patrician blood?"

"Don't you know?" She leads me to the door. "Patricians are royalty. You are a part of the original founders' of Ky's bloodline. My advice to you, miss? Soak it up and revel in the delights Frankfort has to offer. This is a rare gift. Rare indeed." And she walks me out the door and closes it firmly behind me.

The vehicle is waiting outside the hotel at exactly five-thirty, as promised. This is the first time I get to see how the Patricians actually live. Do they really live in mansions, like Judah said? But I'm more excited about seeing Forest, despite Judah's warning.

The vehicle travels through Frankfort for twenty minutes, according to the clock on the dashboard, then rolls up to a black iron gate. The gate opens, and the jeep rolls down a black-top driveway. Trees arch over the driveway, shading the vehicle from the sun. The road curves and an enormous mansion with a red tile roof comes into view. When the driver opens the door for me, I step out and climb the stairs to the front porch, which is huge and graced with a white banister. The doors open before I get a chance to knock, and an older woman looks up at me.

"Miss Carter." She opens the door wider and gestures for me to enter. "This way, please." I step in and she closes the door behind me. "Wait here."

All these maids are probably the most polite people I have ever met.

While she's gone, I study my surroundings. The foyer alone is a three-story tall cylindrical chamber, with a stained-glass ceiling. Sunlight glints off the railing of a spiral staircase. Plants wrap around the edge of the room, and a black leather couch harbors the space in between them. This room looks like something from a palace.

"Miss Carter," Forest says as he descends the marble stairs. He approaches me and kisses me lightly on the cheek. The small gesture makes heat rush to my face. "I'm delighted to host you for dinner. Please, this way."

So formal. I link my arm through his extended elbow

and follow him through the hallway, hoping my embarrassment or lack of Patrician manners isn't too obvious. "Thanks for having me, Forest."

"I thought you deserved a better welcome than a lonely stay at the hotel." He smiles down at me. "By the way, I told you that you'd pass the test. How did it go?"

I grimace, remembering the black tiger and how I almost died. "I passed. That's all that matters."

He stops and faces me. His smile fades and a deep sorrow fills his eyes. "What happened?"

I wave my hand in the air. "They stuck a black tiger on me. It was—it was like escaping the prison all over again. Like Judah's death all over again. And I—" My voice chokes off and I look away.

"I'm sorry," Forest says softly. "I honestly didn't realize they would actually use a black tiger." He reaches out, takes my hand and presses my palm firmly between his fingers. The gesture is oddly comforting. I look at him, at his honest blue eyes, an ocean of raw emotion.

He swallows convulsively and says, "I won't bring it up again."

I nod. Grateful. Because I'm so incredibly ready to move on from the nightmare that was this past week. We continue walking through the hall until we arrive at the dining room. A crystal chandelier hangs from the ceiling above a long wooden table, and the floor is made of black tile. A window runs the length of one wall, allowing the orange light of the sunset to spill into the room. A thin, older man with pale skin, graying hair, and eyes as blue as Forest's sits at the head of the table. He rises to his feet and inclines his head toward me.

"Miss Carter, I would like to introduce my father,

Congressman Thomas Turner." Forest looks at his dad. "Father, this is the girl I told you about."

He talked about me?

Thomas smiles gravely. He wears a crisp black suit with the traditional politician vest. His fedora hangs on the knob of his chair. "A pleasure to meet you, Miss Carter. Please, sit."

"We are still waiting for my brother." Forest rolls his eyes. "As usual, he's running late. Mother won't be joining us. She always works late on Fridays."

I accept the chair the maid offers, and Forest sits across from me.

Thomas leans forward in his chair. "It's remarkable, Miss Carter, that you would be able to escape Frankfort Prison. That place is flooded with Defenders and alarm systems. It's wired to the bone with cameras. Please tell me. How did you manage to escape?"

I gasp because I didn't really expect an interrogation, but then maybe I should have because Judah told me. He told me Forest only wanted to question me. So he brought me here and now I'm trapped by him and his father.

Forest clears his throat. "I doubt Miss Carter wants to relive her near-death experience, Father."

I let out a breath I didn't realize I was holding.

"My apologies," Thomas says with a polite nod. He accepts a glass of champagne from the maid. "Perhaps, instead we could discuss the matter of—"

His words are cut short by the doors bursting open. I glance at the doorway, and every last thought collapses in my brain because Rain.

Rain. is. *here.*

His newsboy cap is crooked, his vest wrinkled, and his white shirt untucked. He pauses when he sees me, his gray eyes flashing with amusement, then smirks and strides into the room. "Sorry I'm late, Father. Didn't miss anything, did I?"

CHAPTER TWENTY-FIVE

Surprise doesn't quite cut what I'm feeling at this incredibly awful moment. It's like a nest of ants decided to take up residence in my stomach and now they're digging digging digging and turning my stomach inside out until I think I'm going to puke. Because Rain isn't exactly the bearer of good news.

He brought me to the prison.

He gave me the Black Tiger Test.

He's the arrogant, smirking son of a jackal who never ceases to bring the absolute worst out of me. And right now, in front of Forest and Forest's father, I desperately need to be on my best behavior.

Yes. Rain's unexpected presence is a serious problem.

I'm not the only one who tenses at Rain's presence. His father's posture becomes more rigid, his brows more furrowed. "Rain," Thomas says. "I'd like to introduce to you Miss—"

"Carter," Rain says with a brilliant smile as he pulls out the chair beside Forest and hunkers down. "The living legend. Pleased to see you again." He lifts his champagne in salute. "Welcome to Frankfort. My brother wouldn't stop talking about you."

"You—you're *brothers?*"

"You're surprised." Rain grins like he's enjoying my discomfort.

"Well, it's just—Forest never said anything about a brother." They're so incredibly different.

"I didn't think it necessary," Forest says.

"Is there anything else I should know?" I ask.

Forest's eyebrows flicker. "Like what?"

A mischievous glimmer sparks Rain's eyes. "Perhaps she'd like to know that you and Olivia Doss are engaged."

The words are like a blow to the stomach. Olivia, the girl who assigned me my career. The girl who kissed Forest on the cheek on Career Day. I wondered if something was going on between them. But *engaged?* Heat creeps up my neck and I swallow hard, wish I could disappear forever.

A muscle jerks in Forest's jaw, but his eyes remain locked with mine. "I meant to tell you, but—"

"But he thought you were going to die." Rain offers a mock-sorry smile and shrugs. "Turns out you're clever enough to escape the most guarded prison in the country, you can talk to black tigers, and—surprise, surprise—you're a Patrician."

"About that." Thomas looks at me. "Did you have any idea you had Patrician blood, Miss Carter? Or was it as much a surprise to you as it was to all of us?"

I tear my gaze from Rain's and stare at Thomas. "I had no idea. I didn't even know you Patricians could

206

communicate with black tigers. Tell me, how is it possible?"

Thomas considers my question for a moment, then curls his upper lip in an arrogant smile, making him look much like Rain. Even with age, he is handsome, like both of his sons. "Let's just say the Patrician genes are…altered. Different than Proletariat genes."

"How so?"

He waves his hand dismissively in the air, the way I've seen both Rain and Forest do so many times. Those two are a bit more alike than I care to admit. "I don't want to bore you with the details. I'd rather hear your story. How did you come to be Patrician?"

I look down at my plate. Sometime during the chaotic moment when Rain entered the room, our food was brought out. A big round plate with a giant steak, potatoes, and an assortment of vegetables remains untouched. My stomach is too tied up in knots to be hungry.

But Thomas's question lingers in my mind. How *did* I become a Patrician?

Looking at Rain, I arch a brow. "Rain was the one who tested me. He should be able to tell you."

All eyes turn to Rain, but he stuffs a bite of steak in his mouth and shrugs. "I took her blood and sent it to the lab. Results aren't in yet." He swallows. Grins. "Hopefully they'll know in two days."

"Two days?" I ask. "*Two days?*"

He nods.

Two days sounds like an eternity. I don't want to stay in Frankfort for two more days.

"You tested her?" Thomas asks Rain. "Why were you placed in that position?"

"Brown had me do it. I was shadowing him for the day, he had some business to attend to, so he temporarily assigned me to the position."

"How did you like Brown's job?" Thomas leans back in his chair. "Do you think that will be the career you choose?"

Choose.

"I don't know, Father." Rain rolls his eyes. "I'm still deciding." He finishes off his champagne and sets the glass down with cool indifference.

"You already turned down the career as a General of Defenders," Thomas says. "I thought you would do well with that title."

General of Defenders? He was offered *that* position? That must be why he was the one who took me to the stadium.

"Yeah," I snap. All eyes are on me. "Why didn't you choose the career as a General of Defenders, Rain?"

He stares at me with those steel gray eyes. "Why on earth *would* I?"

"Oh, I don't know. Lack of emotion? Heart cold as stone?" I size him up. "Perfect attributes of a Defender."

He tilts his head, narrows his eyes. "Ordering a bunch of brainless Defenders around isn't exactly my idea of living life to the fullest."

"And Brown's job? That didn't suit you?" Thomas asks.

Rain stares at me a moment longer, then clears his throat and looks at his father. "No."

"Well, you'd better find something you like," Thomas says. "Time's running out. The rest of the country's graduates have already been assigned their careers. The other Patrician children have chosen theirs. What's the hold-up, son?"

"Ugh. Here we go again." Rain rolls his eyes for the second time and stuffs another bite of steak into his mouth.

"Can we drop the issue?" Forest cuts in. "This is hardly a discussion to have in front of our guest."

"Of course," Thomas says. "My apologies, Miss Carter. Rain's been having trouble making a career commitment."

"At least he has a choice," I say. "Those of us who *didn't* grow up Patrician get arrested for so much as questioning the career assigned to us."

Thomas nearly chokes on his drink. "Excuse me?"

"I think what Miss Carter is trying to say," Forest says. "Is that she appreciates very much how our government provides jobs for them."

I'm about to correct him, but seeing Thomas's face redden makes me realize I'd better not overstep my bounds. He is a politician, he does work for Chief Titus Whitcomb, and he will have me sent back to the prison if I demonstrate any signs of treason.

I smile politely and pick up my glass. "Yes. That's exactly what I meant."

Rain snorts and stuffs his last bite of his steak into his mouth.

"What's the weather like this time of year in the Community Garden?" Thomas asks.

Now it's my turn to choke on my drink. Why are we talking about the *weather*? "Freezing," I say when I recover. "It's winter, and we don't have a cupola to keep us warm."

My mockery goes unnoticed by all but Rain, who snickers across the table.

Thomas continues asking me questions about life in the Community Garden, but the conversation is strained, the atmosphere tense. The rest of the conversation is shallow, and I offer safe answers to Thomas's questions with a fake smile. The whole time, Rain stares at me from across the table, an amused look in his eyes and two fingers planted over two smirking lips. It's unnerving. The tension leaves my body when dinner's finally over and Forest escorts me outside.

Finally.

"I'm sorry about tonight." He leads me to the waiting jeep. "I didn't realize how pointed my father's questions would be. And Rain—"

"Don't apologize for Rain."

"He's a shoddy jackal." He leans his hip against the vehicle and drags his hand down the length of his face. "Don't listen to a word he says." He crosses his arms, stares down at me. "You are attending the Feast of St. Nick tomorrow, right?"

"Um...I don't think so."

Forest's eyebrows furrow. "Why not?"

"I don't really...I'm not...Frankfort material." I peek up at him. "I don't think I would exactly fit in."

"Well, of course you would. You're a Patrician."

I bristle at the way he says that. Because apparently Proletariats wouldn't fit in, but I have Patrician blood, so I'm magically one of the rich kids.

"Please, Ember." Forest takes my hand, and the gesture is so intimate, I have trouble finding my tongue. "Please come. I'd love to see you there."

"Why?" I pull away from him because he's *engaged* to another woman. "Why do you want me to go? So you can show off your *fiancée*?"

He winces and I immediately feel bad. I shouldn't be so snarky, but I'm so incredibly irritable after that dinner with his father and Rain, not to mention seeing all that fresh food that doesn't get past the shoddy Frankfort cupola. And I'm still hung up on what Judah said about never trusting a politician. What's more, Forest never told me about the special power the Patricians have. The power that I don't fully understand. So why *should* I trust him? And why should I feel any obligation to go to that shoddy party tomorrow?

I take a deep breath, let it out, force calm into my voice.

"Listen," I look at Forest. "I'm sorry if I seem harsh. I don't really care about the celebrations. I'm just trying to get through the next few days so I can go home and resume my normal life."

His frown deepens. "You want to return to the...the Community Garden?"

"Of course I do. It's my home."

He looks down, his brows furrowed in thought, then he looks at me, his eyes deep and compelling. "You may not be able to return home that soon, you know. You have until they figure out what's going on with you, and even then, Chief Whitcomb may have other plans."

"Plans? *Titus*, the Chief, might have *plans* for me?" Now I'm really confused. "Why on earth would he give a jackal's nuts about me?"

Forest waves his hand in the air impatiently. "You're an interesting specimen, Miss Carter. A new project that has opened up a new realm of possibilities. Possibilities that Chief Whitcomb doesn't like very much, because if there are other unregistered Patricians out there, it could mean he'll lose control."

Unregistered Patricians?

"Control of what, exactly?"

"Of the people." His voice lowers and he steps closer, intoxicating cinnamon filling the air around me. "People like *you.*"

I blink. What is he saying? Something Mcallister said earlier flashes through my mind. *They can't control you.* What the shoddy rot did he mean by that?

"Whitcomb can't strip me from my home because of some past events I had no control over," I say.

Forest laughs softly. "Whitcomb can do whatever he likes. He's the chief, you know."

Of course I know. Who *doesn't* know?

"Don't roll your eyes, Ember." Forest's smile vanishes and his features become dead serious. "I went to school with Titus. Even then, everyone knew not to cross him. He has a bad temper, to put it lightly."

"I thought you two got along? I thought you said he liked you?"

"He does. But that's because I know how to stay on his good side."

"Yes." I give a whimsical sigh and dust some imaginary lint off my dress. "I suppose spying on the Proletariat in taverns and trying to use us to get to the Resurgence would keep you on the Chief's good side."

If he's trying to fool me by looking shocked, he's doing a good job.

"I wasn't spying on you at the tavern," he says. "And I'm not trying to *use* you. Holy Crawford, Ember. Do you really think so little of me? Do you really see me as some monster whose sole purpose is to *torture* you? What on earth have I done to make you so skeptical?"

I open my mouth, then close it. Because he hasn't really done anything to deserve my doubt. Except not rescue me when my death sentence was set in stone. But he claims he didn't have the power to help me in that moment.

I release a sigh and look at him. "What were you doing at The Tap, if you weren't spying?"

"It's not every day that I get out of my...Frankfort bubble to experience a different side of the population. I just wanted to see what the Proletariat life was like."

"Why would that interest you?"

"As a congressman, it's my job to know how the country is run and how its citizens are doing."

"So you wanted to make sure everyone was working diligently, because lord knows we're the backs you Patricians stand upon."

He winces.

Regret floods my veins. What's wrong with me? I've never been this snappy to anyone. Why do I feel the need to be this way to Forest? Especially after he invited me to dinner tonight? Despite Judah's warning, Forest has done nothing to deserve my bitterness. He's only been the kindest person to me since I arrived to Frankfort.

He clears his throat and opens the jeep door for me. "I can see I made a complete mistake coming out here. I apologize." He bows and strides back toward his house.

No. Don't leave, I want to say. "Why did you walk me all the way out here, anyway?"

He pauses, turns his head slightly. "I was going to ask you if I could escort you to the Feast of St. Nick tomorrow night, but I think I already have my answer."

My heart twists. I open my mouth to respond, but he's already walking through the door and closing it behind him.

CHAPTER TWENTY-SIX

I'm alone the next morning, the fingers of guilt wrapping around my throat for turning Forest down. I almost write a letter of apology to him, but have no idea how to get it to him. I don't really know how to call him on the phoneband, either. And I almost ask LeighAnn, when Judah's warning comes back to me, and I decide not to apologize. What good would it do? He's dating Olivia Doss, so who cares what he thinks of me? Besides, if all goes well, I'll hopefully leave this place in two days and never look back. So it wouldn't matter on what terms I leave, now would it?

Two days. Just two more days until I can go home.

I spend the day experimenting with my new art supplies. I could seriously get lost in painting, coloring, and sketching, and never see another person for days.

By mid-afternoon, LeighAnn enters the room to help me prepare for the party. She brings a hairdresser, River. They bring to my room the most elegant gown I've ever seen.

LeighAnn calls it a Victorian era dress. It has hoops, a thing called a petticoat, and loads and loads of crimson fabric.

"Red is the color of Christmas," LeighAnn explains. "You'll look very festive for the Feast of St. Nick."

River pulls out a small black bag from her satchel. "But first, we do your makeup."

They set me in a chair with the bathroom lights focused on my face and then spread black, thick liquid on my eyelashes.

"You don't need those fake lashes like most ladies wear," LeighAnn says as she brushes the liquid on. "Your eyelashes are naturally long and thick."

If they are already thick, I wonder, why do they need to paint them? Gold powder is spread on my eyelids, then they use a black pencil around the edges of my eyes. And they keep painting my face until I wonder if there will be any piece of me left when they finish.

"You're the talk of the city." River plugs the curling iron in. She takes a strand of my hair and curls it. "When we're finished here, even Chief Whitcomb won't be able to keep his eyes off you."

Oh. Chief Whitcomb. He'll be there. He's *hosting* the party. He *invited* me, after he saw me in the arena and decided I wasn't worth saving. How strange that he would change his mind so quickly about me. Worms begin reproducing more worms in my stomach until I suddenly feel sick at just the thought of seeing this unstable chief.

"Is everything okay, dear?" LeighAnn asks. She must have noticed my sour expression.

"The perfumes are a bit much." If no one notices me by my elaborate dress, they'll definitely notice me by the strong smell that will invade the room at my presence.

My hair is curled, then put up in an intricate braid that crowns my head, with the rest falling down my left shoulder in an inky, black mass. It makes my neck look long and elegant and makes my shoulders look slender. River pins some holly into the braid.

"Now, for the dress," LeighAnn says.

I follow them into the dressing room. River strips me down to nothing while LeighAnn picks up a series of slips and under garments and helps me dress. If I had this much fabric at home, I could make enough clothes for all the girls in my class.

The dressing portion takes the longest. They tie some complicated bodice around my waist, tightening it until my lungs have no room to expand, then pull hoops up over that. And *then* they pull the most beautiful part over my head. The fabric falls over the hoops in lovely layers of crimson taffeta.

River tightens the back of the dress with black shoelace-like strings. Black lace falls loosely over my shoulders like sleeves, but I realize they're only there for decoration, because the strings on the back are what hold the dress up.

"And now, the final touch. A diamond necklace." River tells me to spin around so she can put the necklace on.

Three strands of black diamonds wrap around my neck and connect at the front of my throat, then drip down to a larger white diamond the size of a coin. I've never seen a real diamond.

When I look at my reflection again, I don't even recognize myself. "Can you tell me why I'm being showered with elaborate gifts?"

Both LeighAnn's and River's eyes widen in shock.

"I mean, I'm not ungrateful." I quickly glance at the

camera. "It's just…I was a prisoner two days ago, and now I'm wearing diamonds and lace, attending the Chief's banquet. What's up with that?"

"You're of noble blood, Miss Carter, and you've been pronounced innocent," LeighAnn says. "These aren't gifts. They're what is to be expected for a Patrician like you."

I wish everyone would quit calling me that. Just because I came from the bloodline of the founders of this country does not make me Patrician. Nor should it make me automatically innocent. I mean, *I* know I'm innocent, but that's not why I was forgiven. Since coming to Frankfort, absolutely nothing has made sense and everything confuses me.

After handing me black velvet gloves that reach my elbows, LeighAnn and River leave for their dinner break.

"Your escort will be here shortly," LeighAnn says, and they're both out the door.

My escort. Whoever that is. It's not Forest and that's my fault. My own shoddy fault. I insulted him. I was short with him. I was snappy and cranky and so ready to get out of his elegant presence that I went two steps too far, and he walked off.

And now I'm in this mess.

I heave out a sigh and perch on a stool.

Who will my escort be? Another politician? I imagine some boring black suit offering me his arm, exchanging a few words of mundane small talk, and an extremely boring evening surrounded by Patricians. Nothing like the magical evening it could have been with Forest, who makes me feel worthy and beautiful and *safe*.

Forest, who's engaged to Olivia Doss.

The next few minutes pass by slowly. I know River told

me not to touch anything because I'll get my manicured hands dirty, but I pull off my gloves and pick up the basket containing the paint, brushes, and oil canvas. Painting is probably the last form of art I should do while wearing this dress, but it's the only thing I want to do right now.

After placing a blanket on my lap to protect my dress, I spread the canvas on a desk in front of the window, then select the colors. Tangerine for the sunset. Silver, midnight blue, and onyx for the city and its shadows. And lime, for the tiny patch of the Community Garden I imagine in the distance. The patch that is my home.

I begin to paint.

I don't have as much experience in painting as I would like, using crusty paints on old paper or cardboard boxes, and I've never had lessons. But this is a new, crisp canvas, and these paints have never been used, nor have their brushes, so I take utmost care not to make a single mistake. I pull out a brand new brush, dip it in the thick orange oil, and spread it across the white canvas.

And I completely lose myself.

While I paint, I decide that it doesn't matter that Forest isn't escorting me. I mean, I kind of deserved his cold shoulder. And maybe it's good that I keep my distance from him. As if anything would come out of dating a politician anyway. We're from two entirely different worlds. And he's not available.

I dip my brush into the yellow paint and merge it into the orange, turning it into a coral hue for the sunset. A light knock sounds at the door. I look at the clock. It's already time for the escort to be here. I quickly wipe my hands off on a cloth and cross the room.

"Come in." I pull one glove over a paint-stained hand.
The door cracks open. A slender boy steps in.
And my heart plummets into my gut.
Because Rain, of all people, is my escort.

CHAPTER TWENTY-SEVEN

"Rain," I mutter.

He wears a black suit with a crimson vest that matches my dress. Shaggy hair falls down his ears and into his eyes.

He latches the door behind him and grins. "Don't sound so disappointed." He steps toward me and bows at the waist, as though I were related to Chief Whitcomb himself. "I'm your escort tonight."

"Um…" Every word I've ever learned has decided to take a vacation because none of them want to face Rain. "Actually…I-I don't need an escort."

"Oh." He winces, and I almost feel bad, but then he covers all emotion with a smirky smirk and says, "Well, I suppose you could attend the party by yourself. You probably know how to get to the ballroom. And surely you know all the customs that take place, and I'm sure you've learned the traditional dance of St. Nick. And of course you *won't* skip out because you'll deeply offend the chief if you do." He offers an arrogant half-smile and spins on his heel. "See you there, little apple picker."

Deeply offend the chief? "Wait." The word slips from my mouth before I can stop it.

He pauses at the door and glances over his shoulder with gray mocking eyes. "Yes, Patrician Sister?"

I grit my teeth, but bite back any rude comments. I'm terrified of crowds. I can't go to the party alone. "The chief would be...offended if I didn't go?"

He turns fully around to face me. "Well of course he would. His ego is very fragile. You received a special invitation, yes?"

"I guess."

"So not going would be a complete insult. A proverbial slap to the face of our leader."

I groan. Pull the other glove over my fingers. "I guess you can take me."

"Ah." Winning smirk back. "What an honor."

I loathe how his voice drips with sarcasm. But he's right. I know nothing of the Christmas celebrations. And there's no telling what the chief would do if I offended him. I don't know why he would even care if I showed up tonight, but whatever. According to Forest, he's not a person to be crossed, so why risk it when I'm so close to going home?

"Shall we?" Rain extends his elbow.

I stare at it, wishing it were Forest's. Letting out a sigh, I link my arm through his, catching the whiff of peppermint coming off his clothes. His steps are light as he leads me from the room and down the hall toward the elevator.

"LeighAnn told me you looked magnificent," he says. "But I didn't realize you would leave me breathless."

My cheeks grow warm at the compliment, but I quickly

remind myself that he's probably used that phrase on hundreds of girls, so I shrug it off.

"You know LeighAnn?" I ask.

"Oh, yes. We go way back. She was a servant at my father's house."

Servant. "Such a degrading word used for someone who's supposed to be your equal."

"I'm sorry. Her career included cleaning my father's house and cooking our meals." He grins. "Is that better?"

"Not really."

"Apart from what you might think, LeighAnn and I are pretty close. She was more like the mother I never had."

The softness in his voice takes me off guard. "I thought your mother was alive?"

"Oh, she is. But she spends most of her time at the office, it's almost like she doesn't exist."

"Is she a politician?"

"Of course she is."

"Oh." How strange it must be to have both parents away from home all the time, to feel closer to a maid than to your own mother. My mom was always around, but then her career as a seamstress allowed her to work from home. "So, you promised to tell me the rest of the history of the Patrician blood and...antitoxin."

Rain keeps his gaze straight ahead as we approach the elevator. "In time, Miss Carter."

"Oh, so it's Miss Carter now that I'm a Patrician?"

Now he looks at me and arches a brow. "You've proven your worth."

The elevator doors ding open and he leads me inside. I glance at the street below, then turn to face the silver doors.

The elevator begins its decent down the hundred stories, and my stomach feels like it's floating in space. I tighten my grip on Rain's arm to keep my balance through the swift movement.

"Have you gotten my results yet?" I ask.

"Trust me. When I receive your results, you'll be the first to know."

I'm not sure how much longer I can wait until the mystery of my Patrician blood is solved.

Silence hangs in the air as the elevator descends. Questions fill my mind about who this arrogant Rain is, and how he could possibly be related to the polite gentleman Forest Turner. I shouldn't care. But I do. I have a burning desire to know more about this boy who takes innocent people to prison and commands the Defenders with such an air of confidence and carries a flask of whiskey everywhere he goes.

"So," I say. "You had a chance to ask me personal questions during my test, and you know more about me than my neighbors at this point. Don't you think it's fair that I learn about you?"

"I don't play fair, Carter." He look at me and grins. "I'm a Patrician, remember?"

Strange that he would admit that Patricians don't play fair.

He sighs. "But, I suppose if you ask a few questions, I'll be inclined to answer…as long as they're not *too* personal."

Fair enough. "Why haven't you chosen a career yet?"

"First my father, now you?"

"It's kind of a big deal."

"Yes. It is. Choosing a career is a huge commitment. I have a lot to think about."

"It must be nice being able to take time to think, to *decide* what career you get."

"You have no idea."

When the doors open, Rain guides me through the hallways until we reach large arched doors. Music echoes from the room. I didn't realize the ballroom was connected to the hotel. Two Defenders open the doors for us. Ironic that the Defenders who forced me around the previous week are now opening doors for me.

We step through the archway, and I find myself at the top of a marble staircase. Below is the ballroom, where hundreds of Patricians are dancing. The smell of cinnamon invades my senses. The most beautiful music I've ever heard fills the room.

A dome ceiling curves high over the ballroom. A chandelier hanging from the center in dozens of layers illuminates the room with a warm yellow glow. Arched windows run the length of the far wall, stretching up to the ceiling and peering out to the city. Pillars line the other walls, and a balcony overlooks the ballroom floor. Red ribbons hang from the balcony, and tiny yellow lights dip down the ledge of the banisters like icicles, making me almost miss winter.

Some Patricians mingle around a long buffet table laid out with the richest foods I've ever seen. And, oh my word, there is so much food. I can't even name half the things I see. Roasted meats, bowls of fresh fruits, plates with cheese and rolls of bread. It's a feast fit for a king. Where on earth does all this food come from?

Like me, the women are dressed in elaborate gowns with ruffled hoop skirts, not their usual togas. The men dress in black suits similar to Rain's. And there are so many people, so many *rich* people, that my heart begins to pound, and I stand frozen at the top of the stairs. I've never wanted to disappear more than I do now, and I take a step back. Shrink back into the hallway, out of existence. Rain tugs on my arm and my feet automatically obey his command.

"Don't be shy now," he murmurs in my ear as we descend the stairs. "Most of these people are intrigued by you."

"They know me?"

"Come, Ember. You're the talk of the city. The dramatic excitement of the week. The mysterious Patrician. If you don't *feel* confident, at least *feign* confidence. Command the room. Take control of this situation. Make them love you and fear you all at once."

"How? How in the world does someone do that?"

He lets out a sardonic laugh. "You have a lot to learn about Frankfort, little girl. Lift your chin, look people in the eye when you greet them. Stare them down. You know." He adds a little bounce when we arrive at the bottom floor. "Put a little more pep in your step."

Pep in my step? His words always sound foreign, like an idiom from another time. And his character is so insane for the cold Rain I know. I can't help but laugh. Some of the tension leaves my body as I force my step to match his, lift my chin, and look people boldly in the eye, nodding my greeting.

We weave through the thick mass of Patricians, greeting people, and it takes a moment for me to realize that Rain is purposefully leading me in a specific direction. Where are we going? I look ahead, between the mass of people, and my stomach plummets.

Because we're headed straight toward Chief Titus Whitcomb's throne.

CHAPTER TWENTY-EIGHT

My heart forgets how to pump blood into my system. My feet forget how to walk. All the confidence I'd felt before slowly drains from my body. The chief. I knew he would be here, but I didn't realize I'd have to actually *speak* with him.

Rain and I approach, and the chief's eyes snap to attention. Rain bows at the waist, and I curtsy the way LeighAnn taught me.

"Rise," Chief Whitcomb says.

I straighten, study the man-child who rules this country. He looks even younger in person than he did in his portrait, but has the same green eyes, the same black bowtie, black slacks, black vest over a crisp white shirt. Elegance is the one word I would choose to describe Chief Whitcomb.

And he's staring right at me, mouth slightly agape. He's looking at me like he's seeing a ghost. He looks shocked and guarded and terrified all at once, and I tighten my grip around Rain's arm until I'm sure I'm about to cut off his circulation, because right now, in this very moment, I want to turn around. I want to run out of the room and not look back. Because, even though the chief is supposed to be loved by his people, I was taught to fear him. And by the way he's looking at me right now like he would like nothing more than to kill me with his bare hands, I'm completely terrified.

Then he blinks. His mouth breaks into a grin, his piercing green eyes are suddenly shining like this is the best day ever. "Ember Carter." His voice is fluid. "Welcome to Frankfort. What an honor. What a remarkable honor to have found my sister."

I almost choke. "What?"

"My Patrician sister. We're all like one big family around here, you know. We're all like brothers and sisters with tightly woven friendships."

Oh. My heart rate slows to its normal pace.

"So tell me," he says, clearly amused. "Where have you been hiding all this time?"

"Um." I didn't really expect the Chief to pay me any attention, much less ask me personal questions. "I haven't…been hiding."

"No? Well. Then I'm just happy we found you before it was too late."

"Too late for, um, what?"

"You were going to die on the Rebels Circle, yes?"

Oh. Yes. I was going to die yesterday. And you weren't even going to rescue me. You came. You saw me. And you declared me unworthy of being saved, I want to say, but don't. Don't dare open my mouth because whatever I say might just have me sent back to prison. So instead I say, "Thank you. For your warm wel-welcome."

"No problem." Titus smiles a little. "Please, enjoy the

230

feast. Drink your heart out and indulge. My city, Miss Carter, is your city."

His smile deepens, and he holds my gaze like he's holding onto some kind of secret.

Rain tugs me along, and I'm left wondering what the shoddy inferno just happened. Honestly, if I'd seen Titus on the street anywhere, I would *not* be afraid of him. He seems friendly, genuine, and I would probably open up to him like I did in The Tap with Forest.

Which is a terrifying thought for so many reasons.

"You okay?" Rain whispers.

"Um. He's young."

"Well, yes. He's Forest's age."

"He doesn't seem mean at all."

"Who ever said our chief was mean?" Rain asks. "He's a kind leader who rules with a gentle fist."

That's the lie of the century, what, with people dying at the mercy of black tigers and Rebels Circles and starvation taking up the majority of the population.

"I need a drink." I make my way to the table. My mouth is dry as sand and I need Rain to stop talking while I think.

"Remember, little apple picker," Rain says. "Confidence. Feign confidence."

Oh. Right. People are watching and judging and looking for something to gossip about. I force a bold smile, lift my chin, and add the "pep in my step" as we head toward the refreshment table.

"Good," Rain says. I hear the smile in his voice. "You're already becoming a Patrician."

My smile vanishes and I grit my teeth again.

He hands me a glass of red wine. I remember when he

gave me the flask of hard liquor in the arena, finding amusement in my inability to down it. Wine is supposed to be more refined. People in the Community Garden call it a luxury drink. But when I take a sip now, I wonder why it's called a *luxury*. Because it's bitter and kind of disgusting and it takes all my energy not to spit the shoddy stuff out. Not nearly as bad as Rain's whiskey, but not exactly thirst-quenching, either.

"You okay?" Rain asks. "You don't look so good."

"I'm just more used to the watered-down stuff they serve at The Tap."

Rain snorts. "You're going to have to get used to refined alcohol. It's pretty much all people drink around here." He passes me a glass filled with a liquid that's brighter red than the wine. "Perhaps this will better suffice for now."

I stare at it and begin to wonder if this is another one of Rain's tricks.

"It's punch," he says. "You'll like it. I promise."

Accepting the glass, I take a tiny sip, surprised that Rain is actually right. This stuff tastes really, really good, like pure sugar spiked with the tiniest bit of alcohol. I take another drink, then watch the show before me. The Patricians are already dancing a formal dance, which apparently requires at least four people to participate, and I am so incredibly glad Rain hasn't asked me to dance. Though LeighAnn taught me the main steps, I would rather not look like a complete idiot in front of people who supposedly find me fascinating.

A girl with dark curls whisks up to the table. I recognize her as the girl hanging off Rain's arm when they were spectating us in the arena.

"Rain, you dirty son of a jackal." She lightly shoves him and he takes an exaggerated step back.

"Cherry, what was that for?" He lifts his hands in mock defense.

"You stood me up last night. You said you were going to take me for a ride on the ferry."

He throws his head back and groans like someone's chopping his leg off. "Oh, *no*. I'm *so* sorry, Cherry. My brother invited Miss Carter here to our house at the last minute, and I couldn't miss the opportunity to dine with our newest Patrician sister." He curls long, manicured fingers under her chin and tips it up in the most mocking gesture. "Will you *ever* forgive me?"

Ugh. My stomach turns at this slightly disgusting display before me.

Cherry's cheeks bloom scarlet. She looks away and chews her lip, not like she's in thought, but more like she's trying to look attractive. It works, of course. "I suppose I can let it slip this once."

I snort. I can't help it. She's so incredibly fake.

She looks at me for the first time, almost like an afterthought. "Miss Carter. So happy that you could join us tonight."

"My pleasure," is all I have time to say before two more girls flock to Rain's side. Their flirtatious giggles grate on every. Single. Nerve. Rain smiles down at them, clearly enjoying their attention. He looks every bit the Patrician, with a glass of fine wine in one hand, his hat just crooked enough to make him appear carelessly handsome, his lips tipped up in an arrogant smile. He laughs at something one of the girls says, and I realize even his fluid laugh has the capacity to make all the girls swoon.

Me? I'm disgusted. This is the Rain I know. The one

who flirts and drinks and visits the prison just to patronize so-called criminals. I hate Rain's dark charm and grace and the sensuality that draws women to him like bees to flowers. I hate his arrogance. I hate *him.*

Closing my eyes, I take a deep breath and turn my attention to the ballroom. There's an orchestra in the corner. The musicians must be the best in all of Ky to play in front of the Chief. The melody pouring from their instruments eases my soul, sets my wildly beating heart to a normal pace, and calms my extremely irritated spirit.

Inhale. Exhale. Replenish bad air for good. Everything will be okay.

And maybe it really will. If Titus is as nice as he seemed, then maybe once my records are clear and the mystery of my Patrician blood is figured out, I really will be able to go home.

A familiar voice cuts through the air behind me, and all my tension returns.

"Are you just going to stand there during the Dance of St. Nick?" Forest asks, appearing through the crowd. And I suddenly can't breathe. He looks so incredibly attractive, dressed in the traditional tuxedo with a dark blue vest that brings out the ocean of his blue eyes.

Olivia's arm is hooked through his. White beads crown her dark hair, and she wears a sapphire-blue gown without sleeves. Tall with high cheekbones, full lips, and shaped eyebrows, she is much more beautiful—and intimidating—up close. I haven't spoken to her since Career Day, when Leaf died, and I have to look away to keep from remembering that terrible day. I wonder if she remembers me as vividly as I remember her. I did, after all, punch her.

"Miss Carter, I would like to introduce you to my fiancée, Olivia Doss," Forest says.

234

I force a smile at Olivia and curtsy. "Pleased to meet you."

She curtsies back, and though a charming smile graces her features, her eyes are cold and full of unspoken warnings. Warning, no doubt, to stay away from Forest. I hear the message loud and clear.

"Are they still treating you well at the hotel?" Forest asks.

Small talk. I can do this. "Yeah." I look down at my hands and pretend Olivia's presence doesn't completely intimidate me. "It's a very nice hotel."

I have a thousand questions to ask Forest, but not in front of Olivia. Awkward silence fills the gap between us. Forest is probably still hurt from what I said to him last night. Olivia seems too proud to converse with a peasant like me. And Rain is, well, *Rain*. Still flirting with the girls. Finally, Rain manages to escape the flock of pigeons and steps into our circle. Before he can get a word in, I turn to him, desperate to get away from both Forest and Olivia and these extremely awkward piles of silent seconds.

"Will you dance with me?" I can't believe I just asked him to dance.

Rain sweeps auburn locks out of his eyes and holds his arm out for me. "With pleasure."

"Perhaps we can join you," Forest says.

I grit my teeth, but Rain glances back. "Well, we need two more partners to complete the ensemble."

And before I know it, the four of us are in the center of the dance floor. I face Rain and Olivia faces Forest. Then, as a part of the dance, the group separates and it's just me and Rain.

"You're dancing pretty well for a Proletariat, Rainbow Eyes," Rain says.

"Rainbow eyes?" I ask.

"Your eyes are shaped like a rainbow arches. Always smiling, even when you're having the most miserable time of your life. No wonder none of the guys here can take their eyes off of you."

Guys are watching me? Now I really do want to disappear. "It's because of all the make-up."

Rain smirks. "Nope. You have a natural beauty that shines, even when you're covered in sweat and sand as you race around the arena. And you have a perfect dimple right—" He trails his finger down my cheek. "Here."

I jerk away from his touch. "Don't touch me."

"Why not? Afraid you'll like it too much?"

"I'm afraid I'll cause the same scene here that I caused in the arena when I punched you."

His smile vanishes. And now it's my turn to smile.

"Venus flytrap," he says.

"What?"

"You draw people in with your charm and then you completely decapitate them." His smile slowly returns and he releases my hand, taps my nose. "Very Patrician of you." And then he passes me off to Forest.

I try to remember the dance steps and try my best to not make a complete fool of myself. What will Forest and I possibly talk about? The last time I saw him, I decapitated him, too. I guess it's a nasty new habit of mine when people aren't as easygoing as they were in the Garden. Fortunately, Forest speaks first.

"I apologize for not telling you about Olivia sooner." His hand is warm against mine. His other hand presses against the small of my back, making the butterflies in my stomach take wing.

"No worries." I try to remember how to breathe. "You had no obligation to tell me."

"It would've been right for *me* to tell you instead of Rain. I was working to gain your trust, and now I've completely lost any trust I might have acquired due to letting this information slide."

"It's okay, Forest. You never really had my trust to begin with."

He winces. Oops. There I go again. No filter. Complete decapitation. I swallow hard and offer a smile. "I'm sorry, Forest. I was told never to trust a politician." I shrug, surveying the other dancers. "I've heard too many things about your kind, and I don't really want to get involved."

"Well you don't seem to have any trouble getting involved with my brother."

"Rain?" His name comes out in a strangled laugh-choke. "Are you serious? We're not involved. Had I a choice, he would be the *last* one I would have selected to escort me."

"You did have a choice, though. Apparently I was beneath even him."

I cringe. "It's not like that. I didn't know who would be escorting me. Rain was assigned to be my escort. It just sort of happened."

"If only that were true."

"What do you mean?"

"Rain *requested* to escort you."

I stop dancing. Why would Rain want to escort me after he wanted to watch me burn on the Rebels Circle? I glance at him as he dances with Olivia. But he's not watching her. He's staring at me with a brooding intensity that makes something strange swirl in the pit of my stomach. I blush to my roots and look away. How does he have such power over even those who hate him?

"I wouldn't look so pleased if I were you," Forest whispers as we resume dancing. "Rain is a player, Ember. He only wanted to escort you for no other reason than to be the center of attention tonight."

My smile flattens. "I'm *not* pleased. And why are you telling me this? To get back at me for what I said earlier?"

"No." His golden brows furrow. "I want you to know so that you won't fall for his charming act. So that when he bores of you—and he will—your heart will remain intact." He sighs, staring over my shoulder as we switch hands and walk in a circle. His left hand on my left hand, our fingers interwoven so intimately, and I don't think I ever want to let go. "Listen," he says. "I understand if you don't trust me. Fine. I get it. But if there's anyone you *really* don't want to trust in this room, it's Rain."

I almost laugh out loud. "You don't have to worry about me trusting Rain. Not after what happened during my stay in prison."

Forest glances at me. "What happened in your stay in prison?"

Oh, rot. The last thing I want to do is place a bigger wedge between two brothers who are already at odds with each other.

"Never mind. I'm leaving soon and none of this will matter."

Just as I finish the sentence, Forest passes me on to another suitor with black hair and dark skin. He's handsome and tries to make small talk, but I'm too busy trying to figure out Rain's sudden change in character, Forest's engagement to Olivia, Rain and Forest's relationship, and why I even care.

Another reason for me to leave as soon as I'm allowed. Too much drama in Frankfort. The people thrive on it. There is no trust, not even between two brothers. There's no openness like there was in the Community Garden. Leaf and I told each other everything. There were no secrets among my classmates. If I asked them a simple question, they gave me simple answers. No elaborate riddles that blow up into drama. The people here...they've got nothing better to do than play games with each other.

I'm thankful for a quiet dancing partner for once, so I can think. But then I'm passed back to Rain.

"So, you have the hots for my brother," are the first words that pop out of his arrogant mouth.

I look away, my face warm enough to melt steel. "I barely *know* him."

He laughs. "It's all right. Your secret's safe with me, Rainbow Eyes."

I wonder if anything is safe with him.

"It's not like they're married yet," he continues. "I mean, you could always, you know, stay true to your Patrician blood and steal him away."

And that sets me over the edge. "I'm *not* a *Patrician!*" I rip my hand from his and stalk away, not caring about the scene I may or may not be making right now. But, seriously. Rain is unbelievable. I mean, can't he just let it *go?* Keep his shoddy mouth shut for like *five minutes?*

"Wait." He grabs my arm and spins me around. "You *are* Patrician, Ember. I, as your tester, know that well. Why can't you accept it?"

"Because if Patricians are anything like *you*—" I twist out of his grasp. "—I want *nothing* to do with them."

He blinks, opens his mouth then closes it and looks at the floor.

I choke out a laugh at the look in his eyes and say, "Don't pretend to be offended, Rain. You said yourself that you looked forward to watching me die on the Rebels Circle. So don't stand there and pretend like anything I say could possibly offend you."

"You don't understand."

"Understand *what*? That of all the Patricians, you're the worst? Even worse than Titus."

His gaze hardens. "Don't forget where you are, Carter." His eyes swivel to the people around us, and a muscle jerks in his jaw. "You'll get killed for insulting *Chief Whitcomb*, whether you're Patrician or not." He steps closer, his peppermint breath hot on my cheek. "One word against the chief, and I will report your treason myself."

My body goes hot, then cold. My heart pounds. Is he serious? Then he steps back, and the look in his eyes tells me that, yes, he would report my treason, no problem. He would be more than happy to send me back to Frankfort Prison, to watch me die on the Rebels Circle.

Behind Rain, I catch a glimpse of Chief Whitcomb making his way back to his throne, and I wonder why he bothers keeping me around since I'm innocent. Why a friendly person like him would keep me prisoner. Then it hits me. Frankfort is the golden city. The pride of Ky. Many people dream of coming here. Even Elijah verbalized several times his desire to experience the Christmas celebrations. So no wonder Titus invited me to the feast.

He thinks he's doing me a favor.

Maybe—maybe all he needs is to be informed that I don't really want to linger around here. That I want to go home, resume my career as a farmer, and live close to my dad and brother. I mean, Titus seems like a pretty nice guy. He's warm and smiley and understanding.

He sits in his throne, then his gaze locks with mine. And his brows flicker but then his mouth breaks into a brilliant smile, and I can't help but smile back. I automatically begin walking in his direction.

Rain clamps a hand down on my shoulder. "Where do you think you're going?"

I shrug his hand off my shoulder. "I'm informing the chief that I'd like to go home first thing in the morning."

CHAPTER TWENTY-NINE

"Whoa." Rain's hand is on my shoulder. Again. And he firmly turns me to face him. "Informing? *Informing?* You'd better make it sound more like a request if you really want to go anywhere."

I shrug from his hand. Again. I'm really getting tired of his grabbing my limbs. "I don't see why he would have a problem with me wanting to leave."

"Neither do I. You're just a plain little farm girl who's created quite a bit of excitement here in Frankfort and is now failing miserably at paying off."

The jackal.

"But for some reason," he continues. "I really don't think Titus wants you to leave yet. You see, he's not really the type to invite just *anyone* to his feasts. He doesn't even invite all the Patricians. In the rare instances that a criminal is proven innocent, he sends them home. But *you. You're* an exception, Ember Carter. You're *special.* And not in a good sort of way. In case you didn't know, you're still under custody. You're not free yet."

"I've been proven innocent. My records are clear. I'm as free as you and Forest and everyone else in this shoddy ballroom. So, if our chief truly believes in equality, he won't stop me from leaving."

Rain snorts. "You don't get it, do you? No. He won't stop you. He will let you go and then he will get back at you in a worse way."

My mouth goes dry. "What do you mean?"

"Whether it's forcing you into an awful career or putting you back in prison for who knows what, he'll get back at you."

"Why are you telling me this?" I ask. "When you absolutely loathe me?"

His Adam's apple bobs. "I want to help you."

"Help me? *Help* me? You were anticipating my death two days ago, and now you want to *help* me?" Since when does he care what happens to me? Then it hits me. Rain may not be a politician, but his brother and parents are, and he may not be so different from them. "*Oh.*"

He frowns, tilts his head. "*Oh*, what?"

"You want to *help* me so you can use me to scout out the *Resurgence*, don't you?"

He smacks his hand over my mouth and shoves me into an adjoining chamber, slamming the door behind him. No people here. Just me and Rain. And he shoves me against the wall, his hand clamped firmly over my mouth and his eyes frosting over like ice, and I wonder—I wonder what, exactly, he plans to do with me.

"What is *wrong* with you?" he asks.

My heartbeat pounds in my eardrums, and I'm breathing

too fast and struggling against his grip, but he shoves me against the wall again. Fear paralyzes me.

"Don't *ever* talk about them in public," he hisses. "Don't even say their *name*. Do you *want* to be executed? Do you *want* people to suspect you're working with them?"

I quickly shake my head.

"Then drop it. Pretend you've never heard of them. Because few people, *very few people*, Ember, support the Resurgence. And if you're caught talking about them, you might as well stamp the word REBEL on your forehead." He speaks slowly, as to a child. "If one person hears you even say the name of that rebel group, you WILL be executed."

His passion terrifies me. His warning confuses me. Because I thought he wanted me dead. And now he's trying to keep me alive. He removes his hand, steps back a little so he's not crushing me to the wall, but still has a firm hold on my shoulders. I can't escape.

"You're already a suspect for saving your little friend," he says, very quietly. "That's why Whitcomb doesn't want you to leave. That's why he's placed you in a hotel, under surveillance, where he can watch you while he's supposedly waiting for your blood work to come in. He doesn't give a jackal's nuts why you're a Patrician. Like you said, *who cares?* But he'll let the Patricians believe he's as obsessed with the drama as they are, while watching your every move and listening to every word that carelessly tumbles out of your pretty little mouth."

I clamp my mouth shut. Swallow the tears burning the back of my throat.

"When he catches you speaking of this rebel group, he'll arrest you again, and he'll try and torture information out of

245

you. If you don't speak, he'll kill you. No amount of talking to tigers will get you out of trouble this time."

"Why are—" My voice chokes off, and I swallow. "Why are you telling me this?"

He smirks. Steps back and releases me completely. "Because you have a knack for getting yourself in trouble. As fun as it is to watch rebels burn to death, I don't like it when innocent people die. And I do believe you're innocent. You're incredibly stupid, but you're innocent."

I wipe my nose with the back of my hand. I didn't realize I was this close to crying.

"Now, I'm going to leave you. I'm going to let you sit here and think about your actions," he says, like I'm some stupid child. "I want you to think really hard about whether or not you really want to approach Chief Whitcomb, and if you do, what, exactly, you're going to say. How you're going to say it. How you're going to sound incredibly appreciative and look extra pleasant while you speak the words on your mind. I won't stop you. I won't stop you from talking to Titus. But if you're sent to prison tonight, you can't say I didn't warn you."

He spins on his heel and walks out of the room. And it's not until he's out of sight that I realize I'm trembling. I'm trembling violently because his rage is possibly more terrifying than a black tiger. Rain is...unpredictable. Confusing. So confusing. So incredibly confusing. Gloating about my death one day, then three days later, what do you know, he suddenly believes I'm innocent.

Rain is just about as temperamental as a feral cat.

And now...now I'm terrified of Rain. I'm angry at Forest. And I don't think anything sounds better than going home right now, starvation and all. I'll take hunger over drama any day. I mean, seriously, who would have thought a beautiful city full of glorious luxuries could turn into such a shoddy nightmare?

Frankfort is a black tiger. Beautiful. Dangerous.

I need to get home. I don't care how risky it is to ask the chief, I just need to at least ask, because I don't even know how long he plans on keeping me around. So I step out of the room. I numbly edge around the chamber, around the whirling bright dresses and dashing black suits, and I approach the chief, although I'm feeling eighty times less confident than I was minutes ago.

He looks at me, his eyes widening in obvious surprise and discomfort and then that smile—that dazzling smile. And I force a smile of my own. My most winning smile. A smile like the smile Olivia Doss wore earlier tonight, because Rain told me to look pleasant.

And I think, everything's going to be okay. Everything's going to be fine.

Just. Smile.

I bow to the chief of Ky. "Chief Whitcomb," I say, straightening. "I would like to…*request* permission to go home to the Community Garden."

"When?"

When? I didn't expect *that* to be his first question. "Um. T-tomorrow? Morning?"

Something shifts in his eyes. "You wish to forego the rest of the Christmas celebrations and return to the Garden?"

"Yes."

"But the glorious New Year's parade is only a month away. Surely you want to be here for that?"

Who cares about the shoddy parade?

"No more parties or parades for me, thank you. I only want to return to the Community Garden." A strange courage fills me. "And work in the apple orchard. That's my only request to the greatest chief of all time."

Forest must be right about the chief, because my flattery seems to get to him. The strange spark leaves his eyes, and his smile almost looks genuine. "Very well, Miss Carter. I will have a jeep waiting for you outside the hotel at sunrise."

Wait—what? "You mean, you'll let me go?"

He laughs softly. "Yes, Miss Carter. You are my guest and are free to leave whenever you want."

Shock, then pure joy so consuming that I can't hide my smile.

"Th-thank you, Chief," I bow again. "You are most gracious." And this time, I mean it.

I turn and waltz back through the room, completely unaware of the other dancers around me. That was so easy. For the first time in weeks, things are going my way. *This* is what I'm used to. *This* is what I grew up with. Easygoing people. One simple request granted with one simple answer. And home. I'm finally going home. It's so completely unbelievable.

When I reach the refreshments table, I pick up some spiked punch. My going home is something worth celebrating.

"You've had some change in mood," Forest says as he steps up beside me.

I grin. "Don't worry, Forest. After tonight, you won't have to worry about my wellbeing weighing on your conscience. I'm going home."

"Really?" His brows shoot up. "How did you manage that?"

248

"Easy. I merely *requested* the chief let me go, and he said 'yes.'"

"You asked the chief to let you leave early?"

"Yes."

He clears his throat. "Well...I suppose a congratulations is in order. But I will miss you, Miss Carter. It's a shame you're leaving so soon. I'd hoped...." His voice trails off and he looks past me.

"Hoped...what?" Could Rain be right? Could there be something between me and Forest?

He looks at me again, opens his mouth to respond, but then Olivia whisks to his side in a flurry of blue ribbons. He smiles down at her, then looks at me. "I hope to see you once more before you leave." Then he takes Olivia back onto the ballroom floor.

Disappointment is possibly the worst feeling in the world—next to humiliation. It's like nails on a chalkboard. Sandpaper on skin. Mud stuck to the roof of my mouth and I just can't spit all the grains out. It's uncomfortable and unbecoming and I don't like it.

I don't like watching Forest dance with Olivia on the ballroom floor. I want him to dance with *me*. I want those evening sky eyes to be focused on me, like I'm the only flower that decided to bloom this season. I want that smile reserved for me, and me only. The world must be laughing hysterically at my expense. My decision to leave tomorrow might quite possibly be the wisest decision I'd ever made. Because I don't think I could stand another day in this place.

Not as long as Forest Turner is engaged.

Not as long as I'm slowly falling for him.

"Word on the street says you already approached the

chief." Rain steps up beside me and picks up a drink. How many has he had? Four? Five?

"Are you here to reprimand me?"

"Sounds like you did what I said, and thought really hard about how to approach Titus. I'm proud."

He's back to his old exuberant self. That was quick. Temperamental feral cat.

"However," he says. "You can't leave the cupola without getting a real taste of Frankfort."

"What do you mean?" How much more to Frankfort could there possibly be?

He gestures toward the ballroom. "You think this is all we do here? Have refined get-togethers where we dress up like kings and queens and dance all night? *Borrring.* Allow me show you what a *real* party in Frankfort looks like." He extends his elbow.

I eye it, then look at him. "Are you trying to get me locked back in prison? Chief Whitcomb won't be happy if I excuse myself early."

"Are you kidding? Look at him. He's as bored as I am, all slumped in his throne. This shoddy ball is a tradition started by his Grandfather, an unfortunate job description that falls to whoever is Chief. Notice how the majority of the people look old enough to be your grandparents? That's because they are. Besides, you came. You did your part. Now, you can stay here for three more hours and watch people make mundane conversation and stuff their faces like swine, but if you come with me, I can guarantee you'll have a good time."

I bite my lip and look at Forest gliding across the ballroom floor with Olivia, and my heart twists violently. I really don't want to sit here for three more hours watching *them.*

"Fine," I say. "Show me what a real party looks like."

"My pleasure, Rainbow Eyes. But be ye warned, you'll only truly enjoy yourself if you like to have fun."

CHAPTER THIRTY

Rain leads me out of the hotel and hails down a cab. A few minutes later, we pull up to a tavern with an illuminated sign that says *The Black Tiger*.

I bristle. "The Black Tiger? Really? That's the name of the tavern?"

Rain smirks and offers me his hand as I clamor out of the cab. "Fitting, isn't it? And by the way, this isn't a common tavern. It's a *club*."

"What difference does it make?"

"Only exclusive members allowed."

He shows his I.D. at the door, and I guess his name alone gives him the right to bring any guest he wants, because I don't have to show anything. We step into a dark room with flashing blue and white lights. Music bombards my ears. Not soft orchestra music like in the ballroom, but something harder, faster. Something that encodes with the rhythm of my heart. Unlike The Tap, this place is kept-up well—no chipped tile floors. No smoke lingering in the air. It's like stepping into the future.

We pass an alcove, and I peek in just long enough to catch a glimpse of a man making out with a woman wearing close to nothing. Another girl sits behind him, massaging his shoulders. I quickly look away, heat inflating my face and a sick feeling curling in the pit of my stomach.

"Holy Crawford," I say. "Don't people have any decency?"

"Welcome to Frankfort," Rain says. "We look like refined nobility on the outside, but under the skin, we're nothing but a bunch of desperate jackals." He offers a wicked grin. "We Patricians like to indulge ourselves, live life to the fullest. Y'know?" He winks. "Eat, drink, and be merry."

My gut clenches. I shouldn't be surprised that Rain mingles with this crowd, the way he drinks like a half-starved fish and has two women hanging off his arms eighty-percent of the time. And then I begin to wonder why, exactly, I came here.

We approach the bar, and I take a look around while Rain orders drinks. Girls wearing sheer garments dance on the stage. Waitresses dressed in transparent gowns serve drinks. They're all dolled up, their faces caked with make-up and their hair bleached. I scan the rest of the bar and gasp when I spot naked girls posing as statues. They change positions every once in a while, and everything is exposed. Everything. And my heart pounds and my face burns and I quickly look away.

"I thought people in Frankfort appreciated modesty," I say to Rain. "I guess I was wrong."

Rain hands me a drink. "They appreciate modesty for themselves, of course. Decency is always valued among

Patricians. But when it comes to entertainment, well, let's just say all their morals go down the drain."

I take a sip of the purple drink and wince. It's strong, but the fruity flavor makes it drinkable. One of the men sitting on a couch pulls a passing waitress onto his lap and kisses her, hard.

"So who are these dancers and waitresses and...statues?" I ask. "Patricians who didn't want to become politicians?"

"Proletariats."

I glance at him sharply. "You mean...these people didn't have a choice? This was the career forced on them?"

"Yep."

Shock. It's a strange little emotion that makes everything in the world freeze up. I have to set my drink down, before I drop it, because I'm so completely disgusted, disturbed, and...*angry*. These girls are slaves. No question about it. If they refused to entertain or dress like that, they'd be killed. What if I had been given a career as a dancer? What if I had to stand around, stark naked, still as a statue while snotty Patricians gawked at me? My stomach tightens into a ball.

"Why do you come here?" My voice comes out in a hoarse whisper. I clear my throat, look at Rain, and speak louder so he can hear me. "Why on earth would you come here?"

"It's the best place to collect the latest gossip." His grin reveals absolutely zero remorse. "Now, excuse me while I make my rounds." With two drinks in hand, he strides to the couches and passes one to a Patrician girl. His winning smile in place, he strikes up a conversation. The girl giggles and gestures for him to sit beside her.

I roll my eyes. Rain and his girls. Why did he bring me?

To torture me? This place is sick. Two people beside me start making out. I slip off my stool and turn toward the door. But two girls step in front of me. I recognize one of them as Cherry, the girl with dark curls who approached Rain at the ball.

"Miss Carter," Cherry says, her dark curls bouncing. She smells like sugar and fruit. "You've found where the real fun is at, huh?" She gestures toward the rest of the bar. "Welcome to paradise."

This is the complete opposite of paradise, is what I don't say.

"Rain brought me," I say flatly.

"Ah, lucky you." The other girl cocks a sculpted brow and gives me a once-over. "Rain's latest diversion."

"I'm not his *diversion*."

"Oh?" Cherry says. "Then why did he escort you to the ball? Surely you had your pick of the men in Frankfort?"

Why do I feel like they're sizing me up? "H-he's the only one who showed up at my door."

"He must have chased everyone else off before they could get their hands on you," the other girl says with a laugh. "Even now, he can't keep his eyes off of you."

I glance back. The girl Rain sits beside chats endlessly, but he's staring right at me, his eyes narrowed in thought. What's his shoddy deal?

"Maybe you could enlighten us on your little secret," Cherry says with a giggle.

"There's no secret." I turn back around. "Rain's the biggest rogue in this country. He'll go with just about any girl he can get."

"You mean any girl who gets *him*." Cherry's voice is laced with envy. "He may be the biggest rogue, but he's also the biggest mystery." She looks at him and leans in close.

"You see, Rain hasn't actually slept with anyone."

I jerk my head back. "Why would he? He's not married, is he?"

This brings a giggle out of both of them.

"You don't have to be married to sleep together, dear Ember," Cherry says. "People today only get married out of mere convenience or to promote themselves."

And I'm a little—actually a lot—shocked, because I've never heard of anyone marrying out of convenience or promotion.

"Sleeping around is a good form of recreation," Cherry's friend says. "If you meet a cute guy, why not enjoy an evening of pleasure?"

"Because...it's...intimate." I've never considered sleeping with anyone except the person I plan to marry. It was never an option in my head. It never even crossed my mind. And why, *why* would you sleep with multiple people? That's gross. It's—I scrunch up my nose, and now I feel sick.

A scream comes from across the room. I glance up in time to see a Patrician boy pinning one of the "statues" to the wall. She struggles beneath his weight, but he overpowers her as he gives into his desires. No one helps her. No one cares. In fact, others are crowding around, cheering. My blood runs cold, and I'm confused and enraged and disgusted and I find myself stumbling toward the girl, but someone grabs my arm.

"What are you doing?" Cherry asks.

"Someone needs to *help* her!" I jerk away from Cherry and push through the gawking, laughing crowd. I grab the shoulder of the boy and shove him aside, surprised by my own strength.

"Get *away* from her!" I scream.

He steps back, sweeps his gaze down the length of me, then stares at me with glazed, mocking eyes.

"If is isn't the famous Ember Carter, our newest Patrician sister," he says, grinning. "What's the problem, Miss?"

Everyone's staring now. The laughter has died down and they're waiting. They're listening to what I have to say. Swallowing hard, I turn back to face him.

"You…you were about to *rape* her."

He snorts. "Nonsense. Given a moment, she would have enjoyed it."

A wave of rage sweeps over me and my heart is pounding against my chest and I grab his shirt and shove *him* against the wall. But he only seems to enjoy the gesture.

"The new girl likes to play rough," he says, grinning at me. "Come on, vixen. Gimme a taste of my own medicine." His eyes shine while the others laugh and I want to punch him. I want to shatter that grin off his face. I want to—

"What the shoddy inferno's going on here?"

A hand on my shoulder pulls me out of blinding rage, and I release the boy, turn to face Rain, surprised to find concern instead of his usual smirk. And I'm trembling. I'm trembling from my anger. Rain stares at me a moment, then looks at those around us.

"Show's over, folks. Go about your business."

"Ah, but the fun's just begun, Rain," the boy I slammed against the wall says.

Rain rolls his eyes. "Go home, Brendan, before you puke all over your clothes again and cause a terribly embarrassing scene for yourself."

Brendan's eyes widen, and he mumbles something crude under his breath before stumbling away. The girl is kneeling by the wall, trembling violently. Rain places a hand on her shoulder. She stiffens, about to scream again, but he says something too quiet for me to hear, and she stills, nods, and calmly walks out of the room. Whatever Rain said seemed to have a more calming effect than anything I could have said. Seriously. How does he do that?

He turns toward me. "What the shoddy rot were you thinking?"

"I had to help her."

"By helping her, you just got her in worse trouble, you know that, right? Brendan's pride is shot. You just made his hunt to get what he wants more exciting. He'll be back again. He will look for her again. And next time, he won't let down."

I think I'm going to throw up. "And you're just going to let that happen?"

His jaw tightens. He looks at the floor. "I'll do something about the girl. For now, you should probably go. People are staring."

I glance around, reminded of the people who can't stop gaping because someone actually stood up for one of the statues. I guess they're not used to people being *nice*. "Why did you bring me here?" I turn to glare at Rain. "Why do *you* come here? This place is the worst kind of hell. And anyone who comes here willingly is worse than a diseased, maggot-infested dog. And that includes you, Rain Turner."

His eyes widen a fraction, almost like he's hurt, but before he can say another word, I whirl around and stumble through the crowd. I push through the gawking Patricians. I force myself to breathe.

Inhale. Exhale.

But everything is *not* okay.

I race out of the building and drag fresh air into my lungs. The cab driver gets out of his car and opens the door for me, but I wave him off and break into a sprint. I need to run my frustration off. I need to clear my thoughts. But running is nearly impossible with this ridiculous dress and these shoes. So I kick my shoes off, lift my overwhelming skirts, and bolt across the street.

A loud honk blares at me, and I leap out of the way just before the car almost hits me. Tears stinging my eyes, I run toward my hotel. I need to get out of Frankfort, like, yesterday. Everyone always talked about Frankfort, the golden city, the *utopia*, but I'm realizing now that this place is a nightmare. My own personal hell. A fire-breathing dragon.

And I need to get out before it eats me alive.

CHAPTER THIRTY-ONE

I can't sleep. Everything I saw at the club keeps me awake, my mind fully wired with disturbing thoughts. I was taught that the careers given us are to help better the country. We're all contributing to make Ky a better place. It's what always made Career Day almost acceptable. But after what I saw tonight, my suspicions are confirmed. Everything we do is for the Patricians. Girls getting selected to serve their careers in Frankfort as maids and dancers and nude wall statues? How is that making Ky a better place?

Why?

The question leaves my lips before I even know who I'm asking. But that pull, that powerful presence has filled every drop of the atmosphere, and I find myself asking again, out loud this time. "Why? Why are things so *wrong*? Why can't someone change it?" I open my eyes to the overwhelming darkness surrounding me and whisper, "Why won't you help?"

Thunder rolls overhead and chills flesh out across my skin. What is wrong with me? Why do I bother speaking to thin air? I flop over and bury my face in my pillow when more thunder rattles the windows. Frankfort may have controlled temperatures, but apparently, if you can't keep the sunlight from entering the cupola, you can't keep the rain out, either. It pounds against the window as lightning flashes across the sky and the windows are trembling in fear and then there's a BANG-BANG-BANGING coming from the living room.

I bolt upright. Wonder if I'm hearing things. And then, there it is again.

BANG-BANG-BANG-CRASH

Holy rot. My heart begins to pound and my legs and arms are lead, paralyzed by fear, but I force myself out of bed. I pull on my bathrobe and wrap it tightly around my body like a shield. Has Brendan come to do to me what he almost did to that girl? Has he come to get me back for humiliating him? My stomach turns inside out and I step out of the bedroom.

Darkness envelops the room, but another flash of lightning reveals an open window and curtains whipping wildly in the wind. The wind. It must have blown the window open. No way Brendan could have scaled a hundred-story wall. A sigh of relief and my heart beats at a normal rhythm. I cross the room, slam the window shut, and latch it, and it's once again silence inside my lonely apartment.

Until I hear the faint ringing of sirens. My heart takes a violent leap because they're the same sirens that chased me and Judah through the streets. The sirens grow louder, and then below, through the rain-streaked window, I can see the flashing red and white lights of the Defender Vehicles as they dart down the street—straight past Frankfort Hotel. Holy Crawford. They're not after me. I release another small breath.

All this excitement in Frankfort is going to seriously give me a heart attack. I shake away my fear, decide to ask for ear plugs first thing in the morning, and then remember that I'm leaving in the morning so I don't need earplugs. Because this time of night in the Garden, there's only complete silence.

I wrap my robe more tightly around my body and head back to my room, when someone grabs me and shoves me into the corner. I almost scream, but a strong, cold, wet hand clamps over my mouth.

"Quiet!" a gruff voice says. "I'm not here to hurt you." The voice of a man. Not Brendan's voice. "I'm going to release you now. Do I have your word that you won't scream?"

I swallow hard, then offer a quick nod, and he releases me.

"Very good," he says. "I just need a drink. Can I please have a drink?"

"Of-of course."

"Thank you." He steps back, and I can see his silhouette cross the room. He's tall and brawny and removes something from his belt, then a blue beam of light flashes across the room to the ceiling. Sparks fly everywhere, and I stifle a scream, press my body further into the corner, and watch in horror as he does the same thing to the corner of the kitchen. More sparks fly.

"Are those all the cameras in this room?" he asks.

The cameras. He shot out the shoddy cameras. What is he planning on doing to me with no cameras on us?

He pulls something else out of his pocket. I hear a click and brace myself for another spark of light but only see a small flame as he lights a candle on the kitchen bar.

"You can come out, little mouse." His voice is deep and oddly soothing. "I've no interest in harming you."

For some reason I don't quite understand, I believe him. I step out of the shadows and slowly approach the kitchen bar where he stands. I can see his features more clearly now in the flickering light of the candle. He wears a fedora over dark, curly hair. A thick beard covers half his face, dripping with rainwater. He has green eyes and a scar running from his left temple into his beard.

And all I can think is that I've seen that face I've seen that face I've seen that face—where on earth have I seen that face?

"It's good to finally meet you, Ember Carter." He stares at me.

"And who—who are you?"

"My name is Jonah Walker."

CHAPTER THIRTY-TWO

"W-walker?"

Holy Crawford. *That's* where I've seen him. On tablets passed around by Defenders. In the newspaper headlines. On Most Wanted posters all around the city. Jonah Walker. Dangerous criminal. Report if seen.

What few people know is that he's actually a leader of the Resurgence, which still makes him a criminal.

"I hope you don't mind hosting me for just a few minutes." He juts his thumb toward the window. "Shoddy Defenders are after me."

"H-how do you know I won't report you?"

"After my team helped you escape from that prison?" He looks at me, his eyes glowing emerald in the candlelight. "You would do that?"

"Th-that was *you*?"

"That wasn't me, but it was a member of my team."

"The Resurgence?"

He nods.

"Oh." They must have helped us escape because of Ash and Judah, two people who were a part of the Resurgence. Yet, I'm the only one who survived. How disappointed Jonah Walker must be. "I'm sorry more of your people didn't survive. I was fond of Judah."

He nods. Looks down. "Judah was a good man." He stuffs his pistol back into his belt.

I stare at the gun. I'm no expert, but I've seen enough of what the Defenders carry around. They hold big clunky black guns. But Walker's pistol is white, no larger than his hand, and it made no noise when he shot the cameras out.

"Where'd you get that?" I ask. Surely not from Titus.

"The Indy Tribe."

"The *who*?"

He turns to the fridge "You got anything to drink in here?"

"Um—" Before I can answer, he pulls out a bottle and sits on a barstool, rainwater still dripping off his coat. "Cheers," he says, and begins chugging his drink down.

"So…what are you doing here?" I ask.

"I told you. Hiding from *them*."

"I mean, what are you doing in *Frankfort*. You're wanted by Titus."

"Oh. Yeah. That." He rolls his eyes. "I'm visiting a family member."

A family member? "So, you're a Patrician?"

"You think I would have the free will to work against the government if I wasn't?" He laughs out loud, a deep sound resembling the thunder outside. "No one can control me. *No one*." He takes another drink, sets his bottle down, studies me in the dim light of the candle. "Holy Crawford you

266

look so much like her."

"Like who?"

"How does it feel, by the way?" He ignores my question. "Rising from the place of a Proletariat to a Patrician?"

"Not too different. Should I feel different?"

"Well, you can communicate with black tigers, yes? That's kind of a big deal. Can you command the Proletariat, too?"

"Command the Proletariat?" What on earth is he talking about?

"You know. Like the Patricians do."

"Why would I *want* to?"

"Same reason they do." He shrugs. "Power."

"That's not really...a good reason."

He stares at me and smiles a strange smile. "Ember Carter, you do not disappoint." He lifts his bottle in salute, then chugs down the rest of his drink.

And I watch him. A dozen questions filter through my mind, and I struggle to pick just one that's appropriate to ask right now, when a tap sounds at the window.

"Ah. My comrades."

His *what*?

He strides to the window and opens it. Thunder rolls overhead, accompanied by more lightning and pounding rain. Two girls and three boys climb into the room, all dressed up in thick coats, gloves, and heavy hats. I almost forgot it's winter in the rest of Ky. They pull a black rope in after them, then disconnect it from their belts.

Jonah Walker closes the window behind them and pulls the drapes shut. "Drinks in the fridge."

"Coffee?" a boy with thick-rimmed glasses asks.

"This is Frankfort. I'm sure there's some in there."

He hurries into the kitchen, the others behind. They start making themselves at home, dishing up food from the fridge and pouring drinks, and I really, honestly don't mind. Because there was no way I could have eaten all this food by myself, so it's good to know it won't be wasted.

I study the others, and my eyes are drawn to one of the girls. Strong build. Dark, dark skin. Looks like a lioness. And I gasp. "Ash?"

She looks up from a sandwich she was just about to chomp into and grins widely. "Hey there, Thirteen."

I grin at the use of my prison nickname, as short-lived as it was.

"You—you're *alive*?" I ask.

She looks down at her body as though seeing it for the first time, then looks at me. "It would appear so."

"I thought—I thought—the tigers—"

"Nope. Tigers didn't get me." She winks. "I'm fast and parted from the group before they got to me."

My heart lifts. I just wish Judah and I were smart enough to part ways. If I wasn't there to slow him down, he might have gotten away, too.

I watch the others as they dig into their food. Their clothes are dripping with rain water, their hair matted down, and they look famished.

"So, are you all the Resurgence?"

"Just a small part," Walker says. "We call these brave young souls the Fearless Five. Allow me to introduce Isaac, Levi, Digory, Kate, and of course you know Ash." I nod at them. Levi, the one with glasses who asked for coffee, pours dark granules into a machine. Digory is lanky with red, red hair. I didn't even think hair could grow that color. Isaac is

268

tall and well-built, and Kate is about my height. Her belt is packed full of weapons. I don't think I would ever want to get on her bad side.

"And comrades," Walker says. "This is the living legend. The newest Patrician Sister. Miss Ember Carter."

Kate smirks. "How does it feel to rise above your own kinsmen, Carter?" She takes in my white plush robe. "Enjoying the luxuries of Frankfort, I see."

I look at my robe. "This isn't—I don't usually—" I clamp my mouth shut, shame burning my face to my hairline. "I actually kind of hate it here."

"Good," Isaac mumbles. "Because Frankfort will only destroy you."

"Are you all here to visit family, then?" I try to sound as casual as they act.

"Are you kidding?" Levi, the one with glasses, says while he stares at the machine that's now pouring black liquid into a glass pitcher. He seems like the brains of the bunch. "Walker here is the only one who is Patrician-born. We've just come to help do the dirty work."

"What dirty work?"

Levi looks at me, opens his mouth to respond, but Walker cuts him off.

"We're here to recruit you."

CHAPTER THIRTY-THREE

I blink. "Huh?"

Walker grins. "We want you, Ember Carter, to work with us."

"Y-you want *me*? To work with the—the *Resurgence*?"

"Yes."

I glance at the others. They all seem to pause their eating, all looking at me expectantly, waiting for an answer, and I'm reminded at how much I hate being put on the spot.

"Um. Wh-why do you want...*me*?"

"You're a fighter," Walker says. "Ash told us all about your courage, your speedy stealth, the way you're not afraid to stand up to Patricians and plan suicidal escapes. We need someone with your courage and, um, *un*brainlessness on our side. We want you to help us take down the chief."

Holy Crawford. Jonah Walker wants *me* to help the Resurgence take down the chief. Just to speak of such things is treason. And kind of thrilling.

But, also impulsive.

Because I'm leaving tomorrow. I'm finally going home. But if I choose to work with rebels, my picture will be hanging right up there with Walker's, and I'll never be free to go home again. I won't be able to resume my work as a farmer. I mean, will I even see Dad or Elijah again?

"I-I don't think I can do that."

The others resume eating, some rolling their eyes.

"See?" Isaac says to Walker. "I told you she wouldn't be up for it." He shoots me a glare. "She's too *scared*."

I almost snap that I'm not scared, but then decide that he might be right. I am afraid. I'm afraid of dying. Terrified, really. So, yeah, Isaac's absolutely right. I look at Walker and shrug.

He stares at me. Releases a heavy sigh, the kind I'd hear when I'd disappointed Dad. "Why not?"

"I'm going home tomorrow and I don't want to die."

"Okay. But what if I told you you're *not* going to die, and that you'll get to see your family again once all this blows over?"

"I mean, how can you be sure?"

"I can't."

"Then...no." I shake my head and look down at my hands. "I really just want to go home. I want to live a normal life. I already faced death and didn't like it. So unless you can one-hundred percent guarantee that I'll live through this, I don't want to join your little army."

He presses his lips firmly together and he doesn't really look as happy as he did when he first entered the room. He looks almost...devastated.

"Wait," I say. "You didn't...you didn't come all the way to Frankfort just to talk me into joining you guys, did you?"

"Don't flatter yourself," Kate says as she scrapes the bottom of her bowl. "You're just a side project Walker insisted on taking on. We all tried to talk him out of it, but he wouldn't let up."

Now I really feel guilty. And I don't understand why, exactly, Walker believes in me so much that he would go out of his way to try and convince me to join them. I'm nobody.

He stares at me long and hard, then says, "You'll change your mind." He looks at the others. "Finish up your food, kids. It won't be long before the Defenders know we're here." He swivels his eyes to the broken cameras, and the others chug down their drinks and finish off their food. They stuff more food into their pockets and begin making their way to the door. Except Levi.

"Hurry *up*, Levi," Isaac says in obvious annoyance.

"I'm hurrying. Just hang on." Levi fumbles through the cupboards until he finds a large thick cup with a lid, and he pours the black liquid into it, the whole time mumbling, "Holy Crawford, it's been so long. I've gone way too long without coffee." And then he seals the lid onto the cup, takes the entire bag of granules, stuffs it into his coat pocket, and joins the others by the door.

"Thanks for the food," Digory, the boy with red hair says as he opens the door. He's about to walk out, then hesitates. "And thanks for not sounding the alarm."

"*Should* I sound the alarm?"

Digory's brows flicker as he stares at me for a moment. "Depends. Whose side are you on?"

What kind of question is that? I was only recently informed that there were two sides, and I don't know anything about the Resurgence side, other than Jonah Walker

273

is their leader and they want to assassinate Titus. And so far, Titus has been kind of nice to me so...

"I—I don't know," I finally say.

"Well, you might want to figure it out." Digory grins a boyish grin. "There are going to be questions, now that you're straddling the Proletariat and the Patrician line. Are you for us—the Resurgence—or are you for Chief Whitcomb?"

Chief Whitcomb? His smiling eyes flash through my mind. His warm welcome, the way he let me go home, no problem. Before I can answer, Digory is out the door.

Walker pauses at the door. "We really do appreciate your hospitality, Ember." He looks at me, I mean, really looks at me, studying every feature of my face, my eyes, my nose, my mouth, then says. "It's unbelievable how much you look like her."

"Like *who*?"

"Your mother." He shakes his head in disbelief, and rests his hand on my shoulder. "I really truly wish you would come with us, but I understand your fear. You're still young. Think about my offer. I *will* come back for you. That's a promise." And he disappears into the hallway with the others, leaving me in a haze of eleven-thousand questions, like how in the shoddy inferno did Walker know my mom and why does he want me to join him?

I close the door. It seems too quiet all of a sudden. Like I just hosted a party and now am left to clean up the mess. Alone. The silence of the room is almost deafening against the questions screaming in my head, begging for answers. But no one seems to be eager to explain themselves around here, and I'm left in a haze, clueless and ignorant of everything.

So I return to bed. I close my eyes. I try to clear my

mind.

But I can't sleep. Outside, more sirens wail past. I pull my comforter tighter around my body and close my eyes. Listening to the rain beat against the glass reminds me of home, when it beat against our roof in the Garden. Thunderstorms always remind me of Mom. Elijah would get scared of the thunder and lightning, and Mom would sing, her humming merging with the sound of the thunder, and suddenly storms weren't so scary anymore. I remember her singing lullabies to me at night, combing her fingers through my hair, her soothing voice washing over me.

Follow me, little one, to land of ashes
Where death has its hold so it seems
Where rivers flow free and the water washes
Back the control of the supremes

Tunnels run deep by the northern line
When you follow the emerald eyes
Hidden beneath a blanket of vines
Is a place where our only hope lies

Emerald eyes.

Like Jonah's eyes.

And now *my* eyes fly open. This song is no lullaby. This is a riddle. It's a song of the Resurgence.

Emerald eyes, that's gotta be Jonah Walker. And the northern line is the Ohio River, since that's the river by Louisville, where Judah hinted the Resurgence was located. *Where death has its hold, so it seems.* Louisville is known to be completely abandoned. The dead city. The ashen city, as most

275

people call it. Because half of it's been burned to the ground.

...*the land of ashes*...

Holy Crawford, how am I just now realizing this? And how did Mom know this song? Did *she* know it was a riddle? *Is* it a riddle? Or am I just making that up? Ugh...I doesn't matter. Because I'm *never* going there.

When I finally fall asleep, dreams of green eyes dance through my mind. I dream that I'm in Leaf's cabin in the Community Garden. Darkness of night envelops the outside world, and rain pounds on the windows and roof. Everyone is there. Dad, Mom, Elijah, Leaf, and even Jonah and his comrades. We're all sitting on the floor, the faint candlelight illuminating a map of Louisville.

Footsteps sound outside our door and someone shouts, "Defenders of the Peace. Everyone come out with your hands up."

Walker rolls up the map. Mom blows out the candle.

"Come on," Leaf says. He takes my hand and leads me to the back window where rain splatters against the pane. More shouts from outside, then the door breaks in.

"We have to go back," I say to Leaf.

Leaf turns to look at me. Except this time it's not Leaf. It's Judah. His dark eyes shine in the faint glow of the moonlight. "Whose side are you on?"

A clap of thunder jolts me awake. Lightning flashes across the sky. But Judah's whispers still ring in my ears, as though he were here.

Whose side are you on?

CHAPTER THIRTY-FOUR

I'm going home today. That's the first thought that enters my mind when I wake up, and I grin.

LeighAnn and River arrive shortly after I'm awake. They help me get ready, despite my insistence that I've been getting ready on my own for sixteen years and can still do it alone, thank-you-very-much. I guess they have their careers, just like I'll have mine.

I expect the clothes they give me to be the normal farmers uniform—white wool shirt, brown cotton pants, rubber boots. But they pack the farmers uniform in a suitcase and dress me in an emerald toga fit for a Patrician. It's simple, easy to adjust and put on, but looks so elaborate. I feel like I should be attending another ball, not returning to the Community Garden. They insist on makeup, but I decline. I don't want to look completely Patrician when I return. I want to look myself.

A jeep is already waiting for me when we exit the hotel.

Forest stands beside it, his hands shoved into his pockets. Well. This is a surprise.

Gripping my handbag, I walk toward him. "Shouldn't you be spending the morning with Olivia?"

"You shouldn't go back to the orchard."

I stop. "Why not?"

"Because you haven't found out your whole history yet. Aren't you interested in why you're a Patrician?"

I heave out a sigh and open the jeep door. "I don't really care. I'm sure my dad will tell me if I ask."

"Ember." Forest's voice is low and he touches my arm.

I pull away. "Yes?" I don't look at him.

"Stay."

Now I look at him. "Why?"

"Because Chief Whitcomb is letting you go too easily, and I'm afraid—I'm afraid he might have something else planned. Something dangerous."

"Chief Whitcomb is nicer than I ever gave him credit for. He didn't have a single problem with me leaving. I didn't even have to fight him. I really think you're overthinking everything."

He releases a sigh. Runs a hand through his shaggy blond hair. Looks past me in thought. Then looks right at me. "I think...someone went behind Chief Whitcomb's back, and that's why you're a Patrician. Someone slipped you the antitoxin. The only type of person who would go behind the chief is a spy from the Resurgence. And if you've been working with spies—"

"You think I'm a *spy*? That I'm working with *them*? I'd never even *heard* of them until—"

"Leaf."

"Yes." My voice is a husky whisper at the memory of

278

Leaf. I swallow hard, shove the memory of Leaf back into the deepest compartment of my mind. "For your information, Chief Whitcomb wasn't the least bit angry about my leaving. In fact, I think I've won him over." I offer a winning smile, the same one I used for Titus when I asked to leave. "Your brother is a very good teacher in Frankfort etiquette. Thanks to him, I know how to talk to your kind of people."

He narrows his eyes. "Yes, your smile is very charming, and you acted boldly last night. Very Patrician of you."

Something deflates in my chest at the way he calls me *Patrician*.

"But Chief Whitcomb doesn't care about charm," Forest says. "You think you've won him over, but..." He rubs the back of his neck and looks away.

"But what?"

He studies me. "You think it's really that easy? Resurgence spies were seen in Frankfort last night. They were last seen close to the Frankfort Hotel."

My heart pounds. "And?"

"And your cameras were reported as dysfunctional around that same time."

Oh. Right. I bite my lip and look away.

"Do you know anything about that, Ember?" he asks. "Did you speak to anyone? Did you...have any visitors last night?"

I stare at the ground. And I'm wondering if I can trust Forest, if I can tell him everything and believe he's going to just keep it a secret from Titus, but then I remember how he said he and Titus were friends and he's known Titus far longer than he's known me, so, no. Of course I can't trust him.

"I...didn't have any...visitors." I look at him now; the lie comes easier with every word that tumbles out of my mouth. "If anyone visited my apartment, I slept right through it."

"And when you woke up, there wasn't any evidence that someone had broken into your apartment?"

"Um..."

"I'm asking you, because right now, at this very moment, Defenders are scouting out your room. And if they find evidence that someone was there—other than you—this is your chance to come clean. Tell me right now exactly what happened."

What a mess what a mess what a mess. "The window was open when I woke up. I thought the wind blew it open." That part, at least, is true. Mostly.

Forest stares at me a moment longer than necessary, then sighs and says. "I believe you."

Guilt might be even worse than the feeling of disappointment.

"But I'm not entirely sure Whitcomb will believe you," he says. "You see, the whole thing looks suspicious. And I don't think Whitcomb is just going to let you go after last night."

"But...the cab. He sent this cab. So he must be okay with it."

"Yes." Forest nods. "He had the cab scheduled to pick you up before spies were found in the city. I don't know how far you'll get before he stops you, though. But if he lets you go home, that might be worse. Because that would mean he's automatically pegging you a criminal. And Titus is very good at making bad things looks like accidents."

"What do you mean?"

"I mean, something bad might happen to you, and no one will even suspect it was Chief Whitcomb who made it happen."

"And you know this because...?"

"I'm a part of his...inner circle."

"And you've done nothing to stop these bad things from happening."

His mouth clamps shut, and I have my answer, though it's not the answer I wanted. If he's a part of Titus's inner circle, then he is most likely working for Titus. Nope nope nope. I definitely can't trust him at all. Why is he trying to convince me to hang around?

"I'm sorry, Forest," I say. "But Patrician or not, I'm not Frankfort material, and I couldn't take another day here if I were ordered to. You should go back to your fiancée and forget about me. I'm not staying here. I don't want to get in the middle of—" I wave my hand in the air. "Whatever is going on between Whitcomb and the Resurgence." I sigh and look away. "I just want to go home and live life the way it was before."

"That's just the thing, Ember." He steps closer and brushes a loose strand of hair behind my ear, then his warm fingers slide down my neck, and I have to catch my breath because the heady scent of cinnamon fills the space between us. "Your life will never be the same," he whispers. "Not if you leave now." He tips my chin up and I'm drowning in the ocean of his blue eyes. "But if you stay until after they figure everything out— long enough for Titus to trust you—you may have a chance to have your old life back."

His hand lingers on my chin. I close my eyes and take a shaky breath, try to focus. He seems so honest, so caring, and maybe it's because he's been my one constant since leaving the Garden, but I feel so safe in his presence.

But he's engaged. To Olivia.

I swat his hand away. "So long, Congressman Turner." I offer a brittle smile, then add the formal "May you live a good, prosperous life" in a neat, Patrician accent, and I enter the vehicle, slamming the door behind me.

The jeep veers down the street. Time to move on with my life, leave Forest with his beloved Olivia, who is way more fit to be with him than I will ever be.

And I think of home. Of Elijah and Dad waiting for me. Has the first week of winter been kind? I imagine the apple orchard with a fresh layer of snow covering the field.

We whir through the city, through the tall, glorious buildings stretching hundreds of stories high. The palm trees billow in the breeze. The jeep takes a series of turns until we're finally out of the confining skyscrapers. Ahead, I see life on the other side of the cupola. A white layer of snow blankets the ground, but I couldn't imagine a warmer welcome from this lukewarm inferno I've been living in.

The jeep slows at the edge of the cupola and stops at the gate. The driver rolls down the window as a Defender walks toward us. I recognize him. Tall, muscular, dark skin. Young. Captain Mcallister. Worms coil in the pit of my stomach.

"The city has been shut down," Mcallister says to the driver. "There will be no traffic through the cupola for another day or two."

"Shut down?" I ask from the back seat. I roll down my window, which only goes down a few inches, and look at Mcallister. *Patrician. Act the role of Patrician,* I can almost hear Rain say.

I lift a Patrician brow. "And why has it been shut down,

Mcallister?"

He looks at me, his dark eyes holding a hint of amusement. Then he locks his arms behind his back and steps closer to my window, bends down so we're eye level, and now my heart is beating a bit too fast for comfort.

"Rebels have been spotted inside the cupola."

My heart rate skyrockets. "Oh." Feign surprise. "That is terrible news."

He narrow his eyes, straightens, then looks at the driver. "You've orders to return the *princess* back to her quarters."

I roll my eyes at his mocking tone.

"Yes sir," the driver says.

"But Mcallister—"

Mcallister holds up his hand, cutting me off. "Consider this an extended welcome from the chief." He smiles, then he turns and marches back to his vehicle by the gate.

Oh, rot. I don't want to go back. I *can't* go back. I try opening the door, but it's locked. Of course it is. The driver continues down the street and makes a U-turn back to the hotel. I grit my teeth and lean back, crossing my arms over my chest. I should have known Titus wouldn't be that lenient. Forest warned me. I clench my hands into fists. This was not supposed to happen. I don't care about the festive celebrations. I don't care why or how I became Patrician. And why do I have to pay for the price of the Resurgencies? I'm clearly not one of them, so why can't they just let *me* out?

The answer forms in my head before I finish the question. It's because the rebels came into my apartment. It's because they shot out my cameras.

It's because I didn't sound the alarm when I should have.

Now, no thanks to Jonah Walker and his posse of rebels, I'm in worse trouble than I was before.

We arrive at the hotel, and two Defenders escort me back to my room. "We will stay outside the door, miss." They close the door behind them as they walk out.

Well, rot. I was *this* close to going home, and now…now I'm a prisoner again. Thanks, Walker. Thanks a lot. You saved my life, I saved yours, and now you owe me one.

Pacing back and forth, I try to think of another escape. I could sneak out the window, but I don't have the tools Walker had to scale a hundred-story building. I can't ask for any help— Forest is too loyal to Titus, and Rain would laugh in my face.

Think think think.

I stop pacing and take a deep breath, glancing around my room for the first time since I returned. Someone has cleaned it while I was gone, made the bed, opened the drapes, wiped off the table where I ate breakfast. Sunlight streams into the living room. I walk to the large window and survey the city. Even if I did somehow manage to escape the hotel, it would take a full day just to get out of Frankfort and another full day to travel to the Community Garden. I wouldn't get far before the Defenders caught me.

This toga is uncomfortable, so I strip it off and put on the familiar farmers uniform from my satchel, only these are new, the fabric still stiff, the wool scratchy. Not as comfortable as I'd anticipated, but I keep them on anyway out of pure rebellion. Then I sit on the couch, pull my knees to my chin, and chew my thumbnail while I think some more.

Someone knocks at the door, then opens it before I have a chance to cross the room. Captain James Mcallister walks in, six Defenders on his heels.

I leap to my feet. "Are you going to let me go?"

He looks at me and offers a no-nonsense smile. "Miss Carter, we have a few questions for you, if you have the time."

My heart plummets into my gut. "Time? That's all I've got in this shoddy place."

Mcallister nods at his men, and they take their places around the living room. I wonder how Mcallister could have such a commanding presence when he's twenty years younger than the Defenders he's ordering.

"Please," Mcallister says, gesturing toward the couch. "Have a seat."

I cross the room and plop into the couch. "What's the problem?"

"Like I already informed you, revolutionary spies were found in the city last night." His lips tip down in a deep frown. "They were last seen nearing Frankfort Hotel."

"Oh." This again. I begin to roll my eyes, then see the look on Mcallister's face. So I straighten and feign shock. "That's terrible. Are they still on the run?"

He regards me through narrowed eyes. "Your cameras were shot out last night."

Heat rushes to my face, and I glance away. "I...I didn't notice." I look at the place where the cameras used to be. *Didn't notice?* Who couldn't notice two gaping black holes in their ceilings?

Mcallister seems to be thinking the same thing as he studies me carefully. "So...you claim to have nothing to do with their escape?"

"Correct." I stick to the lie I told Forest. "That...that is correct."

"Very good." He heaves out a heavy sigh, then slaps his hands on his knees and rises. "I'll let Chief Whitcomb know. Until then, two Defenders are ordered to stay by your side. No leaving Frankfort city limits, understand?"

"*Never?*"

"Not until your name is cleared." He snaps his fingers and the other Defenders follow. "After more investigation, Miss Carter, we'll decide for sure whether you're innocent, or working with revolutionaries."

He strides out, closing the door behind him. Well, at least I don't have to go to prison. I'd rather spend my captivity in this plush hotel than in the dungeon. Still, captivity is captivity. I sink back into the couch and drag my hand across my face. I was so close to getting home.

So close.

What am I supposed to do the rest of the day?

I pick the celebration schedule of the week off the coffee table. A lunch is supposed to take place in the Commons. Wherever that is. I don't want to see anyone. Especially not Forest or Rain. How they would laugh at me now. Poor little farmer couldn't go home because she helped the resurgencies escape.

Tossing the schedule back onto the table, I stand, walk to the window, and look once more at the city. The tall buildings make me claustrophobic. I miss the wide open spaces, the fresh air, the whipping wind and the giant sun. The *real* sun. My heart stirs with longing, and I do the only thing I can think of that will make me feel closer to home. I pull out a fresh, large canvas and paint my home the way I remember it.

A little cabin on the brown dirt road, a rundown wooden mailbox, leaning ever so slightly at the entrance pathway, weeds growing all around the base. Apple trees rise behind the cabin, hills and hills of them. Lush red apples grow from the shimmering green leaves. And in the background, way, way far back, stand the tiny buildings of Ky. Far enough away that I feel safe.

And the sky. A sea of blue stretching high above the Community Garden, vast, broad, and *real*. Nothing like the fake sky and fake weather controlled by Frankfort.

This orchard is my home. This is where I belong. Once all this Patrician and spy stuff has blown over, I will go back.

I will.

And THAT is what keeps me going.

CHAPTER THIRTY-FIVE

Not long after I finish the painting, someone knocks at the door.

"Come in."

I brace myself, ready for more Defenders to march in for questioning, but Rain steps in.

"Oh. It's you." I remember the club last night and turn back to my painting, wishing he would leave.

"Don't sound so excited," Rain says.

Ignoring him, I dip my brush into the paint.

"Heard you couldn't get back to Kansas."

"Kansas?" I look at him. "What's that?"

"Inside joke."

"Inside. Like something only you Patricians would understand." I grit my teeth. Rain is full of strange idioms.

"You're Patrician now." He steps up to the window, blocking my view of the city. "It's time you learn everything we know. For example, Titus not letting you go home so easily."

Oh, so he came here to gloat. I keep my eyes fixed on my painting and fill in the soft, blue color of the sky.

"Hate to say I told you so," he continues.

Hmm. I think I should use a darker shade for the sky.

"What? You're ignoring me now?"

"Unless you have something worthwhile to say."

He sighs. "If this is about the club last night, I'm sorry. I was hoping you'd get a chance to enjoy yourself for once, but I see I was wrong. You're too stiff to enjoy anything."

"Enjoy myself?" I look at him now. "Girls, like me, who had no other choice but to follow their degrading career, were viewed as nothing more than decorative objects to be *used!*"

His Adam's apple bobs in a hard swallow. "I'm sorry." He says the words so quietly, I'm not sure he really spoke them. He looks at the floor, juts his jaw out, then looks at me again. And his eyes aren't mocking. There's nothing arrogant in his expression. "I really, truly am sorry, Ember." His voice is gentle, almost sincere. And the way he says my name chips at the walls around my heart a little. "And just for the record, that girl is safe now."

"How?"

"She just is. That's all you need to know."

I don't know why, but I somehow believe him. I look down at my hands. "Why are you here?"

"I came here to escort you to lunch."

The thought of surrounding myself with Patricians again makes my stomach squeeze. "I don't want to go to lunch."

He smirks, all forms of regret and compassion vanishing from his features. "You'll go."

"No. I won't."

"Have you already forgotten? Chief Whitcomb will be insulted if you refuse to attend the holiday picnic."

Chief Whitcomb. Everything is about Chief Whitcomb. And since he stopped me from going home, I'm beginning to hate him again.

"I'm not going." I stare at Rain, determined to hold my ground.

His eyes harden and he suddenly looks angry, and Angry Rain is not a species to cross. He steps toward me and I automatically flinch.

"Ember Carter," he says quietly, as to a child. "You'll go to lunch, if I have to carry you out of here myself."

The look in his eyes tells me he means every word, and I break.

"I—I'm not ready," I squeak.

His eyes roam down my farmers uniform, then linger on my paint-stained hands. He frowns, as though just now realizing what I'm doing, then steps around and looks at my painting. "I didn't know you painted." All form of anger has left his voice, replaced with genuine curiosity. "Where did you learn to paint?"

Heat rises to my cheeks, because I know I'm not very good. I haven't had private lessons like the elite painters I've seen. "I'll go clean up."

I wonder why River and LeighAnn haven't come to prepare me, but then I figure it's another one of Titus's ways to get back at me. No matter. I'd rather get ready on my own. I just wish they were here for moral support against Rain.

After scrubbing my hands, I hurry into my room and strip off my farmers uniform, then I open the closet full of gowns. So many gowns and togas. Some for the ballroom dances like last night, others for evening dinners. But which one is appropriate for a picnic? I leaf through them. Maybe I should put my green toga back on. It's fancy enough, but not as fancy as the evening gowns.

I pull on the toga, run my fingers through my hair, and exit the room.

"You're wearing *that?*" Rain asks.

"Um, yes?"

He scrunches his nose, then shakes his head. "No. You're not." Taking my arm, he practically drags me back into the bedroom. "Where are your maids?"

"*LeighAnn* and *River* think I've left for home."

"Figures." When we enter the bedroom, he releases me and walks to the closet. It doesn't take long for him to pull out a pretty yellow dress with simple shoulder straps. It flares out slightly at the waist and has a white braided belt. Nothing like a dress to wear in winter time, but then, it's never winter in Frankfort. "This will do for the picnic. Now take that ridiculous toga off and put on something more fitting for a late summer lunch." He tosses me the dress and stalks out of the room.

I pull the simple dress over my head and slip my arms through each strap, but when I reach back to do the buttons, I only get halfway up my back. No wonder LeighAnn always insisted on helping me. These dresses are impossible.

"Are you ready yet?" Rain calls impatiently from outside my door.

I grit my teeth. "Not yet." My fingers fiddle with the button halfway up my back. My hand cramps up and I have to take a break. I bite my tongue. There's only one thing I can do, even though my conscience is screaming at me not to do it.

292

"Rain," I call in a flat voice.

"Yep?"

"I need…help."

He doesn't miss a beat before he opens the door and strides in. "What's the problem? We're *late*."

"I can't button up this ridiculous dress." Peeking up at him, I feel heat rise into my neck and settle in my cheeks. "Can you help me?"

His eyes light with a hint of humor and he smirks. "Of course."

I turn to face the window, listening to his footsteps cross the floor behind me. His hands are warm as he gently combs my hair to one side and lays it over my shoulder. His fingers graze my neck and an electric current pulses through my bloodstream. Then he slowly buttons up the dress. I feel his breath on my neck, smell the peppermint, and a strange warmth floods through me, pooling in the pit of my stomach. I let out a soft breath I didn't realize I was holding.

When he snaps the top button, he takes both of my shoulders in his hands and turns me to face him. And I suddenly can't breathe, can't think, can't determine why I feel so vulnerable around him.

And then he tips my chin up until our eyes meet. For a moment I'm lost there, in the gray mystery of his eyes. I never realized how deep his eyes were, how they look more like gray storm clouds specked with silver. And he's searching my eyes, and he steps closer until his peppermint breath tickles my nose and butterflies take flight in my stomach. Emotions that were once disgust and hatred have somehow evolved to something else, something I don't understand. Something I loathe to admit.

And the energy is charged between us.

"You look beautiful, Rainbow Eyes." The way he looks at me makes me almost believe him. But then his lips quirk up into a mocking smile and he says, "Like a Patrician, even." And the moment shared between us completely vanishes. "Are you going to put on make-up?" He picks up a light white sweater and helps me shrug it on.

"I don't want to wear make-up."

"Good. Because we're already late."

The Defenders are still outside when we exit the room. Rain looks at them and says, "I can take her from here. I'll deliver her back to you safe and sound after the picnic." He leads me down the hall to the elevator.

"You have a lot of confidence speaking to the Defenders like that."

"My father is one of the highest politicians in Ky. My brother is in Titus's inner circle. And I've been offered the position as a Captain of Defenders." He looks down at me and smirks. "I guess you could say my confidence derives from the authority given to me by my station."

A jeep is waiting for us outside.

"Isn't the park just down the street?" I ask.

"Two blocks down."

"Can we walk?"

He looks at me like I suggested crossing the line into White Plague Territory. But then he shrugs. "Sure. Why not?"

After telling the driver what we're doing, I link my arm through Rain's, and we're off again.

"So do you accept my apology?" Rain asks. "For taking you to the club?"

The reminder of the club irritates me. "You could earn your forgiveness a lot sooner if you answer some questions for me."

"What kind of questions?"

I look up at him. "What's the history?"

"History? Of Ky?"

"Holy Crawford, no. I've had Ky history beat into my head at school. I mean the Patrician history. Why is it such a big deal that I'm Patrician? And you mentioned something about an antitoxin."

"Oh, rot." He throws his head back in defeat and groans. "I should have known this was your way of trapping me. No cameras around, so you think I'll answer your questions." He looks at me and narrows his eyes. "Sneaky girl. Fine. Now, where to start...."

We cross the road. One more block left. I slow my pace to give him more time to talk.

He must notice, because his lips disappear entirely in obvious irritation. "All right. Fine. Basically, over a hundred years ago, when the White Plague was spreading way out of control, twelve of the best scientists in the country got together and came up with some sort of cure. Well, not really a cure. An antitoxin to save themselves from the White Plague."

"Wait," I say, stopping. "So, the government doesn't have resources to give medicine to the Proletariats, but they have an *antitoxin*?"

Rain stares at me. "Yes." His jaw clenches. He resumes walking, and all I can do is walk beside him and absorb all this information he's cramming into my head. "After the scientists created the antitoxin, they gathered up what was left of the healthy population and corralled them into Ky, then blocked off the White Plagued by blowing up all the bridges that crossed the Three Rivers."

"The plagued couldn't swim?"

"No. Too weak, their brain cells too far gone. The scientists also selected twelve politicians and one leader, Quentin Whitcomb, Titus's great grandfather, to help run the country."

I remember the statue I saw in the Capitol Building with the name *Quentin Whitcomb* engraved at the base.

"To keep the politicians safe," Rain continues, "They offered them and their families the antitoxin as well. But since the rest of the city was considered safe from the White Plague, they chose not to distribute the antitoxin to anyone else except those who could afford it."

"Why not give it to everyone? Wouldn't it be a good idea to take precautions?"

"Because it's very expensive to make, little apple picker, and they certainly didn't have the resources back then, when the entire country fell to its ruins. Now it's pointless to distribute to everyone, because, well, we've all been safe from the plague the past hundred years."

"But they still give it to the rich people?"

"Mm. No. The antitoxin sort of becomes a part of your blood. You can pass it on to your children through your genes."

"Oh. So...Patrician isn't so much as a title of the rich, as it is a marking of the antitoxin in your blood."

"Exactly."

"So, do they still have an antitoxin stored up somewhere? Or do they make it on demand? I mean, it seems like they should have a whole lab full of vials in case another outbreak occurs."

"Now you're thinking like a politician." He grins. "But

honestly, I have no idea if they have some stored up. You see, I'm not a politician, and don't have access to that information."

"Does Forest know?"

"You should ask him. Though I doubt he'll tell you. That sort of information is classified, and one could get in trouble for sharing it."

So, the politicians keep some things even from the rest of the Patricians. Interesting. I guess I thought they were all a part of the same loop.

I have a dozen more questions about the antitoxin, but we've arrived at the park, and listening ears are everywhere. As we cross the street, I catch a glimpse of something racing in our direction. Something big and dark with variegated stripes and I realize it's a black tiger.

And it's leaping straight toward us.

CHAPTER THIRTY-SIX

I freeze. My heart forgets how to beat, then begins pounding twice as fast. I might be having another nightmare but I'm not sure, so I tighten my grip on Rain's arm. He looks down at me, then back ahead, and steps in front of me, as though to protect me. The tiger slows to a stop right in front of him. Rain squats down on one knee and scratches the beast behind the ears like it's some sort of kitten.

An older butler comes jogging behind the tiger. "Sorry, sir. I tried to tie him on the leash, but he was too fast when he saw you arrive."

"It's fine, Jeff. I can take him from here." Rain looks back at me. "I would like to introduce you to Julius."

"J-Julius?" I place my hand on my heart, trying to calm the wild thump.

Rain grins and moves aside, revealing the black tiger wearing a gold collar. "Go ahead and pet him. He won't bite." He winks. "He especially warms up to beautiful

Patricians."

Breathe. Remember to breathe. But don't take a step near the beast. "D-do you just take it everywhere with you so you can see who's Patrician and who's not?" I hate that my voice cracks.

He stands. "I saved him. His back leg was chopped off by one of the prisoners three years ago."

I glance at the tiger. Sure enough—only three legs. Good. Maybe I'll have a chance to outrun him if he ever decides to attack me.

"They were going to put him down," Rain says. "But, I didn't see a reason for him to go. It's not like he did anything wrong."

"Except kill people."

He looks at me, his gaze hardening. "Criminals. He followed orders. The same way Defenders follow orders."

"The way they followed orders to kill Leaf."

Rain closes his eyes and takes a deep breath. When he opens them again, I think—I *think*—I catch a glimpse of empathy.

"Forget it," he says. "Julius is nothing like a Defender." He turns abruptly and merges into the crowd, Julius at his heels. I hurry to catch up and link my arm through his, careful to keep a distance between myself and the tiger.

We're stepping onto more dangerous territory now. My heart throbs in my fingertips at being surrounded by hundreds of Patricians. Defenders gird the perimeter of the park, so I'm guessing the spies are still in town. Can't put Chief Whitcomb in any sort of danger.

Guests immediately notice us.

"Rain," one girl says as she approaches, smiling wide enough to show all her perfect, white teeth. She's not one of the girls I saw last night. How many girls does Rain have? She stands close enough that I can smell her intoxicating perfumes. "We were beginning to think you wouldn't make it." Her voice is soft and sultry.

"Me? Miss a picnic?" Rain flashes his hallmark grin. "Wouldn't miss it for the world." He slips his flask out of his back pocket, screws off the lid, and takes a deep drink.

The girl looks at me, almost like an afterthought. I'm beginning to wonder if I'm not as welcomed into Frankfort as Rain suggested.

"Oh, Miss Carter." Her icy fingers touch my forearm. "How nice that you could come. We're all excited to learn how you, a mere farmer, are actually one of us."

One of us. I force a sweet smile. "It's not official yet. Honestly, I was hoping to return to the Community Garden today, but, alas, I'm not allowed."

"Why on earth would you want to go back there when we offer so much here?" she asks.

"Because my family is there. Why wouldn't I go back? Unfortunately the chief—"

Rain squeezes my arm in a painful grasp and I wince. Heaven forbid I make the chief look mean. And I certainly can't mention the Resurgence.

"I mean, the roads are closed now, due to the massive celebrations."

"Oh." She smiles again, but her smile is too perfect, like she's trying hard to look like a picture. "Well I, for one, am glad the roads are blocked. We've still a month of celebrations to fill up on, and the New Year Parade is the biggest occasion of all. You simply can't miss the parade."

"And I shan't." I mimic her Patrician accent.

"By the way, we all heard about how you stood up for that girl last night." Now her smile fades a little, and I might be seeing things, but a flicker of concern flashes in her eyes. "That was awfully kind of you to do that."

And I'm speechless. Because if it's such a nice thing to do, why isn't everyone doing it? Why do girls like Cherry just stand by and watch and...laugh?

Rain tugs on my arm. I offer a slight curtsy to the girl, and we're off.

"Look at you," Rain mutters. "Making a positive difference in Frankfort in just a few days. The people are really beginning to admire you."

"Then maybe you should let me speak my mind. I could really open up their eyes to what kind of jackal is leading their country."

Rain shakes his head. "Helping a statue? That's heroic. But you've got to watch what you say about the chief. These people have no sense of privacy. They're bound to repeat whatever you say to them, and whatever is repeated will most likely reach Titus's ears."

"Yes, sir," I say sarcastically. "So what am I supposed to talk about?"

"Oh, there are plenty of things us Patricians like to talk about." He takes another drink from his flask. "The weather, the food, each other's clothes, and finally, how great our chief is."

I roll my eyes at his self-mocking statement. At least Rain isn't afraid to make fun of his culture. Forest would defend it to the death. Rain leads me down the trail, winding into a cluster of trees. We pass an alcove where two people are making out. Or as Rain would say, *indulging*. Everything about the tavern last night comes colliding back, and I suddenly feel sick to my stomach.

"Miss Carter."

I look up. Forest steps in front of us, Olivia's arm linked through his.

"Forest," I say.

"I thought you went home." His features are serious, his mouth as straight as his nose.

"You were right." I shrug. "Frankfort's been shut down."

"Yes." He nods. "I'm deeply sorry about that. Well, we are glad you're staying. It's only right that you experience the full excitement of the Christmas celebrations."

"Oh, Forest, don't push the poor girl." Olivia smiles apologetically to me, though I know there's absolutely nothing genuine in her Patrician smile. "She must be going through a lot of culture shock. What, transitioning from the life of a pauper to one of a Patrician and all." She looks at Forest with mock empathy. "I heard they don't get to enjoy the occasional party where she comes from. It's all work, work, work and no play for the farmers."

"We're not *allowed* the luxury of picnics and balls," I snap. Rain's fingers dig into my arm again. Another warning to keep silent, but I ignore him. "We might not have smooth vodka or pet tigers, but I can assure you, Congresswoman Doss, we have parties of our own. They're just more casual."

Forest frowns, then clears his throat "To each his own, eh, ladies?"

Leaning up, I whisper in Rain's ear, "And they're a hell of a lot more fun."

This earns me a chuckle from Rain. The crease between Forest's eyebrows deepens, as does Olivia's scowl.

"Miss Carter," Forest says. "May I have a word with you? In private?"

CHAPTER THIRTY-SEVEN

I stare at him. Forest wants to speak to me in private? What could he possibly want to say that he doesn't want Rain or his precious Olivia to hear? Olivia must be thinking the same thing, because she shoots him a look. He seems completely unaware while he waits for my answer.

I clear my throat. "Um, of course."

He releases Olivia's hand and extends his elbow for me to take. Slipping my arm through his, I cast Olivia a wicked smile, just because I can, then walk beside him, wondering why I suddenly feel like a child who has been caught eating too many apples.

"I can't help but notice how you're warming up to my brother," he says.

"I—I'm not warming up to him. I *hate* Rain."

"Is that why you can't seem to keep your eyes off him and whisper sweet nothings in his ear?"

"Sweet nothings?"

"Just now."

I cough back a snort. So that got to Forest. Good.

"I wasn't whispering 'sweet nothings.'" I slip my arm from his. "And what does it matter to you what happens between me and Rain? You have your own little fiancée to worry about." What right has he to be jealous?

Forest leads me into an alcove, and I'm infinitely grateful for the privacy. "I fear for you. Rain...he's not exactly on Titus's good side."

"Wow. We actually have something in common, since Titus thinks I'm some sort of rebel."

"You don't understand. My little brother doesn't agree with the government. And he's careless and destructive and—" He lets out a hard sigh, looks at the ground, rakes his hand through his hair. "He could easily get you into trouble."

So Forest does have a little bit of concern for me. The thought is touching. But why does he care?

And I'm intrigued by the fact that Rain doesn't agree with the government, when he was the one patronizing the rebels at the prison. These brothers are two walking contradictions.

I place my hand over Forest's. He flinches, then wraps his fingers around mine.

"Don't worry about me, Forest." I ignore the way my heart pounds. "I can take care of myself. If anything, *I'll* probably be the one to get *Rain* into trouble if Titus keeps stopping me from going home."

"You can't think like that. Titus has absolutely nothing against you. He's only trying to protect his country from reckless rebels. I believe you're innocent, but Titus needs...a little more convincing."

"How can you defend him? How can you possibly

defend that pig?"

His eyes widen and he drops my hand like it's a cold fish. But I don't care.

"You saw the injustices in the Community Garden," I say. "You saw the starving children, the work-worn parents. Surely you know the rest of the country is on the brink of starvation while you Patricians live in luxury." I stare at him. "Right? Please tell me you know how completely unfair the government is."

He blinks. The shock ebbs out of his eyes, replaced with a deep sorrow. "Yes," he whispers, then swallows hard. "Yes. There are a great many flaws in our system. But they cannot be fixed with a snap of a finger. It needs to be revised, not replaced, which is what the Resurgence wants to do. They want to replace our leader. That will only lead to chaos and more suffering. But I can assure you, Ember, that, as Titus's advisor, I carry a lot of influence. In time, I know I can help improve the system. If I want to see changes made, I have to stay on his good side, which means no talking behind his back. No insults to his character. No bitterness for his decisions." He offers a gentle smile. "And you, little Ember, would do well to follow suit."

I stare at him, absorbing everything he just said. And my defenses crumble a little. Because this is the Forest I've come to know. Forest, the honest. The compassionate. The leader with a heart of a servant. This is the man I feel infinitely, indescribably safe with. And for reasons I don't understand, he's concerned for me. And for the sake of my family, and everyone in the Community Garden, maybe I should listen to Forest. Maybe I should suck up to the chief. Maybe I should try a little harder to think less about me and more about...everyone else.

"I'll behave," I say. And I mean it. "I'll be patient."

A small smile forms on his beautiful lips, and a warm glow appears in his eyes.

"You have no idea how relieved that makes me feel. To know that you'll try to stay out of trouble. I do care about you, Ember. I—" He swallows, searches my eyes. "—I truly want you to be safe."

And the way he looks at me, like I'm the first star in the night sky, like I'm the first flower in spring, like I'm the sun and the moon and everything that is wonderful, I believe him. Forest Turner wants me safe. Forest Turner cares about me.

I only wish he cared for me the same way I care for him.

Rain steps into the alcove. "Hope I'm not ruining your little rendezvous, but um, the chief is looking for you, Forest."

Forest nods. Stands. Offers his hand and helps me to my feet. "Remember." He squeezes my fingers between his. "Be good."

I nod and watch him step out of the alcove.

"Whew." Rain heaves out a sigh. "That was intense."

"You heard all that?"

He lifts his hands in mock defense. "Hey, I heard nothing. It's not really in me to collect gossip by eavesdropping, but the atmosphere..." He whistles. "I mean, I can feel the charged energy between you two. It's almost suffocating."

I roll my eyes and step past him out of the alcove.

"Hey, wait up." He jogs up beside me, pulls his flask out of his back pocket and drinks deeply. I'm disgusted with how much he drinks. "You can't leave me escortless." He grins, a dimple forming in his left cheek and his eyes dancing, and he almost looks attractive. Too bad he drinks like a fish and flirts like a whore. His tiger prowls by his heels. With only three feet, Julius walks pretty well. The place where his leg used to be ends in a stump. You wouldn't think he was the three-legged wonder.

"We should head back to the picnic," Rain says

"I don't want to go back," I whine.

"No? What would you rather do?"

"Go home."

"To the hotel? Really?"

"No, Rain." I don't even try to hide the irritation from my voice. "I want to go back to the Community Garden. The *orchard.*"

"Ah. I see. Well, that option's off the table, no thanks to your warm welcome of Ky's worst enemy last night."

"I didn't help the Resurg—"

"Spare your lies for Titus and his Defenders. I can see right through you, little apple picker. So let me ask you again, what do you want to do? *Besides* return to your precious little garden?"

I stifle a groan. "What's there to do in Frankfort?"

"Oh, there is so, so much to do here. Like, too much for your bored little farmer-brain to even comprehend. Let's see. There's the Kentucky River close by with a ferry. Did you know Ky used to be known as Kentucky? Little known fact. Anyway. We have a theme park, with actual rides and stuff."

"Like, pony rides?"

"Um…yes. But they also have a roller coaster and a Ferris wheel and—"

"What's a Ferris wheel—"

"Never mind." He flips his hand in the air. "I don't really want to be seen riding with you in a Ferris wheel.

People will think we're official or something. What you *might* be interested in, though, is the library and historical sites."

"A library? Like, with actual books?"

"That is what libraries are known to have."

Rain knows me so well.

"Do you want to go there?" he asks.

"Yes. Definitely." I've always loved reading, but we only had like five books in our whole school. Books are a rare commodity around here. The thought of seeing a library thrills me.

Rain hails a cab. We clamor into the car, and much to my disappointment, Rain shoves Julius in between me and him. And I tense, because the last time I was this close to a black tiger, it was shredding Judah to pieces, and I have to close my eyes against the terror, against the nightmare that still haunts me.

Rain's voice cuts through my thoughts. "So tell me," he says, his voice exuberant. "What's at the library that you want so badly to see?"

"Books," I blurt out. I look out my window, pretend there isn't a man-killing beast breathing in my face. "I want to see what sort of stories I've missed out on."

"Excellent. I know quite a few books that may interest you."

"Do you read?"

"All the time."

Wow. Rain, the uncultured, arrogant prick, *reads*. He's just full of surprises.

"So, is that it?" he asks.

I think for a moment, and I think about Ky and how it's just a massive city surrounded by a ghost town and how past the ghost town is the ashen city, Louisville, a place few people roam. And I wonder where this Louisville is located and if the Resurgence is really hiding out there, but I can't really tell Rain that without him freaking out on me, so I try to keep my explanation basic.

"I've never seen the geography of Ky," I say. "Maybe you could show me the Three Rivers."

"Hm. Okay, then. They might have a map there."

We arrive at the library within a few minutes. I step out of the cab and stare at the beautiful building before us. The library looks more like an old chapel than the snobby glass buildings of the city. The walls are made of limestone and a cupola rises toward the sky. We enter through the quaint double doors, Julius following us inside.

Rain seems to know exactly where he's going, like he comes here often. I follow him through the maze of bookshelves that stretch toward the ceiling, staring at all the thousands and thousands of books, and I think, I could easily live here. I mean, just give me my food rations and water every month, and I could probably make a living just reading books.

Rain begins pulling books from the shelf and passing them back to me. I read the titles. *Peter Pan*, *The Wizard of Oz*, and a whole series titled *The Chronicles of Narnia*.

"These are all classics from the Old Country." He presses the books into my hand. "You might pick up on some of my 'inside jokes' if you read 'em." He spins on his heels. "And one more...ah, here it is." He pulls out an old, red, hardback book called *The Hymnal for Celebration and Worship* and hands it to me. "Add a little musical culture to your life."

I snort. "Celebration and worship? What is this, some

sort of collection of songs to sing to our chief?"

Rain stares at me. "They have absolutely nothing to do with our chief."

Okay then. Once I have my books, Rain takes me on a tour of the library, then leads me into the geography section, and my heart skips with excitement. He slides out a rolled-up tube of paper and unravels it. The poster unfurls, and for the first time in my life, I'm staring at a map of the mega city-slash-country of Ky.

CHAPTER THIRTY-EIGHT

I don't understand how small—or large—it is, until Rain points at a tiny red star that says *Frankfort* at the very edge of the map.

"That's where we are," he says. "And here are the borders of our city. Also known as the Three Rivers."

I look closely at the borders.

"We've got the Ohio River at the top." Rain trails his finger along a curvy, blue line. "The Kentucky River on the East side, which runs right past the capitol building, and the Salt River on the southern border. Then here—" He points to a straight blue line. "—is the channel we built between the Kentucky River and the Salt River."

"Any bridges?"

"Like I said before, all bridges were blown up to keep the plagued out of our territory."

"So there's absolutely no way to get across the rivers?"

He stares at me suspiciously. "Well, I mean, if you know

how to swim—"

"I don't."

"Then, no. There's no way across. Unless you built a raft of some sort."

I suddenly feel claustrophobic. I mean, all this was common knowledge growing up. I'd always assumed there were no bridges, because no one even wants to cross over to Old World where leftover bodies of the plagued have been left to rot. But to know it as a fact now, to know I'm stuck here when I suddenly have the deep urge to leave this inhumane country behind…it's kind of confining.

"There is one bridge." Rain says the words so quietly, I wonder if he really spoke or if I'm hearing things, but then he looks at me, his eyes guarded, his lips settled in a thin, straight line. And he says, very softly, "There's one bridge left in the ashen city that crosses the Ohio River."

I catch my breath. The ashen city. Louisville. Which is apparently a city full of secrets.

"So, where is this… ashen city?" I ask.

He stares at me a moment longer than necessary, then looks back at the map, slowly trails his finger from Frankfort westward, following a line that says I-64, then his finger stops at a dot on the northern river. I know I should stop asking questions now, pretend like I don't care, but my curiosity wins me over.

"So, if I wanted to go to Louisville, how long, do you think, would it take to get there from here?"

He blinks several times, then his serious features break into a grin and he laughs. And he laughs and laughs and laughs and says, "That's quite possibly the stupidest question I've ever heard."

My throat tightens. "What? Two hours by jeep? Three,

maybe?"

"Are you *crazy*?" he asks. "Out of your shoddy *mind*? You *don't* want to go to Louisville. That place is abandoned, full of thieves and...who knows what else. Zombies, maybe."

I snort. "Zombies. Is that what the Plagued have become?"

He shrugs. "Maybe. You never know until you meet one."

The thought sends a shiver up my spine.

"Seriously, though," he says, sobering. "There's no food in Louisville. No people. The city is ashes. It's the ghost town of a ghost town. It's dead and...haunted. The only living beings there are the worst kind of criminals."

"Criminals?"

"You know exactly who I'm talking about." Something in his eyes shifts, and my heart takes a plummet. "Revolutionaries. Like the crew you hid in your hotel room."

"Those are rumors."

"Of course." He chuckles and lifts his eyes to the ceiling. "Rumors."

I look back at the map, trying hard to hide anything that might give me away. "I guess I just wondered what it would be like to live in Louisville. You know, living off the grid, where Defenders and cameras can't watch my every move. It's kind of...freeing, if you think about it."

"You'd be completely alone. And you'd die alone." He rolls the map back up and shoves it into its compartment, then places his arm around my shoulder and guides me out of the aisle. "You're brave, little apple picker, but foolish. Your lack of fear will be the death of you. I can assure you of that. Defying the chief for kicks and giggles? That's cute. But wandering out of the metropolis into the ruins of Louisville? You might as well be asking for a headstone. People who go there never return. I wouldn't risk my life cutting into that dangerous territory if I were you."

I allow him to guide me out of the library, my mind spinning with his warnings. How does he know so much about the Resurgence, anyway? Whose side is *he* on? He thinks the government is corrupt, yet he was at the prison tormenting the rebels and at the club *indulging*. I can't read him. I can't tell if he actually cares about my safety or the Resurgence, or if he's just trying to save his own neck by not getting involved.

Rain mentions walking back to the hotel instead of taking a cab, and I happily agree. Julius walks behind us, and I have to glance back every once in a while just to make sure he isn't about to attack me.

"Don't worry," Rain says. "He's as harmless as a kitten."

Tell that to the people he killed, I want to say, but I keep my mouth shut. Rain is very protective of his "kitten."

This is the perfect opportunity to dig for more answers. "So, Forest said you didn't agree with the government system—"

"Here we go again." He rolls his eyes. "More shoddy questions."

"But your father and brother are politicians. You don't agree with their lifestyle?"

"I wouldn't say that." He smirks. "We get refined wine, picnics, nice clothes to wear, good education...what's *not* to like?"

"Then what don't you agree with?"

"The way we treat the Proletariat."

That's a surprise, that Rain might actually have a grain of

compassion. "You mean the commoners, like me."

"Yes, Rainbow Eyes. Like you and your little family in the Community Garden."

I laugh. I can't help it. He's just so incredibly contradictory it's almost disgusting.

"What's so funny?" he asks.

"Am I supposed to believe that a Patrician like yourself is compelled by *compassion*?"

"Don't get too excited. I have more feelings for Julius than I do for a Proletariat like you."

Of course. Of course he does. I link my arms behind my back. "So, how can the government be fixed?"

He frowns. "I'm not sure if it can. Titus would have to, um, *die*, and I don't see that happening any time soon."

Wow. His solution is completely opposite of Forest's. Forest seems to think chaos will ensue if the chief is killed.

"Why does he have to die?" I ask. "Couldn't Forest have a say in changing things? Don't all politicians have a vote in how to change the government?"

"Of course you'd think that." His lips twist mirthlessly. "Titus wants everyone to *think* he has nothing to do with the way the government's run. He's got it all figured out. He has the commoners thinking it's the Patricians who make all the decisions, and he has the Patricians believing the commoners are treated with dignity. Trust me, Ember, he's got everyone under his thumb."

"Except you, apparently. I mean, if you don't agree with his…philosophy."

"Let's just say I don't accept this place in life so readily. I've been around the city, and by 'the city,' I mean the entire country of Ky. I've seen poverty, though Titus claims there is none. I know this country has its problems, and I want no part in it. That, Ember, is why I don't want to be a politician."

"So what do you want to be?"

"Now we're getting too personal." Rain takes my elbow as we cross a busy intersection. "But, enough about me. What other questions do you have about *Ky*?"

Why does he constantly dodge the questions about himself? What's he hiding? Or does his father do enough nagging about his future that he doesn't want to discuss it with me, either?

"Okay," I say with an irritated sigh. "What about the Defenders? Titus can't have all of them squashed under his thumb, if they don't get paid as much as you Patricians."

"The Defenders are all brainwashed, Ember. As is everyone who isn't a Patrician."

"Brainwashed?" I stop walking, that one word rattling around in my brain. "What do you mean?"

He utters a curse, rubs the back of his neck, and glances around. "I guess...I guess you have a right to know." He looks at me and lowers his voice another notch. "This is why it's such a big deal that you've got Patrician blood, and why Titus is making it such a big deal. The politicians can't control you like they can control everyone else." He stares at me. Speaks slowly. "The antitoxin our ancestors took...it did something to them. Altered their genes or something. And it gave them the power to *brainwash* the unvaccinated."

I feel like time has stopped. Like every thought in my brain has suddenly taken a vacation. Because I can't seem to wrap my mind around what Rain is saying. "Is this some sort of joke?"

He opens his mouth, closes it, looks around, then says.

"Patricians have the power of persuasion. Manipulation. Compulsion. It only takes one word. A look in the eye and an order, and the Proletariat are forced to do *whatever* the Patricians tell them. No strings attached."

"So...all you have to do is look me in the eye, tell me to do something, and I'll do it? No question?"

"No," Rain says simply. "That's the thing. *You're* different. *You're* immune to our power."

"*Power? Manipulation?* Altered *genes?*" I choke out a laugh and try to decide whether to believe him right now, or discard his every word as cow dung. "Do you think I'm *stupid?* That I'll just believe everything you say?"

"Right now? Yes."

And he's serious. Dead. Serious. His eyes unbreakable steel and cold, brutal honesty. And my humor vanishes because Rain isn't often serious, but when he is...A chill runs down my spine, and I look away. "So, you're telling me that all Proletariats are under this...*manipulation?*"

"Only those with careers. After people are chosen for their careers, they go through a training program. They're compelled to follow the rules. To work hard. They're told how great and merciful the government is and to do whatever the chief instructs. They're brainwashed." He looks at me. "But you're immune to our power, which could only mean one thing."

"I'm Patrician."

I've been told that over and over by Rain and Forest and LeighAnn. I've been given the Black Tiger Test. But I feel like I'm just now fully understanding it. And everything makes so much more sense now. I always wondered why the kids at school were so easy to get along with. Why they always did exactly what I said. Why, when they bullied Leaf, I was able to just step in and stop it. Because I was never big and intimidating. The bullies could have shoved me into a puddle, no problem. And I always assumed it was because my mom was taken away. I thought they felt sorry for me, and so left me alone. I had no idea that, the whole time, I was just controlling their minds. It's kind of disappointing, really. Because all this time I thought people actually *liked* me. But they were only heeding to their Proletariat blood.

"I suspected it for a while," Rain says. "Even before your test."

"How long?"

"Since I loaded you on the bus that first day. I told you to be quiet, and just like the little annoying thing that you are, you kept talking. Asking questions. And I knew immediately you were not the average Proletariat."

"Wait. So, you're telling me you knew I was Patrician, and yet you would have just let me die on the Rebels Circle? And what about the Black Tiger Test?" I cross my arms defensively. "You just stood there when the tiger charged toward me."

Rain shakes his head. "You're too smart. I knew you would have figured it out."

"And if I didn't?"

He shrugs and offers a mocking grin. "Would've been a shame to lose you."

He would've just watched. He would've watched the tiger shred me to pieces. He would have watched, and documented, and left the room without a second thought. I shouldn't be surprised by his crass words, but they strike a familiar rage inside of me, hot lava boiling up and consuming my core until my fists clench, and I shove him against the wall and stalk back to the hotel.

"Ember, wait."

I pick up my pace. I hear his footsteps behind me, racing to catch up. I think of Julius pouncing behind me and briefly wonder if Rain will tell his "kitten" to kill me now, and I break into a full sprint.

I hate myself for trusting Rain, even for a second. I hate that I just wasted an entire afternoon with him. Rain is Rain. There isn't a grain of mercy in him. Whatever I thought I saw, whatever compassion I thought he might have, is non-existent. Rain's heart is a black coal that pumps ash into his veins and cinders into his arrogant head.

I'm breathless by the time I arrive at the hotel, and I slow to a trot, nearly colliding into someone stepping out of the doorway.

I step back, almost apologize, but my words freeze on my tongue.

Forest. The older brother. The responsible brother. The untrustworthy politician with whom I feel incredibly safe.

"Miss Carter, what on earth are you doing?"

"I—I'm running from—" I look back, but Rain is gone. Vanished in the mere seconds it took for me to run ahead of him. He didn't even come after me. I turn back around and bite back my annoyance. Why should I care that he disappeared? He's *Rain*.

"Running from whom?" Forest asks, his eyes filling with worry.

"Nothing. Just getting back from the library."

He looks at my books, then at me, and his gaze darkens. "Were you with the rebels, Ember?" His voice is dangerously low. "Please. Tell me the truth."

"No, I *swear*. I was at the library. With Rain." I lift my books as proof. "See?"

He closes his eyes for the briefest moment, then his eyebrows crease. "What were you doing there?"

"Just looking for something to get me through the next few days until the cupola opens again."

"Oh. I see."

Awkward silence. I wish—I wish I could speak to Forest the way we did before. Back at The Tap, when he was a builder and I was a farmer's daughter. When he smiled and laughed and didn't have the pressures of real life creasing his brow. Back when I thought I could trust him.

"What are you doing here?" I ask. "Shouldn't you be with Olivia?" Her name comes out like a curse.

"I came to check on you. I noticed you left the picnic early, and I was worried about you."

My chest caves in. But why should I feel guilty? Why do I need approval from Forest to do anything?

"The picnic was boring." I shrug. "Rain showed me around the city instead."

"I see." He casts a look of disdain down the street. "Didn't realize you were flaunting your time with him." He looks down, and I notice his hands fiddling with a folded piece of paper. A note? "Well. I guess I'll see you tomorrow, then." He smiles, almost regretfully, and shoves the paper into his pocket.

"See you tomorrow," I mumble. I swallow my utter disappointment and push the hotel doors open, desperate to escape the wild, confusing emotions I always feel around Forest Turner.

CHAPTER THIRTY-NINE

I can't stop thinking about the map. It's past midnight. Dark. I should be sleeping, but the map is all I can think about. Because if I could figure out how to get to Louisville, then what are the chances of being able to leave the Community Garden to get there? I mean, what if, somehow, we—Dad, Elijah, and I—really could live off the grid? Grow our own food, make our own clothes, and not worry about Defenders coming after us?

Because nothing about the Proletariat lifestyle is okay. And I can't just pretend like it's okay. Not after everything Rain and Judah told me. Not after everything I've seen here in Frankfort. And now—knowing that the Proletariats aren't even working by their own free will, that they're actually *literally* brainwashed into laboring hours and hours and starving half-to-death for it—I'm more disgusted by the government of Ky than even Dad ever was.

Which makes me wonder...is Dad a Patrician? Did I get

my blood from him? Because, unlike most brainwashed people, he never supported the chief. And if Dad is Patrician, why didn't he tell me? And why is he working as a lowly farmer instead of a politician?

All these questions tumble around in my head until it hurts, and no matter how tightly I close my eyes or how many apples I count in my head, I can't seem to think about anything else. So I switch on my bedside lamp and file through the books Rain gave me. The red hymnal sits at the top of the pile—old, worn, and unassuming. Reading old music doesn't really sound too appealing right now, so I set it aside and look at the other books. I read the inside jackets first, trying to decide which looks more interesting. Ironic that they all have to do with escaping reality to go to a new, imaginary world. Neverland? Oz? Narnia? Ridiculous. And yet...appealing. I could get lost in these easily.

I flip open *Peter Pan* and begin reading, but I can't focus. Reality is pressing down on me on every side. Constricting. Confining. Completely overbearing and demanding that I make a decision any decision some decision just make a decision right now or I'll never leave you alone.

What decision? I wonder.

You know what decision, is what reality says.

Or is it reality? That presence tugs at me again. At my heart and my brain. And I let down my walls, let the pull tug just a little harder and allow thoughts to file through my mind. And I'm thinking thinking thinking I'm trying to decide, should I side with my dad and the Resurgence and everything that is rebellious against Ky? Or should I play a pawn in this game we call life, suck up to Titus, and eventually—hopefully— return home, unharmed, unscathed...and stuck in my old career?

One decision will kill me.

The other will kill my soul.

I rise and walk to the window. Unlike the Community Garden, which would be cloaked in darkness at this hour, Frankfort thrums with life. Lights speck the sidewalks. Loud music filters through the streets, red lanterns dot the trees, and late-night guests revel in the glory of the annual Christmas celebrations.

I rub the sleep out of my eyes, so incredibly grateful that I'm not required to attend the late-night parties. But then I wonder. What would it feel like to sense the joy these carefree Patricians feel? To experience the freedom, the lack of worry about work tomorrow or what the chief will do if they refuse their careers? But how could I join them? How could I ever pretend like the rest of the country isn't on the brink of starvation while I indulge in refreshments and drinks? It would go against everything that was right.

How many people know the rest of the county is on the brink of starvation? I don't know which would make me angrier. If they're so sheltered that they don't know the injustices going on in the rest of the world? Or if they do know and do absolutely nothing about it? Both options make my chest tighten until it's suddenly too hard to breathe, and I need air. I need to get out of this stuffy room and breathe some *real* air, so I pull on my robe and head for the door. LeighAnn told me about this hotel, how the roof is like a balcony overlooking the city.

When I step out of the room, I'm greeted by the two Defenders scheduled to keep an eye on me like a pair of guard dogs.

"I'm going to the roof," I say simply. And they follow

me up.

Cool air blasts into my face when I open the door. My hair whips around my face. I pull the robe tighter around my shoulders and walk to the edge of the roof, glad that the Defenders stay by the door, allowing me some space.

Frankfort is a beautiful nightmare. Lights speck the city like stars. An acoustic melody drifts up from the streets below—upbeat music that defies the warring, angry emotions inside of me.

"Lovely, isn't it?"

My heart leaps into my throat, and I spin around to find Forest walking toward me. Even in the shadows, his golden hair almost glows, his presence ignites warmth, and everything inside me melts at the sight of him.

"What are you doing here?" I pull my robe tighter around my shoulders. I don't know why, but I always feel exposed around him.

"I could ask you the same thing," he says.

Another gush of wind washes over me, and I wipe loose strands of hair out of my face. "I, um, couldn't sleep."

"Neither could I." He steps up beside me at the railing. "I felt bad for leaving so abruptly earlier and decided to come apologize." He chuckles self-mockingly. "I was approaching your doorway, then decided against it, but just before stepping onto the elevator, I saw you leave your room to come up here." He stares at me and seems to look into my very soul. "I saw you," he whispers. "And I knew I had to speak to you."

And my heart's suddenly beating three beats too fast because Forest is *here,* and Olivia's not around to claim her prey, and Rain's not around to ruin the very intimate occasion, and I suddenly wish this night would last forever.

He tears his gaze from mine, breaking my trance, and looks below at the party happening in the park.

"Look at them," he says. "These are the most prosperous people in the empire. The smartest, the richest." His Adam's apple bobs as he swallows. "The most powerful."

"Do they know?" I ask. "Do they know how the rest of Ky lives?"

He looks at me, guarded, and shakes his head. "*I* didn't know. Not until I was in Titus's inner circle. And then it wasn't so much a problem as just an unavoidable way of life. That's how he saw it, anyway. But I wasn't satisfied with that answer. I was actually…*appalled* that people lived on the brink of starvation. *Our* people. People we were entrusted by our ancestors to take care of. That's why I went undercover at The Tap. But the Community Garden isn't the first place I surveyed undercover. I wanted to know how the citizens of Ky were faring. I wanted to see for myself how bad it was, and I wanted to know if there was a reason Titus didn't make finding a solution a priority."

"And…what did you decide?"

He closes his mouth. Swallows hard. Looks back at the people below. "That it is a problem. A very big problem. And we need a solution."

My heart pounds because this is the first time I've ever heard Forest talk like this, like Ky needed to be fixed, like maybe the chief really isn't so perfect.

"I've been trying to push it higher on Titus's priority list," Forest says. "He wants me to find a good solution. A manageable solution. Funny thing is, he keeps me working on so many *other* things in the country, things I consider less important, that I don't have time to work on a solution."

"Maybe the only solution is overthrowing the chief." I meant that as a joke, but the look in Forest's eyes tells me there's absolutely nothing funny about what I just said.

"Chief Whitcomb isn't *bad*, Ember. He just doesn't have his priorities straight. Come on. A part of you wants to believe there's good in Ky, in Titus."

"What makes you think that?"

He straightens. "Because the night we met at The Tap, when you were talking about your conspiracies, you didn't believe the words coming out of your mouth. You were only quoting what you'd heard. But deep inside, I think you wanted to believe Ky was a good country."

I'm taken aback by his perceptiveness. The fact that Forest remembers so much of what I said that night in The Tap.

"Tell me, Ember." And he's suddenly standing so close. His knuckles brush my cheek as he pushes a strand of hair behind my ear. I have to grip the ledge to keep my knees from giving out. "If you were chief," he says. "How would you fix Ky?"

"What—what kind of question is that?" I breathe. "I'll never have that kind of power."

"But if you did." He drops his hand. "Come on, now. Forget about the walls keeping you locked up. No cameras are watching us up here. Dream big. What would you do?"

"Um." I look below, stare at the lights of the city as though I could find the answers there. "Well, I would stop brainwashing people on Career Day."

I peek back at him, wondering what his reaction will be to my knowing this information or if he'll deny it because maybe Rain made the whole thing up. But to my utter disappointment, Forest doesn't seem the least bit surprised.

He just nods and says, "Okay. So people aren't compelled to obey the law."

There it is. The truth. Rain was being honest the whole time.

"So," Forest says. "If people aren't forced into obeying the law, there will be law-breakers. Crime will rise at an unspeakable rate. Then what, Miss Carter? Burn them all on the Rebels Circle? We would lose half our citizens."

I shake my head. "I would stop executions altogether."

"And how would you bring about justice? If people aren't afraid, they will do anything. There would be no peace."

He's right, of course. "I suppose I would do things the old fashioned way and create a prison of sorts. But I would give them a just trial. That's something I didn't have at first."

"Okay, so you would stop the Compelled Training. You would take away the executions. What else?"

I look back at the city, allowing my mind to stretch and think about things a commoner never dares think of. "I would let people choose their careers."

He laughs softly like I'm some ignorant child. "If you let people choose what they do, there would be an imbalance. No one wants to be a waitress or a custodian when they could be actors and singers and artists."

His questions make me realize how little I know. "You're not being fair."

"No?"

"No. We farmers only go to school until eighth grade, then we're sent to work with our parents until Career Day. You politicians, on the other hand, have gone to the best schools in the empire for *twelve* years. You are much more educated in the matter of politics than I am. I'm sure you could provide a reasonable answer. Am I right?"

His brows lift in acknowledgement as he returns his attention to the city. "Good point well made, as always, Miss Carter."

"Maybe that's one thing I would change," I add, thinking of Elijah. "I would allow equal opportunity for education. Everyone goes to school the same amount of time; everyone has equal chance at the career they would want. I mean, isn't that how this country was run before?"

He nods. "Sounds reasonable. You surprise me, Miss Carter. You're persuasive in your arguments. You would make an excellent politician, you know that?"

And the breath is knocked out of me because— "I've never even considered it. It's easier to talk to you than other people."

"Listen, I know I haven't been completely open with you in the past." Forest's voice is barely audible above the sound of the wind. "But you can trust me. You can tell me anything, and I won't repeat it."

Right now, in the darkness, alone in the cold with his warm, gentle hand enveloping mine and his voice a warm caress to my ears, I want to trust him. I do. But then the smirking dark eyes of Olivia Doss flash through my mind. Olivia, his soon-to-be wife. And then I think about how he works directly with Titus, and all my trust takes five steps back.

"What's wrong, Ember?"

The way he says my name in that husky voice makes my walls break down further, but I build them back up, forcing each breath that he takes away from me back into my lungs.

"Does Olivia know you're here?" I avoid his gaze. I hate

sounding like a jealous school girl, but maybe that's what I am. Yes. That's exactly what I am.

He drops my hand, his jaw tightening. "Is that it then? Everything is going to come down to her?"

"Well—yes—I mean." Oh, rot. Why did I have to bring up Olivia? "It's kind of a big deal that you're engaged to the woman who put me in this mess."

His eyes darken. "Don't blame Olivia for your mistakes. She had nothing to do with you attacking the Defender."

"No...but...she drafted Leaf into the Line of Defenders. The one place he didn't want to go."

Forest chokes out a humorless laugh. "She was only there to announce it. There's nothing she could have done to change his career."

"You changed mine."

"That was a drastic step I took. And besides, why should she have changed Leaf's career and not someone else's? This is exactly why you Proletariats are given your careers. Because we assign you where you're needed so there's no unbalance in the system."

"Why do you need more Defenders?"

"You know exactly why."

Of course. Of course I do. The Resurgence. "You need to train a whole army against that tiny, little rebel group?"

"Don't underestimate the power of the Resurgence. They may be small, but they're clever. We'll take all the precautions necessary to keep them from nefarious activity."

"Why can't we just reason with them? I mean, maybe they have the same problem you do with the government. Maybe they just want to see some changes made. Fewer starving citizens and less burnings on the Rebels Circle.

He stares at me as if that was an options he's never thought of before. "I'm not sure they can be reasoned with."

"Why not?"

"Any politician who enters their territory is killed on the spot. Any rebels we arrest have been given the antitoxin, and so cannot be compelled into giving us answers. They keep their mouths clamped shut, offering no compromise. How on earth are we supposed to reason with people like that?"

"Maybe you need a…a messenger."

"Are you volunteering?"

I almost choke on my own saliva. "No. I don't want any association with them. I'm already suspected of working with them, and look where it's gotten me?"

He nods. Looks at the street below. "You could work with us, though, you know. I mean, your mind is Patrician-clear. You're not afraid to verbalize your beliefs, and you're passionate about what you believe in." He looks at me and smiles a little. "Like I said earlier, you'd make an excellent politician. You would be very useful in taking steps to improve our government. Maybe you and I could approach Whitcomb and, I don't know, work together to make Ky a better place."

And I'm suddenly left completely speechless. Because Congressman Turner, a politician in the chief's inner circle, is basically offering me a job.

"As nice as being a politician sounds, I could never do it."

Forest frowns. "Why not?"

"Because I don't think Titus would ever listen." I look at him. Should I say exactly what's on my mind? "You're the one who told me how dangerous Titus is. And now you basically want to instigate him?"

"Not instigate." Forest waves his hand. "*Enlighten.*"

"I don't think he needs enlightenment, Forest. He's the one who told *you* that the rest of the country is starving. And look at how he's living. Like a king."

"Because he is, in essence, our king."

I snort. I can't help it. "If he wants to bring equality to everyone, if he wants to stop the hunger issue, he would have done it a long time ago. I mean, can you imagine? Titus, sitting on his throne, throwing lavish feasts Every. Single. Day. Can you imagine him just giving that all up?"

Forest shoves his hands behind his back, thinks for a moment. "If he's the leader I think he is, then, yes, he will. All he needs is a little pushing. Between your unstoppable passion and my position as his advisor, I think we can do it. I think we can work together to come up with a solution and encourage Titus to execute it."

And it suddenly makes sense. Why Forest is so nice to me. Why he goes out of his way to meet with me when he's already engaged to a beautiful woman. Because he wants to hire me as his assistant. I swallow hard, my pride shot, humiliation painting me red. "I thought—I thought you wanted me to stay on his good side and remain quiet. Didn't you just tell me today to stay on his good side?"

"Yes. Titus is dangerous. You don't ever want to cross him. But there's a way to anger him, and then there's a way to...*charm* him into doing what is right."

"And you think you know how to charm him?"

"After the way I saw you handle him at the ball, I know you're more than capable."

"Yes, but that got me nowhere. I'm still stuck here, aren't I? And after letting Jonah Walker and his posse into my room and not sounding the alarm on him—"

"Wait, what?" His eyes widen.

Oh. *Oh*. Kill me now, because Forest didn't know I let Walker escape.

And now he does.

CHAPTER FORTY

I clamp my mouth shut, but it's too late. The truth already slipped through my non-existent filter and tumbled out of my mouth, and here I am: Ember the liar.

Lies are interesting little webs built by clever little spiders of the brain. Whoever thought it was a good idea to lie in the first place? Did they get away with it? And if they didn't, was it worth it just to buy them some time? Because right now, in this very moment, I'm thinking, it was totally not worth it to lie to Forest.

He grabs me by the arm and jerks me around to face him. "You told me you had *nothing* to do with the rebels."

"I didn't plan for them to come."

"But you were fully aware they were there? So, what, then? Did they hold you hostage? Did they press a gun to your head to keep you from sounding the alarm? Did they threaten to kill your family if you squeaked one little word about them being there?"

My fear is screaming at me to lie again, but my brain is trying to convince me it won't work.

"Answer me, Ember," Forest says. "Answer me now, or so help me—"

"No," I say. "They didn't do any of those things."

He releases me. Blinks. And I feel like I should probably just go ahead and tell him everything. Well, *almost* everything.

"Jonah Walker broke in with his group. They engorged themselves on food, and they left. They didn't tell me where they were going or anything about the Resurgence. They came. They ate. They left." I don't tell him how Jonah said he knew my mom or how he tried to recruit me.

"Why," Forest says, his voice just barely controlled, "are you just now telling me this?"

"Why do you *think*? Just the suspicion that I was working with them was enough to put me on Titus's bad side. Why the shoddy inferno would I sentence myself to prison by telling anyone that the Resurgence was in my apartment and I did absolutely nothing to sound the alarm?"

He laughs a humorless little laugh and says, "Great. Perfect. What a beautiful disaster." He drags his hands down the length of his face, then back up and then weaves his fingers into his hair. "So you helped rebels and then you lied to the chief. How are we ever going to convince Titus that you want to help now?" He slams the rail and I take a startled step back, because I've never seen Forest this angry and it's kind of extremely terrifying.

"I'm sorry," I whisper. It's all I can think to say right now when the calmest person I've ever met is shaking with rage. "I just…wanted to go home."

He barks out a laugh, but he's not smiling. Nothing in his eyes tells me he thinks this is funny. "You're not going home. You're not going home until this clears up. Until you clear this shoddy mess up."

"You mean…you think I should tell the chief what really happened?" Is he out of his mind?

"No." He inhales. Exhales. Closes his mouth then opens it again. "No. At this point, you'd better just stick to your original story. I'm sorry I got so angry. I just—I'm trying to *help* you, and you keep *screwing* everything up."

"Why do you even care?"

His eyes lock with mine. And he looks so distressed and distraught and almost…*destroyed*. He steps closer, searches my eyes, his own raw with emotion.

"I know it's hard for you to believe," he says. "But I truly just want to help you."

I stare at him, confused. Because why would he care for little old me when he's dating someone like Olivia Doss? And why, exactly, does he even want to be associated with me when I keep—in his own words—screwing everything up? Sure, he could care for me maybe. For some ungodly reason, he could actually be concerned for my life.

Or he could just be fueling his campaign as a politician—something Dad taught me. Politicians are always looking for some new way to become more popular, and sometimes those new ways go against the norm. Trying to help the commoners would certainly be against the norm here in Patrician City. And if I remind myself that Forest is a politician—if I try to see him through that lens—it's just a little easier to think clearly. To feel less attached and more level-headed. Because until I understand why he cares for me, I have to take Leaf's and Judah's words to heart and trust no one. And by the way he talks about Chief Whitcomb, I think

Forest might be the last person I should trust.

Which leads me to my next question.

"Forest, are you and Titus…friends?"

He looks warily at me. Unsure. "We grew up together, if that's what you mean."

"No. That's not what I mean. Are you guys close? Do you ever…hang out just for the heck of it?"

His jaw clenches. He looks away, and I know my answer before he gives it.

"Yes." He nods. "Yes we are close. We confide in each other. We're…friends."

"Like. Good friends?"

He looks at me. "Best friends."

I grip the ledge because even though I knew Forest was in Titus's inner circle, I never really pictured them as *friends*. I didn't really know anyone could be *friends* with the chief. And I suddenly feel exposed and humiliated because the *chief's* best *friend* knows me on an uncomfortably intimate level. And I have the sudden urge to hide because I'm standing next to the best friend of the man who basically *owns* my family. And it's a strange feeling, this sense of powerlessness and yet having power. Because Forest is looking at me. He's listening to me. He's offered me a high position in society and he *cares* for me.

And he's best friends with the man who owns my life and controls my fate.

And I think I should probably get back to my room. It's getting late and I need to rest. I need to clear my mind and paint a picture of an apple tree or something.

I unwrap my fingers from around the balcony ledge and offer a stiff nod. "I guess, um, I guess I should go. I'll see you in the morning, Congressman Turner."

Something shatters in his eyes. A look of tortured regret. "Wait."

I pause. "Yes?"

"Do I...intimidate you?"

"No. If anything, you make me feel *safe*." *Too safe*, is what I don't say.

"Then why the sudden eagerness to get away from me?"

I swallow hard. "Because. You're best friends with Chief Whitcomb."

"And?" He takes a step toward me. "Why does that have to change anything between us?"

I'm finding it suddenly hard to breathe. "I—I don't know if I like the chief."

"And whatever you decide about him, you're just going to foster onto me?" Another step closer.

"You are working for him," I breathe. "And I don't know if I can trust him. And if I can't trust the chief, I'm not sure if I can trust his b-best friend."

"You can trust me, Ember." And he's standing right in front of me now, and he's staring down at me with earnest eyes. Hungry, even. And just when I think he's going to change his mind and dismiss me, he steps closer, cups my face, and covers my mouth with his.

And I'm melting. I'm melting beneath the power of his passion. And he's suddenly standing so close, his body pressed against mine, and the heady scent of cinnamon consumes my senses. And his kiss. His kiss is gentle and inviting. His touch promises freedom and joy. And his hands slide down my neck and slip down to my waist, and I can't seem to catch my breath.

I want this. I want it so bad. I've wanted it since I met

him in The Tap, since I saw him standing in the office wearing his politician suit, since he told me he was trying to get me out of prison, and every moment that I've seen him since I was free, I've wanted *this*.

I cling to his vest—his crisp politician vest—like a lifeline, and I'm screaming inside. I'm whispering please hold me. Hold me until the smoke clears. Until the air is crisp and clean and the chief isn't breathing down my neck anymore and I'm free. Free of this chaotic nonsense. Please. Hold me. Hold me until it's safe to come out.

Too soon, he breaks off the connection. He takes a startled step back and he's breathing heavily an his eyes are wide and he says in a raw voice, "I'm sorry. I'm so sorry. I shouldn't have…"

And I want to tell him it's all right. It's fine. I want it too. But then I remember Olivia.

Olivia Doss.

The pretty one. The *smart* one.

And Forest keeps saying *I'm sorry. I'm so sorry*. And I nod. I turn around. I begin walking numbly toward the door, hoping he didn't see the humiliation painted all over my body.

A gust of wind blasts into my face, and I pull my robe tighter around my shoulders, trying to keep out the sudden chill with the same useless effort I try to keep out the strong, magnetic effect I feel around Forest Turner.

CHAPTER FORTY-ONE

The next morning brings with it the same mundaneness I experienced yesterday morning. Except I have the memory of Forest's kiss that thrills me every time I think of it. But I shove it out of my mind, because a kiss, when given out of unfaithfulness, isn't something to be excited about. And by kissing me, Forest was unfaithful to Olivia.

I pace the living room, press the memory out of my mind, and try to think of something else. I'm not used to staying inside for hours with nothing to do. The orchard kept us busy from sun-up till sun-down. But here, there's nothing to do but wait for the results on how I'm a Patrician and hope that no charges are pressed on me for helping the Resurgence out.

Because, even though Forest told me to keep my mouth shut, I'm almost certainly positive he did, or will, tell Titus the truth. Because they're *best* friends.

I walk to the window and look at the park across the

street. Couples stroll along the trails, some teenagers sit on a bench laughing and talking, older people walk their dogs and cats and tigers and—is that a chicken? Such a strange culture here. At least one good thing comes out of being here, though, and that's that I get to soak up the warm weather.

My entire day is wide open. No picnics. No feasts. No interrogations from Mcallister or instigations from Rain or torturous conversations with Forest.

And I want to paint.

I gather my brushes, easel, and paint; grab a blank canvas; and head out of the hotel flanked by my two guard-dog Defenders. Checking for traffic, I cross the street and stroll through the park. It's nice to take a walk by myself, with no one offering me an elbow—because apparently girls can't walk on their own around here.

The leaves of the palm trees are long and green. They billow in the wind and shade the trail from the winter sun. A limestone building stands to my right. It's one of the few buildings in Frankfort not made of glass. Flowers gather at the edge of the trail by the building, glowing orange in the sunlight. I pause and marvel at the long petals specked with an even darker hue of orange. The long stem makes the flower almost look like a swan.

Yes. I want to paint these.

I take a seat on a marble bench, set up my station, and begin to paint. I carefully paint the long stems, then mix the yellow with peach and red to create a sunset-orange glow. After dipping my brush in the orange, I fill in the petals, letting my brush flare out at the curves. Gentle strokes, applied with just the right amount of pressure, can create a masterpiece. Defender Shepherd once told me that.

"You have an eye for color," a boy says.

I blink, momentarily interrupted from my art-trance, and glance at him. And I suddenly have the urge to puke, because Brendan. Brendan is standing *here* and he almost raped that girl the other night but now he's wearing the vest of a dignified politician and he's got a smile plastered on his face that almost looks *kind*.

"You paint well," he says. "Your tiger lily almost looks like the real thing."

Others who have gathered around murmur their agreement.

I swallow down my bile. Blood rushes into my face and I want to walk away. But why should I let this bully scare me off? I was here first. I turn around. Look back at my painting and try to focus on the flower apparently called a tiger lily. Even their lilies are named after tigers.

Gripping my paint brush, I fill in the bold color and eventually lose myself in my painting again. I try to ignore the fact that Brendan is standing entirely too close and I remind myself that the girl is safe now. He can't hurt her. And then I decide that maybe I can do something, something to make him realize what a heartless jackal he is. So I fill in the heart of the flower, making it look more like a girl kneeling on the ground. Her long hair flares out with one of the petals. Her head is bowed. And I use another petal to form her arms splayed on the ground in front of her, bound together. Captive. Slave.

Then in the background I paint a silhouette of a man holding a scythe, ready to chop the flower.

"Wait," Brendan says behind me. "What are you—"

But he doesn't finish his sentence before a loud BANG shatters the silence into a million pieces. A gush of wind knocks me off the bench, and I'm falling, crashing face-first into the dirt. My heart pounds and thunder rolls in my head and I can't breathe can't breathe can't breathe until I'm gasping.

Strong arms wrap around my shoulders, and a solid body lays on top of me, and debris falls around us like blocks of hail and black rain.

"Stay down." I hear Brendan say through the ringing in my ears.

My heart pounds against my chest like a drum. Screams resound all around us. As the debris starts to lighten, another explosion invades my eardrums and shakes the ground. A *whoosh* of air torrents over us. This bang is louder than the last, the gust of air stronger and hotter, whipping my hair in every direction, and now I really can't hear anything but ringing and thunder and then—

"Let's get out of here," Brendan shouts.

I feel his weight lift off me. But when I try to stand, my leg won't move. I look back. A giant piece of scaffolding lies across my calf, pinning my leg to the ground.

"Help me get this off," I shout, but I can barely hear my voice above the chaos. And I'm twisting around so I can reach it, but when I look up, Brendan is gone. He must have disappeared into the smoke and debris with everyone else who's not pinned to the ground. I don't know whether to be relieved he's finally gone or terrified that he left me in the dust.

I cough the smoke out of my lungs and look toward the explosion. The limestone building has a massive hole blown into the side where smoke billows out of the gap and fills the sky. Burning debris falls around me, on me, into my lungs, and I cough it out. I try to kick the pole off, but it's heavy and unmovable and it's pinning me to the ground. Most of the people have evacuated the area, but the few who race past me.

"Help!" I choke, coughing on the smoke and debris. "I need...help."

A man looks down at me and slows down, but then shake his heads and continues. Typical Patrician. No one wants to stick around after two explosions. Not when there might be a third. I can't say I blame them. I cough more smoke out of my lungs, then try to wedge my calf out from under the bar, but my efforts are completely useless. I cough more, my lungs wracking, trying to force the dust and ash out, and I crumple on the ground. I grit my teeth against the pain just now shooting up my leg.

"Ember?"

I look up.

Rain appears in the midst of the falling debris and screaming people. Usually he's the last person I want to see, especially after our last conversation. But right now, when I'm alone and terrified, Rain looks like a knight in shining armor. I would laugh at the very prospect if I wasn't counting on him to rescue me right now.

He jogs toward me. "What the shoddy rot are you doing here?" he shouts. "Why aren't you in your hotel?"

"I'm...*stuck.*"

"Holy Crawford you have a knack for finding trouble."

I grit my teeth to keep from saying something that'll make him decide to walk away. He kneels down beside me, shifts the piece of scaffolding, then, with much effort, shoves it off my leg. I wince at the pain of my foot resetting itself and the stab that shoots up my leg and into my head.

"Come on," Rain is saying. "It's not safe here."

That's the understatement of the century.

He grabs my hands and lifts me to my feet. I take a step, but excruciating pain shoots through my ankle, and I almost fall back to the ground, but he catches me in his arms.

"I've got you," he says so quietly that I barely hear him. He swoops me up and carries me through the falling debris and smoke. I wrap my arms around his neck to steady myself, and I can't help but think of Peter Pan carrying Wendy through the starlit sky. Except Rain's carrying me through ash and falling remnants of the building. No stars here.

He dodges another clump of concrete flying through the air. "Why are you always at the wrong place at the wrong time?"

I roll my eyes. Rain might not know how to fly, but he sure has the same arrogance as Peter Pan.

"I just wanted to paint."

"You can paint in your room."

I don't really want to argue right now so I zip my mouth shut. Sirens blare from the street, and a moment later, a firetruck appears. Firemen leap out, unwinding the hose and spraying water on the smoking building. Rain carries me across the street, far away from the falling debris, and I can finally hear myself think.

"What happened?" I ask.

"Looks like the Resurgence hasn't finished their visit."

A sick feeling curls in the pit of my stomach at the mention of the Resurgence. "I thought Walker was here to visit a family member. Not to blow up the city." I realize as the words tumble out of my mouth that I just totally gave myself away. To Rain of all people.

But he seems completely oblivious, or he's just playing along, because he smirks and says, "Family reunions. They never end well."

Just when we reach the other side of the street, another explosion shakes the ground, sending a gust of wind into us. Rain shoves the door to the hotel open with his shoulder and carries me in.

"What building was that, anyway?" I ask.

"The food bank. Looks like Robin Hood and his gang of merry men decided to break in and grab a handful of food to distribute to the poor."

Robin Hood? Another one of Rain's inside jokes, no doubt.

"Is that what the revolutionaries do?" I ask. "Steal food to give to the needy?" Because if they do, then maybe I do want to work with them.

"Or just grabbing rations for their own camp, the greedy Neanderthals that they've become."

"Why would they want to blow up the building?"

"To burn up whatever they couldn't take, I guess." He pushes the elevator button multiple times, then looks down at me. "Why leave food behind for their enemy?"

The doors ding open. Rain steps inside and gently sets me on my feet.

I grip the railing to steady myself. As we ascend, I get a better look at the chaos in the park. Most of the people have evacuated. Some are trapped under debris, like I was, but firemen immediately set to their rescue.

"Are you sure we're safe here?" I ask. "I mean, what if they blow up the hotel next?"

"We'll be *fine*. No reason for them to blow up the hotel. Especially with you in it, you know, since you helped them escape and all."

I grit my teeth, but don't bother denying that I helped them since I pretty much already gave myself away.

He helps me limp to my room and opens the door for me.

I release his arm. "Thanks, Rain." I wince at the sharp pain in my ankle as I limp to the window and look at the buildings below. Ashes float around the gaping hole, but the firemen have done a pretty good job putting the fire out. Rain steps up next to me. I look at him, surprised he's still here.

"Are you going to be okay?" The concern in his voice surprises me.

"I'm fine." I look down at my foot. "I think I just twisted it."

"Let me have a look."

Before I can object, he takes my elbow and helps me sit in my chair, then bends down on one knee and inspects my ankle. His skilled fingers gently press into the swollen area, making me wince. "Sorry," he mumbles. "You're right. Looks like you just twisted it."

"Good. I don't think I can handle one more piece of drama around here."

He smirks, then stands and strides into the kitchen, returning a moment later with a small bag of ice. "A bit of ice and rest today should help it feel better by tomorrow."

A knock at the door makes me jump. Forgetting my ankle, I rise to my feet, but stumble forward. Rain catches me just before I nose-dive into the floor.

"Easy there." His voice his soft, and I look sharply at him, expecting a smirk, a roll of his eyes, but all I find is zero arrogance and a pound of concern. "You okay?" he asks, and he's searching my eyes, then his gaze slowly travels down my face, as if absorbing every detail, then settles on my lips. His mouth opens slightly, and my heartbeat trips over itself at the hungry look in his eyes.

Another knock. I blink and look away.

"I'll get it," Rain says. He helps me to the leather couch, then leaves to open the door.

I sink into the cushion and pretend to nurse my ankle, but I think my flaming cheeks need the ice more than my ankle does. How does Rain have this effect on me? How can a simple look from him make my heart pound harder than an explosion that almost killed me? Forest is easy to fall for, being the gentleman that he is. But Rain?

Rain's an unfeeling jackal.

The door opens and six Defenders step in, followed by an older man I don't recognize. He gestures for Rain to sit, then makes himself comfortable on the couch across from me.

Crossing one leg over the other, he offers me a no-nonsense smile. "I have a few questions, Miss Carter."

More questions? "Okay...?"

"Did you have any idea about the explosion on the food bank?"

Oh. Great. "No, Mister...."

"*Congressman* Schuster."

"I had no idea."

He closes his eyes and lets out a long, frustrated sigh, then uncrosses his legs and leans forward. "But you were at the site of the explosion."

Oh, Ember, I can almost hear Rain thinking beside me. *Always at the wrong place at the wrong time.*

"I was p-painting."

"Were you, now?"

"I'm sure the canvas is still out there, lying in the debris. I can bring it up as proof, if you wish. I even have some witnesses." Though I didn't get any of their names. And I'm not sure I want Brendan of all people to defend me.

"Not necessary. You could have worked on setting up explosives, then used your painting as a cover up. Now tell me, what is your association with the Resurgence?"

"I have no association with them." I struggle to keep my patience in check.

"Except when you provided shelter for them two nights ago."

"I didn't *know* they were *here*." The lie comes easier every time I tell it.

Congressman Schuster drags a veiny hand across his face, then shakes his head. "You're going to be difficult, I see."

"Oh, come on, Schuster." Rain leans forward. The Defenders aim their guns at him, but he lifts his hands in mock defense, then looks back at Schuster. "If Carter had known the building was going to explode, why would she be sitting in harm's way? If she were working with the Resurgence, she wouldn't be anywhere near them. She would've stayed as far away from the site of attack as possible, to avoid suspicion."

"You've put a lot of thought into this." Schuster narrows his eyes at Rain. "What were *you* doing at the site, Mr. Turner? Have you any ties with the Resurgence?"

"Oh, come on, are you *serious*?" He barks out a laugh. "Congressman Forest Turner's brother, working with the Resurgence? *Really*?"

Schuster lifts a brow, clearly not amused.

Rain heaves out a sigh. "I was enjoying the afternoon

with two *lovely* ladies when the explosion occurred."

A tinge of jealousy pricks me at the thought of him spending the afternoon with other girls. I picture Cherry hanging off his arm and giggling in that annoying, high-pitched voice. Rain pulls the flask from his back pocket and jiggles it, making the liquid slosh around inside. "I was enjoying a little *vodka* to help the boring afternoon pass. Next thing I know, I'm lying face-down in the dirt."

Schuster nods, stands, clearly accepting Rain's story but not believing mine. He looks pointedly at me. "Until further proof, I'll leave you alone, Miss Carter. But with more digging, I can assure you, we will find something, and all your lies will crumble around you, trapping you until there's nowhere left to run." He walks out of the room, the Defenders at his heel. My shoulders relax the moment they shut the door behind them. I sink back into the couch and bury my face in my hands.

"Oh my *word*," I groan, massaging my temples. "What am I going to do? I'm *never* going to leave this shoddy nightmare."

"No need to have a pity party just yet," Rain says as he stands. "They'll sniff around for evidence, and when they don't find any, they'll get out of your hair. Assuming you're guilt-free like you claim."

I bite my lip. Okay. I might be guilty for sheltering the Resurgence. But the explosion? I was an innocent, sitting too close to the site of an attack, painting a picture of a *flower*. "Why am I a suspect and not anyone else?"

"Why do you *think*? The rebels supposedly found shelter in your room. You mysteriously have Patrician blood. You can talk to black tigers. Let's see…what else…" He taps his

chin with his index finger in mock deep thought. "Oh. Yes."
He stares at me. "That incident with the Defender on Career
Day."

I groan and flop back against the couch cushion. "I'm
hopeless! With my luck, I'll *never* be able to go *anywhere* or do
anything without being a suspect of *something*."

Rain's phoneband illuminates blue. He clicks a button.

"Rain, here," he snaps into his mic. He looks at me and
lifts both brows. "Oh. Okay. That's great. I'll let her know."
He clicks the button again and looks at me. "This is
apparently a big day for you, little apple picker." He grins.
"Your results are in."

CHAPTER FORTY-TWO

I jerk upright. "What?"

He grins. "Sonega will let you know the details himself." He holds out his hand and helps me to my feet. "I'll walk you out."

Rain escorts me back out to the street where a jeep waits, a Defender in the front seat.

"Good luck, Rainbow Eyes." Rain opens the door for me.

"You're not coming with me?"

"I know. You must be devastated, but I've got more important matters to attend to. Like rescuing those poor girls I left abandoned in the park." He shuts the car door before I can say anything, and the vehicle takes off down the street. Why did he leave two girls in that debris and choose to stop and rescue me?

What a jackal.

We take off down the street and thoughts of Rain are

left in the dust while new thoughts consume my mind. Like what, exactly, will my results say? How am I a Patrician? Was the antitoxin given to me when I didn't know it? Or was one of my parents Patrician?

We arrive at the building, and I limp to the waiting room, sit in a chair, chew through my cuticles.

"Congressman Sonega is ready for you," a Defender says.

I rise and stiffly enter the room, gripping the Defender's arm like a lifeline. A man with white hair and a neatly trimmed white beard looks up from a large pile of paperwork. His smile is professional, but tired. He rises and gestures toward an empty chair across from his desk.

"Please sit, Miss Carter." He sits back down and shuffles through some papers. "I suppose you know why you're here."

"To hear my results."

He offers a grave nod, then hands me a sheet of paper. I look at it, but it means nothing to me. Just a series of codes and numbers.

"Those codes tell us that the Patrician blood is in your genes." He reaches out and takes the paper back. "But we don't know whether the genes were passed down from one or both of your parents."

So I didn't take the antitoxin. Dad must be a Patrician. But why didn't he ever tell me? And was Mom a Patrician, too?

"Your DNA is being processed now. But we went ahead and looked at your parents' files. Your father was not a Patrician. We have records going all the way back to your great-grandfather. But—what's your mother's name?"

"Tracy."

354

"Maiden name?"

I frown. Carter's my Dad's last name. "I don't know."

"And I don't suppose you know her middle name, either, huh?"

I shake my head.

"That's the problem, Miss Carter. We have no records of a Tracy Carter. We don't know where she came from, her history... *nothing*."

"So you think she was a Patrician?"

Sonega sets the papers down, rubs his face, and looks at me with tired eyes. "We won't know for sure until we get your blood work back."

A loud rapping sounds at the door. Sonega gestures for one of his Defenders to open it, and a balding man in a long white coat steps in. He casts a curious glance at me over the rim of his glasses. His dark eyes look wide and wary as he passes his tablet to Sonega.

"Results are in," he says in a quiet voice, tearing his gaze from me to Sonega. "Very interesting outcome, sir."

Sonega furrows his brows as his eyes scan the tablet. "Hm."

"What are my results?" I ask.

Sonega lifts a finger to silence me as he continues reading. Then his eyes widen a fraction. He fidgets in his chair, then looks up at me, his eyes now alert, full of warning.

"What?" My heart begins to pound.

He clicks a button on his phoneband and sticks an earpiece in. "Chief, we have a Code 3472. What would you have me do?"

Chief? Is he talking to *Titus*? Why would Titus care about my results? I pick at my fingernails while I wait. I assume Whitcomb is doling out orders. Then Sonega nods. "Yes, Chief." He clicks his phoneband and then types something on his tablet. Looking at the lab guy in the eye, he says, "File these records in a secure place until further notice. Forget what you read on them."

The lab guy blinks. Nods. Leaves the room. And I've officially seen what brainwashing looks like. But why did Sonega tell him to forget? I look at him. "What were my results?"

Sonega studies me like I'm a new creature, something he's never seen before. He doesn't look tired anymore, but alert. Almost...terrified. His hands tremble, and beads of sweat collect on his forehead, but it doesn't seem that hot in here.

He clears his throat. "Records confirm your mother was a Patrician."

"Really?" *Mom* was the Patrician? "And my dad? Was he—"

"I don't think so."

I swallow hard. "So...what was her name?"

He stares at me a moment longer than necessary, then blinks and says, "We don't know her name. All we know is she had Patrician blood." He nods a dismissal and begins gathering up the paperwork. "You may go."

"What?" Hardly any of my questions are answered. If anything, I have dozens more. "So...what happens now? I mean, now that you all know I'm not a spy?"

Sonega stops what he's doing and frowns. "Spy? Who said you're a spy?"

"I thought everyone was suspicious of it, after the explosion and all."

"No..."

Great. "I'm not, obviously. It's my mother who carries the gene. Which means I didn't illegally slip the antitoxin."

"Who said anything about an *antitoxin*?"

Why can't I keep my shoddy mouth shut? "Never mind." I stand up, almost turn to leave, but I catch a glimpse of his phoneband illuminating.

He answers it. "Sonega here. Yes. You—you would like her sent to you...*now*?" He nods. "Okay. Yes. Of course." Then he clicks a button, looks at me with a shaky smile and says, "Chief Whitcomb would like to see you now."

CHAPTER FORTY-THREE

Flanked by two Defenders, I'm taken back outside, led into the jeep, and driven through the city to the capitol building.

A Defender is waiting at the front door. He opens the car door for me. "Come with me, Miss Carter."

I follow him into the building, up the stairs, and into the large square chamber with the bronze statue of Quentin Whitcomb where the ceiling arches up into a dome. The Defenders lead me up the marble stairs to the second floor, which overlooks the first floor, then down an open hall lined with tall marble pillars, to a pair of double doors. The Defenders by the door immediately wave us along. No waiting period, not even for a minute, and I wonder, what could be so urgent that the chief could just drop everything to meet with me?

We enter a large room that smells ancient and looks ancient, and I feel like we took a step one- or maybe two-hundred years into the past. The hardwood floor creaks beneath our feet. The ceiling is high. It's engraved and painted with odd designs, and two chandeliers hang from it. There are two fireplaces for this room—one on either side of the room. Beside one fireplace is a door that branches off into another room. The other fireplace is flanked by tall bookcases, packed full of books. A large mirror hangs above the mantel. Tall windows line the opposite wall, and right in front of them, in the center of the room, is a marble desk where Titus sits in a gold-fringed chair.

He props his elbows on the desk, his chin resting on tented manicured fingers. "Miss Carter." His voice is exuberant. "Please, come in." He gestures for me to sit.

I do, in one of the plush, red chairs in front of his desk.

His eyes meet mine, and they're suddenly not friendly anymore, but hardened, forced, and I realize, he hates me. This chief, this supreme leader of Ky, has some beef against me and I have no idea why. Well, maybe I do. Maybe it's because of the rebels breaking into my room and that explosion that I had nothing to do with.

"I assume you know why you've been called here," Titus says.

"Um. Because of that explosion this morning?" I feel like a child answering to a father. "And maybe because you assume the rebels were in my apartment?"

"They were in your apartment," Titus says, leaning back in his chair. "We now have evidence of that."

"Yes. I had no idea they were there, though." The lie comes easily with my life at stake and all.

"Their gun shots should have been loud enough for you to hear."

Actually, no. Not with their fancy guns. The blue lasers

flared out of those pistols as quiet as wind. But I can't tell that to Titus without giving myself away. "I-I didn't hear a thing. And if those guns were so loud, why didn't one of the Defenders on my hall hear it?"

Titus narrows his eyes.

"I don't know how you expect me to believe you, *Carter.*" The way he says my last name is full of loathing...and something else. Sarcasm? "We have proof of your rebellion, so no more lies, please. Now, I've another matter I would like to speak to you about, and that's concerning your conversation with Sonega."

"My results?" I sit up a little straighter.

"Yes." Titus's lips thin out. "What did he tell you?"

"My mom was a Patrician, and that's how I have Patrician blood."

"Anything else?" He leans forward.

"Not that I know of," I say carefully. "Sonega told me I'm Patrician. A man in a lab coat came in and handed him a tablet. Then Sonega called you, and then he sent me away." I briefly remember my stupid mention of the antitoxin.

Oh. That must be what this is about. Maybe I should just spill.

"If this is about my knowledge of the antitoxin, I learned that prior to my meeting with Sonega. He had nothing to do with that."

"Good." Titus shuffles some papers on his desk, not even phased with my mention of the antitoxin. "Very good." He looks at his Defenders, all six of them standing around the room, and says, "Please leave. I would like to speak to Miss Carter. Alone."

CHAPTER FORTY-FOUR

I hear the door click behind me. All the Defenders are gone.

Why does Titus trust me enough to be alone in a room with him when I'm supposedly a rebel who could essentially kill him? Then I remember the cameras in every room and Defenders, who would rush in and shoot me.

I sink deeper into my chair and peek up at Chief Whitcomb.

He stares right at me with a hint of amusement in his green eyes. "I know your secret."

My hands begin trembling. Is he planning on torturing me until I admit to working with the Resurgence?

"I'm not—" I begin, and then decide I need to be a bit more convincing, and I straighten in my chair and look him in the eye. "I swear to you. I am *not* working with the Resurgence. I promise. I never even *heard* of them until Leaf told me, just before he died. I don't really want to work with them, and I didn't *help* them—"

"Not *that* secret," he snaps. And he laughs. He laughs and laughs and laughs and says, "I *know* you helped Walker. That's hardly a secret so quit *lying*. Holy Crawford. If you insist on being a liar, at least learn how to be more convincing."

My blood grows hot.

"Tell me your other secret," Titus says, still smiling that cold, insipid smile. "The one that neither Forest Turner, nor Rain, and not even your little brother, Elijah, knows."

And I'm breathless and so incredibly confused, and I'm racking my brain for some piece of information that Titus is digging for, but I find nothing because my life is an open book and Titus know *everything* about me. What secret can he possibly be talking about?

"I don't—I don't have any...other...secrets."

He blinks. Twice. His smile vanishes and his green eyes harden. "Look at me, Ember. Do I look stupid to you? Tell me, do I look completely naive?"

I blink because this is *not* the way I expected a conversation with Titus to go, and now my heartbeat is tripping over itself and I'm honestly hoping that whatever information he's digging for will magically appear so he can get off my shoddy back.

He stands. "Do I look like a brainless commoner, whom you can just look at and say you don't know anything, and expect me to *believe* you?" He laughs and his smile is back. His wide, brilliant smile that is so incredibly deceiving. "You expect me to believe you don't know?"

Has he gone mad? Officially lost his shoddy mind? But he appears completely level-headed as he pulls out a gun and studies it.

My heart stops. I grip the armrest of my chair, wondering if maybe I should bolt because this psychotic man-child is holding a gun, and he clearly hates me.

"Kn-know *what?*" I ask.

He laughs out loud. The sound seems friendly and jovial, but I know better. And he looks at me, smiling. "Did she seriously never tell you? Your mother never told you the truth about who you really are? Are you *serious?*" And he laughs again. "What a brilliant surprise this must be for you, then. To find out that you don't have just any Patrician blood. You have the *chief's* bloodline. You're royalty. To find out from *me* that you, Ember Carter, are my sister."

CHAPTER FORTY-FIVE

The chief's sister? *Me*? Can't possibly be true...can it?

"I—I think you might have me confused with someone else," I whisper.

"Oh, no. Absolutely not." Titus places his pistol back into its holster. "I just received a call from Sonega. I'm sure you were in the room when he made it. He gave me the code. I had the results sent over and the numbers translated for me. You see, Ember. We have the same DNA. We share the same mother and father—"

"Wait. No. That's where you're wrong. My dad is Andrew Carter."

"That's what your parents told you, yes." Titus walks around to the front of the desk, leans back against it, and crosses his arms. "Andrew Carter took our runaway mother in. But he's not your real father. Aden Whitcomb was your real father."

My thoughts crash all around me, and I'm trying to

think, I'm trying to think straight, I'm trying to process this information that simply cannot be true. Because Aden Whitcomb has been an untouchable icon all my life and there's no way he could be my father. "You're lying. You—you're a *liar*."

He frowns. "I don't believe anyone's ever called me that before. Fitting, that it would be my own sister." He sighs, straightens. "What reason would I have to lie to you? Why on earth would I want a suspected criminal to be my sister? The idea is completely absurd. Almost embarrassing. If Sonega never found out we were related, I might have kept the information to myself. But, here we are. I guess you have a right to know. And now the country will know. You're real name is Ember Whitcomb, and you're the chief's sister."

I stare at him. I blink. I shake my head, stand, and pace. I'm Ember *Carter*, a farmer's daughter. From the Proletariat. My mom loved my dad. She couldn't have been with Chief Aden before my dad. That's simply impossible. And how could I be Titus's *sister*? No.

No, no.

I find myself sitting back down, all these thoughts whirling around in my head like the whirlwinds of a winter vortex. Because, if Whitcomb is telling the truth, then my identity—my entire childhood—was a lie.

"Why didn't they tell me?" I look at Titus. "Why on earth would Mom have kept this information from me?"

"I don't know." He sighs, walks back around his desk and sits down. "According to Father, she was a flighty thing. Overly dependent on her emotions. Never thinking through her actions. Mentally unstable, that one."

I can feel heat rising to my face, but I bite back any remarks that might piss Titus off.

This is a strange, strange situation. The chief, the person I'm most uncomfortable around, happens to be my brother. Maybe. A reunion like this should end with happiness and tears of joy and maybe even a hug, but here we are. Chief Titus Whitcomb, my brother, sitting at his marble desk, staring at me with cool indifference.

"I'm just glad I found you." He breaks the silence. "You've heard the rumors, I'm sure, about my long-lost sister. Mother was caught red-handed working with the Resurgence, and that's why she was executed—"

"So she *was* executed?"

He looks at me, shrugs, and nods. I guess I knew. I knew she was executed. I just hoped I was wrong.

"So," he says. "I had reason to believe that wherever my sister was, she was working with rebels, too. See, when Father arrested Mother, he didn't bother taking you with him, the fool he was. He figured you were harmless. But he never got around to telling me your whereabouts before he died suddenly of a heart attack. So I knew you were out there somewhere, and I hoped Father was right—that you were harmless. And when I found out *you* were my sister, I was quite disappointed. Because, your records don't exactly scream innocence. I thought you were a spy living inside the Cupola. We do not like spies in the Cupola, you know."

I nod.

"But, I'm a good judge of character," he says. "And I believe you're telling the truth about your innocence."

He does? He believes me now?

"I'm just glad that you're not conspiring to rise against me. I'm glad that you seem like a decent girl who really doesn't care for drama or fame."

"Yes. That's exactly right." And my heart pounds because finally—*finally*—things are going my way. "So…what now?" Because I just found out I have royal blood, and I'm not entirely sure what to do with that. This information kind of gives me the same thrill that finding out I was a Patrician did. None. What *does* give me a thrill is the fact that Titus might just clear my records.

"Well," Titus says. "If you're really as innocent as you claim, and if you can avoid raising any more doubts in my mind about you, then I suppose you could have whatever you want and be on your way."

"Wait, what?"

He regards me carefully. "If you agree to return to your home and avoid stirring up drama," he says, "I'll give you whatever you ask for. Within reason, of course."

"You mean I can go home?" Hope. I grasp it. "I can work in the Garden with my dad?"

He nods.

"And…food? You'll provide my family with plenty of food for the rest of our lives?"

He smiles. "I want you to draw up a document stating exactly what you want, and it'll be granted to you." And now he's smiling. A warm, genuine smile that sets me completely at ease. "It's the least I can do for my long-lost sister."

PART III

home

CHAPTER FORTY-SIX

News has a way of spreading at the speed of electricity through Frankfort. News of my royal blood reaches the ears of the citizens that night, and the next morning, I'm showered with gifts, welcome cards, flowers, sweets. The kind of gifts that would make me particularly fond of the people who sent them. It's a popularity contest among Patricians.

I'm treated like royalty by Titus himself. Defenders line the hallway outside my room and even the street below. Titus assured me it was to keep me protected. I'm not sure if that's really the reason, or if he still suspects I'm working with the Resurgence. But it doesn't matter. He's letting me go home. Finally. Not only that, but he's letting me have whatever I want.

I spend the morning drawing up a document. More food to last us the rest of our lives. For Elijah to get to choose his career when he comes of age. Pain medicine for Dad. Art supplies at my request. I feel very Patrician making demands for things we had absolutely no access to, but I might as well take advantage of my position in society.

I wish I could ask for more food for *everyone* in Ky. And equality and justice and basically an entire government makeover, but I doubt that'll pass over smoothly. By the way Titus said I could *be on my way*, I'm thinking he wants to get me out of his hair.

Because of my royal blood, he sees me as a threat. Because that's how Patricians think. It's all competitions and one-upping each other. Family and friendship and integrity don't really get much value around here, which is why I'm dying to get out. When I finish the document, I have a Defender deliver it, then LeighAnn begins preparing me for the afternoon.

Because I have a major interview.

Apparently, I'm the talk of the city. I'm popular now. More so than I was before, when they just thought I had Patrician blood. Amazing how status alone can make people adore you. I was taught to be nice in school. Be honest. Be kind and do unto others as you'd have them do unto you. And that's what makes people like you. But not here. Here, your popularity depends on your status in society. And right now, I'm at the top of the chain, just below Titus.

And I'm not really sure how I feel about that.

A gaudy lavender toga, silver heels, and black ribbons are laid out for me to wear. River fixes my hair in a series of bouncy curls. I've never even had curls until I came here. Now, since that's the only way I've ever been seen in public, it's how everyone else perceives me. Would anyone even recognize me with straight hair and farmers clothes? Probably not.

And I'm not sure how I feel about that, either.

∾

The interview is intense. People watching me. More people watching me on their televisions at home. And I briefly wonder if Dad's heard the news yet. Probably not. This sort of news doesn't usually make it out to the Garden.

After the interview, a host of people line up to meet me. I'm still shell-shocked from being on camera. I mean, the interview was easy enough. I just had to answer a series of easy, shallow questions that were written down ahead of time by the audience. *How does it feel to be the chief's sister? What do you plan to do with your new power? Why do you want to return to the Community Garden? Aren't you happy you found your family?* As if I was some sort of lost orphan. I don't tell them that my *Proletariat* father and brother are more family that Titus will ever be.

And now, all I want is to return to my hotel room and soak in the silence, recuperate from all this exhausting socializing that really leaves me depleted. Better yet, I want to return to the Community Garden. And I will. I will get to return. First thing in the morning, according to Titus.

After the cameras have shut off, people line up to greet me, welcome me home, and pepper me with more questions and shower me with more compliments. Because now that I'm famous and rich, everyone suddenly wants to be my friend. I honestly don't care about making any friends in this shoddy place.

By the time the studio is finally empty, I'm wiped out. Relief washes over me when Forest appears amidst the lights and cameras. We haven't talked since that kiss, but I'm still infinitely grateful for his company, awkward or not.

"You look exhausted," he says. "Come on, let's get out of here." We step outside to the brilliant sunlight. "It's a beautiful day for a stroll," Forest says. "Do you want to walk?"

As if there's ever a bad day in Frankfort with the Cupola.

"Yes," I say. "Let's walk."

He extends his elbow and I take it. I need air. I need to exercise my body, make my heart pump a little extra blood to my brain so I can process everything that's going on.

"So how does it feel?" Forest asks. "Do you feel a little more appreciated? A little less...invisible?"

I smile and look down at the sidewalk. "Yes and yes. Although it's hard to accept appreciation when it has more to do with my family line and less to do with who I am."

"But the chief's sister *is* who you are."

"I did nothing to put myself there. I didn't come to this higher status by my own work. I just happened to be born to two people."

He nods. "Either way, you have the chief bloodline, which means you have power."

"Not really, though. Titus will always be my superior. And after I return to the Garden tomorrow—"

"Hold on." He stops and turns to face me. And for reasons I don't understand, he suddenly looks like someone ripped his heart out. "You're not seriously thinking about going back, are you?"

Why does he care? "Um." I sigh. Bite my lip. Turn away from Forest. "I need to get home, Forest. I haven't seen or spoken to my dad or brother since I was taken to prison. I have to let them know I'm okay. I have to let them know that...that I'm Titus's...sister." Wow. It sounds so strange saying that out loud.

"It's a whole different cultural experience for you."

"Exactly."

He nods. "I suppose I understand."

I look at him. "You do?"

He presses his perfectly sculpted lips together and nods. "Yes. You need to see your family. You're miserable here."

I can't stop a short, pathetic laugh from slipping out of my mouth, because Forest is never this blunt. But he's right. I *am* miserable here. And I'm so glad he understands.

He reaches out and takes my hand in his. "Because of that, I will take you home myself."

I look sharply at him. "You will?"

He offers a small, sad smile. "Whenever you're ready."

"And you think...I mean...will Titus be okay with you leaving him for a day?"

Forest laughs softly. "Have you forgotten? Titus and I are thick as thieves. He'll understand completely. In fact, I'm sure he'd give us his full blessing. There's no one he would entrust his sister to more than his best friend."

Best friend. Forest and Titus are best friends. And Titus and I are siblings. What a strangely small world we live in.

"Are you sure?" I ask.

"Positive."

"But, Olivia—"

Forest tips my chin up, searches my eyes. "Don't worry about Olivia. Just say the word, Miss Carter, and I'll drive you home."

And the truth in his eyes sets my heart on fire. Forest. My one constant since all this craziness began. He's always been there. He's always been my comforter, my safe haven, and I can't stop myself from leaning in and embracing him. He takes a startled step back, but then lifts his hands to my back and hugs me in return.

"Thank you, Forest," I say, my throat closing. "My trip back to the Garden will be so much more enjoyable if you're with me."

He combs his fingers through my hair and the small gesture sends a strange warmth into the pit of my stomach, and I rest my head against his chest. I listen to the steady rhythm of his heartbeat. I close my eyes and inhale deeply, fill my lungs with the heady fragrance of cinnamon. He smells nothing like Rain. Rain smells of rugged masculinity with the occasional whiff of peppermint. But Forest smells clean, fresh. *Rich.* And I want to stay in his strong embrace forever.

"Ember," he whispers, his voice husky. The way my name rolls off his lips makes my blood grow hot. His fingers caress my chin, and he lifts it so our eyes meet. I search his honest blue eyes, so free of malice and deceit. "Everything's going to be okay now," he says. "Your records are clear. Titus trusts you. *I* trust you. And everything is going to be fine for you and your family. Do you understand that?"

No, I want to say. Because I don't remember a single time in my life that I've felt completely safe. There was always the fear of starvation, and then as Career Day drew nearer, there was the fear of the unknown. But everything is known now. Career Day is over. And despite the fact that Leaf won't be there waiting for me when I go home, hope seizes me. It fills my heart like a wellspring, like a fountain of overwhelming joy, and I can't stop a smile from easing on my lips.

"You have a cute smile." Forest taps my nose. "You

should smile more often."

And I think, I probably will smile more often. Because everything is going to be great. Everything is going to be fine. After tomorrow, everything is going to be A-OK.

"Thanks, Congressman Turner, for offering to help," I say. "Chief Whitcomb already gave me the clear to leave first thing in the morning."

He offers a lopsided grin, and for a moment, he looks like Rain. "I'll be at the front of the hotel at eight o'clock."

Relief washes over me like my first hot shower. "Thank you, Forest."

"No problem. I'll see you at dinner tonight."

Oh. Dinner. Of course. The feast Titus prepared in my honor, as a welcoming home of sorts. How could I have forgotten about dinner? I nod, then I step through the doors of the hotel.

LANNING/SHANE MICHAE
FLIGHT 4047 GATE B21

JUL 15
Conf. #: UKDCBR

FROM TO   FLGT#   TIME   FB   BOARDING TIME
IND ATL 4047   2:10 PM R   1:40 PM

Boarding
Group
B

Position
20

(subject to change)

LN LANNING
FN SHANE
MN MICHAEL

B20

INDK0006   DENVER

CHAPTER FORTY-SEVEN

Meals seem to be the way Titus corrals people together in this city. If he ever plans on killing people in one large group, I'm almost positive he would do it by inviting them to a banquet. By the time lunch rolls around, I'm wearing a slimming black toga with a still-darker velvet sash. I feel like a black tiger. A knock sounds at the door at noon, and I smile through gritted teeth, ready for Rain to step in.

Instead, my escort is someone I've never seen before.

"I'm pleased to meet you, Miss Carter," he says with an exaggerated bow. "My name is Azar Smith."

I glance behind him. "Where's Rain?"

"Mr. Turner had business to attend to. I'm afraid he won't be able to make it today."

I'm surprised at the stab of disappointment I feel at his words, but I shake the feeling. I should be relieved I won't have to deal with Rain and his antics. But over the past few days, he's kind of grown on me. I guess his cynicism reminds me of Leaf, and his recklessness is refreshing in a city full of snotty Patricians. And, honestly, I feel like I can be completely myself around him.

Ah well. Too bad.

I link my arm through Azar's extended elbow and walk with him down to the commons. He's quiet. His features are straight.

I glance out the window. "Looks like a storm's brewing. You'd think this giant Cupola they spent so much money on would keep out the rain."

"Yes. Quite the storm." He doesn't so much as glance out the window as he presses a button on the elevator.

At least Rain makes me laugh. He makes the Frankfort experience somewhat tolerable. But now, escorted by a man as stoic as Mr. Smith, I'm not sure I'm going to make it through the meal. I might not even make it to the commons before I pass out by complete boredom.

The meal is served buffet style. As in, stuff-your-face-until-you're-too-full-to-walk-while-people-starve-in-the-rest-of-Ky style. Mr. Stoic leads me to a table, then offers to get my food. After he leaves to fill my plate, my eyes skirt the room, just to make sure Rain isn't here and merely didn't want to be in my presence today. Because that would be completely offensive. *I'm* the one who turns *Rain* down. I take in half the room before I hear a familiar voice slice through the air behind me.

"Ember Carter Whitcomb."

I cringe at my new/original last name. I don't think I'll ever get used to hearing the chief's name with mine. I slowly turn to face my terrible instigator.

"Olivia Forest's Girlfriend Doss." I grin. Forcefully. "Glad to see you've come to celebrate my welcoming party. I assume you had nothing better going on."

"Oh, I'm not here for you, *Princess* Whitcomb. I'm here for him." She dips her chin and I follow her gaze across the room to Forest. And just the sight of him makes my heart forget how to beat. "*I* wanted to do something *fun* today, but he insisted we come here. He wanted to welcome back our chief's sister." She looks back at me, and arches a sculpted brow. "I have to admit, though, Carter, this party isn't like anything I'm used to. I'm bored out of my mind."

"You and me both."

"So, why are you still here if you're so bored?" She rests her forearms on the back of the chair beside mine. "As the chief's sister, I thought you could do whatever you wanted. I seriously thought you'd hightail back to your little garden by now. But, I suppose you need to soak up your fame a little longer, don't you? You're quite the Patrician, down to the very last blood cell. You must—"

"I'm leaving in the morning." I grin like I didn't just completely cut her off. "First thing. Didn't Forest tell you? He's the one driving me home."

Something shifts in her eyes, and I almost regret saying that, because far be it for me to cause any tension between Olivia and Forest just before I leave. And now I really do feel like a snotty Patrician.

"He's driving you home?"

Guilt lodges itself in my throat but I swallow it back down. "Yes."

"Hm. Well, good riddance. It'll give you one last chance to humiliate yourself by staring at him with those pathetic puppy dog eyes like you really want to kiss him but you *know* you're just not good enough for someone like him."

"Kiss him? *Kiss* him? I'm sorry, but I want nothing to do with your Congressman boyfriend." Biggest lie ever. I want *everything* to do with Forest Turner.

A soft laugh escapes her and she runs a slender finger down my shoulder. "Oh, Ember. You were always bad at lying. Lying to Forest. Lying to the chief about the spies in your room."

I forgot how open everyone's lives are in Frankfort.

"But," she continues, "I can see right through you. I know you have a thing for Forest. And *you* know he's engaged. But you also know that there's no way he could ever go after a measly little farm girl like you. Not when he has a successful woman on his arm, like me. But for some reason, Forest has taken an interest in you. Call it pity. Call it self-promotion. But it's there. So listen to me and listen close. It's common knowledge that the lion kills the male cubs to stop any future rivals from challenging him for the pride. So, keep your distance, little kitten. Or you'll have the lion to deal with."

And she smiles that brilliant Patrician smile like she didn't just completely decapitate my pride. What good is it to have the chief bloodline when no one's going to respect you anyway? I could probably stake my claim in this society. I could probably claim my bloodline, my status, accept the title of a princess and have ultimate rule just below Chief Whitcomb, and people like Olivia wouldn't get away with threats like that.

But it sounds like a lot of work to live in nobility, to deal with all the drama. And I just want to go back to my simple life in the Garden. So I watch her. I watch her walk away. And the worst comeback I can come up with in my head is, *stupid lion.*

I scrunch up my nose to hold the sudden flow of tears back because what she said kind of hurt, and what she said is true. I am a measly farm girl. And Forest belongs to Olivia. And after tomorrow—after tomorrow I will resume my life in the Garden and I can forget all this chaotic emotional experience in this purgatory known as Frankfort.

I look up to find Forest staring at me from across the room, his hands shoved into his pockets, and I almost look away, but then I think, Olivia's right. I need to stay away from him. And I need him to not take me home tomorrow.

Mr. Stoic arrives with two plates of food and places one in front of me. "Here you go, miss."

I stand just as he sits. "Thanks. I'll be back in a minute."

His solid features finally transform into something resembling disappointment, but I'm already off before I can feel too bad. Forest is starting to walk toward Olivia's table when I catch up with him. I grab his arm.

He turns and smiles politely down at me. "Good afternoon, Miss Carter. I hope you're enjoying the feast prepared in your honor."

"I would honestly have been happier if the food was distributed to the poor and not stuffed into the Patrician's mouths—" I stop short at the devastated look in Forest's eyes. "I mean. Yes. I'm enjoying it."

Despite the fact that your girlfriend just ripped me a new one, is what I *don't* say.

"Forest, can I…have a moment? Alone with you?"

He casts a glance at Olivia who happens to be glaring at us.

"Perhaps later—"

"No. I need to talk now."

He furrows his brows slightly, then looks at Olivia and holds up a finger, signaling her to wait. I turn and smile too sweetly at her, ignoring the death threat she gave me earlier. Then I link my arm through Forest's and lead him out of the banquet hall. We walk through the hallway and into another empty room where curious stares aren't everywhere. The last thing I need are wagging tongues gossiping about how I'm trying to steal Forest away from Olivia.

Taking a shaky breath, I look at Forest. "I don't think you should take me home tomorrow."

He frowns. "Why not?"

"I just...don't think...it would look too good. I mean, you're engaged to Olivia, and I don't really want to stir up drama on my last day here—"

"Did Olivia put you up to this?" His jaw tightens.

"No—*no*," I say.

"Then you don't wish to spend time with me?"

I want to spend all the time in the world with you, I don't say.

"No," I say.

He reaches out, gently takes my elbows in his hands, and the warmth of his touch sets my skin on fire.

"I really want to go with you," he says quietly. And the honesty—the *desperation* in his voice rips my heart open. "I really want to meet your father and brother," he says. "I want to see where you live. I want to meet your friends. In fact, I was hoping—" His voice catches, and he swallows. "I was *hoping* you would let me stay...for...a few days."

And now I'm confused. Because why would a congressman show any interest in farm life? Maybe he wants to see what life is like in the Garden. He told me that before, how he dresses up like the citizens so he can see how they live.

Or maybe he really is attracted to me. Because he did kiss me, once. And Forest isn't really one to go around and just kiss anybody. Either way, he needs to know.

"The Community Garden is nothing like Frankfort," I say. "We've no plush mattresses to sleep on or fresh food to eat."

He offers a crooked grin and pushes a strand of hair behind my ear. "I think I can handle myself."

He holds my gaze and I want to look away—I *need* to look away but I can't. I can't because his eyes are drowning me in their sea of blue, and I want to look at him forever I could stare at him forever and it hurts my heart that he belongs to another girl.

"Please," I say. "Don't come." Because it'll make my soul ache if I have to linger in your presence a moment longer when you're completely unattainable.

His jaw clenches and unclenches. "I'll see you tomorrow at eight." And he spins around, and walks out of the room.

An invisible weight seems to lift off my shoulders. I wasn't really ready to say goodbye to Forest yet. I'm not sure I will ever be. Smiling, I head back to the dining hall, steeling myself for a long, boring lunch with Mr. Stoic.

Fortunately, Mr. Smith didn't have the patience to wait for me. His plate lies empty next to mine. A tinge of guilt eats at me for abandoning him, but it's short-lived as I find Rain sauntering my way, his flask in hand, as always.

"You ditched me for lunch," I say through clenched teeth. "Too *rainy* outside for *Rain*?"

He smirks. "Didn't think you'd miss me. Turns out you have deeper feelings for me than you care to admit."

I roll my eyes and shove past him to my table, smiling to

myself when he follows. "I was just surprised. That's all."

"Surprised?" He pulls out a chair, turning it so the back is facing me, then straddles it and rests his arms on the back and his chin on his arms. "Or disappointed?" He picks a grape off my plate and pops it into his mouth.

"Surprised. I thought, now that I'm sister to the chief, you'd want to escort me everywhere for the sake of popularity."

"Ah yes. The mystery of your Patrician blood is finally out." He grins. "How does it feel to be royalty?"

I shrug. "The same. I guess."

"The same?" He snorts and plucks another grape. "You had less power than the lowest Proletariat three nights ago, and now you have more power than Forest. And you feel the *same?*"

I look down. "I don't—I'm still powerless against the chief, and the chief gets the final say in everything."

"Yes, but you're not powerless against everyone else."

"True." What I don't say is that I unknowingly grew up with this sort of power. I've always been able to tell people what to do, persuade them to be on my side, apparently because of my Patrician blood. So it doesn't really excite me to suddenly have power. In fact, it's kind of disappointing. I mean, I feel kind of guilty because I've been carrying around all this power all my life, wielding it just because I could, and I didn't even know it. I honestly thought people just liked me. Now I wonder how likable I really am.

I look at Rain. "Well, one good thing comes out of this power. I don't have to take any more grief from you." I grin. "One offensive remark, and I could have you sent to the black tigers."

His brows shoot up. "And Chieftess Whitcomb strikes. I

have to admit, Carter, you're kind of sexy when you go all macho on me. But don't worry. I'll make up for all the mean things I said to you. Tonight."

My eyes widen and he laughs out loud at the look on my face. "Not *that*. No offense, but I'm not really interested in getting my hands into your pants—er—dress. I have a cool place to show you. A historical site that might interest you."

"Oh. But isn't the chief giving a speech or something?"

"Trust me. If you didn't like the Feast of St. Nick, which is supposed to be *fun*, you won't like the chief's festive speech."

"But won't he be disappointed if I miss it? I mean, I think he's going to say something about my being his sister…or something."

"Who *cares*? Seriously, when did you start worrying about our beloved chief's feelings? Is it because he's your brother? You suddenly *care* about him enough to sit through his incredibly boring speech?"

"I don't care—"

"Then what's the problem? I mean, doesn't being the chief's sister give you an out? Aren't you allowed to do whatever you want? Why not take advantage of your new status and live the hell out of life?"

He's right. I don't have to go to any speech. The last thing I want to do is dress up in uncomfortable clothes and surround myself with more Patricians and then be in the spotlight for however long Titus wishes to put me there. And after that lecture from Olivia…well, I really don't want to go to any more festivities.

"Fine," I say. "What sort of historical site do you have in mind?"

He grins. "It's a surprise." He takes a swig from his flask and winks. "Meet me in the lobby after dinner, yes?"

I feel a wicked grin spread across my face. There are few things that I like more about Rain than I like about Forest, but this is one of them. His spontaneity. His recklessness. And this will give me the perfect opportunity to say goodbye to him forever.

"I'll meet you," I say. "But you have to promise not to say a word about it. The last thing I need are people going on about you and me..." I roll my eyes. "*Together*."

Rain's lips quirk up into a knowing smile. "Come, Ember, who do you think is the king of classified info around here? Me." He taps me on the nose, and the gesture is so playful the tension eases. "This will be our little secret."

CHAPTER FORTY-EIGHT

When eight o'clock finally rolls around, I leave the room to meet Rain, slightly excited about the surprise. He said something about a historical site.

I step out of my room, and the Defenders immediately take their places behind me, as they're instructed to do. Titus assures me it's for my safety, but I think he's still a little suspicious that I'm working with the Resurgence. And I don't fight him. I don't refuse the Defenders. Because I need Titus to trust me if I want him to leave me alone the rest of my life.

Rain is waiting outside, leaning against his vehicle, his arms crossed, his vest unbuttoned, and his newsboy cap slightly crooked. He looks just like he did the first day I saw him, when he led me out of prison and brought me to Frankfort.

He looks at the Defenders and rolls his eyes. "Can you send your guard dogs back, please?"

I look back at them. "They're instructed to watch me."

"So? You have Patrician blood. Brainwash them into *un-*watching you."

Oh. I forgot I could do that. "I-I don't know how...to...manipulate them."

"Ah. Well. Let me show you." He looks at the Defenders and says, "Thanks, but I'll take her from here. Go back into the hotel and play Rock-Paper-Scissors until Miss Carter returns." And without question, they bow and return to the hotel.

"Wow," I say. "That was easy."

"Eye contact and an order. So, so easy." He opens the passenger door for me. I'm surprised he has any manners at all.

I slide into the front seat, then he takes the driver's seat.

"So where are we going?" I ask.

He looks at me and grins. "To church."

"Church?"

He revs up the engine and pulls out onto the street. "Didn't know there were any more around, did you?"

Church. The very word is ancient. All religions had been banished hundreds of years ago, though Dad told me some people still worship their deities in secret. But with the banishment of religions came the burning of churches. I didn't know any still existed.

"Why are we going to a...a church?"

"Everyone needs a little culture in their lives. Religion is a huge part of our history." He shrugs and turns down another less-populated street. "Besides, the building's pretty dope. And it's one of the few places not wired with cameras."

"So, it's abandoned?"

"Yes. There's a part of Frankfort that's been completely abandoned. This church is a part of that...abandonment."

The vehicle glides smoothly through the city. I let out a breath once we're a good ten blocks from the hotel and everyone who resides there. The buildings eventually become older, evolving from beautiful glass to chipping bricks. Weeds sprout out of the sidewalks, and the traffic thins. Rain turns down a street eaten away by age. Then he slows the vehicle down and parks in front of an old brick building. The front of the building is tall and square, with the shape of a castle on the top, and a *t* standing tall on the roof. Three, long stained-glass windows line the side of the building.

"It's beautiful," I whisper.

"Wait 'til you see inside."

I follow him up the steps to the quaint arched red doors, one of the few parts of the church that isn't crumbling. Wrapping his hand around one of the brass handles, he pulls with force, and the door creaks open. When I step inside, I'm greeted by the musty scent of mildew. Paint peels off what's left of the crumbling walls. A gaping hole in the ceiling allows sunlight to flood into the sanctuary. The wooden benches are crumbling, and the carpet is disintegrating. Light shines behind the stained-glass windows, creating a rainbow glow from the glass. But despite all the oldness, this place is arcane, carrying within itself a certain…nostalgia.

"Beautiful, isn't it?" Rain asks from right behind me.

All I can do is nod.

"This is one of the few churches in Ky that hasn't been burned to the ground," he says.

"Why did they keep it around?"

"I'm not really sure." He shrugs and slowly begins walking ahead, between the benches, his hands shoved into his pockets. "I suppose it's smaller than the others. Humble.

And this part of the city had already been abandoned. The government saw no threat in this place."

I follow him toward the front of the church. Above the podium is a picture of a man hanging by his hands on a post. Blood drips down his arms and feet. It's so gruesome, so incredibly disturbing, that I have to look away.

I step up onto the stage toward the podium. An old book lies open, and I touch the pages, but they crumble beneath my fingertips. Notes on the page tell me it's a songbook. I read the faded words. *O come, O come Emmanuel, And ransom captive Israel, That mourns in lonely exile here, until the So…*. The rest of the words fade out on the page.

"That's my favorite hymn." Rain steps up beside me.

I catch a whiff of his peppermint breath. "You know it?"

"Mm-hmm. They may have burned all the churches down, but a lot of the hymnals were kept and taken to Frankfort Library for culture's sake. Every hymn in those books alludes to this religion. Every verse speaks a message. And this specific song, ironically, is an advent hymn."

"Meaning…"

"It's a Christmas song." He grins. "And next week just happens to be Christmas. What are the odds of you learning about this hymn *now*?"

"I—I don't think I could ever learn it. See?" I point at the place where the words fade out into the crumbling page. "I can't even read past the second line."

"But you have this exact hymnal in your hotel room, yes? I believe I gave it to you the other day at the library."

"Oh. Yes."

"Have you cracked it open yet?"

I chew the inside of my cheek. "No." Honestly, I was too interested in the other stories to bother looking at songs from the past. "But I don't think it would matter. I don't understand half the words in the first line. Emmanuel? Israel? Is this another language?"

"They're words from another lifetime. Israel represented a tribe, a chosen people of God."

I tense. It's so strange hearing someone talk about God, or religion at all, when that kind of talk has been banned for so long.

"Emmanuel means 'God with us,'" Rain continues. "It's a name representing God's son, who made it possible for God to be with us in a very personal way by dying on a cross."

"Cross?"

He dips his chin toward the picture of the man hanging limply on a stake. "The thing that looks like a little *t* is called a cross. It's the old world's version of the Rebels Circle."

"And God's son died on it? So he could be...with us?" This reeks of contradiction.

"Yes."

"Why?"

"Because people were forgetting about God, and he wanted to draw them back to Himself by becoming one of them. Hence, the name, *Emmanuel,* God with us."

"But, isn't God supposed to be all-powerful? Like, why didn't he just rewire the people's brains so he could control them and keep them from forgetting him?"

"Kind of like the way the chief controls the Proletariat?"

My mouth clamps shut.

Rain sighs. "God wants to be our *companion,* not our puppeteer, Ember. So, in order to show the people a new way of living, a way of *love,* he sent his God-Son, hoping to strike up a relationship with each individual human so he could know them in a personal way."

"By dying. On a cross."

"Yes."

"Why? Why does he *care*?"

Rain stares at me. Blinks. "Because he *loves* us. Because he didn't just throw a bunch of random humans on the planet and find entertainment in watching them figure their pathetic lives out. He chose each human specifically, *individually*, with much thought and pride and...*affection*. God *knows* you, down to the very last blood cell. And God wants to be known *by* you on an intimate level."

And I feel it. The pull. The longing for something higher, bigger, more powerful and all-consuming and there's no denying it. There's no denying the presence filling the gaps in the atmosphere surrounding me, filling the cracks in my spirit and in all the empty spaces in my soul, and I want to ask—I want to ask who this God is and why he cares about me and how can I find him and when can I set up a meeting with him.

But then I realize I'm being drawn into ancient mythology, not reality, and I look away from Rain. I clear my throat. I think of the pure ridiculousness of his words.

"It's a shame God's son died," I say. "It was a waste. Nobody in Ky has a personal connection with God. Not anymore."

"At least not that you know of. But tell me, Ember. Haven't you ever experienced the power of nature? Haven't you ever felt another presence standing near—so near you felt like it *knew* you? God is everywhere. From the strokes of nature to your beating heart. His Spirit is all around us. Haven't you ever...*experienced* a voice calling out to you in the wind, in the trees, in the music of nighttime field frogs or in the warmth of the sun? Haven't you ever watched the life bloom in the Garden, and wondered where that life came from?"

"It came from seeds," I say. "Which came from the sower."

"Yes." Rain steps closer until I feel his peppermint breath on my ear. "You are the Garden, Ember," he says. "And God is the Sower."

And now I'm not breathing. Because I always imagined it like that. Like me being the packed dirt wanting to grow something useful, just waiting for the seeds to drop and take root. Waiting, like the apple trees I've grown up watching, to produce fruit.

"So…so, where is he?" I say when I find my tongue. "Where is…God?"

"Here."

My eyes dart around the dim room, finding no sign of another being, then land back on Rain. I lift a brow. "He's invisible?"

"But you feel Him, don't you? You can sense him calling out to you?"

"Or I'm just a little creeped out right now because we're in a haunted church with a picture of a dying corpse, and you claim there's a spirit lingering around here." I chuckle. "No wonder the chief abolished religions. He was saving his people from their own madness." I release another nervous laugh.

But Rain's not laughing. He just stands there staring at me. Unblinking.

Until he does blink. Then he looks away. "You're right."

He looks around the room, his eyes landing reverently on the picture of the man on the cross. "The one thing we *don't* need in this dire government is the hope that after this life comes a perfect eternity."

Does Rain really believe in all this stuff? Somehow I can't imagine a cynical guy like him buying into myths. But then, Rain is full of odd surprises. And the way he talks about this God being with us, right now in this very room, is unnerving, because religions are something most people laugh at nowadays. And Rain certainly isn't laughing.

I release a shuddering breath, shake the strange feeling, and glance at the rest of my surroundings. An alabaster bowl sits on a shelf, collecting dust. A small sculpture of a baby angel lies crumbled on the floor. Pillars line the walls. A small table stands just in front of the podium, holding an old brass candleholder, a silver chalice, and a plate. It almost looks like someone lived here and dined alone at that table. An odd shiver rushes up my spine.

"This place is…eerie," I say.

"I know. That's why I like it."

I study Rain as he steps back down from the podium and walks toward the tall stained-glass windows, studying them like a painting in a museum. And the realization hits me. Rain—the nonchalant, reckless boy—has a soft spot for art, music, and ancient cultures. My heart stirs at the sight of, not a politician's son who's content with the world as it is today, but a lost boy yearning for the way things used to be. That's why he reads all those classics. That's why he knows that old hymn.

That's why he sometimes talks like he's from another time.

"So, why did you bring me here?" I step down from the

podium and walk toward him. "Surely not to talk about God?"

"I wanted to talk to you about Titus." He turns to look at me. "Now that you see Titus as your brother, what do you think of him?"

"Um…He's still the same person. So I don't think much of him."

"No?"

"No. He's not fixing the starvation issue. He kills people who challenge him without a just trial." People like Judah and Leaf.

"The chief and his Patricians believe criminals deserve their executions," Rain says. "That it's a just punishment."

"So, you're defending them now?"

"I'm not defending them. But perhaps the Patricians only need someone to shed light on the truth. They need someone to show them the very real conditions of the rest of Ky, and then push them into taking action against it. They need to be shown another way to live." He slowly walks toward me. "And who can do that better than a farmer-turned-royalty?" He smiles a little. "Who can do that better than a girl who grew up in these very unfair conditions, and then rose to the place of power?" He stops right in front of me. "Who better, than you, Ember Carter Whitcomb, could flip this government on its head?"

CHAPTER FORTY-NINE

"Me?" I laugh, though there's nothing humorous about his words. They are simply ridiculous. "I am *one* person. I may be able to open one person's eyes, like Forest's, but not an entire city's."

I step away from him and run my fingers along the chipped wall. The paint crumbles beneath my fingertips. "If I say one thing about the injustices of Titus, I would be considered a rebel. He already has his suspicions about me working with the Resurgence, even though I told him that I know very little of those people. Titus made it clear he wants me out of his way. If I stuck my nose into his ruling methods, I would be considered a threat by him and burned upside down on the Rebels Circle, because I seriously don't think he holds any measure of affection for me." I look back at Rain. "I'm sorry, but I would rather keep my life a few more days than risk it for nothing."

"Nothing?" His laugh is hollow. "*Nothing*? How many

people's eyes would be opened to the truth, Ember? There are too many people here for Titus to fight against. The Patricians are the shoulders on which he stands. But what happens if those shoulders were removed?"

"Titus falls."

"And with his fall, a new leader would have to be elected. And you, with your royal blood, would be just the candidate. If you could make the people love you more than Titus, if you could step in, shake this government so much that the people adore you, you could establish a new government. A new way. Justice and freedom. Now tell me this, Rainbow Eyes, is it worth your life to save an *entire* nation?"

Words evade me. Would I risk my life if I knew I could save millions of people? If it meant offering them a new system, a new way of living? If it meant bringing justice to the Proletariat?

"There is no certainty," I say. "Even if I did shed light, even if I did die for the sake of justice, there is no guarantee that anything would ever change. And I can't risk my life with no guarantee of change." I chew my lip, wishing that he would stop staring at me like I just beheaded his pet tiger. "I just want to get home to my family, Rain. I don't want to get entangled in politics. I don't want to interfere with Titus's way of ruling. I just want to go home. I just want to be *free.*"

"But will you ever really be free?" He steps closer and wraps his long fingers around my chin, tilts it up until our eyes meet. "After all you've seen here—the unlimited food, the comforts, the luxuries—will anything *ever* be the same?"

He's standing so close, I lose all train of thought, and I jerk my chin from his grasp, turn around so I can think. What's Rain asking of me? To stand up against the chief? To give up my life? It's too much. Too much for me to take on. I was raised to live a simple life, make simple decisions. But since coming to Frankfort, nothing has been simple.

Forest wants me to work *with* the chief.

Rain wants me to *defy* the chief.

I only want to go home and forget *everything.*

And that's exactly what the chief wants, too. So what's holding me back?

Rain places his hand on the small of my back. I can feel his warm breath on my neck, and the warmth spreads through my body, and I close my eyes, trying to remember how to breathe.

"Ember," he says from behind me. "Look at the window."

I open my eyes and lift them to the long stained-glass window in front of me. Something about the art moves me, makes me feel small and makes me want to do big things.

"That window is made up of broken glass," Rain says. His voice is lucid, almost musical. "Every distinct color has its own separate shard of glass. And the pieces are put together so perfectly, so *precisely,* that it creates a picture, a pattern, a masterpiece that only *those* colors, with *those* shapes, in *that* pattern, could create."

He steps around so he's facing me. His gray eyes burn into mine like rain clouds, thunderclouds, like lightning searing into my very soul.

"Colors. Shapes. Patterns," he says. "Three simple things that, if puzzled together, can form something so incredibly majestic."

I know he's trying to tell me something, use the window as a metaphor. But what? He begins pacing in front of me, hands locked behind his back.

"Without color, the windows would be plain." He gestures impatiently with one hand. "No pattern, no order, no rhyme or reason. Everything would be random, chaotic, and kind of ugly. And if the shards of glass weren't so incredibly unique, if they were just squares and squares and squares of colorless pieces, this window would look like megapixels on a dull computer screen. There would be absolutely no art about it."

He stops pacing. He looks at me.

And all I can do is swallow and say, "It's so unlike you to speak in riddles, Rain. What, exactly, is your point?"

He smiles a little, continues pacing. "Those three things––colors, shapes, patterns— come together to create something…messy, but clean. Something chaotically organized. Something *beautiful*. Kind of like three *other* things that, if put together in such a way, could create something beautiful." He looks at me, really looks at me, and says, "Person. Location. Time."

He pauses, allows me to process the information. "*You* are the person, little apple picker. The defiant, outspoken, reckless…" He presses his fist against his pursed lips like he's frustrated. "*Powerful* person. Location." He continues pacing again. "Somehow, by fate or God, whichever you choose to believe, you, a Patrician with the mindset of a Proletariat, were brought to Frankfort, the most influential place in the country, during a time of turmoil. A time when some of the most powerful people—politicians like Forest included—doubt the…*ethics* of our government." He speaks faster, his voice slowly rising, becoming slightly more musical. "Common citizens, like your father, are becoming aware of their dire circumstances and looking for another way of life.

The government is more fragile than it's ever been, Ember, and Titus knows it." He spins on his heel and looks pointedly at me. "Now tell me this, little apple picker, how those three things, coming together so perfectly, aren't a recipe to create something...*beautiful*? Like, say, a new society, perhaps?"

"Um..." I swallow hard. Because Rain just crammed a mouthful of thoughts down my throat, and I'm not really sure if I'm supposed to chew or swallow or spit them out completely. Because what he's proposing is, essentially, treason. And, honestly, I didn't think Rain cared about the government at all, seeing as he chose not to walk the life of a politician, nor the life of the Resurgence. And I realize Forest is completely wrong about his brother. So, so wrong. Because Rain isn't shallow. He's not looking to one-up everyone else. He is a genuine person looking to right what is wrong.

Which is kind of exactly what Forest is trying to do. Do they ever even communicate? Because the only emotion I've ever seen between the two is resentment, but they could work really well together.

But my main questions is...why *me*? Why not Forest, Rain's brother and Titus' best friend? Why not Cherry who practically drools after Rain and is studying to be a politician herself? Why have I become his target? Because I'm vulnerable? Or is it just the fact that I'm the chief's sister? Why would that even make a shoddy difference?

I sigh and shake my head. "What makes you think this would work?"

"Because you have the chief's bloodline." His voice has hardened now. It's not musical. Not soft like it was moment ago. It's hard like steel. And his eyes...they're burning coals that look deceptively calm. "You have Alpha Blood."

"Alpha Blood?" I ask, scrunching up my nose. "What on earth are you talking about?"

He heaves out a frustrated sigh. "Don't you understand *anything?* Your bloodline surpasses any other bloodline. You have ultimate control." He steps closer, and before I know it, he's got me backed against the wall, and my heart is pounding pounding pounding. He stops inches from my face, his peppermint breath filling the air between us. "Do you remember what I told you about Patrician blood?" His voice is soft again. "How, if you are born with the antitoxin blood in your veins, you can control the Proletariat?"

"Yes."

"Okay. Let me try to explain this in a way a simple little farmer like yourself will understand." He takes a step back, looks at the floor and skates his thumb along his lower lip. And I'm grateful not to have the intensity of his gaze on me. "There are four blood types. And I'm not talking A or B or AB or O or any of that shoddy stuff. I'm talking, Alpha, Beta, Gama, and Delta. Are you listening?"

Yes, I think. *I'm listening. I'm enraptured by your every word, I'm trying to understand this information that was somehow withheld from the rest of the world, and I'm trying to wrap my mind around one more impossible thing that you're about to lay on my mind like a grenade.*

"Okay," Rain speaks slowly as to a child. "You have more power than the average Patrician. You see, when the antitoxin was first created, there was a special dose made only for the chief. A dose that gave him *ultimate* control. So his direct commands to the Proletariat would stand above any other Patricians' command. They did this so there would never be any confusion as to who is leader. They did this to keep control."

406

Control freaks.

"What you're saying is, if the chief gives a direct command to a Defender, and then a Patrician comes along and tries to change it—"

"It won't work. A Patrician cannot override the chief's direct order."

"But you just told my Defenders to go play rock, paper, scissors, and they obeyed."

"That's because they answer to a general. Not directly to the chief. Regular Patricians can override other Patricians' orders, but they cannot override the chief's orders. However, the chief can override the Patricians' order. Does that make sense?"

I nod.

"Great. Now, that's Alpha and Beta blood. Chief being Alpha Blood, regular Patricians being Beta Blood. And then there's Gama and Delta Blood. Delta is the lowest of the low. The brainless Defenders you see walking around? The laborers who do their work with extra enthusiasm even though they're working twelve hour shifts for zero pay and even though their children are, um, *starving*?"

"That pretty much sums up everyone in the Community Garden."

"Yes. It pretty much sums up everyone in *Ky*—" He holds up one finger. "—except for us Patricians." He offers a self-depreciating smile. "So, those brainless inhabiting ninety-percent of Ky are Delta bloods, and easy targets."

"And Gama? Who are they?"

"Gama bloods are Deltas who took the antitoxin."

"So, they're not *born* with the antitoxin in their blood, but they've taken it, and so can't be controlled anymore?"

"Right." Rain grins. "Exactly. They can't be controlled, but neither can they control anyone."

"So there's a cure for brainlessness."

"Yeppers."

I blink, look at the floor, try to process this very new information. Alpha, Beta, Gama, and Delta blood. And I'm Alpha. And everyone in the community garden is Delta. And the Patricians are Beta. Which would make the Gama people like Judah.

I look at Rain. "Is the majority of the Resurgence Gama?"

He shrugs. "Probably. I mean, they've stolen a vast amount of antitoxin—don't ask me how, *I* don't even know where it's located— and they give it to refugees. Sometimes they'll kidnap a Defender or two and give them the antitoxin, too, so they can no longer be brainwashed."

"Wow," I say. "I'm beginning to like the Resurgence more and more."

Rain snorts. "Don't even joke about that. They're Neanderthals who love nothing more than to watch people die in cold blood. The only reason they *rescue* Defenders and refugees is to grow their own army."

I know they're not Neanderthals. They had more advanced equipment than we do. But I don't tell Rain that. As for loving to watch people die in cold blood? I have no idea. I don't know how Jonah Walker thinks, how cruel he could be, because I hardly know him. I shrug and step past Rain. I don't really like being cornered like this.

"So," I say. "You're wanting me to rival my brother, Chief Whitcomb, and possibly take his place as chief." I look at him and smirk. "And if I succeeded? What then? You want me to work as your puppet? You want to rule the country through me? Is that your true intent?"

He gives a brief shake of his head. "I've no interest in leading this country, Ember. But I do know changes need to be made. And I feel like you're just the candidate for the job, you know, because how long is it going to be before another person is born into the chief bloodline and understands the living conditions of the Proletariat first-hand? And even when Titus does get married and starts popping out heirs, how do we know they will be *good*?"

"So what am I supposed to do?" I whisper hoarsely. His speech has me eating out of the palm of his hand.

He steps in front of me and tips my chin up. "You assassinate Titus and lead the nation to greatness."

CHAPTER FIFTY

Assassinate Titus? I choke out a laugh. I can't tell if he's serious or not, but he's not smiling so he must be, and for the first time, I actually wish he would crack a smirk and tell me he's kidding. But he doesn't. His gray eyes are so intense, his voice full of more passion than I've ever heard from him. My hands tremble.

I clear my throat. "I am only one person, Rain. And Titus is hardly accessible. He's always surrounded by his shoddy Defenders. Even if I started brainwashing them into letting me by, I couldn't get through all of them before he ordered one of them to shoot me." I shrug. "There's no way I could do this on my own."

"What if I told you that I have people who can help? What if I said that, within a week, you could be chief?"

I want to laugh out loud. I want to cry. I want this conversation to be over. Because in order to get the attention of a large mass of people, I would have to do something drastic. And the act in itself, to defy Titus, could get me killed.

Would get me killed.

And I'm not ready to die.

I swat Rain's hands off my shoulders, filled with a certain irritation I haven't felt since Judah's death. Actually, make that *Leaf's* death. "I *just* got out of an execution," I snap. "And *you're* telling me to stay here, put my life on the line and kill my brother, *hoping* a bunch of Patricians will just let me lead? As far as I can tell, the Patricians love their chief, so I don't think they'll be very happy about me killing him."

"They wouldn't know it was you. *You* don't even have to do it. I've got it covered. All I want you to do is be willing to take the helm."

And be chief. A leader. A leader without the education. That sounds like a disaster, like a government preparing to collapse on itself.

"Nope," I say. "Sorry, Rain, but I'm not willing to die for a plan that might never work. I'm not willing to lead a country to its possible ruin."

He barks out a laugh. "It's *already* ruined."

I whirl around and stalk to the door. Rain has clearly lost his shoddy mind, and I am officially done with this conversation. Unbelievable. He brought me to this church, knowing I loved art. He's trying to weasel his way into my heart, acting so intimate, telling me ancient myths and showering me with compliments, like some sort of pathetic romantic.

"Ember!"

Ignore him. Keep walking. Don't look back.

"EMBER!"

His voice is raw and loud and holds so much authority I

freeze in my tracks. My heart is pounding, and I slowly turn around, tears stinging my eyes because I feel like a child again. I feel like a child who's in so much trouble. And his eyes are the gray waters of a churning sea threatening a hurricane, and he saunters toward me. I try to decide if I should fight or flee but all I can do is stand here and remember to breathe.

"Who do you think rescued you from that dungeon pit?" he says.

My heart lodges in my throat, not allowing any words to exit my mouth.

He stops right in front me. "Who," he says more gently this time, "set off the fire alarm and led you out of prison the night before your execution?"

"The Resurgence," I say too quickly. "Walker said it was one of his men."

"Walker is a liar, and most likely said that to earn your trust."

"Why would you say that?"

"Because," Rain says. "It was me. *I* was the one who rescued you."

I blink two times too fast. "You're lying. You're a *liar*."

He smirks. "What can I do to prove it to you?"

Prove it? How can he prove it? I glance at his torso, briefly remembering the tattoo on my rescuer's side. "Lift up your shirt."

His head jerks back. And he snorts out a laugh. "Really? If you wanted to see my bod all this time, all you had to do was ask—"

"The boy who saved me had a tattoo on his left side, lower waist. Lift up your shirt."

He stares at me long and hard, his jaw clenching, then

takes the hem of his shirt and lifts it up just enough for me to see a tattoo.

The tattoo. The exact tattoo my rescuer had. A symbol I just learned is called a *cross*. Except this one is fancier than the simple cross standing on top of the church. This one has intricate designs woven within and a circle outlining the center.

"It's called a Celtic Cross," he says, lowering his shirt.

I look at him, putting the pieces together in my head. Because Rain. Rain Turner rescued me from my execution. Which means I owe Rain my *life*.

I shake my head. "But—but you couldn't have been the one who rescued me. Why did you—why *would* you—"

"Because I knew you would prove useful in my plan," he says. "And, what d'ya know? You're *more* than useful. You're a necessary piece in reestablishing the government. You're Titus's sister, the one we've been waiting for to execute our plan."

Something he says echoes what Judah said: *when we find Titus's sister, and if she supports our cause, we'll have ourselves a new leader.*

And I wonder...

"What do you mean, *our* plan?" I ask.

Rain clamps his mouth shut.

No. It couldn't be. There's no way. He just called Walker a liar. But I have to be sure.

"Are you—are you working with the Resurgence?" Because that would make so much sense. Why Jonah came to recruit me in my hotel room. Why Rain's trying to recruit me now.

"We're getting off subject," he says too quietly. "Work with me, Ember. Help me fix this economy. Help me bring

414

Ky to a better place, *please.*" He holds out his hand, looks at me with so much vulnerability I wonder if this is the same Rain who gave me my Black Tiger Test.

But I shake my head, because fear. Fear is an unwelcome guest that I don't really want to entertain any longer.

"It's not worth risking my life." I squeeze the words through gritted teeth, then turn around.

And walk out of the church.

I'm so over Frankfort and people telling me what to do. So much has happened in such a short time. I need a break. I need time to process Rain's offer and Forest's offer and the fact that I'm Titus' sister. Maybe down the road I'll be able to think more clearly. Maybe then I could choose a side and muster up some courage to *do* something. But I just feel like my brain is on survival mode and I need to get home. I need to be some place safe. I need to decompress.

And *then* I need to come up with a plan.

The sky has darkened to a dusky gray since we arrived, and a cool wind sweeps in from the street. I stand by Rain's car and wrap my arms around my shoulders. I wish I was wearing my warm wool farmers clothes, but LeighAnn was so intent that I look nice for Titus's speech.

Titus's speech.

Which I skipped out on. For *this.* Will anyone notice I wasn't there? Of course they will. A seat with my name on it will remain empty. Everyone, including Titus, will know I wasn't there. I curse and dig my fingers into my hair. If I was planning on staying on good terms with Titus, I should have stayed on my best behavior. Now, because I skipped out on the speech, Defenders may be watching me more closely when I get back.

Defenders.

How angry will Titus be when he finds out I not only skipped out on his speech, but didn't have the Defenders with me while doing so?

I have the sudden urge to hurry back, return to my hotel before Titus declares me guilty. *Again.*

Rain finally steps through the red doors. I wonder what he's been doing in there this whole time. Praying to his unseen God? I wish I could tell him this God doesn't exist. If he did, wouldn't we all be living in peace by now? Where is this paradise he promised? Why would an all-powerful God allow a government to erupt into this mess when he supposedly *loves* us?

I slide into the front seat and Rain starts the engine. As we glide down the street, he slips his flask from his back pocket, screws off the lid and takes a drink.

Unbelievable. "Do you really think you should be drinking right now?" I snap.

"It helps take the edge off."

"I need you sober while you drive, Rain. Not drunk."

"Here, have a sip." He smirks and passes me the flask. "Looks like you could loosen up a bit yourself."

I shove his hand away.

"Come on, apple picker. Take a drink. I *swear*, you'll feel much better if you do."

"No, thank y—"

He shoves the flask into my mouth. The metal scrapes against my teeth, and I wince, bracing myself for the burning fire of whiskey to consume my mouth and set my stomach aflame. But the liquid is almost bland on my tongue, carrying with it the faint flavor of...*peppermint.* I cough as he lowers the canteen.

"What *is* that?" I say, wiping my mouth.

"Peppermint tea. It helps with the migraines."

"I didn't know you got…migraines."

"Well, it's not exactly a topic that just flows into conversation."

"So, what, do you have a migraine every day?"

He shrugs like it's no big deal. Like maybe this was something he's had to deal with the majority of his life. "Most days."

That explains his constant irritability.

"But…you're not always drinking tea," I say. "I mean, the stuff I tasted in the prison was pure liquor. And the night at the ball, you couldn't stop drinking."

"Occasionally I need something a bit stronger than tea. Have you met the other Patricians? It's all drama with no break. Besides, it's not easy playing the part of a, um, *player*, surrounded by empty-headed girls."

"You *pretend* to be a player?"

"Um, yes." He smirks and shakes his head. "Do you really think I enjoy surrounding myself with shallow, self-absorbed girls? Puh-lease."

"Then what's the shoddy point? Why hang out with them at all? And why do you carry that flask around everywhere you go? Why do you let people make assumptions about your addiction to liquor and your obsession with girls?"

He shrugs. "I have an image to uphold. One that includes looking like a fool to the one person I want to assassinate."

I stare at him. Could he possibly be telling the truth? But now that I think about it, I've only seen him drink real alcohol in public. Never when we were alone. Not only that, but even in public, he rarely reeked of alcohol. He always smelled of peppermint. And when it comes to girls…Cherry said herself that no one's ever slept with Rain. Considering how free Frankfort culture is, and how popular Rain is among the girls, I guess it's a wonder he hasn't slept with anyone.

I cast a sidelong glance at him. Who is this Rain Turner? Where, exactly, does he stand? He takes bets on people's deaths, yet he doesn't agree with the executions. He flirts openly and allows people to think he's a drunk, but he hardly ever drinks and apparently doesn't give a jackal's nuts about those girls. He wants to assassinate the chief, but he thinks the Resurgence is made up of a bunch of cold-blooded Neanderthals.

"What about the club?" I ask, trying to dig deeper into who this person is. "Why go there if you don't agree with the system? And why did you take me there?"

"I go to the most renowned bar because it's the best place to collect information from tipsy politicians. And I'm not talking about gossip. I'm talking about *classified* information."

"Classified information?"

"For my plan."

"Which includes assassinating Whitcomb and does *not* include working with the Resurgence?" Just clarifying here.

"That's right. And I took *you* to the club because I knew it would piss you off. I wanted you to see the black heart of Frankfort. I wanted to show you how corrupt Patricians could be."

I roll my eyes. His plan worked. I hate Frankfort more than ever. Still. Rain is a mystery I'm afraid I'll never unravel.

"What are you thinking, little apple picker?"

"I'm thinking that I don't understand."

"Understand what? I tried to be very clear for your simple farmer brain."

I grit my teeth. "I don't understand why you put so much work into creating such an unlikeable image. Why you let people think that you're a miserable drunk desperate to get your hands on any girl who lets you."

"All assumptions." He looks at me. Something shifts in his eyes. "But what do you think of me, Ember?"

His question takes me aback. Why does he care what I think of him? I swallow hard, thinking of all the times I saw a girl on his arms, all the times he was drinking...except he wasn't drinking all the time. And he did save me from those explosions.

My silence must confirm his fears, because his lips thin into a tight line and his hands whiten on the wheel. "That's what I thought."

A tinge of guilt pricks me, quickly followed by fear. Maybe I've gone too far. Rain is as fickle as Titus, his pride easily stung, his actions unpredictable. And my life is in his hands. So I keep my mouth shut the rest of the drive back to the hotel. Thunder rolls overhead, and raindrops splatter on the windshield. When I'm dropped off at the hotel, I hardly have time to close the car door before Rain speeds off.

Why is he angry? Because I offended him? Or because I wouldn't go with his plan? If he's so determined to flip the government on its head, why doesn't *he* do it?

And then I realize, I never even told him I was leaving in the morning. This was our last conversation, and it ended miserably. How fitting, though. Because our first meeting didn't go all that well, either. He was leading me to my death.

LeighAnn and River are nowhere in sight when I arrive in my apartment, but I'm glad to be alone. After a hot shower—probably my last hot shower ever—I change into comfortable clothes and curl up in bed, pulling the covers over my head. I should soak up the comfort. Appreciate the soft sheets rubbing against my bare legs and the fluffy pillow beneath my head, because it'll only be scratchy wool blankets and rock-hard pillows after tonight.

But I can't sleep. I can't even get comfortable. Raindrops pound on the window outside, matching the rhythm of my chaotic thoughts. Everything Rain said whirls around in my head like a monsoon until an old poem I learned in school begins to take form.

I opened my eyes...

I squeeze my eyes shut tight. But the poem by Shel Silverstein flits through my mind like an unstoppable train.

I opened my eyes and looked up at the rain....

I cover my head with my pillow.

And it dripped in my head and flowed into my brain...

Plug my ears.

And all that I hear as I lie in my bed....

Don't finish don't finish don't finish—

Is the slishity-slosh

of the rain

in my head.

Rain. It's not so much rain that's in my head, as *Rain*. And his words. His treasonous, suicidal words. They're all I hear. *Assassinate Whitcomb Assassinate Whitcomb Assassinate Whitcomb*. His words keep sloshing around in my brain until I'm quite positive I'm going crazy.

And all that I hear as I lie in my bed is the slishity-slosh, the slishity-slosh, the slishity-slosh of the rain, rain, rain, Rain

I throw the covers off my head and sit up. Enough. I will not think of Rain. I will not think of his offer to kill the chief and take the helm as Ky's leader. I won't do it. Because I'm *not* built to lead. I'm *not* ready to die if this all fails. And I'm *not* willing to get sucked into politics and drama. In fact, that's exactly what I'm trying to *escape* from.

But maybe—I sigh and press my palms on my eyes—maybe I can think up a plan when I get home. When people aren't breathing down my neck and I have complete silence for like, a week, *then* maybe I'll have the balls to stand up to Titus and become chief of Ky.

Me. Chief of Ky. Snort.

But I can't even think about that right now. Not with all the things that happened in just the past two weeks.

I switch on the light, look for a distraction, and immediately notice the hymnal lying on the floor by my bed. Discarded and forgotten, while *Peter Pan* sits on my end table half-read. And I feel the pull, the strange silent voice. Picking up the hymnal, I flip through the pages.

"Every hymn in those book alludes to this religion. Every verse speaks a message."

Does Rain really believe this shoddy stuff? I scan the titles as I flip through until I reach the familiar title, "O Come, O Come Emmanuel." Rain's favorite hymn, huh?

Flopping onto my stomach, I read the lyrics. I read each verse, each word carefully, trying hard to decipher their meanings. But there are still some foreign words, and I don't get it. Does Rain like this song because of the words or the melody? What does the melody sound like, anyway?

Picking up the book, I sit at the piano in the living room and dig into my memory of the brief piano lessons I took in music class so long ago. I always thought it was funny, how they don't allow us Proletariats to own any extravagant things like pianos or pursue extravagant careers like being musicians or artists, but we still had to learn the arts in school. Just an old tradition carried down from our ancestors, I guess.

I place my thumb on middle C, then try to follow the pattern of the notes with my fingers. Once I get used to the rhythm and keys, I look at the verse while playing, and place the words with eerie melody.

O come, O come, Emmanuel
And ransom captive Israel
That mourns in lonely exile here
Until the Son of God appears
Rejoice! Rejoice! Emmanuel
Shall come to thee, O Israel

My hairs stand up on end. This haunting hymn stirs something foreign that I usually try to keep locked down. And deep longing for something I don't fully understand invades my spirit. I play the song over and over, reading each verse, wondering why it tugs at the core of my heart and why this melody, these words, the theme of this song make my eyes burn and my spirit ache. Maybe because Ky is too much like Israel. My country, my people are mourning something from the past. And where is God? Like captive Israel, we have been exiled, and now we're waiting for the promise of liberation from the chief.

Finally, with my soul raw with emotions and my eyes wet with tears, I flip the book closed, crawl into bed, and succumb to the darkness, wondering if we will ever be free or if God will ever decide that we're worth rescuing. And I drift off into a light sleep, but even in my dreams, the third verse comes to me, eerie, haunting, yet filling me with anguished, undeniable hope for Emmanuel.

Disperse the gloomy clouds of night, and death's dark shadows put to flight. Rejoice, rejoice, Emmanuel shall come to thee, O Israel.

CHAPTER FIFTY-ONE

Luck is one of those things that creeps in and out of life like the seasons. You can experience a whole string of luck and then a new strand of misfortune. You could always be lucky or never have luck at all. Is it attitude that gives someone luck? Or is it the decision to be hopeful or despaired? The glass is half-empty or half-full and a person controls which it is by their outlook on life? Or is it God who gives luck? Either way, luck is a simple word that can encompass the difference between life and death. And I realize that right now, in this very moment, I'm favoring on the side of luck.

Because I'm going home today.

Lying in bed, I stretch my legs out to the tip of my toes, stretch my arms above my head, inhale a breath of hope, and grin. I'll get to see Dad and Elijah today. Does Dad know I'm the chief's sister? What will he think when he finds out? Will he be disappointed in my choosing to come home instead of claiming my position in the capitol?

So many questions.

I hope he has all the answers I'm looking for. Like why did mom run from Frankfort and why did she take me and not Titus, and why didn't she ever tell me the truth about where I came from?

I pull on my green toga. I would usually wear the farmers uniform that LeighAnn brought up, but I want to look my best for Forest.

After I finish cramming everything into my satchel—including all the food and the soft sheets I just can't imagine leaving behind—I look around the room. The room that's held me captive the past four days. A week ago, I thought I was going to be executed. And now, here I am, sister to the chief and on my way home with any requests at my disposal. I don't care what Rain said about me not being able to forget what happened here. When I get back, I'm going to try my best not to ever think about this place again. And soon, it will be as if nothing ever happened. The only change will be having a few more luxuries and a bit more food to eat.

And Leaf being gone.

Leaf.

My heart collapses at the mere thought of his name. Between prison and my learning I'm a Patrician and my relationship with Forest and Rain and then finding out I'm related to the chief, I haven't really had a chance to grieve. And this—*this* is something that's going to hit me all over again. Leaf is gone. And I will never see him again. I won't get to tell him all my newfound secrets, and I won't get to ask him how he knew so much about the Resurgence.

I let out a shaky sigh. At least I *am* returning. Gotta focus on the positive.

"Optimism is a good trait, Ember," I can almost hear Elijah say. *"But if you always see the glass as half-full, you'll never have the incentive to change anything."*

I close my eyes as those words sink into my soul like a dagger. Here I have the perfect opportunity to make changes for the better, either working with the Chief like Forest said, or working against him with Rain. What would Elijah have to say about me taking the easy way out? I won't hear the end of it when he finds out. No doubt about that.

Well. I made sure he could choose his career, and if he still wants to be a politician when he turns sixteen, he'll have the perfect opportunity. Then he can do whatever he wants to make this country a better place.

I won't get to see LeighAnn or River before I leave, so I leave a note saying, thank you and goodbye. Then I place it on the counter, gather my satchel and coat, and take one last look at the room. The pictures I painted of the city and the apple orchard prop against the wall by the window. They would be a nice commodity at home, but I want no reminders of this place. Although I'm not sure I could ever forget Frankfort...or this whole experience. But I leave them behind, anyway. If Titus holds true to his word, I'll have unlimited paints and brushes and canvases to create new pictures.

Forest is already parked by the curb when I step outside, as promised. With the vehicle still running, he gets out of the front seat and opens my door for me.

"Good morning, Miss Carter," he says with a nod.

And just the look in the ocean of his eyes is enough to make my heart melt. If going home isn't enough to make me excited, a road trip with Forest definitely tops it off.

"Good morning, Congressman Turner."

"You sure you want to go home so soon?"

"Absolutely."

"I wish you would stay."

I catch my breath, suddenly feeling stupidly hopeful. Like maybe he decided that he doesn't like Olivia and he likes me instead, so I look at him. "Why? Why do you want me to hang around Frankfort?"

He blinks, like he's shocked I don't know the answer. And his lips open, then close, and he looks past me and swallows hard then looks at me again and says, "So we can, you know, try to talk to Titus together. Like we had planned."

And my heart sinks into my gut like a large bite of food I forgot to chew.

"Oh," I say, looking away. "*That.*" That's why he wants me to stick around. To work as, like, his coworker. To brainstorm on how to make this country a better place. To convince Titus to make some changes. Problem is, Titus doesn't like me very much. That's obvious. And if he was interested in making changes in Ky, I have reason to believe he would have done that already.

I look at Forest. Offer a smile. Wish that he had the same feelings I have for him. "I'm going home, Forest. I don't want to stay here and get wrapped up in politics. If you don't want to take me home, I understand. I could find another way."

His lifts his hands in mock defense. "Hey, I'll take you. Hop in."

I take my place in the passenger seat, he closes the door behind me, and soon we're off.

"So how does Olivia feel about you taking me home?" I ask.

He winces. "Um. About that. We kind of...broke up."

Wait. "What?"

He glances at me, unsure. "I, uh, broke up with Olivia. Last night. We're not dating anymore."

I can't stop my mouth from dropping open, and I seriously hope this has nothing to do with our conversation last night.

"*Why?*" I ask "I mean, I thought you loved her?"

"She was...tolerable. I never really loved her, though. It was all business." He shrugs. "But—I don't know." He drags his hand through his golden hair and down around the back of his neck. "When I met you, Ember, I felt...a spark. A thrill of excitement. I'm not sure how to explain it exactly. It was the first time I'd ever felt that way around a woman. I craved your presence. And when I saw you were arrested, when Perseus announced your death sentence." He shakes his head. "I was *devastated.*"

He glances at me. "You see, I don't usually go out of my way to rescue criminals. And yes, I know what you did wasn't intentional, but usually I don't interfere. Even though it wasn't me who rescued you from prison, I wish it had been. I wish that escape had never happened so that the next morning, before your execution, it could have been me who saved you. And then you could trust me, Ember. You could understand that..." Words seems to falter him, and he swallows, stares ahead at the street. "That your happiness means more than life to me."

Holy Crawford. He *does* care for me. In *that* way. It's not all just an act. He's cared for me this whole time. That kiss wasn't a pity kiss or a ploy to advance himself as a politician. It's been real all along. This charged energy between us has been real. And if he broke up with Olivia…what does that mean? Could there maybe be a chance for us?

"Ember, say something." He looks nervous, his thumbnail biting into the steering wheel.

"Um…I think you made the right decision. I don't like Olivia."

He bursts out laughing. I hardly ever see him laugh, and seeing it now makes my heart smile.

"Well, that's honest," he says.

His happiness eases my tension and makes me feel like everything really is going to be okay.

"I'm also really happy that you're the one taking me to the Community Garden," I say. "Are you still planning on staying for a few days?"

"Yes. I mean, if that's all right with you. And I don't have to stay in your cabin if you don't want. I can stay in the hotel."

"I would love for you to stay in our house, but that decision really is up to Dad. I should warn you…he's not too keen on politicians."

He grins. Laughs a little. "I know, Ember. You made that quite obvious at The Tap when I first met you."

When we first met. How strange. I feel like I know him quite well, but it was less than two weeks ago that we met. If he's going to stay in the Garden for a few days, it'll give me a chance to get to know him on a more personal level. I'll get to see him, how he really is, unmonitored, without the constant worries of daily life hounding him.

Sirens blare in behind us.

My entire body tenses, my grip tightens on the car door, and I glance at the rearview mirror just in time to see two

Defender jeeps dart down the street.
   Straight toward us.

CHAPTER FIFTY-TWO

Oh. Oh no. Not again. I'm so close. So incredibly close to leaving Frankfort and all its unnecessary drama behind, and I suddenly wish that Forest would speed up, take us out of this cursed city once and for all before we're stopped.

But, ever the law follower, he pulls the vehicle over. "I'm sure there's a good explanation for this." His jaw is tight.

Right.

True to my bad luck, the jeeps pull over, too. One behind our vehicle, and one in front.

"Stay calm," Forest says. "In fact, don't say a word. I've got this."

A Defender walks with his gun in hand straight to Forest's door. Forest rolls down his window. "What seems to be the problem?"

"We've orders to arrest Miss Carter."

"Arrest?" Forest laughs mirthlessly. "She's already been forgiven by Chief Whitcomb. Tell me, who gave you orders to arrest her?"

"Our orders come directly from Whitcomb."

Directly from Whitcomb. Which means that no one can stand against it. Except...*me*. Because I have Alpha Blood. Leaning over Forest, I look the Defender in the eye and say, "Let us—"

"—Ember don't—"

"—go."

The Defender's eyes flicker, and he steps back, blinks, nods.

Wow. That *was* easy. The thrill of power courses through my veins.

A shot rings out.

A gun shot. Loud and deafening. And my head is suddenly pounding and I'm living my escape from the prison all over again, and then I see it. I see the Defender I'd just compelled stumble. And fall onto the road.

My mind starts buzzing. My heart is pounding. What the shoddy inferno just happened?

Forest utters a curse. "I was afraid that would happen."

"What? *What* just happened?"

"Titus is always one step ahead." Two Defenders begin walking our way now, and Forest speaks quickly. "The Defenders were told that if one decides to let us go, the other will shoot him. No doubt, if you manipulate this one, another will shoot him and take his place, and so on until all six Defenders are killed."

I grit my teeth. As much as I want to leave, it's not worth a needless bloodbath just so I don't have to face Titus again.

The Defenders part ways at the front of the vehicle, one coming to my door, the other to Forest's.

"You will both step out of the vehicle," Defender number two says.

Forest glances at me. "Ember—"

"It's fine." I grab the door handle and yank it open. "Let's just get this over with."

The Defender on my side of the vehicle grabs my arm as I step out of the car. "You will come with me, Miss Carter."

My heart stops.

Because that voice is too incredibly familiar. And maybe I'm just imagining it. Maybe, like everyone else in Frankfort, I have officially lost my mind, but I look at my Defender just to be sure.

His uniform is buttoned up to his chin and his hat shadows his eyes. But he's no taller than me. And he's thin and wiry and that face. I would recognize it anywhere.

"L-leaf?"

It can't be, though. He died. I saw him. I saw him get shot and fall on the stage and—*oh*. He didn't die. They kept him alive. He's *alive*. I can't stop the flood of emotion filling my entire being, like a wave of hope has decided to consume me. Because Leaf is here. His brown hair is cropped short above his ears, and his hat and red uniform make him look a little stiffer than the Leaf I'm used to, but he's here. *Alive*.

Without thinking, I lean in and embrace him. But something's off. He doesn't hug me back—he actually stiffens. He grips my arm and steps back. And he stares at me like he doesn't even know me. *Oh*. He's been brainwashed. Like every other Defender, he's been manipulated into thinking a certain way.

"You…do remember me, right?" I ask.

He blinks. Smiles a stiff smile. "Of course I remember

435

you. But you're wanted by Chief Whitcomb."

Chills spread out across my skin. "Do you have any idea why?"

"Of course not. I don't question my chief."

My heart sinks a little at his lemming way of thinking. At the fact that he's not who he used to be.

His features remain expressionless. His eyes, once filled with laughter, are cold and...dead. He pulls an electroband out of his pocket.

"Leaf...You've gotta let me—"

"Ember." Forest's voice cuts me off and I look sharply at him. "Remember what happened to the last Defender."

I look at Leaf, and realize I could persuade him into letting me go. But then he'll be shot. Titus really is one step ahead.

"Chief's orders are to arrest you," Leaf says. And he takes my hand and straps the electroband around my wrist. And I need to know. I need to know just how far gone Leaf is.

"So, what about Jonah Walker? You hid him in your house once. H-how do you feel about him now?"

Leaf looks sharply at me, and now there's an emotion in his eyes. Rage. Anger. Disgust. "Say that name again," he says very quietly. "And I'll put a bullet through your head myself."

My lungs collapse. But I nod, my heart pounding, and follow him to the jeep. I want to tell Leaf everything. I want to tell him that Titus isn't good and that he's fighting for the wrong team. I want to tell him everything I learned in Frankfort about our blood, and I want to tell him to let me go and that I'll rescue him. I'll give him the antitoxin. But I'm afraid anything I say will only get him killed. So I keep my mouth shut. I fight back the tears of betrayal, because my best friend is arresting me. Because my best friend threatened to kill me.

And there's everything wrong with that.

I glance back at Forest. He starts to follow, but the other Defender stops him.

"Don't worry, Ember." He shoves the Defender away. "I'll go meet with Titus right now." He leaps back into his vehicle and speeds off while Leaf shoves me into the backseat of the jeep. After closing the door behind me, he takes the front seat and the driver pulls down the street.

I can't believe it. Leaf, my best friend is one of them now. No wonder they didn't kill him or arrest him and send him to the Rebels Circle for treason.

Because Leaf, my best friend, is a Delta.

There's no need to arrest someone who can just be brainwashed. They must only arrest Gama and Beta Bloods. Because their brains can't be overwritten. But arresting a Delta would be a complete waste when you could just convince them to act a certain way, to think a certain way, to become a part of an army and defend a flawed country.

And I decide, this will be one more request to make of the chief. I'll ask him to give Leaf the antitoxin and let him live in the Garden with us. That is, if Titus will listen. Why does he want me, anyway? I thought my records were cleared. I thought he believed me when I told him I was *good*. And now he's arresting me. And he's turned my best friend against me.

He just made this whole manipulating the government thing personal.

A homicidal impulse wraps around my heart, its claws reaching up my throat until it's hard to breathe. I hate Titus.

I've hated him since the day I met him. I hate his brutality. His inhumanity. His *games*. I hate his need for control over everything and everyone.

Control over people like Leaf.

My nose gets congested, but I swallow the lump in my throat and glance at Leaf sitting in the front seat. I'll get him back. I don't know why the chief wants to see me. Or why he intends on torturing me by making Leaf bring me. But I'll figure it out. And we'll settle it like siblings. Then I'll get Leaf back.

We arrive at the capitol building minutes later. Strange that I was here just two days ago to find out I'm the chief's sister. What sort of unswallowable info am I going to learn now?

Leaf shows the guards his badge at the door, and I can't help but feel just a little bitter.

"You already earned your badge, huh?" I ask, not making any effort to hide the mockery from my voice. He glares at me, but I shrug. "I just thought it took longer, but you must have really pleased the chief."

He shakes his head and leads me inside, up the marble stairs, and toward the chief's office.

This is when the fear begins to take a hold of me. Because Titus is emotional and unpredictable and all-powerful. My heart pounds harder and harder the closer we get to his office, until we reach the double doorway. I feel something sticky on my thumb, and look down to see that I'd picked right through my cuticles because of my nerves, and now blood smears across my finger.

The doors to Titus's office open and Leaf leads me in.

My fists clench at my sides as we approach Titus, who sits smugly at his marble desk. I know Rain and Forest told me to at least pretend like I like Titus. But I can't. I've never held any fond feelings for the chief, and after seeing how the Patricians live, I like him even less. And with this brainwashed version of Leaf standing beside me, it's proving harder than ever to plaster a fake smile on my face for the person I've come to hate.

"Ah, sister," he says, a brilliant smile on his face. "How nice to see you again."

CHAPTER FIFTY-THREE

I try to smile as I stop in the center of the room beside Leaf. "Nice to see you too, brother."

His jaw hardens. He rises from his desk and walks toward me, a bowl of grapes in hand. "Hungry?" He holds the bowl out.

I shake my head. "No. Not really."

"No? Not even for one grape? They're awfully delicious. The best around Ky. I believe you know who manages the vineyard, yes?"

Yes, I almost say. Ilene and Charlie Jackson. They're one of the few people I got to say goodbye to before everything went to hell. Charlie was just barely able to walk. He was old and wiry and knobby and sometimes I would go over and help them harvest their grapes. But I keep my mouth glued shut.

"I had the Jacksons work extra hard during harvesting season," Titus says, inspecting the grape between his fingers.

"So we could have fresh grapes through the winter. And wine, of course."

My stomach tightens into a cold, hard knot.

"They worked so hard, in fact." Titus looks at me, frowning. "That I'm afraid a one of them might have died off. The man. What's his name?"

My mouth drops open and a shocked breath escapes me. I just saw him less than two weeks ago. He seemed fine. I cover my mouth because I think I'm going to throw up.

"Ah, doesn't matter," Titus says, waving his hand in the air. "It wasn't too bad a loss. He was getting old and slow. I just had a couple newly careered Prots replace him and his wife."

"His—his wife?"

"Well, she was pretty slow too. And was going to be useless without her husband around. I had her killed off and buried."

Grief then rage is flooding my blood stream, and I'm a train wreck just waiting to happen and the train is coming— it's coming at 200 mph and I shut my eyes tight and the train crashes into the front of my brain and it's smoke and fire and flying debris and loud thunder, but I take a deep breath.

Inhale.

Exhale.

Replenish bad air for good. Open my eyes. And despite the explosives still going off in my head, I force all emotion out of my eyes, bite back my tears.

"So," Titus says, grinning and clearly amused. "Do you want one?"

And my eyes are burning and I my heart is pounding and I want to punch him. I want to slap that stupid smile off his face and shove all those grapes down his throat at once until he chokes.

Instead I take another shaky breath. Slowly let it out. "What do you, um, what do you want with me, Titus?"

"I want you to eat a grape. Just one. Just one little grape to show your appreciation to Charlie, to show that his hard work didn't go unnoticed."

And now I can't contain it anymore. I can't hide it. "I'll *die* before I accept anything from you."

He grins. "Ah. There she is. The rebel."

"I'm-I'm not a rebel. Just because I have some measure of humanity does not make me a *rebel*."

"I'm not talking about your pathetic humanity, my dear sister. I'm talking about this." And he pulls a small slip of paper from his pocket and unfolds it and holds it up for me to see.

It has a drawing of an apple in flames.

It's the paper Leaf gave me on Career Day. I automatically look at Leaf to see his reaction, but he stares emotionlessly ahead. I look at Titus. "Where did you get that?"

He laughs a little, stuffs the paper back into his pocket. "Rain claimed he found it in your cell."

Rain? Rain. Rain *betrayed* me. Makes sense, I guess. He rescued me from prison so I could help him assassinate Titus, and when I refused, he saw no use for me. What a heartless jackal.

Well. Two can play this game. "Rain wants to assassinate you."

His eyes widen a fraction.

"He just told me last night. He wants to assassinate you and make *me* leader."

Titus bursts out laughing. He laughs and laughs and laughs and says, "Seriously? You expect me to believe you? Tell me why, exactly, he would claim he wants you as his leader, and then turns you in? I'm sorry, but spouting out drastic accusations is a poor form of defense."

"Rain doesn't like you."

"Rain Turner doesn't like anybody but himself. It's what I admire about him. He's self-centered and looks out for number one. He's a sloppy, miserable, self-absorbed drunk whose one goal in life is to one-up his brother."

I almost laugh because that's not at all who Rain is. And he has everyone fooled. He seriously plays his role so well, he even has the chief tricked into overlooking his cleverness.

"Listen, Titus," I say. "I'm not a part of the Resurgence. Can't you understand that? Why can't you understand that? Why is that so hard for you to understand?"

"Hm." He taps his chin and stares at the floor in mock thought. "Let's see. Perhaps because you attacked a Defender," he says, counting on his fingers. "You hid Walker and his gang in your room." Two fingers. "You were at the site of the explosion caused by the Resurgence." Three fingers. "And, oh. You've kept your true identity from me for sixteen years."

"I had no idea we were related—"

"I didn't believe you the first time you told me, and I don't believe you now. So, tell me." He perches at the edge of his desk, sets the bowl of grapes down, and crosses his arms. "When you spoke to Jonah Walker, did he offer you payment for your help? Did he even offer to take you out of Frankfort with him? Or did he just use you, then abandon you to the fate of crime?"

I press my lips firmly together, because Jonah *did* offer

me sanctuary, and I refused. But I have a feeling telling Titus that will only fuel his belief that I'm with the Resurgence. There's nothing I can say that will change his mind about me. So I straighten. Try to turn this back around on Titus. "Forest said you were good at playing mind games."

This gets his attention. His eyes spark with something…reminiscence? Regret? But he covers it quickly with a polite, Patrician smile as he pops another grape into his mouth. The grapes that Charlie picked with his last few breaths of life. My stomach twists.

"Forest," Titus says, chewing his grape. "He's had quite the thing for you since he found out you were my sister. Hungry for power, that one."

"I thought—I thought you two were friends?"

"He criticizes my character by saying I'm good at playing mind games, and you think we're friends?"

Well, shoot. I shouldn't have brought Forest into this. "He didn't speak lowly of you," I say carefully. "He actually spoke highly of you. He just said you were…dangerous."

"Ah. Well, you should have listened to him and not invited rebels to come into your room. I honestly don't know why he insisted on having anything to do with you. He knew of my dislike toward you from the very beginning, yet he still insisted on *helping* you. He wanted to *help* you out of prison. He wanted to *help* you adjust to Frankfort life. He wanted to *help* you go home. He's the exact opposite of Rain. He's always looking out for others, and mark my word, that will be his downfall." He looks at me. "In fact, I think it already is."

"Leave Forest out of this."

He smiles a little. "I'll speak to Forest myself to judge his true character. As for you, you can say your goodbyes to the world. I already have your execution scheduled first thing in the morning."

Wait—what? "But I haven't been proven guilty!"

"You've proven yourself guilty several times. The only reason I let you get by with it was because I was hoping you'd slip up, reveal a secret of the Resurgence. But you're pretty ignorant and useless, and I think I'm finished with you." He straightens and begins walking around to the other side of his desk.

"But…I'm your *sister*!"

He spins around. "And you think that you get off the hook for sharing my blood? If anything, you pose more danger than the average criminal."

"Because of my Alpha Blood."

His eyes harden. "Someone's been telling you secrets."

"Rain has."

He smiles a little. "Well, Rain's right. It's because of your Alpha Blood and your ridiculous empathy for the brainless Proletariats. You pose a threat to me and my leadership, and I simply don't need the extra burden of worrying about you overthrowing my position hanging over my head." He locks his hands behind his back. "But, first things first. Leaf is your best friend, yes?"

I look at Leaf. He still stands erect, his chin held high, his eyes void of any emotion. The Leaf I knew is gone. But he has to be in there somewhere. He just has to be changed back—reversed—given the antitoxin.

Knowing I tread on dangerous grounds with Titus, I shrug and look back at him. "I knew Leaf in school. I wouldn't say we were *best* friends."

"Except that you would give your life up for him, like you almost did on Career Day."

My spine tenses. one. vertebrae. at. a. time.

"It's sort of funny, isn't it?" Titus asks.

What? What's funny? Nothing about this situation is funny.

"It's funny," he says. "How you were willing to give up your life for Leaf, and now here he is, delivering you to your death sentence. It truly is ironic. Poetic, almost."

No. Nothing about this is poetic.

Titus nods at two Defenders standing by the wall. They march to my side. One of them pins my arms behind my back, and my heart pounds because what the shoddy inferno is Titus planning on doing?

"Close your eyes," he tells the Defenders. And I wonder why he's telling them that, and then I realize it's so I won't compel them. Because compelling requires eye contact.

"Leaf," Titus says.

"Chief?"

Titus pulls a dagger out of his belt and studies it. Then he presses it into Leaf's palm and says, "Stab your wrist."

CHAPTER FIFTY-FOUR

That's exactly what Rain told me to do during my Black Tiger Test. I didn't do it. But Leaf does. Without hesitation, he presses the blade hard against the vein in his wrist.

"Leaf, no!" I scream.

But Leaf isn't looking at me. He's looking at Titus. I try to bolt toward him, but the Defenders hold me tight.

The blade slices through the skin, and crimson blood begins streaming down his wrist. I glare at Titus. "Now have him wrap it up."

Titus stares at me a moment with a look akin to pity, then after what seems to be an eternity, he nods at Leaf. "Wrap it up." He pulls a kerchief out of his back pocket and tosses it to Leaf. Leaf, now extremely pale, obediently wraps the wound and my racing heart slows, the anxiety ebbing away.

"I've learned my lesson," I whisper hoarsely. "I-I won't ever challenge you. I'll stay out of your way. I'll never even tell anyone we're related."

"I'm afraid everyone who's important already knows. You're still dying tomorrow, by the way."

"Fine. Whatever. Let Leaf go, and I'll be happy to die however you please."

He stops pacing. He looks at me. Then at Leaf.

"You know what?" he says. "I don't really want you to die happy. Leaf here is a pathetically useless Defender. He's small and weak and lanky and easily disposable." He shrugs. "I think I'll kill him." And he looks at Leaf and says. "Take that knife, and stab your throat."

I hardly process what Titus is saying when Leaf sinks the dagger into his jugular.

"No!" I scream. I twist my arms from the Defenders, but their hold is tight, firm as steel.

Leaf begins gasping. A gurgling sound rises up from his throat and he coughs up blood. He falls to his knees, vomiting, choking on his own blood.

"Leaf, stop! Pull the knife out!"

But he doesn't obey, and I remember I have to make eye-contact for compulsion to work, and Leaf isn't looking at me.

"Titus, stop him!" Tears sting my eyes, blurring the vision of Leaf, now convulsing on the floor.

But Titus just stands there, arms crossed, as though watching some humorous show. And I'm pulling against the Defenders. I'm shouting out profanities. I'm wishing the whole world would just pause for a moment, let me butt in for once just let me stop the madness.

Leaf's body goes still. The Defenders release me and I race to his side.

"Leaf!" I jerk out the dagger, tip his head back, trying to

clear his airway. But it's too late. He's not breathing and blood is everywhere. His eyes are open and unfocused. When I check his pulse it's non-existent.

This time. This time he really is dead.

My breath freezes in my lungs. Everything around me stops. I cover my mouth and tears stream down my cheeks—they stream down my cheeks onto the tile floor. It wasn't supposed to happen this way. He was dead and then he was alive and he was supposed to *stay* alive, but he's not—he's not and what the shoddy inferno is *wrong* with Titus?

"You didn't have to *kill* him!" I scream through my gulps of tears.

"It's the price of being close to a rebel, my dear Ember," Titus says. I look at him through my tears, and he shrugs, his green eyes dancing. "You might as well go ahead and consider your family dead, too."

Red red red everything I see is red. And I'm on him. My hands wrap around his neck, and I'm strangling him, and I hate him I hate him I hate him.

We tumble to the ground and my fist cracks into his nose.

An electric current bolts up my arm, and my body crumples to the floor. I curl into a ball, the shock of the band making my body numb.

"Leave my family out of this," I say through gritted teeth.

"After what you just did?" He stands and wipes the blood seeping from his nose. He looks at the blood on his hands, then glares at me. "No one has ever made me bleed before." He laughs. "Of course it would be my own sister."

He walks to Leaf and picks the dagger up off the floor,

then strides toward me. The look in his eyes is the very definition of evil. My blood races through my veins as he approaches, and I realize he's going to end this quickly. He's going to stab me in the heart. I'm going to be dead right now. I close my eyes, waiting for the blow. Instead, a sharp pain stabs my thigh.

Titus pulls the dagger out of my leg, and I can't think past the blinding pain as the dark crimson seeps through my green dress.

"Just a little something to remember me by," he says. "Tonight, while you bleed in prison, waiting for your death with no knowledge of how your dad and brother will die or how badly they will beg for their sorry little lives, you'll have this wound to remind you that I am all-powerful, all the citizens of Ky love me, and no one can take me down." He leans in close, his breath on my ear. "Not even you, little sister." He stands, then kicks me hard in the side, and it's in that moment of excruciating pain that a hot flame grows inside me. It rises up and chokes me and I want Titus dead. I want him to pay for everything he's done to me, to Leaf, to the Jacksons and every other Proletariat in Ky.

I want to assassinate him.

"Get her out of here," he mutters.

One of the Defenders grabs my arm and yanks me to my feet, then leads me, one leg dragging, out the door. He shoves me into the jeep, and I cover my wound, trying to stop the bleeding, but trying even harder to stop my rage from completely blinding me. My leg is throbbing, but the pain is nothing compared to the pain in my heart. Leaf is dead. Killed himself, and not by his own choice. Now Dad and Elijah are in danger. And Titus needs to die.

"Son of a jackal!" I kick the seat in front of me, but the

rough movement sends searing pain into my leg, and I hunch over and puke on the car floor.

Minutes later, the tall, round glass building appears ahead. The prison. Midmorning sun glints off the windows, making the building look beautiful and glorious. But I know better. This is a place of death, not beauty.

The Defender drags me down the concrete stairs to the underground prison that smells like the crotch-rot of hell. I can hardly process where we're going, which turns we take, how long it takes us to arrive at the pit of the prison. I can't stop thinking about Leaf, convulsing on the floor, a river of blood coating his neck.

We step into the same shoddy room where I was kept before. Except the chamber is completely empty because all the other prisoners either escaped or died less than a week ago. And Judah. Judah's not here to keep me company this time.

The Defender presses a button, the electric shield goes down, and he shoves me into the first cell. I stumble to the ground, then stretch my throbbing leg out to ease the pain. Titus probably already has jeeps headed out to the orchard to collect my family. And since I'm dying tomorrow, there's nothing I can do.

Nothing.

Letting out a moan, I lay my head on the cold concrete floor and give into my grief.

Hours must go by. Hours and hours in this pit of loneliness and despair. The bleeding in my leg has stopped, but my dress is caked in blood, as are my hands. And I have a terrible headache, but then what is a headache when you know you're going to die soon? I wish Judah were here to keep me company. Heck, I'd even take Mcallister. But it's just me. Alone. With my fears of my impending death and regret that I didn't take Rain's offer to work with him to assassinate Titus.

Because I really really really want to kill Titus now.

But Rain is a traitor. He never cared about my life from the beginning, and I guess I knew that, but it still hurts.

Because I was sort of starting to care about him.

Everything he said last night tumbles around in my brain, begging to be heard. Not the assassinating the chief thing. The Emmanuel thing. About God being with us on a very personal level.

Because I'm feeling it again. I'm feeling this very real presence begging me to call out to it. Maybe I'm hallucinating or maybe I'm desperate, but I feel it so strongly that it almost gives me hope.

God wants to be known by you.

How, though? How can I know this God who completely evades us? How can I find something that insists on staying hidden?

SEEK ME.

Chills spread across my body, making my heart shudder and my brain think things I shouldn't be thinking. There's something about facing death that makes me question...*everything.* There's something about the great unknown that makes me want to *know* the Great Unknown.

And I want to know Him. I want to know this Power, this Being, this Creator who created me with much thought and pride and affection. So I close my eyes. I focus on the

454

energy surrounding me. And I whisper one word.

"Please—"

But I can't finish the silent prayer, because praying to nothing is the first step to insanity.

The door slides open, and Forest steps into the chamber. I sigh in relief. I can't really stand with my throbbing leg, so I just sit here, pathetic, and look up at him. After hours of crying, I must look like a wreck. But Forest doesn't look any better, honestly, with red-rimmed eyes and disheveled hair and his usually pressed politician's clothes wrinkled.

"Are you okay?" I glance over his body, looking for bruises, anything to tell me Titus beat him.

"Fine." He looks at my leg, frowns. "Faring better than you, obviously." He glances back at the Defender who accompanied him, his jaw clenching. "They won't let me take you out of here. Not even to talk. But I spoke to Titus. And he told me your sentence."

I look down.

"Don't worry," Forest says. "I'm going to speak to him again in the morning to get you out of here."

Wow. Déjà vu.

"It's useless. *Titus* is useless." I look at Forest, my heart pounding with hatred. "He made him kill himself—" My voice chokes off in a sob. "He made Leaf—" And I can't finish. Because it's too much. It's too difficult to say aloud and I want to refuse to believe it but I can't. I can't. Because I saw it with my own eyes.

Leaf is dead. *Again.*

"What he did was obviously wrong," Forest says. "I don't know what came over him, but Titus…." He sighs. "I grew up with him, and he *can* be reasoned with."

I stare at him. "Are you out of your shoddy mind? Titus is *psychotic*! If you want to try to help, forget Titus. Go to the Garden. Find my family and save them."

"He's not going after your family. He only said that to scare you."

"How do you know?"

"Because I already spoke with him once. And though he's determined to believe you're a threat, he doesn't care about your family."

Somehow I find this hard to believe.

"Listen," Forest says. "If you want to be angry, take your rage out on Rain. He's the one who smoked you out. He's the reason you're here. And don't worry—I already gave him what was coming to him."

I wonder what he means by that, but then I decide that I honestly don't care.

"Whatever came over Titus today will pass. He'll sleep on his dramatic decision tonight, and he'll release you tomorrow. He'll listen to me. I know he will." But by the look in his eyes, I wonder if he really feels that certain. He plants his hands on his hips and looks at me. "Is there anything else I can do for you before I leave?"

I think. I think of my family and wish Forest would go save them because he sure isn't going to be able to save me. I think of Leaf and wish Forest would give him a proper burial. I think of the government as whole and wish he would just fix it. But he can't do any of those things any more than I could have.

Because Titus is in ultimate control.

"No," I whisper.

Forest nods. "I'll see you in the morning, then." He offers a smile that hardly sets my mind at ease, and then he walks out of my life forever.

Forest doesn't show up again before the Defenders come to my cell to escort me out of the prison. I get an entire bus to myself, similar to the one that brought me to Frankfort in the first place. The stink of exhaust fills the air. I lean back on the cold, metal seat and watch the city pass by in a blur of silvery blue- and gold-tinted windows.

When we pass through the cupola, the day turns from sunny spring to overcast and cold with a light blanket of snow covering the ground. Winter has begun in the rest of Ky, and I can't help but feel as though I've stepped out from a dream—or a nightmare—back into reality.

After we cross the dam, the bus takes an exit off the interstate and veers toward the perimeter of Frankfort, a dusty plain containing the Rebels Circle. A place known as the Outer Ring. And I notice a crowd of people sitting on bleachers, like they're about to watch some sort of sick show.

Squinting through the front window, I can see the thirty-foot stakes standing in the distance, the sunlight glinting off the rings on the top. I shudder and look away. This is how I'm going to die. As the rebel who helped Jonah Walker and his gang. And where are *they* now? Why aren't they helping me now? And do I regret my decision? I did for a while. But now that Leaf is dead by Titus's hands, I want the Resurgence to revolt. I mean, if Walker's comrades take down the government, take down *Titus,* then sparing Walker's life that day in my apartment would have been worth my own.

The bus pulls to a stop. When I step off, a freezing wind

blasts into my face, and my body tenses.

"Everyone has the freedom to choose their actions," a Defender says as he grips my arm. "You chose to turn your back on our country. And with that decision comes your execution."

"Don't kill her!" Someone shouts from the bleachers. I look over to see the Patrician spectators stand up.

"Give her one more chance!" Someone else shouts.

"Offer another trial!"

Others begin shouting their agreement, telling the Defender to spare my life, to let me go, and I realize, all the people came here to fight for me. How touching. And how strange, that I was a nobody less than a week ago, and now the *somebodies* are speaking for me.

But the head Defender pulls a gun out and pulls the trigger and a loud BANG consumes my eardrums, and suddenly I'm being yanked toward one of the posts. He ties the end of the cord around my ankles. Without warning, the cord sweeps me off my feet. My head hits the ground hard before the cord pulls me upside down into the air. I catch glimpses of the glorious buildings of Frankfort, glinting silver and gold within the Cupola. Then I begin to spin and the rest of Ky appears before me. Shabby and shaded by winter clouds, it's never looked so cold or dejected. And then everything begins spinning faster and faster as I'm pulled into the air like a hooked fish.

The spinning stops when I reach the top of the circle. Blood rushes to my head. My heartbeat thrashes against my eardrums. I can feel it pulsing in my neck and cheeks and behind my eyeballs, and I can't breathe, I can't remember a single time I've ever been this terrified. My hands hang limply in the air while my body swings helplessly like a freshly killed chicken being drained of blood.

A whistle blows.

The Defender lights the end of long post.

And then I feel it.

Extreme, unbearable heat radiates from below.

I automatically look down, but heat burns my eyes, forcing them shut. This is what utter terror feels like. Like there's no hope and these are my last few breaths of life. I'm going to die today—now—this very moment and I'm not ready I'm not ready I'm definitely *not* ready.

And I wonder, what was it all worth? What was the meaning of my life? I was raised. Given a career. But before I could do anything worthwhile, I was taken to prison, refused to help Rain, and now here I am. Dying with nothing—*nothing*—to show for myself.

Because I'm a shoddy coward.

The fire grows hotter, the incalescence creeping around my body like a snake in flames. And for the first time in my life, I say a full prayer.

God—Emmanuel. Save me. I will do whatever you ask. But please please please save me….

My skin radiates with heat. My face burns—my lungs burn—everything burns. My heartbeat pulses in my fingertips, and I inhale the stink of gasoline. Smoke fills up my lungs. I cough until my chest hurts, and my coughs choke into labored breathing, and I'm gasping, my body clawing for any particle of oxygen.

And I try—I try to inhale—but I can't—even—breathe—

Consciousness is slipping away. And a familiar tune takes its place. Music plays from somewhere faraway, and yet, right here, inside my mind. Familiar and achingly haunting. And I try to place the words until they finally come to me like a distant echo.

O come, O come, Emmanuel…

Another cough. My lungs. They burn. But the song won't stop.

…Disperse the gloomy clouds of night…

Black spots creep at the edge of my vision.

…And death's dark shadows put to flight…

And then there's nothing but *rejoice rejoice rejoice rejoice* and a faint ringing in my ears and the slow thud of my heartbeat until I surrender to complete silence.

Darkness.

And death.

CHAPTER FIFTY-FIVE

When I open my eyes, I am standing in the apple orchard, the sun casting coral hues across the fields and the trees almost glowing green. Long grass billows around my knees, shimmering in the light. The sun is so bright, so incredibly bright it makes my eyes hurt.

Someone walks toward me, wearing a cloak more radiant than the light behind him.

EMBER.

The strangely familiar euphoria fills me at the sound of his voice. And I'm elated. The very definition of joy overcomes me. Welcoming and love wrap around me until I don't think I could ever feel more welcomed or loved anywhere.

This is what I've been looking for.

This resplendent Being in front of me is the One who's been calling me, drawing me in all this time.

EMBER.

And I want him to say my name again and again and again. I want him to speak and never stop speaking. I want him to take me in his arms and never let go.

EMBER.

He's standing right in front of me now, looking down at me with a gaze so piercing, I know he can see into my soul. I'm seized by the power of his presence. And I fall to my knees, because, standing in the glory of this...*Being*, it's all I can do.

His hand rests on my shoulder, and everything I felt seconds ago—the joy, acceptance and love—magnifies. Ten. Thousand. Times.

EMBER.

Yes?

PREPARE THE WAY.

For what?

FOR MY PEOPLE.

People? What people? I have no idea what he's talking about. I don't remember where I came from. All I know is that beauty is all around me. Everywhere. Contentment fills me up like fresh water, flowing over the sides and spilling all around me.

I am in paradise.

OPEN YOUR EYES.

They're opened.

OPEN YOUR EYES.

I try but it's too hot. Heat. Heat everywhere. On my skin, my eyelids, my lungs. And then I'm falling. My arms automatically flail out to grasp anything to stop my fall, and then I land on my back on the hard ground. The air is knocked out of my lungs and my eyes fly open. The apple orchard has vanished. Everything is a gray blur instead of resplendent light. Forest Turner appears through the haze. He pulls me into his arms, his eyes wide.

"Ember!" I can barely hear him through the ringing in my ears. "Oh, *Ember*. I'm so *sorry*." And his voice is raw and pained like he's been crying, then he pulls me to his chest. The movement is too quick. The blood drains from my head too fast. Darkness invades my vision.

And again.

There's nothing.

CHAPTER FIFTY-SIX

No dream this time. A soft voice draws me out of darkness. My face hurts. My leg throbs. Too painful to breathe. I blink my eyes open to find Forest looking at me. Behind him, bright fluorescent lights blind me and I blink my eyes closed.

"Can you hear me?" he says.

I nod. Something's covering my mouth. I reach up to smack it off, but Forest stops me.

"It's a medicated mask. Your lungs were singed from the heat of the fire. It's helping your lungs heal."

The fire? Everything comes tumbling back into my memory like a nightmare, and I jolt up.

"Hey," Forest says, covering my hand with his. "You're okay now. You're *safe*."

I lay back down, my heart still pounding at the memory of my near-death experience.

But I didn't die. I was taken to another place. A place of

perfection and beauty. I want to go back. Why can't I go back? Why have I been dragged back to this hellhole?

I peek at Forest. "What happened?" I croak.

"Turns out having you burned wasn't exactly the popular thing to do."

I cough. Inhale. The medication coming through the mask feels so soothing to my lungs.

"Also," he says. "Rain—"

"That arrogant son of a jackal—"

"—had proof of your innocence."

I blink. I don't—I don't understand.

"He turned me in..." I wheeze. "And now...he...*helped* me?" What's his shoddy deal?

Forest nods.

"And Titus...listened to *him*?"

"Yes." He smiles. "And Titus pardoned you, Ember. Because everyone wants you alive. He's allowing you to go home."

All his words jumble in my head, and I struggle to piece them together. "I'll believe it...when I'm home."

"I think he means it this time. I mean, he placed you here, in the most renowned hospital in Ky, receiving the best medical treatment imaginable. Your leg's already mostly healed. And soon your lungs will be as good as new."

"What about my family?" I rasp, looking at him. "Did he—"

"They're fine. Titus didn't touch them. They're still at the orchard, waiting for your return." His smile lifts every single doubt from my mind. Tears prick my eyes, and I collapse on the bed. He combs his fingers through my hair. "You're free of guilt. Your records have been wiped clean. This time, Ember, I'm really going to take you home."

Home. The thought should calm me. I should be excited. But, even if I did go home…will anything ever be the same?

Though he betrayed me, Rain's words still echo in my mind: *Will you ever really be free? After all you've seen here, will anything be the same?*

And then the vision comes back to me with full force. The love I felt. The Being beaming brighter than the sun, telling me to set his people free. Was any of that real? It *had* to be. The Presence…I *felt* it.

"What's wrong, Ember?" Forest takes my hand in his and squeezes.

"Nothing. I just…had a weird…dream." Forest wouldn't understand. He would say it was the life-flashing-before-your-eyes thing. But I'd never felt more alive than I did when I was dying. I'd never experienced so much beauty. So much acceptance. So much…*love.*

PREPARE THE WAY.

For what? His people, He said. But how? My stomach tightens at the uncertainty, the command to do something I don't fully understand. But right now all I can think about is going home.

Although I'm not as happy about going home as I should be. Honestly, I feel robbed. I feel like I was just tortured for Titus's amusement. Like maybe he's just letting me go now because he thinks I learned my lesson. He thinks he put me in my place, and I'll never ever challenge him again because look what happens when you challenge the chief.

He burned me to claim his place as Alpha.

But I almost *died* today. No thanks to Titus. No thanks to Rain. But, hey. I'll go home. I'll pretend like everything is fine, like I didn't just almost lose my life at the hands of my psychotic brother. I'll pretend...until I have the perfect opportunity to strike.

∾

We leave the next morning. Forest drives me out of Frankfort.

Again.

We pass through the cupola.

Again.

We drive across the Outer Ring.

Again.

I'm failing to feel as excited as I have the past two times I almost went home.

Surprisingly, no Defenders stop us this time. I glance at the Rebels Circle, the place where I was supposed to die. And I have the sudden urge to throw up. I turn away and shove down this terrifying, sick feeling invading the pit of my stomach.

"So...what did Rain tell Titus that helped earn my freedom?" I ask Forest.

"He somehow found the footage from your apartment before the cameras blew out."

"*What?*"

"I don't know what he did to make it look like Walker was never there. But whatever he showed Titus won the chief over."

How the shoddy inferno did he manage that?

"Whose side, exactly, is Rain on?"

"His own," Forests says. "Rain is always out to promote

himself. He tried to suck up to the chief by turning you in. When that didn't sit too well with the majority of Frankfort, he saved your neck."

"Son of a jackal."

"I know—I know you must hate him now, but just know you kind of owe him a big thanks."

I choke out a laugh. "I'll *never* thank him. And please don't ever try to settle things between us." I look at Forest, dead serious. "I'm afraid if I ever see Rain again, I'll rip his esophagus out with my bare hands. It's because of Rain I almost died."

"It's because of him you're still alive."

Of course. Of course it is. Rain took me to prison. Then he rescued me from prison. Rain betrayed me to Titus. Then he rescued me from the Rebels Circle. It seems he enjoys using my life as a means to gain more popularity among the Patricians.

Ugh. I feel sick to my stomach just thinking about Rain. And I don't want to feel sick. I'm going home and I should feel pleasantly excited. So I force all thoughts of Rain out of my head. And I look out the front window at the snow-laden city of Ky.

The vehicle whirs down the interstate for a few minutes, much faster than the prison bus that brought me here, then takes a few turns down alleyways toward the Community Garden. When we arrive, the gates creak open, and we slowly drive down the gravel road through the fields. All bitter thoughts dissipate like the morning dew at sunrise, and my heart floods with warmth at the sight of my home.

A fresh blanket of snow covers the ground. Field hands wearing heavy winter clothes walk down the road. Some look at my vehicle as it passes by and tip their hats in respect. I wonder why until I remember the windows are tinted. They think a politician rides in the vehicle instead of one of their own. Well, I guess a politician is riding in here. We drive through the square, then take a turn down the road that I walked every evening to drop our rations off. The road Leaf and I raced on our last day together. This is where I belong. And my eyes are burning with the overwhelming sense of homecoming.

Gravel pops beneath the wheels of the car, and I squint ahead. I want to see the apple orchard as we near the place that has consumed my memories and dreams and paintings the past weeks. Workers are still out, pruning the trees. One of them leaps off his ladder and stares at the car, then takes off running toward the cabin. And my heart takes a violent leap.

Elijah.

It's real. I'm here. I'm really home. We pull into the driveway, and I take in the view of our cabin, smoke curling out of the chimney just like I remember. I may not have been gone for long, but it seems like a lifetime. When I open the door, Elijah races toward me waving his arms.

"Ember!" He throws himself into my arms, practically knocking me over.

"Hey, easy kid." I wrap my arms around him, tears spilling freely down my face. I laugh and squeeze him so tight, I don't think I'll ever let him go. I dig my fingers into his shaggy hair, inhale deeply the wild, free scent of my little brother.

Dad emerges from the cabin and stares at me like he's seeing a ghost. "Ember," he chokes out. He stumbles toward me and crushes me to his chest. I wrap my arms around his frail form, feel the outline of his ribcage and think about how we'll never go hungry again.

I'm vaguely aware of Forest approaching, placing his hand on the small of my back. And a strange warmth fills me. I pull away from Dad and wipe the tears off my cheeks with the heel of my hand.

"Dad, Elijah, this is Fore—Congressman Turner."

"You can call me Forest." He extends his hand to my dad.

I'm almost afraid Dad won't take it, considering how little he thinks of congress, but to my relief, his hand envelops Forest's.

"Hello," Dad says. He looks at me. "I'm so happy you returned." He wipes a tear off his face. "But I didn't realize a Congressman would escort you."

I laugh. "A lot has happened, Dad. But in the midst of all the chaos and confusion, Forest has been the one constant." I swallow hard, still shaken from what happened yesterday. "He's always been there for me. He's always been on my side."

"Well," Dad says. "Anyone who's a friend of my daughter's is welcome in my house." He gestures toward Forest. "Please, come in." He turns and leads the way to the cabin. A frigid wind sweeps in from the east as we head toward the cabin.

Elijah slips his arm around my waist.

"You got a little meat on you while you were away," he says.

My mouth drops open and I jab him in the side. "I wasn't even gone *two weeks*. Besides, you'll get a bit meaty too. Just wait and see, little squirrel."

"Ew. No. Just because you're back does NOT mean you can call me that."

I laugh and tussle his hair. Forest's hand finds mine, and the warmth spreads throughout my entire body, pooling in the pit of my stomach. When I look at him, his blue eyes are almost glowing with a joy I haven't seen in them since the day I was rescued from the prison pit, and I can't fight down my own happiness. Now that I'm home, I can finally let it out. Joy is a wellspring of hope pumping through my veins and my spirit, and I know I made the right choice coming home instead of fighting the chief.

At least for now.

At least until I come up with some plan to take down Titus.

One glance at my beloved orchard, wiry trees and dead ground covered with a fresh layer of snow, and Rain's words trickle into my head: *You are the Garden, God is the Sower.*

My mood darkens, that he can still influence my thoughts, even when he's not around. Even when he's a traitor. I'll never trust Rain again.

And I'll never trust Titus Whitcomb, either. The hatred in his eyes just two days ago tells me he has more of a personal vendetta against me than me just being some possible rebel. This has something to do with us being related. It has something to do with his fear of me challenging him, despite the fact that I have zero interest in doing so.

But if I've learned anything, it's that life is too short to worry worry worry all the time. Titus is all powerful and there's not much I can do except play the role of a good girl until my moment to strike at him for all the cruel things he's done arrives.

The only thing that matters right now, in this very moment, is that I'm home. My family is alive. And Forest Turner cares for me. With one arm wrapped around Elijah's shoulders and the other linked through Forest's elbow, we walk up the steps and enter our cabin that has always been filled with warmth, laughter, and most important of all, family.

CHAPTER FIFTY-SEVEN

Later, after sunset, Forest leaves for the hotel in the square, giving me time with my family. As much as I love having him here, I appreciate the gesture. I need some time alone with Dad and Elijah.

The fire is lit, the flames licking the air and radiating heat throughout our cabin. The music from Elijah's harmonica fills the silence, and the smell of soup from dinner still lingers in the air. I unpack the paints and canvases I brought from Frankfort and begin painting. I'm not sure what I'm painting yet, but cerulean is the color I select. Dark blue, like Forest's eyes. His eyes that, just a few nights ago, were filled with torturous longing and frightening temptations. And that kiss we shared that night. The kiss that set loose ten thousand butterflies in my stomach that still refuse to fly away.

That kiss that only made me realize how attracted I am to him. It made me want more. And now he's here, in the Community Garden. And he broke up with Olivia. And there might maybe be a future for us.

"Are you okay?"

I look up to find Dad staring at me like he can't believe I'm actually home.

"Yes." My voice comes out hoarse, and I clear my throat. "I mean, now that I'm home."

"Do you want to...talk about it?"

I look back at my painting, the memories of prison and the black tigers and my near-death experience souring my sweet thoughts of Forest.

"Not really," I mutter.

But memories of Frankfort take up camp in my mind. After Titus gloated about Charlie and Ilene's deaths, then killed Leaf right in front of me, and then almost killed me, plus his threats about going after my family, I want to give Titus a taste of his own medicine. But...could I ever return to the golden city, even if it meant taking Titus down? Just the thought of returning to that nightmare makes my stomach hollow. Is it even possible to take Titus down if I'm not working with Rain or the Resurgence? I turned them both down, and now I have no idea how to get in contact with the Resurgence, and I don't ever want to see, much less *work* with Rain again.

But what if...what if help could be found from across the river? Outside of Ky? I remember Walker mentioning something about the Indy Tribe, the people who gave him that tiny, quiet gun. Who are they, and would they be willing to help? And Jonah...he said something about possible survivors across the river. Hope grows in my chest like a well-watered plan, like a sapling finally willing to produce fruit.

PREPARE THE WAY.

Maybe this is what God meant. Maybe I'm not supposed

to be the one to take down Titus or take on the role as a leader. Maybe I'm just supposed to prepare the way for those who *are* meant to do that, whether it means the Resurgence or the Indy Tribe.

"Did you know there's a bridge?" The words slip from my lips before I have time to really organize my thoughts. But I look at Dad and decide to finish. "A bridge that crosses out of Ky territory?"

Dad nods.

"Do you—" My breath hitches. "Do you want to…cross it?"

Dad blinks. "Do *you*?"

"Maybe. I haven't thought about it much, but I think we should leave. Just get out of here. I mean, Titus knows I'm his sister. He's never going to let up. He's always going to be suspicious of me." I swallow hard and look back at the blue paint smeared across the canvas. "I think I just want to get out of this place." I don't bother telling him my thoughts on recruiting any possible survivors from across the river.

Dad frowns. He crosses his ankle over his knee and drags his hand across the back of his neck and looks at the floor. "Let's wait until things cool down a bit. Let's wait for Forest to leave, because as much as you trust him, I don't."

My heart sinks, but I nod. Dad hates politicians. Of course it would take him longer than an evening to warm up to Forest.

"Let's wait," he continues, looking at me now. "Until Titus believes you're not a threat and not watching your every move, and then we'll leave Ky."

His words lift every last grain of apprehension off my shoulders and a my heart skips with the thrill of leaving. I'm

477

so ready to get out of Ky. And, even though I knew Dad would be on board, to hear him say it out loud makes all the difference.

"Promise?" I ask, just to be sure.

"I lost your mother to the chief. I almost lost you, too. I don't want to take that risk again. When the chief least expects it, we'll hightail the hell outta here." He holds my gaze, his features serious, but his eyes filled with so much hope. "You have my word."

END OF BOOK ONE

ACKNOWLEDGEMENTS

First of all, can I just say thank YOU a million times for reading this book? Thank you for taking a break from life and choosing my book as an escape. I hope you enjoyed reading *Black Tiger* as much as I enjoyed writing it. And even if you didn't love it, I hope it still left you better off for having read it.

I thank God for placing the passion for story in my heart and giving me the courage to pursue my dreams. I started writing when I was in a dark place, and this newfound obsession completely flipped my life. Thanks, God!

Michael. My love. My hero. My other half. Thank you for believing in me.

Digory and Aravis: Thank you for having patience with Mama while she had conversations with the people in her head, and for patiently enduring the constant clickety-clack of typing while you were nursing on her lap. Good babies, both of you.

Loads of love to my parents for their continuous

encouragement and support. Becki and Luke: Thanks for being my very first readers EVER...and *still* cheering me on. Nicole: Thanks for asking questions about *Black Tiger* that have forced me to write it into a better story.

To Ron, Donna, Jim, and Ashley, thank you for spending time with the littles so I could regain my sanity. Kathy, I love all the writerly gifts you sprinkle me with. They make me feel almost official. Katie and Kristen, thank you for fan-girling with me over all our favorite books.

Davy, thanks for helping me organize all my scattered thoughts on the cover into one solid idea. You're welcome to build a tiny house on our land any time.

Emily, thanks for being generous with your time and meeting with me to get author pictures done so I didn't have to resort to selfies.

And now for the three Sarahs who have majorly impacted this story...

To Sarah Grimm, my wonderful editor and friend and one of the first people who made me really believe this book was worth publishing: Thanks for reading multiple versions of *Black Tiger* and making it ten times better. Every. Time.

To Sarah Monzon, my inspiration and publishing mentor: Thank you for your continued interest in *Black Tiger*...even two years after you read the crappy first draft. But most of all, thanks for challenging me to think about going indie. And for answering my dozens and dozens of questions about the publishing world.

To Sarah S., thanks for being a reader, a fellow writer, and a friend. You were there on my bad days and my good days, listening to my woes and rejoicing through my small victories. I still can't believe how God brought us together under such random circumstance, but I'm so glad He did.

Lara Willard, you offered to do a simple beta read for the very first draft of Black Tiger, and instead did a full content edit, helping me transform this story into something so much better. Thank you for being generous with your time and skill. You're going to go far, my friend.

Andy, Tracy, Elijah, Jonah, Ember, and Judah: thank you for letting me use your awesome names. And also for staying up late at night reading this book and begging for more. You're an amazing family!

Levi, Isaac, Katie, and Ashley, thank you also for letting me use your names for the Fearless Five. Katie and Ashley—thanks for reading my books and getting your friends to read them.

To all my wonderful beta readers and friends who eased the writing journey with encouragement, gifts, chocolate, coffee, and wine: Thank you. My stories would have never made it this far without you. You're seriously amazing.

And if you made it this far, thanks again to YOU! A writer can't be an author without readers. ♥

Black Tiger Playlist

1. *The Sower's Song* by Andrew Peterson. This song matches the mood at the beginning in the Garden.

2. *Radioactive* by Imagine Dragons. Basically the *Black Tiger* theme song.

3. *Jaded* by Bleach. When everything basically goes to hell after Career Day.

4. *Sail* by AWOLNATION. This song was on repeat while writing the prison escape scene.

5. *Aftermath* by Fever Fever. Beginning of Part II

6. *Riptide* by Vance Joy. When Ember learns the truth about the Patricians.

7. *Demons* by Imagine Dragons. Pretty much every scene with Rain.

8. *3 Rounds and a Sound* by Blind Pilot. Rooftop scene with Forest.

9. *Land of the Living* by Gungor. The church scene.

10. *Swing Low Sweet Chariot* by Brady Toops. I listened to this song on repeat while writing the Rebels Circle scene.

11. *Casualties* by American Aquarium. Last two chapters.

Dear Reader,

I hope you enjoyed reading *Black Tiger* as much as I enjoyed writing it. If you want to read more about Ember and Rain and Forest and what happens to Ky, stay tuned for Book Two, *Ashen City,* coming soon. You can visit my website at https://sarabaysinger.com or follow me on social media (@sarambaysinger) for future updates on The Black Tiger Series.

Also, I LOVE hearing from my readers, so if you want to connect, you can find me at any of the links listed below.

Website: https://sarabaysinger.com

Facebook: https://www.facebook.com/sarabaysingerauthor

Twitter: https://twitter.com/sarambaysinger

Instagram: https://www.instagram.com/sarambaysinger/
https://www.instagram.com/readingontheburrow/

Pinterest: https://www.pinterest.com/sarambaysinger/

Made in the USA
Lexington, KY
29 December 2016